S0-BQI-908

THE
KAISER'S
COOLIES

THEODOR PLIVIER

THE
KAISER'S
COOLIES

TRANSLATED FROM THE GERMAN BY

M A R G A R E T   G R E E N

New York · HOWARD FERTIG · 1988

First published in English in 1931
Published in 1988 by Howard Fertig, Inc.
80 East 11th Street, New York, N.Y. 10003

Library of Congress Cataloging-in-Publication Data
Plivier, Theodor, 1892-1955.
 The kaiser's coolies.
 Translation of: Des Kaisers Kulis.
 1. World War, 1914-1918—Fiction. I. Title.
PT2631.L6K313   1988   833'.912   87-23698
ISBN 0-86527-378-2

Printed in the United States of America

THEODOR PLIVIER

THE
KAISER'S
COOLIES

TRANSLATED FROM THE GERMAN BY

M A R G A R E T   G R E E N

NEW YORK

A L F R E D · A   K N O P F · 1 9 3 1

Facsimile of the title page of the original edition.

Originally Published As
DES KAISERS KULIS
Copyright 1930 by Malik-Verlag A.-G. Berlin

CONTENTS

1. Shanghaied!

"DIERCK!" And again:

"Dierck! Shake a leg!"

The sleeping man shook off the hand on his shoulder and turned heavily towards the bulkhead. He wanted to be let alone; he knew anyway that he was on board a leaky hulk. He couldn't forget it, even in his sleep.

The boatswain himself came into the fo'c'sle to wake the watch below: "Dierck! Jan! Get a move on!"

At last he roused them—two men and a boy. It was hard work. They hadn't been in their bunks an hour. And then the preceding days—it had been going on for four stretches of twenty-four hours.

They sat in their bunks with legs dangling, still dazed with sleep. There was no need to put on their sea-boots; they had slept in them. The lamp that hung from the deck-beam was still swinging to and fro. Each time that it swung to port and reached its farthest point, you heard a wave breaking on deck, and then the rush of the water as it ran off. The ship was making no headway; for four days she had drifted sideways on in Spanish waters, rudderless, her engines broken down.

The boy sat hunched up on his blankets, his head dropped on his breast, and he closed his eyes again. So long as the men sat and dozed, he needn't stir either. One of them was staring at the lamplight, his eyes wide with sleep. The other, whom the boatswain had called with Dierck, was lighting his pipe and taking a few hasty puffs. You couldn't smoke on deck because of the wind.

"There were seven of us when we turned into the cabin."

"Seven—and the wind has risen!"

Someone opened the companion hatch. The opening sufficed

3

to let in the shouting on deck, and it brought the men to their
feet. The boatswain spoke, short and sharp:

"Where are you? Quick, the tanks!"

"That's what it is, the deck-cargo," said Dierck.

"The oil-tanks!" bawled Jan.

They dragged themselves up the ladder and clambered
through the hatchway. At first they were like blind men, feeling their way step by step; then they saw the foaming crests of
the tall waves that beat against the ship. One patch of sky was
clear, showing pale, washed-out stars. The forms on deck stood
out in a misty, blue light: groups of tanks and the watch on
deck.

The tanks were lashed together and to the hand-rail in lots
of fifty, and there were ten such lots in the prow. They were
empty, but nearly the height of a man and made of heavy
metal. The watch was engaged in tightening the ropes that had
gone slack. They pulled on a wire cable: "—Hoi—ho, hoi—
ho! Again! And then again! Pull boys, pull, blast you! Come
on. . . ."

There were three of them with the mate.

Jan and Dierck joined them.

The boy was under fifteen.

"Look out for meat-hooks!" sang out the leader. In places
the cable had rusted and the loose ends of wire tore the palms
of their hands. They had to use care and first to smooth down
the sharp ends as they caught hold, but afterwards to throw
their whole weight into the work: "All together! Pull boys!
Pull! . . ."

When the breakers swept over the deck, they all stood up
to the middle or chest in water. The ship listed over to port.
The upraised starboard side faced the waves, immobile and lifeless like a wall.

Dierck was working with the boy, who was belaying the

<<<<<<<<<<<<<<<<<<<<<<<<<<<<<<<<<<<<<<<<<<<<<<<<<<

wire cable after drawing it through. Suddenly he noticed that only three of the watch were there, with the mate and the boatswain.

"Where are the other two?" he asked.

"On the bridge," replied the mate. And after a time—for, after all, this Dierck Butendrift was a fellow who knew how to work—he even offered an explanation: "They've got their legs crushed."

Then the trouble began, on the back of a wave over which the ship rode with a rocking motion: one lot of tanks broke the wire ropes that held them in place. This set the liberated tanks in motion with a deafening noise; they crashed against the hatches and reels and against the main-rail, slid back again, and loosened the ropes that held the remaining tanks in place.

The men worked like mad. Their bodies were soaked beneath the thick covering of their oilskins. There were six of them against fifty monsters let loose; indeed, there might be a hundred. The worst of it was that they could not see the tanks. It was only at the last moment that they appeared, ghostly and blue, and whizzed past till they crashed into some obstacle. The rolling motion of the ship endowed them with uncanny life and destructive force. The men could work only during the short pauses when the ship was level, seizing one or other of the tanks and throwing it overboard.

The crew had taken refuge on the second hatch.

But standing up there might prove dangerous—the waves were washing over the deck. "Three trips back—" said one. They knew the story. A whole watch had been washed overboard.

The pale, gleaming faces pressed round Jan. Butendrift was a finely built, brawny fellow, but Jan Geulen was the most active of the crew. They had unanimously chosen him as leading hand at the beginning of the voyage.

"To work!" ordered the mate.

Nobody stirred. The tanks made a devilish noise, iron crashing against iron.

"No, we won't go on. We've done!" said Geulen.

"Refusal to obey orders!" The mate noted it without excitement. As a matter of fact, he was glad. He had an excuse for leaving that murderous deck. He clambered up the ladder to the bridge in order to report.

A frothy crest rose above the main-rail, swept on to the second hatch, broke, and foamed across the deck—a fiery tongue, gleaming yellow and licking up all around. And the ship was a flush-decked vessel, a type that was built twenty years ago, with only one part raised high, and that the bridge, resting upon iron girders.

The captain was a placid man. In the ports of the Levant, where his crew, and even the mates, carried on all manner of shady commercial transactions, he sat in the saloon and made nets for his father, who was captain of a fishing-cutter in the Baltic. Now, however, he spoke good High German: "So they refuse? I'll enter that in the log." And he laid special stress on the word "log." As captain he exercised police authority on board, backed up by the Naval Court and prison.

"No! We won't! Not till it's light!"

And they stuck to it. They kept watch till day dawned. To the leeward on the bridge stood the captain with the first and second mates, and on the windward side the crew, huddled together. In the middle, in front of the chart-house and the darkly towering funnel, the compass bowl gleamed in the pale light. When the howling of the wind ceased for a moment, you heard the stokers below in the stoke-hold.

The boatswain, who occupies an intermediate position on board and is counted neither among the officers nor among the crew, stood alone. After a time he joined the crew. He discerned Jan's face, with whom he felt most at home.

"No more ships carrying a deck-cargo for me!" said Karl Kleesattel, the boatswain. "Just let me get home," answered Jan, "and nobody'll drag me into this sort of thing again." They drew back their heads and huddled down so as to present as little surface to the wind as possible, for it was a stiff nor'-wester. Every half-hour one of the men went into the chart-house in order to relieve the watch with the two injured men.

The clattering of a few tins can frighten horses. And here were tanks, oil-tanks with double bands, hurled like projectiles by the rolling motion of the ship. Blows with the force of a twenty-five-ton hammer every time the ship listed over and plunged! How long would the hatches stand against such a battering?

Two bells in the morning watch.

Day broke. It rose from below, out of the sea, with a heavy, leaden light. They could see the whole deck now. The bul-wark was demolished and the ends of the main-rail swept away, as well as the leaden fo'c'sle companion. The fo'c'sle was full of water.

"I knew there'd be some disaster!"

Dierck Butendrift had felt it in his bones for weeks, a dull, paralysing sensation, a foreboding of coming events. So that was it! If the tanks smashed a hatch, the ship would inevitably sink like a tin bath with a hole in the bottom.

When it was light, Butendrift was the first to descend to the main deck. He thrust his long, windmill arms among the iron columns as they whirled to and fro, seized one after another of the dangerous objects, lifted it up, and hurled it along its curved path into the sea. The rest worked in companies of three. Strained and worn for lack of sleep as they were after the preceding days, they yet achieved a feat for Titans.

That same day the firemen got the engines started again. Black and smutty, the pennon of smoke from the sloping funnel drifted across the water. "The 'old coffee-mill' is running again!" With one boiler only, but it was running. Making slow way, but it was enough to enable them to steer her.

The following night they saw the glow of Bishop Rock Lighthouse, which cast its powerful beams thirty miles out into the Atlantic from its perch on the outermost of the Scilly Islands.

The voyage proceeded without mishap.

In the Channel the *Lesbos* received the wind and current on her stern. And in the North Sea, which lay, a great, glassy marvel, beneath a burning and quivering July sky, they forgot those days in Spanish waters.

During the calm weather they cleared the way into the holds. They were busy down below: there were the slings and the gear for discharging the general cargo. The boatswain had found nowhere to store these but the first hatch, the very place where the wine from Samos was laden. Quite by chance they discovered that one of the casks leaked. They brought pails directly, one for the firemen and another for the sailors. These were filled and taken to the empty coal-bunker. The mates had the water-jugs on their wash-stands filled. The paragraph in the mercantile marine regulations which prescribes prison for anyone who takes from the cargo, etc., had nothing whatever to do with the matter. Where there is no plaintiff, there is no judge! The captain sat in the saloon and packed the nets that he had made on the voyage in his trunk.

The ship listed a little to port. One of her sides was dented and the deck smashed. She moved across the broad, shimmering surface at the pace of a slow freight train, always at the centre of an emerald, circular mirror.

Hours passed, a night, a day. . . .

And again the sun beat into the hold so that one forgot the cosmic distance of the heavenly bodies and seemed to be breathing burning gas. Days like that are rare on the North Sea, but when they do occur, a man's blood contracts between the temples.

Butendrift was seated in the bows on the windlass. The sun blazed upon his shaggy head. It was his watch below and he was basking in the hot air, making up for the drenching days.

So that wasn't it, the adventure in Spanish waters! But what was it? He couldn't throw off the strange feeling of something uncanny brewing. He crouched motionless on the prow and gazed fixedly into the empty, glittering world.

The water lost its green transparency and became dull and milky. That was because they were near land, and dirt was carried out from the wide river mouths. To starboard lay a flat sand-bank. Ahead, from below the horizon, smoke ascended. It was not the narrow smoke-pennon of a steamer, but rather such a broad blanket of fog as hangs over cities, only it emitted black puffs, thrusting a sinister wedge into the quivering summer sky. Men-of-war!

"Manœuvres," said the boatswain.

He had served his time, first in the Second Naval Brigade and then on the little cruiser *Nymphe*. Butendrift had never been called up—not that he had actually shirked; it wasn't that. But before he was on the present steamship, he had been on foreign sailing-vessels.

"The first German port for four years!"

One of the firemen on watch below came forward to the bows too, wearing wooden clogs and a cloth round his neck. The three looked unkempt and dirty, with coal-dust on their faces and arms and clothes. Since the men's quarters were flooded, they had slept and lived in the empty coal-bunker.

The squadron of men-of-war was approaching with meteor-like rapidity. They were armoured cruisers flanked by destroyers.

The mate called to the boy:

"Moses, look sharp, get to the flagstaff!"

The boy ran aft and stood beside the flagstaff.

The grey iron-clads steamed one behind the other, keel following keel in a straight line, ploughing up great waves with their bows. Karl Kleesattel knew their names: *"Seydlitz! Moltke! Von der Tann!* They're in the front line, and they'll get most knocked about if it really comes off some day!"

And now the foremost of them was opposite the *Lesbos*.

"Dip the flag!" roared the mate.

Moses lowered it, hoisted it, and lowered it again, three times over. There was no one to be seen by the flagstaff of the iron-clad. Beneath the forward guns stood the crew in their shining white ducks, drawn up in long lines, and on the bridge were officers in blue uniforms fastened high at the neck. No one touched their flag. No notice was taken of the salute of this tramp steamer lying battered and listing in the water.

The fisherman's son on the bridge of the *Lesbos* spat vigorously through his teeth. That was his comment. Moses hoisted the flag again, slowly and without special instructions.

"Full speed. Twenty-eight knots!" said Kleesattel. And the fireman added: "Eh, lad, if you ever meets the English! All the papers was full of war talk when we were in the Levant. That affair with the Austrian, now—there's something wrong." Butendrift kept silence. His eyes roamed absently over the broad path of foam which the squadron had left behind in its progress.

Land was now visible on the other side. It lay beneath the sun's orb, darkly hatched. They passed outward-bound steamers and navigation marks—buoys and beacons. A sailing-ship with her sails hanging limp was drifting down-stream with the tide. The land on either side closed in, nearer and nearer.

The channel of water was like a shining, metallic ribbon. On the banks were apple-trees, meadows, and tea-gardens. Then the first signs of the city: a red brick factory; heaps of coal, clumps of grass, children playing; and women watching the ships as they passed.

The air was smoky and full of dancing particles of dust.

Warehouses. One-armed cranes. On one side an ocean giant in process of construction, a-buzz with a whole tribe of busy workmen no larger than ants. On the other side labyrinths of piled-up tenement barracks. A tug ahead of them and one behind towed the *Lesbos* into port.

The second mate stood with the port watch on the after deck; the first was with the starboard watch on the fo'c'sle. The ropes and wire cables rushed through the hawse-pipes, first fore, then aft: "Belay!"

The ship was fast to the quay: two hundred casks of Samos wine, two hundred and fifty tons of sweet almonds, three hundred tons of Smyrna figs, and a thousand tons of potatoes from Malta.

Next morning the mate's voice called down to the bunker: "Pay hands!"

Hot water, soft soap, clothes to wear ashore.

On the harbour steamer that carried them across the river to the city bank, they pressed round Geulen and Butendrift: "They'll have to pay us for that!"—"The company needn't have accepted a deck-cargo."—"The starboard watch has had forty hours' overtime and the port watch thirty-six."—"Johnny'll lose his leg." Both the injured men had been taken to the seamen's hospital as soon as the ship reached port.

At the Mercantile Marine Office the names of the ships paying off their crews were called out. Now it was the turn of

S.S. *Lesbos*. The sailors and stokers stepped to the counter window. Each in turn received his sailor's book and his wages, sixty marks per month. For the overtime worked in throwing the oil-tanks overboard, by which they had saved both ship and cargo, they received nothing. "From Gibraltar to the Scilly Islands, forty hours' overtime," said Butendrift. The official turned up a book and read a paragraph from the mercantile marine regulations in a monotonous voice, according to which nothing was counted overtime that was due to *force majeure* or the act of God. Then, without altering his tone and hardly raising his spectacled eyes, he said: "You will receive your book and your wages in the central office."

A stoker also was told to go to the central office.

When Dierck entered the office, he immediately recognized the man behind the desk, with his bald, perspiring head and short, sturdy build—a plain-clothes detective! "Your book is not as it should be—your military service. You must please go to the police-station," he said.

The stoker was marching five paces ahead of him between two policemen. The man on Dierck's left wore a cap, and the one on the right a peaked one. He had a full, fleshy face, and even with his tall cap he barely reached to Dierck's eyes. Both policemen were trained in boxing and ju-jutsu. Dierck could hoist the topgallant yard alone in case of need. He knew that if he gripped their two sturdy necks firmly, their skulls would crack together. He knew of cases when it had been done, but he did nothing and submitted to be led through the dusty, crowded streets.

Daddy Lampel had to lend a hand himself; his assistant had more than enough to do. He hurried to the tables laden with drinks and back to the counter with empty glasses. Beer! Spirits! Grog! When the coloured glass panes of the orchestrion flamed red, and the lamps above the tables were put out so that the bar was in semi-darkness, people's faces grew indistinct and the scent of the women seemed hotter and more intoxicating. When light returned, particular objects penetrated the thick clouds of tobacco-smoke—groups of people, wooden tables, and models of ships on the walls. The men's complexion was of that rich bronze which only the sea gives—the soft trade-winds and monsoons of the tropical seas and the heavy counter-currents which blow from the poles in the temperate zones.

> "*Sumatra, Borneo, Java,*
> *And the Great and Little*
> *Sunda Islands in the Pacific,*
> *Sumatra, Borneo, Java . . .*"

They sat at a round table and repeated the same refrain dully and ceaselessly; only now and then one of them dropped out to raise his glass and clink it with the others and drink. They were a crew that had been paid off that day from a sailing-ship which had gone to the west coast of America in ballast and returned to Hamburg with a cargo of saltpetre—a ten months' voyage. They had money in their pockets.

"Your health, Allan!"

"Your health, Jan!"

"Do you remember that long, sandy beach and the rubbish we sheltered under at night, and the old, battered tins we made our soup in? Fred, Fatty, Tin-box. . . ." Jan Geulen of the *Lesbos* had met a pal with whom he had been "on the beach" on the west coast.

"A damned bad time," said the Irishman.

"Yes, them was times!" answered Geulen.

In the dance-hall couples were revolving—heavy, steaming

bodies. A rough fellow with a face like a seal's held the belly-dancer in his arms. Her back and shoulders were light brown and she wore glittering bracelets on her arms and ankles. A sailor in a striped blouse from the south of France was dancing with the Dutchwoman who had previously given an entertainment with performing pigeons, and a Negro with a girl in a poppy-red dress.

"*Lesbos*, Levant Line," shouted Geulen in a loud voice so that the other should catch what he said in the noise. A tall, blonde girl who danced past the table at that moment turned to look at Jan. The man dancing with her had a shock of fiery red hair; he had no jacket and his shirt-sleeves were turned up; you couldn't help noticing his arms, with muscles like a gorilla's.

> "*. . . and the Great and Little*
> *Sunda Islands in the Pacific . . .*"

Some dock-labourers came in from the street carrying empty coffee-cans. They stood at the counter and ordered spirits.

"Damned drudgery!"

"It's this shift system."

"I've accounted for eighteen hundred today."

He and his gang had inserted eighteen hundred rivets. And work was still going on in their wake. In the shipyards and the dry and floating docks it went on uninterruptedly in day and night shifts. The ships moored to the quays loaded and discharged with feverish haste.

"There's something in the air."

It was the man of the eighteen hundred rivets who spoke. He was a big, broad-shouldered fellow with a broken nose. He seized his glass, and his hand was stained with soot and oil and looked like a big, black pair of tongs.

"The dockyard fellow's right. Have you read the proclamation?"

They had read nothing and knew nothing, and they hadn't time to bother; they were entirely occupied in making their money spin. They'd taken ninety-six days on the voyage from the west coast of America. The orchestrion played, and there was Black Bess, and Fritzi, and all the rest. The "seal" had known the belly-dancer before; his face lighted up when she came and stayed with him for a bit.

The long-legged blonde sat down beside Geulen. "So the *Lesbos* has put into port again?" she asked.—"Yes; midday yesterday. She's alongside the Levant Quay."

"Where are the others, then? Nobody else has been here from the *Lesbos*."

"Two are in hospital. And they nabbed a couple this morning at the Mercantile Marine Office. There was something wrong with their army papers."

The girls were as keenly interested in the arrivals at the harbour as any ship-broker.

"My name's Lena."

"And you work?"

"Yes, that too—I'm a saleswoman in the perfumery department of a store. Before that I was a seamstress, with my sisters. I didn't like staying at home."

"Extra!" called a newsboy. "Extra! French Deputy Jaurès murdered!" The song about the Sunda Islands was sharply interrupted. People bought papers. The sailor in the striped blouse left the girl whom he had on his knee, stood up, and uttered four or five sentences which none but his own countrymen understood. But hands were raised and caps taken off.

"He was a left-winger."

"He spoke against war."

>>>

"Jaurès murdered!"

"Landlord, a drink all round!" It was the dock-labourer with the broken nose who called for it, with a reverberating voice, right across the room. Holding their full glasses in their hands, they rose to their feet, the crew of the sailing-ship, some Swedes and Finns from a Russian steamer, the dock-labourers, some Frenchmen, and the women.

"Your health!"

"Good luck!"

And again and again: "Here's to Jaurès!"

Chairs were pushed back and tables crowded together. Jan gave one toast, then the Swedes, then the Irishman: "*Skool Swenska!*"—"Here's good luck to Ireland!"—"We'll all hold together!" The rough faces were animated and reserve was broken down; they felt as one man. The gigantic crocodile under the roof of the bar seemed to wake from a prolonged sleep. The dusty models of ships on the walls, the outrigger canoes of cannibal islanders, and the sails of ancient caravels and full-rigged ships seemed alert for fresh adventures.

The landlord made the orchestrion strike up and gave his assistant a signal to clear the tables of empty glasses. The atmosphere was favourable—drinks all round!

"I like this place best," said Lena. "I generally go to the Eldorado or the Guardsman's Ball-room. Real fine. Carpets. Cloak-room. But it's livelier here. If I was a man, I'd go to sea, too. You explain everything so nice."

Jan went on with his yarns: hookahs, barking dogs, veiled women on one coast. Hats like cart-wheels, mule caravans, and fandango-houses on another. And islands that rise from the sea with coco-palms, huts raised on piles, and naked natives.

"But life on board isn't all like that. Sometimes a ship has a deck-cargo, oil-tanks or something like that. Or else the voyage is long, and there's nothing to eat but salt meat and dried potatoes. Oh yes, I've quite made up my mind, I'm going to look out for a situation on land, working on a crane, perhaps on a harbour steamer. I'm not going to sea again."

Again the red panes glowed from the orchestrion, and couples revolved and stamped in the dance-hall. Those seated at the tables beat time with their fists on the boards. The revolving blades of the ventilator looked like an immense exotic insect in the dim light.

Jan Geulen was left sitting alone.

Lena was dancing with another man.

That damned deceptive light from the silly lamps! Lena really wasn't bad. She was standing by the counter now with the chap she had before. It was the red-head, and he was talking vehemently. . . .

"He's a fireman, he's been ashore a long time. Doesn't want to go to sea again."

If only the music would stop and the lights come on again. What a broad chest the fellow had! Gently, gently! What was wrong? Had he gone mad?

Had he really gone mad?

Jan leapt to his feet, and the others who were near rushed to the spot. But it had happened so quickly that all they could do was to catch the girl as she collapsed, her face a mass of blood and fragments of a broken beer-glass.

"I can do what I like with her! It's nothing to do with you!"

The fellow was possessed by a devil. He had not only the strength, but the swiftness of a wild beast. He defended himself with heavy blows against the sailors who were pressing upon him. His face seemed to gape open as he fought, and nothing was visible but the sombre gleam of his eyes. The landlord was shouting into the telephone. People were throwing chairs and glasses about. The whole bar was roused. The red-haired fireman twisted himself like a spring from the grip of arms and hands, leapt to the ceiling, and smashed the lamp.

"These damned affairs with women!"

"Stifling air!"

"Blast Heini!"

Then the trampling of heavy boots was heard. Everybody thronged to the door and out into the street. But already it was too late. The way was blocked by a chain of sturdy figures wearing peaked caps and carrying truncheons.

"The cops!" cried one of the girls.

"The cops—"

Police!

The side-street, too, was barred. The points of helmets glittered between the peaked caps. The little shopkeepers put out their lights and shut and bolted their doors. A shrill whistle gave a signal. The crowd in Daddy Lampel's bar made a move. "That's what they call 'morality'!"—"They only want the womenfolk!"

The "seal" had the belly-dancer by him. "Kuddl, come here!" someone called to him. "Take your girl with you. We're going to break through at the corner." Kuddl was slow of speech. "Break through!" he repeated, and added: "Jimmy!" That amounted to a promise: you can count on me.

"No exit!" cried the police.

"Make way!" snorted Kuddl, the seal.

With Jimmy at his side he hurled himself against the chain of police, and behind the pair was a wedge of faces, shoulders, and arms. The chain snapped under the violent assault. Jimmy was already through and others followed. But Kuddl was heavy-footed when it came to running. He had thrown one man to the ground and pushed a few more aside. But the "cops" surrounded him and barred the way. The helmeted force fired blank cartridges and received reinforcements. The whole crowd was driven back and bottled up.

A tall inspector of police spoke:

"The women may pass."

"The men are to line up here."

The inspector mustered his haul. He let the Negro, the man from southern France, and a few dagos go. All those who had fair hair and looked stiff and German were made to stand in rows, one behind the other.

"Form fours!"

"Detachment, march!"

The column began to move.

They all woke up in the drill-shed of an infantry barrack, all who had been ordered to the Mercantile Marine Office, or got together in bars and dance-halls. Human material forcibly collected in accordance with paragraph 78 of the Regulations respecting military service. In normal times one ordinary-sized room was enough for those "not recruited at the usual times," known as "A.G.'s" (*ausserterminlich Gemusterte*), with which the Navy supplemented its ranks, in addition to the regular spring and autumn drafts. But times were not normal, and everything was done convulsively and on an enlarged scale.

After their identification papers had been examined, they lay down on the floor. Then they heard doors banging, the building opposite began to hum with life, and heavy boots clumped across the hall. The military routine was beginning suddenly in the midst of this human swarm so precipitately dumped together.

"Shake a leg!" Not one of them but knew the force of that formula from his life on board ship and when keeping sea watch. But this was not the hand of one of their own number, one of the deck watch, shaking them by the shoulder: "Turn out. Shake a leg!" This was something different: ammunition boots that clattered noisily and strange, peremptory voices.

They sat up, one after another; their bones were stiff from lying on the hard boards. "They've got us this time!"—"If I'd been drunk at least! As sober as a fish! And my wife is coming today."—"Once I was in Newcastle, New South Wales. Went from one pub to another. Couldn't see anything but the lamps finally. And next day when I woke up with a head like lead, I was on board one of them cursed wind-jammers. Shanghaied! An A.B. at three pounds ten a month, when wages in port were five. But yesterday evening, and this now! This is the worst shanghaiing affair I've ever known."

The petty officer routed the last of them up from the floor.

"Prepare for medical inspection."

They washed, were given coffee, and undressed.

That was five o'clock in the morning. It was not till after nine that the inspection began. There were a major of the Medical Corps, the major who made the entries in the register of recruits, clerks, and medical personnel. At one end of the hall were the firemen, at the other the seamen: two groups of naked bodies, and faces dulled with waiting.

They were measured and weighed and everything was reduced to a formula.

"Next man!"

One figure separated from the group, walking on clumsy legs like a young ox. He was a sailor from a fishing-vessel and had been paid off after four trips to Iceland.

"Jump to it!" admonished the petty officer.

"Five foot ten!" announced the clerk.

"Hundred and sixty pounds!"

The doctor tapped his chest and listened to his heart, which he marked on his breast with a blue pencil.

"Bend your knees three times!"

Poor fisher-lad! His legs were all right on the rocking deck of a ship; he'd never practised bending his knees.

"Fit for service," said the doctor.

"Navy," wrote the major.

The doctor mopped the perspiration from his brow. "Good material, Major. The finest material, these A.G.'s."

"Go on; next!"

"Five foot nine; a hundred and thirty-six; chest: thirty-five: thirty-eight and a half."

"Where did you get that scar?"

"Crushed between two chests when we were loading cargo."

The doctor placed his fingers beneath the man's testicles:

"Cough! Now again!"

"About turn!"

"Lift your foot!"

"The other!"

"Fit for service."

"Navy," wrote the major.

Outside, the clock struck eleven.

"At four minutes past eleven my wife's train is due." He was a man with a greyish skin and long, hairy arms, a fireman who had been on a six months' voyage to the Far East. He felt as if a hand were gripping him round the abdomen, and then right up to his throat.

"The robber-gang!" he choked.

And then again:

"The damned robber-gang!"

It was just as if he had not spoken. In front of him a man with tattooed back, seat, and legs did not even turn round. It was close and stuffy in the hall. The smell of sweating bodies filled their nostrils and became increasingly oppressive.

It was a heavy job, and the doctor was no longer a young man. He suffered from a neurotic affection of the heart. His knees trembled and a cold sweat broke out on his brow. He tapped and listened, felt throat organs, inquired into venereal diseases, into the diseases of the men's parents, tested their sight and their sensitiveness to colour.

"About turn! That foot! Now the other!"

"No flat-footedness so far. Heart! Lungs! First-rate! Not an ounce of superfluous fat!"

"What is your name?"

Rather a clumsy lout, but bones like a horse—and such muscles! His head was wrapped up in wadding and bandages and only one eye was visible.

"What's wrong with your head?"

"Yesterday evening—"

He said no more, but regarded the doctor with his one exposed eye; it was Kuddl Bülow, who had defended the belly-dancer at the street-corner and knocked down half a dozen policemen with his friend Jimmy.

Fit for service. Navy. To the grey iron-clads!

The doctor had to send for a glass of water. He felt the beating pulse beneath the collar of his uniform. He saw the naked bodies through a mist, without faces, just bodies, firm, wholesome flesh. Grouped bundles of muscle that had hung from sheets and halyards of ocean-going vessels, had put on weight in the struggle against wind and ocean, and had a statuesque appearance. The seamen's hard backs, shoulders, and arms gleamed a dull brown, whilst the firemen's skin was grey like parchment.

"Go on; the next!"

"L.49. Weak heart. Fit for garrison duty."

The group was dwindling. Those who had been examined were allowed to dress. The doctor had unbuttoned his uniform at the neck; his flabby cheeks were flushed.

"Fit for service!"

"Fit for service!"

Two were permanently unfit, and six fit for garrison duty;

the majority were "A.G." for the North Sea naval station. The major made out an order to the railway authorities, requisitioning three coaches.

Jan Geulen had received a few blows from a man's fists on his shoulders and temples. Afterwards he saw with intensified, feverish clarity the row of houses plunged in darkness, transparencies fading away, flags blown against the walls, grey and colourless, and the long chain of street-lamps past which they were led.

When he was roused in the morning, he hardly knew what had happened. His head spun. The fat landlord, the blonde girl, the red-haired fireman, the faces of sailors and policemen, all whirled round and round.

If only he could spew it out. That was the thing. If he could be sick, he would get rid of that cursed pressure in his head. But he couldn't, and the buzzing went on. He stood stupefied in the perspiring swarm of humanity, his head sunk on his breast, his legs dully heavy. He let them push him on to the weighing-machine as if he were a dumb beast—weigh him, measure him, tap him.

He was in the front rank. Over on the other side of the chalk line the crowd of firemen were huddled. Legs and abdomens. They didn't know what to do with their arms; first they raised them to their sides, then slid them down their thighs to the knee. Limbs and faces a grey, colourless mass.

Geulen pricked up his ears.

"Dierck Butendrift—six foot. Thirty-eight and a half: forty-three."

The doctor called the major and had the measurement taken again. "Incredible, such a chest circumference! Magnificent! A unique case in my experience."

They dressed and then waited till those who had been

brought in last had fetched their possessions from the doss-houses or ships. Then they had to fall in in the barrack-square in fours, rank after rank.

"Detachment, march!"

Through the streets to the station.

Jan and Dierck were seated together. The carriage doors were not locked, but at the stations sentries patrolled past the windows. The men in the carriages sang soldiers' songs and sea shanties. Some had even adorned themselves with tinsel and paper flowers like conscript peasant lads travelling from their villages to the garrison towns to which they were assigned. They improvised wind instruments with combs and tissue paper.

"O Susanna, lovely Anna. . . ."

The small stations flew past the windows, dusty barns roofed with corrugated iron, and then the wide, purple heath. At one turnpike children were standing, little girls with thin arms and long, well-grown legs. They stood and waved.

In Bremen one or two who had been recalled on leave got into the train. Two men from the *König Albert* and one from the *Prinzregent Luitpold* joined Jan and Dierck in their compartment. The man from the *Prinzregent* wore a silver band on his cap.

"Here we are again, still three hours from Puddleton." The sailors called the city and district of Wilhelmshaven "Puddleton" and "Puddleshire" because the ground was so wet. "Where have you been, Alwin?"—"In Berlin," answered the fireman from the *Prinzregent*. "My first leave for eighteen months. A fortnight, but after five days I got this confounded note: 'Return immediately.' "—"It's just the same with us. I'd like to know what's up."

"You've got another new commander on the *Prinzregent*!" The recruits stopped speaking and listened. The three men on leave belonged to the 1911 class and would soon have finished their service. "Only three months more, and we're through with it."

"Are you going to Wilhelmshaven too?"

"Yes, in the Second Naval Brigade."

"Kids!" said one of the sailors from the *König Albert*, who was proud of being at the end of his term of service and able to reckon himself as an old tar. "Rot!" said the fireman. "We don't make any difference on the *Prinzregent* between recruits and old hands. We all stick together."

"And there's need, too," he said, turning to Dierck and Jan. "Service on battle-ships is often hard enough at best."

The sailor from the *König* changed his tune. "A pretty slip of a fellow!" he said, indicating Dierck Butendrift. "Been to sea—?"—"Oh, yes, sailing-ships. My last job was on a steamer, the Levant Line."

"Wilhelmshaven! All change!"

"Good-bye for the present, boys. My name's Alwin Köbis. When you're allowed out of barracks, come and see our *Prinzregent* some day, or come some evening to the Navy Bar."

Everyone was busy in the barracks, and the sleeping-quarters were full. The recruits were quartered in cellars, with straw mattresses.

During the night Jan started up. It was warm. The fresh straw and the men's breath gave out a sweetish smell like that of a cow-byre. In the wedge of light cast across the cellar by the moon he saw gaping mouths and hands like fingerless gloves. One man against the wall was snoring. And Jan could not get to sleep again. Fragmentary thoughts chased through his brain, rising like bubbles from unknown depths and bursting on the threshold of his consciousness.

>>

Oil-tanks—men-of-war with broad, black pennons of smoke
—a hand with bent fingers, as if it were trying to hold something
fast. That was how his mother's hand had looked when he
ran away from home. He had to pass through her bedroom in
the night. What a time it was since he had given it a
thought! . . .

The fireman from the *Prinzregent* that day, Alwin Köbis:
"Come to the Navy Bar some day—!" It was such a lean
hand—

At last Jan Geulen fell asleep again, sunk in contemplation
of the disjointed pictures painted by his pulsing blood. And
then came morning, and the stir of three thousand young men
waking up, the hum in the corridors and lavatories, and the
shrill voices of warrant-officers on duty roused him.

On the first day the recruits were entered in the Navy register. They all had the same distinguishing mark, "A.G.," and
the same year, 1914. Then they were clothed in identical shirts,
pants, and boots. Their hair was cut short, quite short. Their
skulls looked like bright, polished bullets afterwards, one almost
exactly like another.

The lieutenant commander strode along the line.

He saw long skulls and round skulls, flat ears and protruding
ears, determined jaws and receding chins, long, bold noses and
modest little organs of smell: a terrible variety, showing blind-
ness on the part of Nature which did not fit into the system
and must be corrected.

"Count off!" "One," began Butendrift at the right-hand
end. "Two," "Three." . . . Each man turned his head and
bellowed the number in his neighbour's ear.

"These recruits must be licked into shape."

And the chief petty officer gave instructions to those in charge
of the men's training—the petty officers, chief petty officers,
warrant-officers: "Rub them up! A double polish! You're up

against A.G.'s, men recruited outside the normal terms. They're unreliable seafaring men, and they've got to be licked into shape."

The work began. The men, drawn up in divisions, marked time, jumped over obstacles, and made about turns.

"Form fours!"

"About turn! March!"

"Halt!"

The ranks stood in the sand of the barrack-square under the hot sun of the North Sea coast, with its moorland and marshes. "Left face!"—"Right face!" "Lie flat!"—" 'Shun!" These movements were repeated for hours on end, till their bodies steamed, their muscles trembled, and their eyes and mouths were glued with dust and sweat, till their buttocks burned like fire, and every thought and every independent impulse was stifled, so that nothing remained but the dull response of circus-horses to the whip.

Then they received instruction in the barrack cellar.

They could sit down, and their eyes fell to. Upon their exhausted, unresisting brains the articles and rules of military rank were impressed. Warrant-officers and petty officers repeated eternally and monotonously the same idea: ". . . is forbidden, under penalty. Confinement to ship, brig, cells, degradation, prison, the firing squad!"

"Those men are asleep."

And the red-faced petty officer shouted:

" 'Shun!"

"Sit down!"

" 'Shun! Dismiss!"

They did not dismiss fast enough. There was only one door. The sergeant wanted to see nothing but boot-heels and cap-bands. The last to leave had to go out into the barrack-square for more drill. So they filed through the door: five times; ten times over. Afterwards a number of them reported injuries to the arms and legs.

Their training continued: insignia of rank. A pyramid of gold embroidery rose before their eyes. The petty officers wore anchors embroidered on their sleeves, sub-lieutenants a gold stripe on the sleeve, lieutenants two, and so on, till you reached that bugaboo who was one mass of glittering gold, the arbiter of life and death: "His Majesty the Emperor and King, Supreme War-Lord and Lord High Admiral of the German Fleet!" answered the recruit, goggle-eyed.

The use of the word "I" in addressing others was forbidden. Seaman Bülow, Seaman Geulen, Seaman So-and-so, answers, begs, obeys, speaks of himself in the third person, and becomes at last a nameless cipher in the human stores of the High Sea Fleet. ". . . three hundred, sir. A cruiser has a complement of a thousand, a battle-ship one thousand four hundred."

Next day brought the same routine over again. They drilled till the area of the barrack-square had been trodden out and rooted up by the impact of their bodies, till the red-brick buildings which enclosed the square seemed to collapse at the ends of the world and to rotate in mad delirium. Then boot, trouser, and bag-inspection, and instructions. And so on the third, fourth, and fifth day: the same movements, the same food, and at night the same foul smell.

It was the sixth day, after the midday meal, in the short pause between drill in the barrack-square and instruction. They were lying on their straw mattresses, and the sweat-soaked rags clung to their limbs. Some were plunged in a deep, dreamless state of relaxation, others lay with open eyes. Two hundred and fifty men were off duty, and not a word was spoken in the vaulted cellar.

Outside the low, barred windows the dusty road burned till it lost itself amidst the fallow fields. Suddenly a cry pierced the sleepy, heavy atmosphere, uttered by a man who had been looking out of the window. They sprang to their feet and crowded round the cellar windows, bunches of heavy faces. Not all could see, but all were conscious of the unnatural stillness, and all heard the roll of the drums.

Three men, with a drummer on the left and the right. The one in the middle held a sheet of paper. They were marching through the street in its midday stillness. They wore dress uniform, three marionettes of more than life-size with jerky, oscillating movements, bathed in the summer glare. Every fifty paces they stopped and the man in the middle, a sub-lieutenant, read in a loud voice:

> "Proclamation: I hereby decree: the German Army and the Imperial Navy shall be placed on a footing of readiness for war in accordance with the plans for the mobilization of the German Army and the Imperial Navy. August 2, 1914 shall be the first day of mobilization. Berlin, August 1, 1914. Wilhelm. IMPERATOR REX."

The tavern and doss-house Old Capetown also hung out a flag, a breadth of black, white, and red material which floated from the ridge of the roof almost down to the pavement. All the houses in the city were beflagged. Banners on all sides, and the boom of patriotic songs. Infantry marching in columns, with roses in their buttonholes and the barrels of their rifles, and the smell of sweat and leather in the air. Women in blouses and summer hats ran beside the troops marching out and distributed gifts—chocolate, cigarettes, and matches. War reports affixed to the walls of houses, a bearded veteran of '70 wearing the Iron Cross, Red Cross recruiting posters, and a hundred other appeals—all attracted the crowds as they strolled past and gathered them in noisy, disputing groups: "No more parties! We are all Germans and only Germans!" "Our Army! The Navy! Hurrah!"

Outside the door of Old Capetown stood the tavern guests, seamen who would also be called up within a few days. "Liége has fallen!" "Yes, the Army's all right! But the Navy's different. We haven't enough ships. Think of the English fleet, and then when it's joined with the French and Russian!" "To hell with that! When they come, we'll show 'em."

"Hullo, Admiral."

"Mornin', Turu."

The boatswain Kleesattel of the *Lesbos* and the red-haired fireman from Daddy Lampel's bar shook hands. "It'll begin tomorrow. We may find ourselves on the same ship again."

An artillery column jolted across the causeway.

"The women are simply off their heads."

"Just look at that Freda!"

"Which is she?"

"That one with the sunshade." The stoker pointed to a woman who was almost under the horses' hoofs. She stuck flowers in the cavalrymen's sword-frogs and nearly sprained her arm in the process. Her blouse was soaked with perspiration. The outline of her upstrained bust showed plainly above her corsets. Her husband, carrying his walking-stick and newspaper in his gloved right hand, ran breathlessly behind her, but resolutely maintained his amiable grin.

"I'd give her what for!" said Turu.

His real name was Turuslavsky.

"Now let's go and have a last round of drinks." "I must go on. I've something to see to." Stanislaus Turuslavsky turned round and elbowed his way, with rhythmically elastic tread, along the crowded street, without letting himself be pushed to right or left. Kleesattel looked after him. "We were together on the *Nymphe*, he in the stoke-hold and I on deck. He's a fighter! Once in Wilhelmshaven he cleared the whole picture-house, all by himself!"

Old Capetown, the Philadelphia Bar, the Red Sand Light-house—they went on from one tavern to another. The men couldn't drink as fast as they were treated. Drinks all round. Even the landlords weren't stingy. And in the evening, when the little bars down by the water were shut, the fun went on up in St. Pauli.

Everywhere business was brisk. And altogether—the world was suddenly transformed. The whole town had become one family. Everybody knew everybody else. There was a coal-heaver standing beside a pale carpenter, and together with them a stout gentleman whose firm dealt wholesale in furs. "Drink another glass, gentlemen! Where are you going?" "Arys, East Prussia. Against the Russians and the Tsar."

Karl Kleesattel was with several men, one of them a fore-man who was already wearing the new field-grey uniform with the gold braid of a non-commissioned officer. His father-in-law, a master baker, was with him: "My business has never been so brisk. I ought really to be in the bakery. But as my son-in-law is off tomorrow . . ."

They ascended the steps of a bar, out into the street. The air was thick with the smell of inhabited cellars and overcrowded houses. From the harbour a siren uttered a long roar and then died away—a ship hauled to another berth. There were no more arrivals and departures; the last had sailed on the previous day.

The Reeperbahn [1] and the amusement centre in St. Pauli!

---

[1] *Name of a street in St. Pauli, a quarter of Hamburg largely occupied with seamen's taverns and places of entertainment.*—TRANS-LATOR.

Beer- and coffee-houses. From the dark upper windows transparencies and flags hung almost down to the heads of the
passers-by.

Kleesattel, the man in field-grey, and his father-in-law and
wife were looking for seats in one of the large restaurants.
With difficulty they found four empty chairs. The music played
without interruption, and everybody sang patriotic songs. Stran-
gers raised their glasses to one another and shook hands.

"We'll be back by Christmas, Lottie."

"The achievements of our civilization are menaced. We must
defend our wives and our homes!" Kleesattel could not suppress the thought that in fact all he had to defend was a sack
stuffed with sea-boots, oilskins, and his working clothes. But
there you are, and the devil take it! The town was aflame with
enthusiasm. And he couldn't escape from the narrow limits of
his own personal interests. "The future of our nation is at
stake!"—"And the German ideal!"—"We must establish our
position in the world market."

The master baker had loosened his collar and tie.

The band was playing a flourish of trumpets.

A man with a protruding stomach beneath a white waistcoat
stepped up on the platform: "A special edition. The German
steamship *Königin Luise* has laid mines outside the mouth of
the Thames. In pursuing her the English cruiser *Amphion*
went down with a hundred and thirty men on board."

The man with the protruding stomach wiped the perspiration from his forehead. A tempest of applause broke out in the
room. People leapt to their feet and congratulated one another.
Karl Kleesattel felt the master baker's moustache, wet with
beer, against his cheek. Pah! He'd give the fellow one in the
eye! But the whole town was either exultant or tipsy. And
here was this wife, Lottie! She sat at the table with a tor-
mented, strained, absent look in her eyes. "The *Amphion* sunk.

That's all right," said Kleesattel, and got away from the baker.

"Yes, yes, our blue-jackets! All honour to them!"

People shook him by the hand, as if he had piloted the steamship to the mouth of the Thames. "Our sailors will teach the English a lesson!" Kleesattel thought of the dreadnoughts that he had seen off Malta a few weeks earlier, of the open maws of the 13.5-inch guns, a long row, almost beyond the reach of the eye. A single one of those shells weighed 1,463 pounds.

"The English dreadnoughts aren't made of cardboard, either," he said. Astonished faces, suddenly hostile: "What does the fellow mean—not made of cardboard? What are they, I should like to know?"—"Is he in the Navy at all?" Kleesattel had to defend his assertion: "The English have three times as many ships as we have. They have heavier guns. They've even got fifteen-inch guns!"

"But our ships are built of better stuff!" said the master baker, soothing ruffled feelings.—"And German shells carry farther." —"They've greater explosive force."—"German armoured ships are the best."—"And the German spirit!"—"That's right," said Kleesattel. The warrant-officer who instructed them on S.M.S. *Nymphe* had said the same.

The head waiter made his way between tables; he was perspiring and both hands were full of glasses of foaming beer. A brass band, with drums and kettle-drums: "*Deutschland, Deutschland über alles.*" They all leapt to their feet—even Kleesattel. They sang standing, so that their voices rose to the glass chandeliers beneath the ceiling: ". . . *über alles, über alles in der Welt!*"

A constant stream of transports of reservists who had been called up poured into the seaport of Wilhelmshaven. The barracks, drill-sheds, and dance-halls were packed. Kleesattel was quartered in one block of the Second Naval Brigade.

During the first night there were shouts and whistling signals in the dark corridors. An air-raid warning!

The block was packed to the very roof with troops. In the cellars lay recruits who were undergoing their first military training. They all dashed down into the courtyard. Karl Kleesattel, in stockinged feet, splashed into a puddle. "There! There they are! Above that dark cloud."—"No, no! Farther to the left." There was nothing to be seen but heavy masses of cloud approaching from the west, behind which shone the moon. When Kleesattel returned to his room, someone had stolen his straw sack. He slept that night on the bare floor.

And so days passed in monotonous guard duty, interrupted by hysterical spy-hunts, blind alarms of air-raids, or the destruction of a mine floating shorewards. Or else they were collected in working parties and sent to the shipyard to coal ships.

When they were off duty, they lounged in the bars of Wilhelmshaven or sat in the barrack-rooms, wrote letters, played cards, or gossiped about happenings at the front. Some volunteered for duty at sea, but only a few. The majority stayed in the barracks and waited. "Volunteer! Not me, I wouldn't do that." "If I gets my orders, that's different. Orders is orders, and you needn't blame yerself if anything goes wrong."

On the thirteenth morning at parade:

"Two, four, six . . ." the petty officer counted forty-two from the right, including Kleesattel: "Pack your kit! Fall in in front of the commander's office!"

In front of the commander's office there were already men from other companies, two hundred and eighty in all, including the firemen: a crew for a small cruiser. An officer addressed them:

"Seamen, firemen . . . an honourable duty laid upon you

. . . the small cruiser *Ariadne* to be put in commission again
. . . His Majesty the Emperor, hurrah!"

"Hurrah—ah—ah!"

The band played a chorale.

"Detachment, march at ease!"

The little cruiser *Ariadne* had been put out of commission
six years before and lay amongst the disrated "old iron" of the
Imperial Navy in the marine cemetery.

2. The Wet Triangle

KLEESATTEL was look-out-man in the crow's-nest. From up
there he had a wide view all around. The ship beneath him
looked like an elongated ellipse, pointed to the fore. The guards
behind the guns of the antiquated ship looked foreshortened
and huddled from his point of vantage.

The *Ariadne* was on patrol duty.

Four days in port, four days at sea.

They passed by the third battle-squadron. The modern ships,
with their powerful guns in turrets, lay at anchor, protected by
a stretch of sand-banks, by a belt of mines, and by a screen of
small ships forming a wide circle thrust out into the North Sea.
The *Ariadne* steamed on at twenty knots.

That strip of sand to the left was the island of Wangeroog.
The old church tower at its western point, which had been
a landmark seen from far and wide by homebound ships for a
couple of centuries, had now shrunk to a mere heap; it was
being entirely dismantled so as to give the enemy no indication
of where to make for port. West of Wangeroog lay Spiekeroog,
Langeoog, and then Baltrum, and after that the chain of East
Frisian islands as far as Borkum; beyond that, Dutch territory
began.

From Borkum, in the Ems estuary, to Sylt, on the coast of
Holstein, the patrol boats cruised in wide circles right across
the North Sea. There were destroyers and armoured fishing-
boats. Behind these effectives light cruisers patrolled.

The line from Borkum to Sylt represented the base of the
"Wet Triangle," whilst the East Frisian and Holstein coasts
formed its two sides. The apex was in the estuary of the Elbe,
near Cuxhaven; it was a dismal area, generally wrapped in
fog, shallow water with banks, quicksands, and short, sharp

waves. The volume of water which the great rivers, the Elbe and Weser, here pour into the North Sea, seems to dissolve in mist when it comes in contact with the colder sea-water. The masses of mist lie flat on the surface, and the wind rolls them up into nebulous islands and blows them hither and thither.

The *Ariadne* zigzagged from east to west.

Every half-hour she altered course.

After two hours the sentries were relieved, and after four hours the whole watch. The watch below was mending clothes. They sat together, ten at a table, and mended undergarments or sewed marks on their clothes. Some, under cover of the piled-up heap of mending, risked a game of skat.

"Harry's deal." Harry Mathieson, who had been a boiler-maker at the Blohm and Vose works in Hamburg in peace time, shuffled the cards and dealt. "Spades are trumps."—"All right, but not so loud," said one of them warningly.—"To hell with that; Weiss is the petty officer on duty; he won't say anything."

Karl Kleesattel was seated at the next table, and round him was a little crowd. He was elucidating certain questions of tactics. "We can't do much with our handful of pop-guns. But there's no need. We and the other small cruisers are just feelers put out, don't you see? Then the armoured cruisers will come along. And behind the armoured cruisers is the High Sea Fleet."

Kleesattel was again called "Admiral," as he had been when he was serving his time, because he was so well up in nautical technicalities. "When you've served your three years in the iron-clads and poked your nose into a book now and then, it's nothing to wonder at," he said. "Of course you mustn't bother about service regulations. There's nothing there except how to behave in the presence of your superior officers, and how important your oath on the colours is, and how many stripes a vice-admiral has, and a lot more rubbish like that."

"Yes, all that balderdash! They'd much better explain to us what it's really all about. And especially where the war's being fought now."

The "Admiral" laughed compassionately. "You're on the wrong tack there, they can't do that. Why, then you'd be as clever as the officers. They won't allow that! What is your battle station? Breech at the second port gun! Right hand on the crank-handle, left hand down! Half-turn right when you close! Half-turn left when you open! You've got to know all that. And perhaps, too, how to shove a shell into place, if the loader gets knocked out.

Weiss, the petty officer, a short man with springy movements, patrolled along beside the tables. He stood still for a moment and listened. He had a pock-marked face, large cheek-bones, and the half-veiled expression of a big, good-natured boy. "Always thoughtful, lads!" he said, and sauntered on slowly. Kleesattel realized why, after almost nine years' service, Paul Weiss hadn't risen higher and still had only one anchor on his sleeve.

Suddenly and unobtrusively the cards disappeared.

The sailors bent over their sewing.

The officer of the watch had appeared on deck. His uniform, clinging to his tall, lean person, had an unfamiliar, Sunday-like appearance. "A reservist from Silesia, a Civil Servant." " 'Shun!" The lieutenant had stepped up on an ammunition box and stood there as if he were on a platform, holding in his hand the Commander-in-Chief's order of the day, transmitted by wireless.

". . . BRITISH FORCES ARE PATROLLING ONLY BETWEEN THE NORWEGIAN AND SCOTTISH COASTS. NO ENGLISH SHIP HAS YET BEEN SIGHTED IN ANY OTHER PART OF THE NORTH SEA. THE BRITISH GRAND FLEET IS

AVOIDING THE NORTH SEA ALTOGETHER AND
KEEPING BEYOND RANGE OF OUR GUNS.
NEVERTHELESS, THEY MUST AND WILL COME
ULTIMATELY. THEN WE SHALL SETTLE
ACCOUNTS. ON THAT DAY OF SETTLEMENT
WE SHALL BE AT HAND WITH ALL OUR
BATTLE-SHIPS!"

The lieutenant had also brought the latest issue of an illustrated paper for the entertainment of his division. He read two
poems out of it, one about the *Goeben* and *Breslau*, which had
broken through off Messina, and the other about a sub-lieutenant
who dashed into the midst of a hail of bullets with drawn sword
and fell dead with a cry of "Hurrah for His Majesty!"

"No one can equal us there!" cried Lieutenant Alvens rhe-
torically, with a sinister, fanatical expression. A lock of hair
had fallen over his forehead, and his eyes stared wide, like those
of the heroic sub-lieutenant in the poem. The men stood as
motionless as the movement of the ship allowed and looked past
the officer to the iron bulkheads or out through the scuttles,
following the grey volume of smoke as it faded away.

"Dismiss! Stow away clothing!"

"What else could a lieutenant chap like that do, anyway?
He's been taught nothing but how to die. Courage in civil life
now, that's a very different matter."

The sailors drifted back again and packed up their mending.
Underclothing, uniforms, sea-boots, all were laid together in
the little lockers. Exactly according to rule, each tidily arranged locker looked precisely like all the rest.

The one and only thing on the ship which had been left
to the private use of the men was the interior of the locker door,
a surface of sixteen inches by twenty. Karl Kleesattel could find

no use for this surface. The man with the locker next to his had hung up a picture of a group, a crew with a life-buoy and the name of the ship in the centre. His neighbour on the other side had a woman, with the heads of a boy and girl beside her, as well as picture postcards of a little town among the mountains. "The wife and kiddies. The little chap's the eldest," he had told Kleesattel a few days earlier.

At supper they had to hold their tin cans of tea and keep them level all the time. The *Ariadne* trembled when she moved at high speed, like a shaking fever patient. "Damn these tin basins. You can't put them to your mouth, they're so hot."—"Nothing but bread and margarine," grumbled another man.—"A sausage relish twice a week. The bacon-cutter won't give out any more," declared Harry, who was cook and had for a week to receive the rations and carry them forward.

After the meal the men lit their pipes. The bare compartment was warmer and cosier when it was full of blue clouds of tobacco-smoke. "It's really just like peace time. I always thought of war as something quite different."—"So far we've just been straying about in the mist. The battle-ships are lying at the mouths of the Elbe and the Jade."—"When the English come, they'll all steam out. Didn't you hear the order?" "Pipe down."

The benches and tables were hoisted up and hung beneath the deck-beams. A little later and all the men were lying in their hammocks, swinging rhythmically to and fro with the motion of the ship. They were slung one above another in two or three tiers. The rows of lamps were put out. Through the confused mass of outstretched hammocks the dim lights that burned through the night glowed red.

The men did not fall asleep at once. They went on talking in low voices, about the war and the possibility of a naval attack. "The English won't come. And until our troops have captured Antwerp and Calais, we shan't attack either," said

≪≪

one.—"The Commander-in-Chief isn't up to much. But the Admiral of the first squadron, he'll make things hum." Able Seaman Kühnle, from the Swabian hill country, was telling the man in the next hammock about his little Lolo: "He's only four, but eh! he knows what he's talkin' about. The day before I was called up, I was goin' home with him in the evenin'. 'Little stars!' he says, and raises his arm. 'Little stars high up. Lolo tan't reach 'em! But Daddy tan't reach 'em neiver!' The little chap was real proud of it."

"The boilers are clogged with dirt. We've got to put into the shipyard." "When we get into port, we're going to Kiel to have the boilers cleaned. If we stay over Sunday, maybe we'll get leave and go to Hamburg."

"Fiete! Are you asleep?" No answer.

Somewhere a couple were still whispering. Then their voices ceased. The red lamps grew more and more befogged. The ventilating motors worked convulsively at pumping out the stuffy air from the sleeping-quarters. You could hear their even hum, and from time to time a wave beating against the ship's side.

At midnight the watch changed.

After her spell on patrol duty the *Ariadne* did not make for Kiel, nor did she go into dock for repairs. The cleaning of her boilers was put off to some future time. After four days in harbour she was cruising once more in the outer estuary of the Jade.

In the crow's-nest Karl Kleesattel was perched up among the clouds, above the bridge and the two funnels, in a half light that belonged to neither night nor day; he was soaked to the skin by the damp in the air. The sea was smooth, but above it volumes of dark fog towered and billowed. He thrust his hands into his pockets. He could only bury his face in his collar up to the mouth. He had to scan the horizon ceaselessly,

and the floating, eternally shifting layers of fog. He could see
three or four miles, no farther. A man's heart beat more slowly
in that grey chaos.

Suddenly he started up.

On the port bow a booming issued from the fog. There was
nothing to be seen, only the seething outlines of great masses
of fog. There it was again, a dull, thunderous roar. And again,
and yet again! In the intervals of volleys fired by heavy guns!

The *Ariadne* altered course.

She ran on into the fog at a high speed. On deck all was life
and stir. The crew sprang to the guns and took their places at
the telephones and transmitting station. The stokers' watch
below vanished down the ladders to the stoke-hold. Clear decks
for action!

The gun-pointers adjusted their instruments. The am-
munition-conveyors clattered and raised shells and charges
on deck from the magazines below the water-line. The stretcher-
bearers lined up in front of the dressing-station. Down below in
the stoke-hold the firemen bent in front of the furnace doors
and emptied their well-filled shovels with the wide sweep of
their strong arms down the craters—several yards in depth—or
stirred the red-hot glow with heavy pokers. Their bodies gleamed
red in the fire-light. The sweat made white channels in the
coal-dust that powdered their skin. In the engine-room flashing
metal, piston-rods, all in furious motion. And between them the
oilers with oil-smeared arms and balls of cotton waste in their
hands. The steam pressure from ten boilers that was here transformed into power set gleaming, blue steel rods in motion
and sent the propeller-blades pounding furiously through the
water.

The chief engineer at the centre was connected by voice-
tubes with the separate parts of the engine-room. All the boiler-
rooms reported steam pressure up to the red line.

"One hundred and twenty-four revolutions!" he reported to the bridge.

On the bridge, in the captain's hands, all the threads were gathered: guns, engines, navigation, wireless telegraphy. And the link of wireless made him and his ship just an outstretched feeler of the heavily equipped battle-cruisers steaming up astern. The light cruiser's task is to make contact with the enemy and to keep in touch with the flagship of the reconnaissance forces, and report on the position.

For three hours the *Ariadne* had been steaming at a high speed. The look-out had been reinforced by one man. Harry Mathieson stood shoulder to shoulder with the "Admiral" in the crow's-nest. Neither of them took the glasses from his eyes.

"Can you see anything?"

"Nothing."

"But they're firing heavier than ever."

"A dirty business!" said Harry. "I never cared for war and all that military stuff. But once you're in it, you do your bit. Did you see how the boys handed the shells? And the stokers —they're all above the red line. The old hulk's never steamed as she's doing today."

"If only it would begin soon!" answered Kleesattel.

Mathieson searched the horizon astern. "Still no sign of our battle-cruisers."—"That's only because it's so hazy. They're following close in our wake. Just like in the manœuvres. When we knock up against the English and report, they'll appear."

It grew rather brighter. There was a break in the foggy atmosphere of the gigantic "wash-house," but out beyond, the damp mists continued to rise.

"Admiral, do you see?"

"Yes, right ahead!"

"Ship right ahead!" the look-out reported to the bridge. "She's bearing straight down on us!"

"Three funnels. That's the *Köln.*"

"She's under fire."

"She's in flight!"

Another vessel issued from the wall of fog, a gigantic grey colossus. The *Ariadne* called the ship with her searchlight. The ship did not reply.

"A battle-cruiser!"

"A British ship!"

From the bridge they recognized the ship's silhouette. The bridge sentry, messengers, guns' crews—each man passed on to the next what he had heard. The *Ariadne* was one single bundle of strained nerves. Rigid faces below the ventilation shafts and pump shafts leading to the magazines and engine-rooms.

"What's going on on deck?" voices asked from the bunkers and engine-rooms and stoke-hold. "What's that above?" called Seaman Kühnle up the ammunition-conveyor of the shell-room aft.

"A big British ship."

"Four turrets: 13.5!"

"Flagship *Lion.*"

"And what about our ships?"

"Not in sight yet."

A second battle-cruiser of the same class hove in sight, the *Tiger.* Sixteen heavy turret guns trained upon the little *Ariadne.*

"Hard a-starboard!" ordered the commander.

"Hard a-starboard, sir!" replied the helmsman.

The *Ariadne* reversed her course and tried to retreat into the fog at full speed. The *Lion* fired from her foremost turret. Smoke rose from the muzzles.

"Like an express train clattering across an iron bridge," observed Harry Mathieson. He choked at the words. His eyes were glassy. Kleesattel recognized the ship—he had seen her

a few weeks earlier off Malta! She was swarming with sailors
then. Yes, he ought to have knocked in that Hamburg master
baker's teeth! That Red Cross sister in Bremen—how long and
slender her legs were!

A second and a half!

Two fountains rose out of the sea a few hundred yards ahead
of the ship. "Fifty-five hundred!" announced the fire-control
for the information of their own gunners. "Fifty-five hundred!"
the voice-tube men repeated to the gunners.

"Salvo—fire!"

The gun-pointers—for the foremost starboard gun it was
Petty Officer Paul Weiss—jerked the trigger-lanyard. A deafening roar. The gun sprang back on its mounting. Each shell
thirty-two pounds of iron. Mere peas, which ricocheted ineffec-
tually against the heavy armour-plating of the battle-cruiser.

The *Ariadne* was 2,600 tons.

Each one of the battle-cruisers was 30,000 tons.

The five men serving each of the *Ariadne's* guns stood un-
sheltered on deck. The eighty serving each British turret gun
stood behind thick protecting walls of plate armour.

The next salvoes fell astern. The enemy had zigzagged
towards them and got their range. And now the gun-flashes
were directed on the *Ariadne* from two points. The brown cordite smoke rose like a wall.

The *Köln* had vanished in the fog.

The *Ariadne* had turned her stern-post to the battle-cruisers
and offered only a narrow target. The shells crashed beside the
vessel. Columns of water, green and resplendent, rose like
crystal arches and then fell on her deck. Five hundred, or perhaps a thousand, tons of water falling from cloudy heights—and
the force there is in water! The ship's whole frame creaked
and shivered and then suddenly dropped down like an over-
burdened mule sinking on its haunches.

Below decks all was confusion. Glasses, instruments, and controls were smashed. The lamp filaments were shivered to dust. On the quarter-deck blood-stained, battered faces rose from out of the ebbing water. The tall Lieutenant Alvens was carried away with broken arms.

"More revolutions!" the captain insisted.

The wireless telegraphic apparatus tapped out an S O S.

"Fire!" came the order from the gunnery-officer.

The stokers worked like devils under the lash. Coal-barrows, pokers, clattering furnace doors! The sweat-soaked rags stuck to their thighs. Their lungs and chests worked like bellows—steam! steam!

On deck, by the guns: charges rammed home, breech closed! See through the telescopes the grey phantoms approaching. When the gun lies true on its mark, fire! Suffocating fumes from the powder. Smarting eyes. Throats burning and parched.

When the smoke disperses, on again without a pause.

Each shell thirty-two pounds of iron, and a hundred and sixty pounds each broadside.

The *Lion* and *Tiger* fired at long intervals, but with every salvo they hurled over six tons of steel and dynamite into the air.

"Hullo, you on deck!"

Fireman Turuslavsky stood at the bottom of the ventilating shaft.

"Are our battle-ships in sight?"

The seaman up above—a link in the chain of those handing along ammunition—put down his burden. His neighbour had disappeared. Something was stuck to the side, flat and broad like a stretched cow-hide, and trickling down on to the deck in red and grey streaks.

What were those firemen for ever wanting?

The sailor put his head down the ventilating shaft.

"Are our battle-ships in sight?" repeated Turuslavsky.

"Shut your bloody mouth!" bellowed the sailor from above, down into the darkness.

Turuslavsky gripped his coal-shovel and resumed his place in the row. The pressure in the boilers was near bursting-point. But the engine had reached the limit of its powers.

"She's too old, the damned hulk."

"Too slow to get away."

Ammunition-porters and look-out-men and the blackened faces of those in the guns' crews, all kept turning their eyes eastwards whence heavy reinforcements might come. And again and again all living flesh stooped and crouched when the air reverberated with the onrush of the shells.

"Karl—!"

"Harry! Old chap!"

They gripped and held one another, and each saw the other's pale face like the mirrored reflection of his own, caught in a flash. Then they drew in air with a deep breath. The mast was still standing:

"It's the air pressure. You can't do nothing against that, Harry."

An earthquake must be like that. Just the same upward thrust in your guts. But floating vessels have more spring and soften the shock. All the same, your whole body is shaken to the very bones. Your nerves are a-tremble.

And it wasn't the end yet, what was going on on deck—that gurgling downward plunge and the blaze that shot up as high as the crow's-nest and blinded their eyes. Kleesattel recovered his sight, he could still hear, he reflected and observed.

The shell had smashed through the deck and exploded in the bows. A rush of air at high pressure whistled through the hole it had pierced. Coal-dust! Smoke! The dust settled in a dark cloud, emitting sparks. The ascending smoke was of a dark ochre-brown. Through exits and man-holes, and finally even through the hole pierced by the shell, a flood of half-naked, blackened bodies emerged. The stokers! They were leaving their posts. The bunker coal had caught fire. The stoke-holds were full of smoke. Five boilers were out of action.

The *Ariadne* was now only making headway at half speed.

The machinery attached to the forward gun was out of ac-tion; the sights and telephone had been swept away. Petty Officer Weiss took his bearings over the barrel and chimed in only a little behind the other guns.

"Salvo—fire!"

They crouched behind the smoke of their guns, five men at each gun. A handful on the bridge and at the searchlight and signal stations. At the foot of the bridge and round the sockets of the funnels stood the fugitive firemen. Everywhere clutch-ing hands, and jaws so tightly set that the bones showed white through the cheeks!

There was no more ammunition for the after guns. The am-munition-conveyor had been blown in. The magazine was plunged in darkness. The men were groping past chests of charges and piles of shells, up to their waists in water, till they reached the iron ladder.

"Get on, Kühnle. Open the damned thing!"

Seaman Kühnle hung beneath the hatch, clinging to the lad-der with one hand whilst with the other he shoved with all his might against the door. He paused without speaking and then tried again.

"Can't you move it?"

"No! I'm damned if I can," he gasped at last.

On armoured deck I and II also, the watertight hatch stuck fast and couldn't be moved a fraction of an inch. A blow had bent it. Something between fifteen and twenty men were huddled together, clinging in the darkness. Their pulsing blood counted the hammer-strokes as they listened to the pattering of tools against the hatch from outside.

The commander with artificers was trying to liberate the imprisoned men. Several firemen, Stanislaus Turuslavsky carrying a big hammer in his hand, came to the deck. The fire burst forth. Boots and fragments of all sorts were transformed into flying ammunition. Men's bodies were swept across the empty space like dry leaves and hurled against the iron bulkhead. Turuslavsky and the other firemen on their way to the hatch lay on the ground like fish cast up on dry land, gasping for breath. The artificers had disappeared and so had the wounded men who had been laid on deck on stretchers, and the sick-bay attendants, the doctor, and the commander. From the heap beneath the bulkhead rose a long-legged ghost and staggered through the compartment; it was Lieutenant Alvens. The blue flames enveloped him as they ran across the deck. His arms were like madly flapping banners. The men who were making their escape upwards over the wreckage heard the sound of his high-pitched, jerky voice.

And now the shells were coming in a long, level flight and tore the sides of the ship. Seething steam and black, curling smoke poured out of every crack and crevice. The lights went out in the stoke-hold aft. The compartments were full of smoke, and it swept across the decks. Those who could still use their legs cleared the stern and dragged the wounded along with them. Midships from the navigator's bridge telephone wires and voice-tubes, riddled with shot, came tumbling down like mutilated iron intestines. There was nothing to be seen of the bridge, funnels, masts; they were lost in a thick veil of smoke which the battered ship trailed after her in a broad path.

For the past half-hour the sky had arched above the ship

and crew like an immense, booming metal bowl; now it was suddenly still and stopped its swinging motion.

The *Lion* and *Tiger* had ceased fire.

They could no longer see anything in the smoke.

Two boats were still seaworthy, being only knocked about by splinters above their water-line. They were launched. Then the wounded were let down with ropes. Stumps were bandaged as well as could be managed. One leg that was still hanging by a fragment of flesh was amputated with a knife.

The rest of the crew crouched in the bow.

Their eyes were inflamed and their voices hoarse.

"There are still some under armoured decks I and II."

"And some in the magazine aft."

"All the watertight compartments are flooded."

"Petty Officer Weiss is aft with one or two men." A hundred pairs of eyes stared fixedly astern into the raging witches' cauldron, seething with steam and smoke. The charges and shells lying beside the guns exploded. The hull was one burning, red-hot mass. The flimsy armoured deck beneath their feet grew hotter and hotter, so that it was unbearable in the forecastle.

An officer's uniform, four gold stripes on the sleeve—the captain. He spoke just a few words.

Why did the German High Sea Fleet not arrive? Why was the *Ariadne* forced to submit to being shot at till she caught fire? He did not answer these questions. He ended with "Three cheers for His Majesty the Emperor!"

A shadow fell upon the glassy red chaos, a group of human forms supporting one another and helping one another along. Paul Weiss and his men. Scorched and exhausted, they came towards the bows. The men from the armoured deck were not with them.

The captain gave the order:

"On life-belts! Abandon ship!"

The sea-gulls were screaming. A wind sprang up, sweeping in a mighty curve from the North Sea. Increasing in force, it pierced through the banks of fog, whipped and rent the veils of mist rolling out from the river mouths, and forced them upwards.

It was nearly evening. The low sun was still veiled, but a wider stretch of sea was visible. With the rising north-west wind behind, the North Sea was swept into the Triangle. The rising tide dashed over the flat sands and broke in short, choppy waves.

Plaice and flounders dived down and lay behind sand-banks, in sheltered basins and hollows, flat on their bellies. With the inflowing stream of salt water came shoals of cod-fish with big maws, and fish of prey armed with teeth, and swam level across the bottoms. Flat-fish quivered and scattered a sprinkling of sand over their mottled backs.

A storm from the north-west!

A flat, clean-swept sky—foamy wave-crests—gulls rushing through space in rapid curves and plunges. Small vessels were making way against the sea, pitching and shipping water. Destroyers and small cruisers were searching the grey battle area where the shots had made havoc in the fight.

"Patrol boat *187* sunk!"

"*Köln* sunk!"

"*Mainz* sunk!"

"*Ariadne* sunk!"

Four ships with twelve hundred men. Four immense patches of oil drifted upon the sea, viscid mirrors radiating far around; the waves rebounded from them and broke against the edges. On their gleaming, violet surface chests floated and mattresses and corpses borne up by cork jackets. And in between, arms moved that had swum to the point of exhaustion, and livid green faces stared.

The destroyers and cruisers put out boats and took on board those who were still living, and afterwards the dead. Then they steered for land, scudding slowly before wind and sea.

The light-ship in the outer estuary of the Jade, Wangeroog, Schillig Road: the incoming vessels had to pass the squadron of battle-ships which lay at anchor against the flat silhouette of the land.

The little cruiser *Frauenlob* steamed past at half speed. Her after funnel was torn open. Amidships a shell had carried a gun away, and aft, just above the water-line, a great hole gaped. The *Stettin*, too, had one of her funnels torn open and riddled by shell-splinters. A half flotilla of destroyers followed in line ahead in the wake of the cruisers.

On the battle-ships the officers and crews had fallen in for divisions below the foremost turret guns: "Three cheers for S.M.S. *Frauenlob*! For the *Stettin*, the *Rostock*, the *Danzig*!"

The crews of the small cruisers stared at the gigantic gun-turrets and broad, curved sides of the iron-clad—fit adversaries for the *Lion* and *Tiger*, for Admiral Beatty's battle-cruiser squadron. They had never raised their anchors from the sand that day and had lain where they were. Mechanically, and only in response to commands, the light cruisers answered the booming roar from the battle-ships. The answering hurrahs from the destroyers were feebler and fainter still.

One vessel with a direct hit in her stem had her bows plunged deep below the surface and was under water up to the foot of the bridge. But she still steamed on with her own engines. The young captain on the shot-riddled bridge stood rigid like a wooden figure, his eyes fixed on the Admiral's flag at the main of the fleet flagship. The crew and the men rescued from sinking ships stood on the quarter-deck, dirty and drenched, whilst the "Hurrah!" from a thousand throats on the battle-ships echoed above their heads. Not an arm was raised. The vessel steamed dumbly past the big ships.

The procession ended with the "bone-collector," with the Red Cross on her funnels and sides, her flag at half-mast. On her deck lay the gathered-up corpses, covered with an ensign. In her cabins the wounded men who had been picked up out of the sea lay writhing in pain, wrapped up in woollen blankets. From all the cabins you could hear the cries and groans of men burned and scalded with steam and mutilated.

Silence fell, too, upon the battle-ships. The crews of a thousand men stood in sombre groups on deck and gazed after the ship that glided slowly past and faded into the gloom.

When the recruits were engaged in rifle-drill the next morning, a company of men marched across the barrack-square, a disorganized, moving mass.

"Bülow! Don't stare like an owl!" bellowed the petty officer. "Order arms! At ease!"

The group approached; they wore wooden clogs, and their trousers and shirts were smeared with blood. Most of them had no caps and the cap-bands of the rest bore their ship's name in gold and silver lettering: S.M.S. *Ariadne.*

Butendrift recognized one of the besmeared faces: Boatswain Kleesattel of the *Lesbos*. His head and half his face were hidden by a bandage. Butendrift wanted to call out: "Bos'n!" But he could only signal secretly. Kleesattel jogged past without noticing him in the line.

" 'Shun! Trail arms!"

"Quick march! Double!"

The petty officer remained standing on the spot. Until he gave another order, the recruits moved away from him, and as they ran, they were able to exchange a few words. "Those were from the *Ariadne*."—"Good God, what a sight!"— "Picked up out of the water. They got the clogs from another ship." Butendrift was marching on the right. He turned half round. "Jan! Karl Kleesattel was among them."—"Yes, I saw him."

An hour later, before the midday meal, boat-inspection. The recruits stood in the corridor on the top storey of the barracks. Each held in his hand a pair of short boots, polished bright, and called 8.8 after the light calibre of the ship's guns.

The chief petty officer, a chief mate of long service, strode along the line. He was in a bad humour in spite of his new uniform, which had been conferred upon him only the day before and which he was now wearing for the first time—collar, tie, and peaked cap.

"He looks like a groom!" said one man.

"Like a commissionaire," said another.

"That's just why he's so wild," Geulen divined.

He stopped in front of Seaman Bülow: "What, you call those boots clean? Out of the window with them! Out, all 8.8's! Downstairs and fetch them up again!"

The boots were thrown out of the window down into the barrack-square. They turned and went. Only the petty officers and the newly rigged-up chief petty officer of recruits stayed in the corridor.

He tramped to and fro with long strides.

Hell! He had to work off his rage on somebody. There was no one he could talk it over with. . . . These goings-on of the Promotion Board—a uniform with a tie and collar instead of being promoted warrant-officer—putty medals! China commemoration medals! Eighteen years' service at sea! And then these miserable togs as a reward! . . . A uniform without a sword! Required to salute!—He must still turn off the pavement on to the causeway for every green sub-lieutenant! That

was the Tirpitz system—economy below, extravagance above!
The company had fallen in again.

"You blasted swine! I'll give your silly legs something to
do. Do you call that standing straight? Out with your boots!
Again: down you go!"

The chase began all over again. But they no longer grazed
and hurt themselves on the stairs. The recruits had grown
accustomed to the system, and even in formation they retained
a certain independence and, when occasion arose, developed a
common habit of going slow. "Lord, how they must have trodden on our little fellow's toes!"—"He's annoyed about the
naval defeat."—"The *Mainz* went down, too."—"They
say that not a single man was saved from the *Köln.*"

The two hundred men were late for dinner. Butendrift and
Geulen, carrying their full bowls, searched all along the tables.
The men from the *Ariadne* were sitting together. The seamen
were already provided with fresh clothing. The firemen, who
came from another barracks, were still bundled in the same
dirty things in which they had been picked up out of the water.

"Abandon ship! Very different from when they used to say:
'Swimmers outboard!' No headers and no fancy tricks. They
dropped into the water like sacks. One jumped right on to the
small of my back."—"Did you see Josh? He'd tied a hammock
under his arms."—"We were in luck. The *Danzig* and the
Stralsund came along at once and sent out boats. But you ask
my friend from the destroyer!"

The man sat motionless before his bowl, his face sunken, dark
rings round his eyes.

"How long were you actually drifting?"

"Just after eight in the morning we sighted two destroyers,
and then some more joined them, and afterwards a cruiser
with four funnels; *187* went down bows first. I was already
in the water."

Geulen and Butendrift elbowed through the men standing round the tables. They had discovered Karl Kleesattel.

"Hullo, bos'n."

"Eh! Dierck! Jan!"

He wrung their hands.

"You've had another nasty knock."

"Oh, me, that's only a scratch on the forehead. But the others . . ."—"Why did our big ships stay at anchor? That's what I'd like to know," said one man. "The approach of the English was reported just after eight, and it wasn't till two that we got into the fight."—"I don't understand that either. They lay only two hours' steam away and didn't move an inch. Not one of the English ships would have got away."

"The second squadron lay off Cuxhaven and had got up steam for full speed. And the first and third in Schillig Road, too. But the Commander-in-Chief never gave the order to set out. The battle-cruisers were at Wilhelmshaven and they didn't set out till it was all over."

The seaman from the destroyer began to tell his story in a low voice, as if he were talking to himself; his eyes had a faraway expression.

"We had a raft—four of us. All we could do was to cling fast to it. Each wave broke right over our heads. And Lord, how our eyes and noses smarted! If only those two had held fast to the corner! The raft was all tipped up and suddenly it keeled right over. When we came up again, there were two of us, Hermann, of the ventilating motor, and me.

" 'Hermann,' I said, 'hold fast, like this, with your stomach and legs. And when the spray comes, shut your mouth.' Hermann just looked at me, didn't say a word. Then we saw a boat, not far off; she rose on the crest of a wave and was gone again in a jiffy. We spat and spewed, we were that wretched.— 'It's no good hanging on . . .' said Hermann. 'If you reach dry

land, just listen: Duisburg, 26 Linden Street.' I'd no idea what
he meant, I was just staring at the sky; it was all green, with
stripes. But I did remember 'Duisburg, 26 Linden Street.'

"Then nothing happened for a long time.

"Suddenly I opened my eyes and grabbed hold of the raft;
something had jerked it, and the waves were much bigger. I
was all alone. Hermann was drifting a few yards away in his
life-belt, head downwards, just like the others before. 26 Linden Street! But I shall never get to Duisburg."

"To barracks. Now, jump to it!" came the warning voice
of the petty officer on mess duty. Dinner-time was nearly over
and the mess-room was gradually emptying.

"Those heavy guns!" said one man, recalling the scene.

"They pounded through the thin armoured deck as if it
were cardboard."—"And they set fire to everything in no
time."—"But the English shells have fuses that act without delay. Else they wouldn't have torn away the thin metal of the
funnels, but simply pierced it," observed Kleesattal.

"Time! Off to barracks!"

The petty officer on mess duty had also been in the China
war; he, too, was an old chief mate in a new uniform.

3. Coolies

MARIE GEULEN at Mülheim in the Ruhr sat in her kitchen, which had been allotted to her and her children because she was a munition worker at Thyssen's Rolling-Mills and Steel-Works. She was writing a letter to her son Jan.

Little Katie, not quite eleven years old, leaned against the folds of her dress. The two little boys, who were even younger, were busy at the corner of the hearth. They had turned over the coal-scuttle and were transporting its contents from one place to another. They were playing at mining. Mother Geulen let them do as they liked. That kept them quiet for a bit, anyway.

"Be a good girl and keep quiet, Katie. Mamma's writing a letter to Jan. Telling him to come home some day and bring something for Katie."

"Something for Rudi, too!" cried one of the little boys. "I want a railway, a real one with rails. Like what Christian Schulz has got."

"And I want a drum and a new helmet."

"Jan's in the war. He ain't got no money; he can't afford things like that."

Katie resigned herself: "If he ain't got no money, he's to come all the more. Just tell him to come."

The woman wrote:

> *My dear Jan,*
> *It's four years now since we seen you. Katie's grown quite a big girl and Rudi and Johnny often asks for you. I'm not very grand these days. The stabbing pain in my left side is worse. I'm working at Thyssen's now, making shells. I earn a lot more than at the looms,*

*but everythink is so dear now. You remember
Mathes Höckens. He's in the Navy too, and
has been home on leave. Maybe you can get
leave too. Just now as I'm ill. Last week I had
to stay two days in bed. Your luving Mother.
The Höckenses sends kind regards.*

Then she addressed it: Seaman Jan Geulen, North Sea Patrol
Flotilla, Patrol Ship *Blaue Balje,* Wilhelmshaven.

Katie took the letter to the post. She held it with the greatest
care pressed against her small breast. The street was an absolutely straight row of houses, like grey concrete boxes. On the
balconies clothes hanging out to dry swelled in the wind. A dim
light showed behind uncurtained windows.

A wind blew round the corner and brought damp air from
the big slag-heaps, laden with heavy, strong-smelling gases.

The letter dropped into the box.

Katie looked up into the sky, reddened with the glow of furnaces. Blast-furnaces and factories, and beyond, fields and a
town. And then more fields and factories and towns—

The first winter of the war came and went. Squalls and hail-
storms and rain-clouds swept landwards from the North Sea.
Hazy weather, poor visibility.

A flotilla of eight fishing-vessels, led by the flagship *Blaue
Balje,* groped their way at half speed through the narrow nav-
igable channel of the Jade.

On the after deck a number of seamen were occupied in passing a rope up on to the poop. Later it would be needed to make
the ship fast to the quay. The sailors wore woollen jerseys, and
knitted caps on their heads. When a squall of rain swept over
the deck, powdering their garments with shimmering, grey

drops, it didn't matter much. The wind soon dried everything again. Only their hands, which drew the hempen hawser across the deck and passed it on to the next man, were wet and dirty and clammy with cold.

But trouser pockets are an extraordinary comfort, and if need be, you can pass on the rope with one hand. Behind, on the poop, which was higher than the deck, stood two seamen who took the rope from the others and coiled it in wide round bights. One of them—he was called the "Square" because of his broad, solid build—put first one hand and then the other in his pocket.

The captain saw him.

A sailor with hands in his pockets presents an unseamanlike appearance. And at the moment Captain Kessel, in command of the patrol flotilla, had nothing more urgent to do. The officer of the watch was responsible for navigation, and, in the last resort, the experienced subordinate to him, a captain in the merchant service who held the rank of warrant-officer. He was piloting the *Blaue Balje* through the channel and past the flat sand-banks.

A man with his hands in his pockets on duty! On the flotilla flagship! The captain felt insulted, just as if someone had spat in his face.

The sailor aft on the poop hadn't a notion that he was excit-ing such disgust. "Let me take it a bit now, Kuddl," he said, and relieved his comrade so that he, too, might have a chance to warm his hands. So then the Square coiled the rope, and Kuddl Bülow passed it to him, also with one hand only.

The captain on the bridge began to pace rapidly to and fro.

"Slackness everywhere on the ship! It's beyond anything! Send for the master-at-arms at once!"

The master-at-arms, who acts as policeman on board, clam-bered up on to the bridge. "You sent for me, sir." "The man aft, with his hand in his pocket!"

"Yes, sir." "Report him directly when we put into port. And the other who is coiling the rope too!"

"Very good, sir."

Black balls were hoisted at the signal-mast at the harbour entrance: the lock was open to let in the ships.

The vessels put in, one after another. There was room for all eight of them at once. In the next lock, No. II, was a ship which filled the whole space with its length and breadth: the battle-cruiser S.M.S. *Blücher*.

Bülow, the Square, and an able seaman were sent ashore to make fast the ropes. They stood by the mooring bollards and waited for orders from the ship.

"What's up in the *Blücher*?"

The whole crew was standing in line on deck, and the ship's band was there too. Muffled music came wafted across.

The song: "I had a comrade . . ."

The flag was at half-mast. A file of sailors in dress uniform came down the gangway marching in slow step and carrying biers, four men to each.

"Nine groups," Able Seaman Gog counted them.

Nine groups: nine dead!

The crew of the *Blücher* stood at attention, gazing straight out into the fog. So, too, the party sent to throw the ropes ashore stood at attention, their arms at their sides.

Between the two locks the dead were laid upon the flagstones. Then the crew were permitted to move again. They tried to keep out the cold, stamping first with one foot and then the other and beating their arms across their breasts.

"That'll go on till the lock opens," said the Square. "Come over here."—"The old man's below deck. Come on, we'll go across," said Able Seaman Gog.

The three went up to one of the men from the *Blücher*.

"Got a match?"

"Yes, here you are."

The man offered him his match-box.

"Mighty bad weather at sea."

"Lucky for us that it was."

"Why are you going into the lock alone? What about the rest of your squadron, the *Moltke* and *Seydlitz?*"

The seaman from the battle-cruiser glanced up at the deck of his ship.

"I mustn't say anything about that. But it's true all the same. They left us in the lurch close to the English coast. We couldn't make as much speed as they could."

"The *Sedylitz* and *Moltke* got back four days ago," declared a man from the other fishing-vessels. "We passed them off Wangeroog, just as we were putting to sea."—"If it weren't for this beastly weather and the fog, it wouldn't be only nine lying here. None of us would ever have seen the lock and Wilhelms-haven again. We sailed round Skaw Cape to Kiel, and then here through the canal."

"Simply left behind?"

"We're not fast enough and the old hulk is badly built, too. Six turrets! We can't bring more than four into action, the others are just so much ballast. The *Blücher's* no good for cruises like that to the English coast; we're all agreed about that on board."

The water in the lock had reached the level of the inner harbour. The gates were opened and the ships could enter.

"Slack off on lines. Let go!"

The hawsers splashed into the water. The men returned on board. The *Blücher* steamed in, her ensign had been hoisted to the mast-head again.

The other lock, too, was opened, and the fishing-vessels put in.

The *Blaue Balje* likewise entered the dock.

The crew was stationed on deck, one half fore on the fore-castle, the other aft on the poop; the *Blaue Balje* had a crew of seventy, and was equipped with three 3½-inch quick-firing guns. There were only twenty-seven men on the fishing-boats, and they were provided with only one gun. After the experiences of the battle of Heligoland the fishing-vessels were provided with some sort of armament and used for patrol duty. Their material value was slight; their loss was less serious and their replacement easier than with destroyers and light cruisers. True, when they came in conflict with enemy forces, they were even more defenceless and certain of destruction than the antiquated cruisers resuscitated from the cemetery.

But crews don't count, only ships!

The water in the harbour lay like dark ink before the bow of the *Blaue Balje* and flowed away beneath her keel. The shore was veiled in grey twilight. The steel skeletons of ships in process of construction, of working-sheds, engine-houses, and ships moored to the piers towered in the air, ragged and dim. Flames leapt up from smithy fires and then sank and were extinguished. The whole area of the harbour and shipyards, which had once been wrested from the Frisian marshes by titanic efforts, steamed and shook with damp and cold and looked as if they were strain-ing to return to the sea. Two ships of the third squadron, the *Kaiserin* and the *Prinzregent Luitpold*, lay at the coaling-wharf, and the swarming throng of their crews extended like a black trail from the decks to the shore—two thousand men with shov-els, baskets, and barrows.

The captain brought his ship to the quay. A tricky piece of work. "Slow! Hard a-starboard! Midships! Port five. Mid-ships! Astern!"

"Stop engines!"

"Make fast! Finished with engines!"

"Draw fires!"

The *Blaue Balje* was firmly moored to the wall of the quay with ropes fore and aft. It wasn't always managed so smoothly; there had been other very different occasions, as witness the dents in the ship's sides. But Captain Kessel had learned from his expert subordinate, the merchant captain now in the Navy, with whom he held no communication except through his lieutenant.

That for the sake of authority.

The personal intercourse of officers in the Imperial Navy with their subordinates was restricted to commands and injunctions, or at most to the ordinance and infliction of punishments.

The Square and Kuddl Bülow were summoned to the captain's office. Beside them stood the master-at-arms with their conduct-books. It was only on such occasions that the sailors set eyes on their conduct-books, and then it was only the covers. They knew nothing of the contents. The books followed them from ship to ship. Every captain entered in each book his observations on its owner's abilities and character; they constituted a kind of register of souls and gave practical hints to the next captain. Penalties imposed by the courts were entered in red ink, and when once a man had a red entry in his book, he was lost.

" 'Shun! Eyes right!"

The master-at-arms on the right, then Bülow, and lastly the Square went rigid and jerked their heads to the right.

Captain Kessel remained standing.

His face was red and healthy, soft with plentiful warm water. He led a regular life, always got enough sleep, and could breathe all the fresh air he needed up on the bridge. At this particular moment his face was distorted to a grimace, his teeth clenched and the lower jaw protruding a little. That made him look energetic and fierce; and that, too, was for the sake of authority. He had no other cares, and his superiors ordained dramatic gestures and rewarded them with marks of distinction, silver scarfs, and uniforms adorned with gold braid.

"You had your hands in your pockets on duty! On my ship, the flagship, the *Blaue Balje*!"

The pair stared at him.

Kuddl Bülow couldn't grasp it all at once. And even the Square wasn't sure what was the matter. Their hands in their pockets! Who wouldn't put his hands in his pockets when it was cold and his work made it at all possible? To put their hands in their pockets is one of the most elementary rights of seamen, even in the Imperial Navy. And on the *Blaue Balje*—a filthy old bucket! Was the captain loony?

The pair simply stood there and stared at their captain with pale-blue, unblinking eyes. They couldn't explain anything to that fellow.

"Well, haven't you anything to say? Three hours' extra duty for improper behaviour towards superior officers! Master-at-arms, their conduct-books!" With the conduct-books in his hand the captain withdrew into his cabin.

The pair remained standing, rigid and motionless.

"Them three hours aren't because of your hands," the master-at-arms informed them. "Them's because you behaved so silly. You oughter say: 'Yes, sir!' when the captain asks you anything, and not stand there like a couple of new-born babies."

A whistle sounded on the forecastle.

"Working parties fall in!"

The men appeared, with boatswain's chairs, scaling-hammers, wire brushes, and ropes. The period in dock, always longed for as an interval of rest, now began. Stages were let down the ship's sides, narrow planks suspended from two ropes, which swung with every movement of the man seated upon them. Boatswain's chairs were hoisted up the funnel. One man swung in each chair, and three or four at once on the stages. They knocked and scraped off the rust, and nearly everyone risked keeping one hand in his pocket. They ought really to have held themselves steady with that hand, according to the old seaman's saw: "One hand for ship, one hand for yourself." "But, confound it all, you can manage like that."

Bülow and the Square were still standing outside the captain's cabin. The captain kept them waiting a long time. His cabin-boy had taken off his long cloak and leather gloves, and he was washing his hands. The cabin-boy, who was anxious to retain his position, had made the temperature of the water exactly right. His boots, his shore uniform, and his overcoat lay ready.

Captain Kessel had a home ashore for the spells in harbour, a modest little place, only three rooms, but it was war time and one mustn't demand too much. His lieutenant managed with two rooms, and the comrade on the patrol boat who sometimes lay alongside when they were on patrol duty and come on board the *Blaue Balje* for a glass had only one room and only one bed in his room.

While his cabin-boy was lacing his boots, the captain glanced through the two men's conduct-books. He had no time to read them. But he could see pretty well. There was only one entry in Seaman Bülow's; the other had a record of punishments occupying several pages.

That knocking and hammering! The metal sides of the ship reverberated beneath the blows of a hundred hammers. The dockyard labourers were already on board, with pneumatic riveters and oxy-acetylene welders. In the forehold a bulkhead was being built in. There were no further orders he need give, and there was an expert to supervise the work, the junior officer from the engine-room—an engineer or something of the kind in civil life.

"Hurry up!" said the captain to his cabin-boy.

"Ready, sir."

Captain Kessel stepped out on deck with the conduct-books in his hand.

" 'Shun! Eyes left!"

"Seaman Bülow, six hours' extra duty for unseamanlike behaviour while on duty!" The Square, because of his previous convictions, got three days' double duty.

"Dismiss!"

After an about turn the pair disappeared in the direction of the forecastle. The master-at-arms resumed possession of their conduct-books. A minute later the captain left the ship and passed along the gangway to the shore. A few paces behind him his cabin-boy jogged along carrying his suit-case.

In the fo'c'sle it was not much warmer than elsewhere on board. The engine and boilers were being overhauled and repaired and there was no steam for heating purposes. None the less, there was always a number of men crouching in the fo'c'sle and evading work for a bit. They kept their pipes lighted, and when they blew the smoke through their nostrils, they had at least a faint illusion of warmth and comfort.

"What did the skipper want with you?"

"Three and six—that's nine hours' extra duty."

The Square took off the blue shirt that he had been made to put on in honour of being reported to the captain. "I've got three days. We had our hands in our pockets when we passed the ropes," he said.

"And that in the *Blaue Balje*!" added Kuddl.

"In the *Blaue Balje*? What does he mean? He must have a screw loose."

"*Blaue Balje*, flagship of the flotilla of fishing-vessels," interposed Geulen. "Nothing wanting but the band. Then we can have drill with music, like in Big Fritz."

Able Seaman Gregory Gog was doing duty as petty officer.

Otherwise he was just an able seaman and received his pay accordingly. Tirpitz economy!

"Hurry on up. The lieutenant is ramping round on deck and asking where the men are," said Gog.

He detained Jan Geulen for a moment:

"Just listen, Jan. I was down in the dockyard a little while ago. There was a fireman from the *Prinzregent*, a man called Alwin Köbis. He said I was to remember him to you, and you're to go to No. 15. Butendrift from the *Seydlitz* will be there too, at three o'clock."

"I'll see about it. But I've just had a letter from home. Perhaps I may get leave." The men cleared out of the fo'c'sle and went on deck, back to their work. They were let down on to the stages with ropes or hoisted up on to the funnels and masts in boatswain's chairs.

Modern ships are all iron. And iron needs care; it needs a skin to keep off fog and sea-water, and calls for a perpetual fight against rust. Scaling-hammers, paint-brushes, and tins of red lead or body-colour are things with which seamen have to do, summer and winter.

The firemen, too, get their share of work. There are furnaces to overhaul, fire-bars to be replaced that have been burned through, the packing on vent-holes to be renewed, boilers to be punched out. And what a job that is! The men have to crawl on their stomachs into narrow shafts. Oil merely daubs you, but hammer-slag and ashes! The yellow calcareous fur that rebounds from the sides beneath the reverberating hammer-blows powders your chest and abdomen and legs and fills all your pores with dirt! And it's hot in those cavities. The ships cannot wait in port till the furnaces and boilers have cooled. Work starts as soon as the fires are drawn. Clear out the ashes! Out with the fire-bars! Get into the boilers! And the parts to be replaced, fired cast iron, the weight of them! One false grip, one slip of the hand, and there is a bleeding, raw wound.

"Damned filth! I'd rather my mother . . ." You can't get on without swearing.

They thought of the deck-hands up above, scrubbing at the masts in fog and wind— "They're living like princes compared with us."

"A seafaring life for ever! That's all right. But this bloody war! Ten hours a day when you're in dock. And that for a dime. It's coolies we are, the Kaiser's coolies!"

The captain had a home ashore, a bed, and somebody in the bed, too. So had the lieutenant, and even the junior lieutenant, fresh from school.

Whilst the firemen swung their hammers and sat hunched up under the rain of loosened calcareous fur, they found time to give vent to their anger:

"Officers' whores! They won't do it for a dime!" "And you can't get home on leave."

"If the first and second boilers aren't finished, you've got to stay here and work overtime. Then you won't go ashore to-night," called the engineer down into the boiler.

> *"To go ashore what need have we,*
> *The shore from the ship's board we see."*

"All right, sir."

"To the devil with him!"

A party of firemen in clogs clattered across the flags and up the iron ladder. With eyes grown unaccustomed to the light, as grey and dusty as rats that had had to wriggle through ash-heaps, this gang of firemen came up on deck. All hot and soaked with sweat as they were, they exposed themselves to the icy cold air, puffing at their cigarettes with long, eager breaths.

"August, give us a light."

"Here you are."

"What does Jan want with the lieutenant?"

"Shut up, can't you?"

"Seaman Geulen asks for three days' leave to go home. My mother—"

"Keep your letter. Anybody can write that sort of thing. You haven't a year's service to your credit yet, and you've already been under arrest three times. Dismiss!"

Jan Geulen took up his paint-pot again and withdrew. Two men hoisted him up the foremast. The lieutenant clambered down the gangway ashore, stared at the ship fore and aft, and then set off slowly towards the dockyard gate.

"He's sneaking off, too."

"In a cloud of smoke. Five marks each, his cigars."

"And 'August' is going ashore this evening. If no leave is given, he'll climb over the dockyard wall. You can bet your bottom dollar! By Gad, he will!"

The firemen couldn't stand the fresh air for long. They turned as yellow as boiler-ash and froze to the marrow of their bones.

"Back again to the sweat-hole."

"Just look, there's Iron Harry."

One or two allowed themselves a few minutes longer. They still took pleasure enough in the technical matters to admire the vast proportions and powers of the floating crane which was passing the ship. Even the engineer doing duty—a chief assistant engineer who had come on deck to look for his firemen—stopped for a moment.

"Iron Harry," a distinguishing feature of the Wilhelmshaven dockyard, held a submarine aloft suspended in slings—a whole ships with guns, engines, and boilers, with holds and quarters. He swung the boat across the wharf-basin to the other side, like a cat with a mouse in her claws, and put it down there on land.

"That's a marvel for you!"

"Some engine!"

"Look how far the arms jut out."

"That lifts two hundred and forty-five tons."

"Come on, now, down again into the filth," the engineer admonished them.

August alone stayed behind. He was out of humour that day and cared for nothing. He had put on his greasy overcoat.

"Half a minute, sir," he said, and tramped across the deck down the gangway to the dockyard closet.

Those closets! Several dozen were crowded in between the sheds and the workshops. They weren't water-closets, but concrete dung-pits, with one seat for every fifty men. Four wooden walls and a roof. Whilst the vessels were in dock, the closets on board were closed so that the water in the harbour might not be fouled. And that is not all: the dockyard closets served a second purpose: that of a meeting-place for the stokers and deck-hands of the different divisions. And all the abuse and humiliations they were forced to swallow in their destroyer, cruiser, battle-ship, or fishing-vessel they here spat out again.

The closets were the club-houses of the crews. In them you were even less liable to interruption and observation than in the public houses of an evening. Here the men criticized conditions in the Navy and the fleet's enterprises, slogans were coined and express messages dispatched. The wooden walls were adorned with scribbled epigrams.

For instance:

> *Equal grub and equal pay,*
> *And the war'd not last a day!*

Or:

> *Party strife we know no more,*
> *All's forgot but jam.*

Or:

> *Not for our Fatherland we fight,*
> *Nor Germany's fair name.*
> *We die to champion rich men's right*
> *And win for blockheads fame.*

The epigrams did not grow stale; fresh ones were constantly appearing. And the men read them, so that they cropped up unexpectedly even on board, scratched on the face of a heavy gun-turret or on a captain's cabin door.

Amongst these dockyard closets there were certain quite exclusive resorts; for instance, No. 15, where by no means everybody was admitted, unless he could present better credentials than just the grimy clothing of a coolie.

"There's two stout gents at the door. You know, regular riff-raff of the squadron. You can read their criminal record in their faces right away and in their greasy rig-outs. 'Busy,' they shout at anyone they don't know." "You just let them be, they're all decent fellows! There's nothing wrong with them."

"I'm not going aboard my old tub, not till the job's through," said August. "Let the sneaking P.O. report me if it amuses him. When I'm under arrest, at least I needn't work till I drop."

"The *Frauenlob*'s still in dock."—"Astonishing, that! Put in commission in 1902. Every inch of her clatters and rattles when she's been a day or two at sea."—"Just the same sort of old bucket as the one you were in, Stan."—"Just the same, coat and trousers to match," answered Stanislaus Turuslavsky. "She was out of commission, too, like the *Ariadne.* They fetched her from the cemetery, too, when war broke out."

Turuslavsky was a fireman on the fishing-vessel *Spiekeroog;* he had even been promoted to the rank of fireman first class.

"Say, you smoke a good brand."

"Salem No. 4," said Turuslavsky.

Three o'clock.

Jan Geulen put his brush in his paint-pot.

"Hullo, you on deck! Square!"

"Hullo, Jan."

The Square loosened the rope by which Jan Geulen was hoisted up the mast and let him slowly down. Jan held fast and descended foot after foot till he touched the deck.

"There now, Square, I'm going to take myself off to the dockyard for a while."

They both went forward. Geulen got the Square to pour paraffin over his hands and rubbed off the paint.

"I'd like to know why you go all the way to No. 15."

"I might just as well ask why you don't stay in your own mess when you're off duty, but crowd along with Kuddl and Frank and the rest in the bos'n's store-room."

It's the same in every ship; there are always cliques who get together whenever duty permits. And so it is with squadrons that cruise together and lie in port at the same time, and even with the whole fleet. But these latter circles are much more loosely knit and have less opportunity of meeting. Nevertheless: from the ships that happen to be in harbour there are always a few who meet at familiar places.

"I'll tell you why the same men always sit together, Square. One man's nightingale is another man's stork. One man likes split peas, and another can't swallow them. There's differences everywhere. There's seventy of us in the *Balje*. To be drowned and go down to the fishes together, yes, that's all right. But to live together—not if we know it. How many are there here on board that you nearly knock down a dozen times every day, and yet you've never spoken a word to them?"

"That's true, Jan."

"See? And yet the others aren't so bad. There are some smart chaps among them. Only you don't notice them."

"Yes, I expect that's what it is."

The Square spoke High German. He didn't mean it as a gibe this time. He just felt like it. But Jan talked like a book, too.

"Now I'm off. You see how it is, Square."

"Right. If the bos'n asks for you, I'll say you've just gone."

No. 15 was brisk and lively.

All day there had been coming and going there. But during this afternoon hour everybody met. A few were already acquainted from the Second Naval Brigade and other stations where they had been together. Others had become acquainted while their ships were in dock.

Jan saw a number of acquaintances. There was Alwin Köbis of the *Prinzregent Luitpold*, Karl Kleesattel, a man from the *Helgoland*, several from the *Blücher*, and others besides.

The filth beneath the seats was not yet frozen; but it was fairly cold and the foul smell had lost something of its strength and pungency. The caustic ammonia exhalation was mingled with tobacco fumes. The smoke, the men's breath, and the warmth of their fifty bodies ebbed away far too quickly.

One man wearing the *Blücher* cap-ribbon shook Köbis by the hand. "I didn't think I'd ever see our Idiots' Club here again. We were over the other side off the coast. We bombarded Hartlepool along with the *Seydlitz* and the *Moltke*; five hundred rounds. But then we turned and scooted full pelt. When they gave chase, the *Seydlitz* and *Moltke* made off. We, with our twenty-two knots, had to rattle along alone. Lord! How the stokers slaved! They got the speed up to twenty-three and a half. But she snorted like a grampus, and, by Gad, the waves! You'd oughter seen the *Blücher* galloping over them green mountains. The fog was like a curtain all round. That was what saved us. The English never spotted us."

"Jan, you idiot, how are you?"

"Eh, Dierck, mornin'."

"Yes, the Idiots' Club. There ain't nothing worse'n clever- ness. That's extra true in the I.N. If you've bitten the apple, don't let 'em know. It's the stupidest farmers has the biggest 'taters. And in the I.N. they decorate stupidity with orders and distinctions, quick promotion, and home leave. But if you've got anything in your noddle, you're an old wiseacre and one that sets up to know everything. And you really are a silly ass, for you're looking for trouble when there ain't no need."

Such were the arguments which had led the frequenters of No. 15 to call themselves "Idiots" and "the Idiots' Club." "Even if you ain't one, make as if you was."—"And if the gents midships treat us as if we were only half there, we'll work for them with half strength. That's only as it should be. They can just see how they work their ships that way," said Alwin Köbis.

"Plenty of folks! Good attendance today."

"We'll have to find another pub to meet in."

The men sat and stood around in groups. In the half light you couldn't see from one end of the room to the other. But it was full of the buzz of voices, and on all sides groups were discussing what went on in the fleet.

The light was turned on—two hanging lamps, yellow and unfamiliar. Jan greeted the "Admiral." Since the battle of Heli- goland he looked a different man. A great scar cut across his forehead and through his left eye. He was still in the Second Naval Brigade, and generally with some working party in the dockyard.

"And it's just the same with the seventh half flotilla. Ships *115*, *116*, *117*, and *119*! Old hulks, not worth a nickel, and they were sent to sea. Without reinforcements, of course."

"That was in October. We happened to be in Emden harbour when they put to sea. They were bound for England, or the Channel. Most of the men on board had volunteered for the job."

"We never saw a trace of them again."—"They were shelled off the mouth of the Ems. The fleet was anchored in the Roads. Just like that time when patrol ship *187* and the *Köln* and *Mainz* and *Ariadne* were betrayed."—"Betrayed! That's just it. And who betrayed them? Who, I ask. I don't want to malign the Commander-in-Chief, but he's no grudge against England!"—"And he's got an English wife, too."—"It's not all above-board. The Commander-in-Chief can't show a clean record."

"They've gone to the bottom," said the "Admiral." "It's too late to save them. But there's the *Blücher*. Put in commission in 1908. A ship of 15,800 tons and 32,000 horse-power. She looks quite imposing if you see her in port and just glance at her from the outside—at least, if you understand nothing about ships and don't know that her guns are constructed so that one will knock the other over! Bad design—built wrong and too slow."

"The Admiralty in Berlin knows that quite well," interposed Köbis. "That's why before the war they only allowed the *Blücher* to be used as a training-ship and for experimental purposes."

"And the Commander-in-Chief has put that slow-going, broken-winged bird in the same formation as our newest and most modern battle-cruisers." Kleesattel became absorbed in arguments concerning radius of action, coal-consumption, the mounting of gun-turrets midships, and other questions of naval architecture.

Alwin Köbis pressed close to his side. He wore grimy dungarees. His face was black from shipping coal, his eyes sombre and fanatical:

"The *Blücher* in the same formation with the *Moltke*, the *Seydlitz*, *Von der Tann*, and *Derfflinger*! It's plain enough what that means. We don't need no 'Admiral' and no theories to understand that. Every boob can see that. If a cow's expected to gallop along with racehorses, she soon gets puffed."

"He's right there."

"We're betrayed."

"Only what can we do?"

"It's all up with the *Blücher*. She won't stand another cruise like this last one."

"And these donkeys here on board sit and write a letter to the city of Lübeck and collect signatures. 'It's so quiet on board,' they write, and ask the Lübeck City Council to send us some harmonicas."

> *"God's curse on England*
> *And our Commander-in-Chief!"*

A sailor from the *Blücher* wrote it on the closet wall, his hand trembling and clammy with cold. The thronging mass of coal-blackened faces and grimy figures crowded closer round Köbis. Outside it was now quite dark. The threads in the two electric lamps were almost burned out and their light was feeble.

One of the watchers entered: "Not so loud, Alwin."

Alwin Köbis went on speaking calmly:

"All that about the Commander-in-Chief and his English

wife and treason is rot. It isn't that at all. One of those battle-ships costs money. Eighty million marks! And you know, you've read again and again in the papers, what an age it takes the Admiralty gents to bargain with the M.P.'s in the jaw-shop in Berlin before they get the money voted for a ship like that. Well, they don't want to lose her, else the admirals and officers will lose their jobs. That's why they leave those ships lying snug in the Jade.

"At the front on land, now, it's quite a different story.

"There it's men that counts, and if one regiment is decimated, another is got together. You don't spend money on building regiments; they grow of themselves again.

"But they've got to show some enterprise with their fleet, else they'll get no more money to go on building after the war. So they scour the ship-cemeteries and send the crews on board and out to sea: with shouts and hurrahs, to a hero's death. That way they score twice over. In the first place they get rid of their old iron and needn't even break it up. And besides that they've made a glorious demonstrative gesture. Down among the dead men with flying colours! Three cheers for His Majesty the Emperor!

"The Berlin Admiralty couldn't get its propaganda cheaper. The *Blücher* has a crew of 888; that means 888 notifications of death to the relatives. They don't even need stamps, they go free as official communications."

"But what are we to do?"

"That I can't tell you. You must find out that for yourselves. I'm off to my eighty-million-mark tub. I shall just be in time for mess. Then I shall roll up in my hammock."

"Well, so long, till tomorrow."

"So long, Emil."

"Till tomorrow, Dierck."

"Tomorrow after three o'clock here again."

"Right, unless we're off to the Roads."

They separated individually or in groups. The "stout gentle-men" at the door had quit their posts. Gradually No. 15 emptied and resumed its identity with all the other dockyard latrines. The atmosphere surrounding the men who had stood there face to face was dissipated. All that remained was the foul and loath-some smell rising from the pit out of fifty openings.

A group of men trudged past dumps of coal, railway trucks, and staring, black rubbish-heaps. They passed the *Seydlitz*, the *Moltke*, the *Derfflinger*, and *Von der Tann*. Then they came to their own ship. Her broad bulk lay heavily upon the water. The mighty barrels of her turret guns towered up against the cold, wintry sky: S.M.S. *Blücher*.

One after another they slowly ascended the gangway.

4. Corpses

FOUR weeks later.

The Second Naval Brigade, fifth company. The corridors and rooms were plunged in darkness. The crews—recruits newly allotted to their units, and, among the old hands, men fit for garrison duty or sent from hospitals and detailed from their ships—lay asleep in their bunks, two and three, one above the other.

Only in the guard-room on the ground floor was there a light burning. Half the watch were also in their bunks. They wore their clothes, with belts and bayonets, and had pulled their caps over their eyes to ward off the glare of the lights.

The other half of the watch were on sentry duty outside the clothing store, the armoury, and the office of the company-commander. None of these were important positions to man, and they stood half asleep. Each of them had evolved a peculiar method of losing consciousness while standing and holding his rifle, and so falling almost a hundred per cent asleep. Only the sentry before the barrack gate could not do that. He had to move in order to keep warm.

The able seaman and petty officer of the watch were best off. They sat at the table in the warm guard-room. The seaman was a sailor who had been rescued when the battle-cruiser *York* had struck a mine and gone down some time previously.

The sailor from the *York* had fallen asleep with his head resting on his arms. The petty officer stared at the night-order-book lying in front of him; he was overcome with drowsiness, and his thoughts were far away.

Outside, the wind whistled against some obstacle—a chimney or the ridge of a roof.

The petty officer of the watch started up. The letters scribbled

80

beneath his eyes marshalled themselves in distinct columns: company orders. There was the night-order, underlined in red because of its importance: "Call the hands at twelve o'clock. Dress: dungarees, sea-boots. 12.15, fall in in front of the barracks to receive spades; 12.45, march off."

The watch beside the book pointed to ten minutes to twelve. He shook the *York* sailor out of his sleep: "Get on now, call the relief. And then the Chief P.O."

The man on duty switched on the light in the corridors and dormitories. The hard, white light penetrated the eyes of the sleepers.

The boatswain's whistle sounded shrilly through the corridors. "Turn out! Dress: dungarees, with sea-boots!"

Like a heavy wheel beginning to turn, the barracks were roused to activity. Benches were shifted; doors banged, steps sounded. The recruits in their dormitories, too, had been called.

"All hands fall in in front of the barracks!"

The courtyard lay like a black cloth. Above the tower of the signalling company you could see the outlines of flying cloud masses illuminated by the moon. Spades were distributed.

The group-leaders numbered their men and reported to the platoon-leaders, and they in turn to the Chief P.O. The company had fallen in.

"By fours, count off!"

"Squads right, march!"

They marched out of the barracks gate in their sea-boots, carrying the spades over their shoulders. On through the streets, across glebes and fields.

A row of poplars stood swaying in the wind.

Gradually the company, snatched from their slumbers, began to grow animated. Red glowed in tobacco-pipes. The men surveyed the desolate, flat landscape.

Every tree looked like a ghost.

"I wonder what's up."

No answer. The silence of the marching column was uncanny.

What could it be again?

It wasn't difficult to imagine.

But nobody would touch upon it.

Two days before, the fleet had put to sea. It didn't sail far out. The battle-ships were already back again in the Roads. But one squadron of cruisers was still absent: the *Seydlitz*, *Moltke*, *Derfflinger*, and *Blücher*.

Petty Officer Weiss was in command of the party.

There were lanterns shining behind a hedge—ship's lanterns placed on the ground. And in front of them figures moving and casting long shadows: sailors in sea-boots, with spades in their hands.

They were digging a trench.

"Working party, halt!"

Petty Officer Weiss reported:

"Relieving party present!"

"Break ranks. Carry on digging trench!"

They had dug to the depth of a man's waist, and now the work continued. It was heavy moorland soil, and every spadeful required an effort. The clods of earth were saturated with water and stuck to the spades by force of suction, resisting the men's efforts as they shoved forwards with their arms. It seemed as though the earth were determined not to submit to being torn open.

A cold wind blew across the field.

Their foreheads were covered with sweat.

"Damned foul mud!" snarled one man.

He met his neighbour's eyes, and, with a chewing motion as if he would gladly swallow the words, he bent down and seized one of the cold, resisting clods with his hands.

"Surely they haven't sent those battle-cruisers into action, Weiss? It wasn't a full squadron—the *Von der Tann* is in dock."

"Haven't they? Much more than that—but you just get on digging. They'll dig for you, too, when your turn comes."

They didn't talk much, but worked tenaciously with set teeth. Their boots stuck in the heavy soil. Underground water trickled in from above. They helped one another out. They suspended their quarrels and shared their tobacco.

A strange and powerful influence emanated from the trench. Day broke, a pale grey and yellow light.

Petty Officer Weiss measured the labour accomplished: six feet deep and two hundred and fifty paces in length. A big grave. Room for three hundred men.

That same afternoon the ships of the cruiser squadron came into port. First the *Moltke* and *Derfflinger*; the *Seydlitz* dragged behind, battered by shells. She steamed against the sea with full engine-power, but slowly and painfully, her quarter-deck awash and her lower decks full of water.

Her two after gun-turrets, the Cæsar and Dora, were not trained fore and aft. One of the long gun-barrels pointed skywards, the others drooped down on to the deck. The turrets looked strangely rigid, as if all life had suddenly gone out of them.

The other turrets were at rest.

The High Sea Fleet lay in the Roads—the first, second, and third squadrons of battleships. No command was given in those ships to "man ship"; there were no reverberating hurrahs. The men, called by their comrades from below, stood on deck in sombre groups.

There was no light and no colour beneath that accursed sky, no morning, nor any evening. The blanket of cloud lay flat above the masts. The daylight descended as if through a vault eaten by rust, and accumulated in gloomy pools round the eternally motionless ships.

And so night fell: dark vapours crept over the broad, armoured bodies, and the crews cowered in the casemates like men forgotten and buried alive.

"No more shore leave."

"When will it end? We're rotting here by inches."

"Listen! Come on deck quick; the *Seydlitz* is coming into dock."

"Where's the *Blücher*?"

"What's become of the *Blücher*?"

"The *Seydlitz* had had a direct hit. In her quarter."—"Look at her turrets, the Cæsar and Dora."—"Those turrets are done for."—"She's down by the stern."

"Her pumps are working!"

The great centrifugal pumps of the *Seydlitz* were freeing her hull of water. It swirled out of her sides like mill-streams, broke in foam, and lay like bright mirrors in her rear.

"Her flag is at half-mast!"

"They've dead on board!"

It wasn't only the gun-barrels, black and desolate, towering skywards or prostrate on deck as if they had been struck dead. The whole ship abaft the beam was heavy and seemed inflated.

And now men came out from the fo'c'sle. They went aft to clear the mooring ropes and stood together motionless at the stern like carved figures.

Cæsar and Dora turrets, with twice eighty men, had been gutted by fire. A direct hit from behind through the armoured deck and straight into the turrets. Several thousand pounds of cordite blazed up and a bluish red tongue of flame shot up masthigh.

For long-drawn-out seconds it hovered above the ship.

The cordite blazed up, but did not explode.

The turret crews were killed on the spot.

But below the armoured deck stood the stokers' watch below and the spare hands. They were still alive and waited for the order to intervene. That order never came, but another had been passed down from the bridge: "Flood No. 3 compartment."

Three men—the commander, with a C.P.O. and an able seaman—made their way through the compartment, which was full of poisonous gas. The hand-wheels were burning hot, but the three seized and turned them. The sea-cocks opened, water flowed gurgling into the compartment and plunged the after part, with all living creatures in it, beneath the surface of the ocean.

The spare hands were still alive. They were drowned like rats in a trap. They drifted through the compartment with dangling limbs and hanging heads.

The centrifugal pumps of the *Seydlitz* disposed of eight thousand tons of water in an hour. The pulsing suction of the engines lowered the level of the water in the compartments, and the corpses of the spare hands sank to the deck like sediment.

The men at the stern stood like carved figures.

By the bows, too, a party stood by the mooring ropes.

Their faces were turned towards the long line of battle-ships lying firmly moored by heavy iron cables, protected by the sandbanks that stretched ahead of them and by the belts of mines and cruisers beyond. With the big ships anchored by iron cables before their eyes, a cry broke from the crew's midst: "Iron hounds!"

The word flew through the casemates, through the coal-bunkers and stoke-holds, spread to the bridge, to the officers of the watch, to the staff of the battle-cruiser squadron, to the Admiral himself!

A thousand men stood on the deck of the flagship *Friedrich der Grosse* crowding against the life-lines, their faces close together.

The captain called from the bridge:

"Give them three cheers, my boys!"

"Three cheers for our victorious ships!"

"Hurra—ah—ah!"

From the hatches and casemates of the *Seydlitz* her crew issued in a grey torrent.

The captain called upon his men for:

"Three cheers for the *Friedrich der Grosse!*"

The response of the crew was a harsh, undisciplined roar. Flats were raised and the cry rose, plain and distinct:

"Iron hounds!"

"Iron hounds!"

"Iron hounds!"

S.M.S. *Seydlitz* entered the lock and brought her cargo from the Dogger Bank action into harbour. S.M.S. *Blücher* had no more need of locks. She had been left behind because of her slow speed—in nautical language, she sank—and was shelled and knocked to bits by a tenfold superior force. The survivors of her crew of 888 men lay flat on their bellies, glued to the deck. And so the *Blücher* turned on her side, lifted her rudder once more, and vanished into the depths.

For the dead of the *Seydlitz* and *Derfflinger* a grave had been dug. The same working party that had dug out the earth stood in double file beside the *Seydlitz* as she lay moored to the quay: the fifth company of the Second Naval Brigade.

Night had fallen. The lamps cast pools of light upon the flags of the quay. A dull gleam lay upon the harbour water, like melted asphalt. The dark silhouette of the iron-clad towered aloft.

"Fifth company, as burying party, fall in!"

A detachment of dock-labourers had already gone on board in the lock with gas-masks, gloves, and oxygen apparatus. The hatches leading down to the turret-shafts, where the dead lay, were opened, beside the watertight hatches to below the armoured deck.

Three hundred men belonging to the company and the thousand survivors among the crew set to work. Carrying long electric cables, they forced their way into the turrets and the armoured deck.

A gang of dock-labourers stood beside Cæsar turret.

The hatch through which the turret was entered from below was so narrow that the men were obliged to climb in one by one. The first man was inside and they handed the electric torch in after him. Before the second, who was only then putting on his india-rubber gloves, could follow, the torch reappeared through the hatch and fell on the deck. The bulb burst with a faint detonation. Then the man emerged again. He did not climb, but dropped heavily on to the deck. His face was deadly pale.

"What's wrong?"

"Nothing. I'm all right again. . . ."

But his forehead was beaded with perspiration.

A lieutenant spoke:

"These dockyard fellows! They can't even clear a turret like that. Now the man's smashed the torch."

"Lieutenant!"

"Yes, sir."

"Tell the commissary chief to issue rum all round. Those aft in the armoured deck, too."

"Yes, sir."

A new torch was produced. Another dockyard workman climbed into the turret. What was wrong? He knew there were dead men there who were to be carried out. But when he raised his light, he saw in the white glare of its two hundred fifty candle-power so unexpected and fantastic a scene that the walls of the turret began to spin round and he was obliged to lean against something.

There was number one of the gun's crew standing just as he had done in action: his eye at the telescopic sights, one hand grasped the wheels by which he had turned the pair of heavy gun-barrels, the other hand on the firing button. Number two had his hands on the range-corrector.

Number two and the rest of the men all stood as if they were still alive—as if they were at gun-drill and the turret-commander had cried: "Halt! Turret crew, halt!"

And yet it was not like that at all. They stood as motionless as figures in a collection of waxwork celebrities. Their faces had lost all colour and lacked even the dull, phosphorescent blue shimmer of death. Their eyes were just deep, charred cavities.

The dock-labourer stood rooted to the spot. He stood as if stunned and waited for another to follow from outside. Only then did he hang up the torch.

The pair felt like interlopers at a party to which they had not been invited, as they stood in the midst of that dumb company.

They approached number one.

They felt impelled somehow to exorcize this horrible, spectral company. These men beside the guns whom they were to remove were not like iron and ship's wreckage which you carried away to be broken up. No, no, not that! If only they hadn't been standing, if at least they were lying down, stretched out or huddled up, as the dead do lie.

The first labourer gazed at the grey, eyeless face. He hesitated once more. He began to speak in a shaky voice, stammering an explanation, a prayer for forgiveness:

"Do, now, let go of the wheels and the gun. You've done your bit." He had to force the words out of his mouth. "You've done your bit, mate. To the very last. It's all right."

He called to his fellows:

"From the other side, mates."

They wanted to lay number one down, first number one and then the others, and hand them up through the hatch on to the deck. But when they stretched out their hands and touched him, something unexpected happened.

The labourer saw sparks dancing before his eyes. Like a man who has gazed at the sun, or as if he could wipe out the image, he brushed his hand across his forehead. The other man stared in stupefaction at his empty hands and the india-rubber gloves, which were suddenly powdered with grey dust.

They had heard a faint cracking—and all that was left was dust on their hands, their trousers, their boots.

The dead man had vanished.

Dust and white fragments of bone!

The heat and afterwards the fact that the room was hermetically closed had caused this phenomenon. The turret had served as a crematorium when the powder-chamber was gutted. The dead men had been consumed to ashes. All that held their bodies together had been the clothes, which were burnt to shreds and had stuck to their skin.

Number two, likewise, crackled and crumbled to dust at a touch. He had turned the range-finder to 19,000 metres. That was his last act.

He, too, had done his utmost.

They had all done their utmost.

But they would have achieved just as much by staying in port. The English ships opened fire at twenty-one thousand metres— a difference of two thousand metres. Two thousand metres short of the enemy ships the German shells reached the limit of their range and dropped into the sea.

A duel with unequal weapons!

The armoured deck aft, comprising the officers' mess, berths, and cabins and those of the captain and the commander of the reconnoitring units, and the passage-ways where the spare hands had been, were plunged in darkness, like an immense grotto with an inextricable labyrinth of caves behind caves. The water still stood knee-deep.

The bilge-pumps had ceased work.

As the men pushed on, the harsh glare cast by their lamp-reflectors now revealed in the darkness a battered-in bulkhead falling awry, now bathed in chalky white a pyramid of debris, or again threw circles of light upon the water as it slowly flowed out through the scuttle.

The water only flowed away as fast as the ship, still sunk deep beneath the surface astern, was raised and the port sank. And you saw objects being swept aloft: pieces of wood, chests, garments. And amongst them the bodies of the drowned men.

Over a hundred hands were engaged in the work of clearance. Everything was dragged forward and carried ashore through the mess-decks on the port side and down gangways— splinters of iron riddled with shot, broken lockers, garments, casks, boxes, and tins swept up from the smashed provisions-room and hurled about, and the bodies of the dead.

The interior of the shell-battered hull seemed to be swarming with water lice: cap-ribbons of the *Seydlitz*, of the men in the working party from the Second Naval Brigade, and of sailors belonging to ships lying in port.

These latter, under cover of the darkness and the general confusion, made their way into the compartments of the battle-cruiser. They approached nervously and with timid steps, like visitors in the morgue, and glanced at the scene of desolation and at the faces of the dead.

The rising sea-water had obliterated the look of convulsed horror from those faces. The distended heads with starting eyes, the inflated bellies, and the soft, slippery skin—they were unfamiliar and loathsome.

The poison generated in corpses! Nobody gave it a thought.

The commanding officers had not even enough gloves to supply the whole crew. The men drank rum again and again. A P.O. stood beside the lieutenant at the scuttle and filled mugs without a pause.

Every time a man came out he swallowed one.

"Get on with it! No slacking!"

"He's a damned heavy one."

"Come and take him by the feet, you knock-kneed beggar."

A hundred and sixty dead! Twelve tons of human flesh! And besides that the iron, the wrecked lockers, the burnt-out shell-cases, and the ship's stores!

Beside the ship and the pile of corpses the heap of rubbish rose higher and higher: steel and wood, splintered and torn; garments; sacks of soaked rice; flour; tins of corned beef, sliced herrings, and sausages.

Beside the bodies was a heap of powder with white splinters. The effect of the air and dampness was to turn it grey, so that it looked like carbide sludge.

Carrying loads and drinking rum!

"Keep your dirty hands from your mouths, lads. Else you may as well dump your own carcasses beside the rest. The whole lot is poisoned from the shells. Picric acid."

The lieutenant held a bottle of eau-de-Cologne in his hand; he dabbed his forehead with it and held a handkerchief in front of his mouth.

"It's all very well for him to kick up a dust about picric acid. With herring and sardine sausage inside him!" "My belly is full of acid anyway from the damned chow they give us." "I don't mind about a little picric acid, if there's some fat along with it."

The light fell upon one side of the heap of debris so that it could be seen from the ship. But the other side was in darkness and was swarming with sailors who burrowed into the pile like maggots, searching for anything edible. They stepped into the light of the lantern with the tins of preserved food they had found in order to read the labels.

" 'Finest Norwegian Sardines in Oil'—good!" The tin was slipped into the man's trouser pocket.—"But look here: 'Chicken Soup'! What's that?"—"Not turnips, anyway; stuff it in."—"And here: 'Sheep's Tongues'? 'Canned California Pears'?"—"You've had no schooling! Tongue and sweet stuff. Pack it all up. German greetings and English grub! Hurrah!"

Butendrift, too, was in the working party engaged in the clearance. He was carrying chests and dead bodies with one of his messmates.

"I've had enough of it. Once more, and then we'll take ourselves off. Are you coming ashore with me?"—"If we can get through the gate!"—"The sentries will let us through wearing the *Seydlitz* cap-ribbon."

"All right, then."

"Just this one here."

"A young snotty."

It was a midshipman of seventeen. His boyish face was distended and looked like a balloon. "That was the lad with the pile of books we found a little time back—Moltke, Emerson, *The Power of Suggestion.*"

"I was on look-out duty with him once," said Butendrift. "He told me something about the books then. The horizon, and the eye, and the whole of life are all circles. He was no fool—and look what he's like now."

At the very moment when they were both bending down to lift the dead midshipman, a hand was stretched out and tapped Butendrift on the shoulder.

Butendrift turned round.

Alwin Köbis!

"Morning, Dierck."

Köbis pressed his hand.

"I just wanted to see—I didn't know in which turret you were for action stations, Dierck. We're lying in the Roads, and we get no leave. I smuggled myself across in the mail-boat."

"No, my station was forward in Anna turret."

"*Prinzregent Luitpold,*" the other *Seydlitz* sailor read on Köbis's cap-ribbon. "You're from the *Prinzregent*—one of them damned dogs on chains!"

"You let him alone," retorted Butendrift.

"We were just going to knock off and go ashore, Alwin."

"Good, let's go together. I saw the 'Admiral.' He's outside loading up. We'll take him too."—"First we'll carry this lad out, one of the snotties. They had their lockers on this deck."

Carts were driven alongside the ship—lidless boxes drawn by two horses. They had been chartered by the Admiralty from a coal-merchant for a certain number of journeys. They had previously been cleaned and scrubbed as well as possible, but the type and their unusual purpose were known to all. The sailors loaded the bodies into the carts, piling them one upon another up to the edge.

No roll of drums, no ceremony.

That was yet to come, at the funeral.

This was just labour, reckoned by weight.

P.O. Weiss stood beside the cart. He was tipsy, but he stood as straight as a die. His duty was to note the number of dead loaded into the cart. Impossible—it meant adding numbers together. But he set down stroke upon stroke like an automatic machine. The reckoning was right. For there was the little heap of ashes, and that made up the difference.

"Weiss!" said a voice beside him.

Paul Weiss did not turn his head. His eyes remained fixed. There was a question within him swelling to vast proportions—a polypus-like tangle of wild ideas with gigantic, far-reaching arms.

What was it?

The sea and the sunny comradeship of men who had been welded together to the death within the steel enclosure of the ships! We belong together to the death!

Did not Admiral de Ruyter stay with his ships, did he not go on giving orders and caring for the welfare of his hard-pressed ships after a cannon-ball had torn off one of his legs and he lay on deck with the shattered bone? We belong together! And only death can release us from the duty of standing by one another! Didn't that good old tradition still hold?

These lieutenants and commanders were no de Ruyters and Störtebeckers—no, indeed, they weren't. Too many bright buttons, too much soap and pomade and suchlike rubbish! Those smooth-shaven asses—to the devil with them, with their homes ashore and their women. But the old greybeards, the captains and admirals—those in high command?

P.O. Weiss had had faith in those.

And there was something in it.

Admiral Spee went down with his two sons and two thousand men. Captain Müller of the *Emden* remained to the very end and was the last man to leave his ship after she had been smashed by shell-fire.

And if that hadn't been the spirit, would he have gone into the Navy, would he and his comrades then have stuck it for nine and twelve and fifteen years in the cramped decks and casemates? Would they have borne in silence the hardships and privations of the service, and the frequent chicanery and slights?

Hell, no! Not one of them!

What did it all mean? They let the *Blücher* sink and abandoned her unprotected to superior English forces. Why did they take her with them, if she was too slow? And no battle was necessary to ascertain that! But better to be in the *Blücher* than in that *Seydlitz* and the squadron that came back.

The Admiral gave the signal to retreat when the *Blücher*

already lay smashed and riddled with shot, bleeding from a score of wounds. And the men, Admiral! Your comrades the sailors were still on board. They were still standing behind the guns sending salvo upon salvo from the smoking wreck.

They saved those ships, Admiral!

But I fear something else was smashed then: the spirit that leads ships and fleets to victory.

P.O. Weiss was still making strokes on the block. Through every four strokes he drew a slanting line and put them ten by ten, one below the other.

"Hullo, Weiss."

The "Admiral" stood beside him.

"What do you want, my boy?"

"I want to disappear for a bit."

"Well, don't be nabbed. And drink a glass to this poor, dumb devil here. Listen a minute before you go—there's a case of Scotch whisky behind that rubbish there. Just bring me a bottle."

The "Admiral" brought him a bottle. Then he slipped away with Köbis and Butendrift into the spacious darkness of the dockyard. The whole area of harbour and dockyard was surrounded by a high brick wall. The sentries at the gates were provided by the ships lying in port. Every twenty-four hours they relieved one another. One of their duties was to examine the passes of the men who wanted to go through the gates. Only of the men; the officers did not require any. When an officer went through the gate, the sentries drew up and stood at attention.

It was the crew of the *Moltke* that were on sentry duty that day.

Neither Butendrift nor Köbis nor the "Admiral" had a pass. The sentry would have seen anyway from the dirty dungarees worn by the three sailors that they were sneaking off. The three raised their hands as they passed and showed a slip of paper. The sentry nodded. He would have let them pass just the same if they had shown him a match-box or their bare hands. The mere gesture was enough, in case they should be observed.

Not far from the gate was a basement tavern, a low room, but fairly large. In front stood the counter; the room was partitioned and had a platform. Only seamen and firemen were seated in that part. Butendrift, Köbis, and the "Admiral" were not the only ones who had come in their dungarees. There were a few from the *Seydlitz*, too.

The three passed through an open door into a back room. Tobacco-smoke; a round table; faces leaning heavily on the men's hands. One, a sailor from the *Moltke*, was speaking. The others listened.

"They tell us nothing. They never tell us what it's all about. We steamed west all night at full speed. So we could put two and two together: we were to make a demonstration off the English coast, just like six weeks ago. A few hundred shells into a town and then off and away, full pelt.

"This time it happened differently.

"In the morning when it grew light—the *Kolberg*, which was ahead of us, had already reported enemy cruisers and destroyers—we sighted clouds of smoke on the starboard beam as well, five of them. I was sitting at the same table as the coxswain for action-rudder, who had just been on the bridge. He heard the captain say to the navigator:

" 'Those must be enemy destroyers, pilot.' 'No, sir, the bow waves they throw up are too wide,' he answered.

"And while they were standing and taking their bearings through their instruments, a gigantic fountain leapt up out of the water a few hundred yards ahead of us, the impact of a big shell. Then we knew that we were in for it. Battle-cruisers, five of them! Mighty thick clouds of smoke! They were still two hundred ten hectometres distant."

"When was that?"

"In the morning, just as it was getting light."

"That was before nine," said Butendrift. "Exactly 8.45. I know that from one of the wireless operators. Our gunnery-officer sent a wireless message to the C.-in-C. just at that time."

"At 8.45? We were scrubbing the decks and polishing brass then," interposed Köbis.—"And we were lying in the Wilhelmshaven Road and drilling! Drill with music!"—"It wasn't till eleven that the dockyard lighter came alongside and carried away our surplus stuff, our kit and the chairs and little tables from the officers' quarters."—"It was just after ten that the *Blücher* was first hit. By 10.40 her after deck was in flames. By eleven there was smoke issuing from all her hatches, and yet she was still shooting!"

"Mates! Just listen, boys—"

Köbis fairly bellowed: "A squadron in action! Against superior forces! And the rest of us quietly in harbour, scrubbing the decks and polishing brass! The *Blücher* sinking and the *Seydlitz* in flames! And we're at drill! Jumping-jack drill with music!

> *Lott is gone,*
> *Lott is gone,*
> *Jule is at death's door!*
> *Who will now,*
> *Who will now,*
> *Have the clothes they wore?*

What sort of a naval staff is that?"

The "Admiral" interrupted him: "You needn't get excited about that. There have been other cases. But what about our gunnery? They've always told us we have the best guns, with the longest range. The English opened fire at a distance of twenty kilometres!"

"Actually twenty-one. I work the range-finder on the *Derf-flinger*."

"There you are! Two hundred and ten hectometres, that's twenty-one kilometres. And our heavy guns only have a range of eighteen, or at most nineteen kilometres."

"That's so. We were shelled for a bit and could only pepper the water with our own shells."

"And the material's good. Our production is tip-top. But the mounting of the heavy guns is all wrong. I read that before the war. It was pointed out to our Admiralty staff before the war. And the reason is that experts have no say in our Navy. The architects and naval engineers are only admitted as subordinate drudges."

"It's the same everywhere," exclaimed another man. "There's the Wilhelmshaven dockyard, a shipbuilding concern with eighteen thousand workmen. And who's manager? A naval officer with absolutely no technical training."

"And the Kiel dockyard."

"And Danzig."

"And the Admiralty in Berlin—well, you know yourselves! Wherever they ought to have a trained expert, a technican or engineer, there's a naval officer who is entirely ignorant."— "And he can't help himself, for as soon as he's learned the ropes, he's promoted. Then he's sent away somewhere else."—"All the ships laid down are behind the English design."

"Our whole fleet is rubbish, just built to make a parade in peace time. When it comes to the point and they really go for us, we just have to let them shoot us to jelly like dumb beasts behind our armoured sides."

Gradually silence fell again in the room. Outside there was a clatter of glasses and the trill of a voice singing a song.

"And what about the *Seydlitz*? How was it there were all those dead under the armoured deck?"

They all turned and looked at Butendrift.

He was staring at his hands, still stained with carrying the wreckage and the corpses. He wasn't fond of talking, but at last he began:

"My station is in Anna turret. You know how a man sits in those turrets like in a big safe and knows nothing of what's going on outside. Only once, though, the breech had just snapped to, and the ship shivered. You felt the grinding right in your bones —a direct hit. Afterwards, in port, I had a look at it. It was a direct hit on the ship's side and it knocked in one of the armour-plates several millimetres. But then came the second direct hit, that set Cæsar and Dora ablaze. It came from above, and then we knew well enough that there was trouble. It was as if the ship had received a blow on her stern. Once I saw a mouse that was caught by the hind quarters in a trap—a sort of lid with a brick on top. That was how the ship sank aft for a moment. She shook herself and rose again. We could see how it was from the lights in the turret. But they burned up brightly again at once.

"Then the bridge called to us just as usual: 'Anna turret!'

"And the voice-tube man answered as usual: 'Anna turret, all clear!'

"Then after a bit:

" 'Dora turret no longer answers.'

" 'Cæsar turret no longer answers.'

"And we loaded and fired again and again, till we got the command: 'Cease firing! Halt, turret crew, halt!'

"When we scrambled out of the turret, the light was different. We had turned and were steaming home at full speed. Nothing to be seen of the English. And there were only three ships in our squadron. The *Blücher* was missing. And there was something else different, too. At first I didn't know what it was. But then I got it—the clear ring of the turbines, ninety thousand horse-power, was hoarse and dull, a struggling, choking sound.

"The ship's resonance was different from usual.

"The two after turrets were gutted by fire, the magazines flooded, and the whole of compartment No. 3 was under water. I heard that in passing. I remember the stokers' watch that was just coming from the engine-room and crossing the deck. Not one of them called out 'Hullo,' and there was no clatter of clogs, and altogether the lot of them seemed to be walking on tiptoe, as if the whole hull was one single cabin where the captain was asleep and mustn't be waked.

"And the mess-decks! There are fourteen of us at table. Five were absent. Two were in Cæsar turret and one in Dora. I didn't ask about them at all. But the two others, Paul and the Hamburger!

" 'Where's Paul and the Hamburger?'

" 'Aft!' someone answered.

"And I can see his face as he said it, and the faces of the others, and suddenly I noticed how quiet it was below. I couldn't swallow the piece of bread I had just bitten off. 'Them under the armoured deck, the spare hands, didn't they let them out first?' 'They're still in there.' "

Butendrift had never in all his life managed to make so long a speech. He sat absorbed in his own thoughts. The "Admiral" thought of the words with which Paul Weiss had sent him on his way: "Drink a glass to this poor, dumb devil here." And he raised his glass and drained the contents, slowly and reflectively.

The others cowered motionless in their places.

After a while Butendrift raised his head.

And then, as though they woke up one after another:

"The ship was saved."

"But the men—"

"The *Seydlitz* and *Moltke* and *Derfflinger*! But the *Blücher*! The *Blücher's* crew! And the men on the *Seydlitz* in Cæsar and Dora!"

"Cannon fodder!"

"And what for? A mere demonstration cruise!"

"A worthless demonstration!"

"If only one of those cursed English airmen would come and drop a bomb on the fleet flagship! Straight on to the C.-in-C.'s cabin!"

"We needn't sit here and moan, and we needn't wait for an English airman. If I had my way, not a man would lift a shovel next time a few ships are ordered to make a raid. Either the whole lot go—or none at all."

The "Admiral" leapt to his feet. The scar across his forehead and through his left eye showed on his face like the red stripe made by the lash of a whip.

"Our ships are no good, the engines are too slow, the guns too short-ranged, and the command rotten. And all the time their lordships think they're the only ones that understand anything, and that we don't know anything about it."

"They only reckon ships and forget it's not ships but men that fight," interposed Köbis. "All we can do is to shout the truth out loud, and tell every deck-hand and every stoker what's wrong."

"We'll do that."

"Then we'll see."

"But only the truth, not a word beyond," Köbis stipulated. He did not sit down again, but settled his cap on his head. "I must see that I catch our boat."

The others called the waiter and ordered beer and sat together a little longer.

⟫⟫⟫⟫⟫⟫⟫⟫⟫⟫⟫⟫⟫⟫⟫⟫⟫⟫⟫⟫⟫⟫⟫⟩⟨⟨⟨⟨⟨⟨⟨⟨⟨⟨⟨⟨⟨⟨⟨⟨⟨⟨⟨⟨⟨⟨⟨

5. His Majesty

THE Commander-in-Chief had been superseded in his command.

The Chief War-Lord, His Majesty the Emperor, was on his way to Wilhelmshaven in order to inspect the ships.

The order of the day for the ships lying in port:

"4.30: wake crews; 4.45: mess; 5 o'clock: all hands change into black shoes, dress uniforms, blue trousers, blue shirts, overcoats; 6 o'clock: fall in for divisions, inspection by captains; 7 o'clock: crews line up in the dockyard."

For days the casemates and mess-decks had been busy: the men blacked boots and steamed and ironed trousers, shirts, and overcoats. Officers of divisions and petty officers carried out bag-inspections. It seemed as though the whole Navy were one vast workshop where old clothes underwent renovation, with the ratings and officers at the head as foreman brushers and patchers.

Rarely had those in authority devoted so much attention to the ships' engines, the torpedoes, or the guns as they now did, before the imperial visit, to the merest speck of dust on the men's trousers and jackets. To say nothing of the crews' state of health: in that matter captains were content with what was known as "short-arm inspection." Once a month the crews had to line up, with trousers open, hold their genitals in their hands, and present them to the doctor as he strode past.

The moment had arrived.

Whilst His Majesty, still far away, lay on his pillows in the sleeper of his special train and flew at a tremendous speed across the country, the crews were lined up on the ships in the dockyard at Wilhelmshaven. They stood in long ranks, as straight as a die.

Slowly the outlines of ships and sheds appeared against the

dawning light of the sky. The coal-dumps, as high as houses, assumed a grey colour.

" 'Shun! Eyes front!"

They stood there like some pattern, like dolls used as targets in a rifle-range. The officers of divisions passed hurriedly along the lines, shifting and pushing particular men. Cap-ribbons two fingers' breadth above the eyebrows! The blue-lined edges of the woollen jerseys to reach to the collar-bone! These jerseys were especially important and had to cover the whole v-shaped front, a rule included in the clothing regulations of the Imperial Navy by the very particular desire of Her Most Serene Highness the Empress Augusta Victoria, who could not abide hairy male chests.

The approval of the Supreme War-Lord was at stake, and with it orders and decorations. And well-disciplined crews of faultless appearance were just as important as a naval victory—perhaps they meant even more.

An hour had passed.

Two hours had passed.

The dockyard was bathed in the full light of a winter morning.

Officers of divisions, lieutenant commanders, captains, and squadron-commanders had held preliminary reviews. The last touch had, so to speak, been given. The men, as they stood with hands and faces blue with cold, might only move their knees. Man is made of peculiar stuff. You couldn't teach a monkey or a circus-horse this trick of: "At the knees—at ease!"

At last: the moment had arrived!

The officers stood six paces in advance.

" 'Shun! Eyes left!"

A motor-car rushed past, and then another. Two shining white enamelled cars, they swept past and had vanished in a flash. Twenty to thirty thousand men stood lined up. Those in the dockyard stood erect and smart, those on the gun-turrets, bridges, and upper works of the ships waved their caps three times at an accurately prescribed angle.

The cars stopped short beside the fleet flagship, *Friedrich der Grosse*, "Big Fritz." The doors were swung open. Light cloaks, shining buttons, high collars of uniforms. The Emperor strode rapidly past the crew of the *Friedrich der Grosse*, as if he had to walk miles along ranks of soldiers. And all the time has face was gloomy and convulsed.

The officers and crews stood like a wall.

They continued to stand after the Emperor and his retinue had boarded the ship and disappeared into the Commander-in-Chief's quarters.

At last they were allowed to stand at ease, at first only to the extent of their knees. Afterwards, however, real movement was permitted. The tension was broken. The officers separated from the ranks and gathered in informal groups.

The sailors, too, had now an opportunity of expressing their feelings. "He's not much to look at, when you come to think of it."—"The old chap with the scrubby beard is Admiral Tirpitz." —"My feet are like lumps of ice. And my hands and ears; to hell with 'em!"—"That fellow on the Emperor's right is the new Commander-in-Chief."—"Well, now, don't he look a sissy?" —"I couldn't see nothing, only the car."—"There's hot sausage and potato salad this evening, in honour of the occasion. There always is when the Emperor comes."

In the battered cruiser *Seydlitz*, which the Emperor wished to inspect, carpets had been spread. The long strips led down to No. 3 compartment, in which drowned corpses had so lately floated.

The majority of the crew were lined up beside the ship; but not all of them. "Wherever is Willy?" asked one of the *Seydlitz* men. "And Louis, and the Danziger?"—"Lord, man, their faces ain't fit for review. Them and the working parties are sitting down below in the bilge." Several hundred men had been penned into the ship's bottom below the water-line for the duration of the inspection in order that they might be concealed from the Supreme War-Lord.

Breakfast in the Commander-in-Chief's cabin.

Inspection of the battle-cruiser *Seydlitz*.

For the time being, the crews were allowed to withdraw to the mess-decks, but not to sit down, for that might crease their trousers.

Hours passed. More orders!

The crews were again lined up for review. The officers stood beside Big Fritz. Up above on the ship's deck stood the Emperor, the familiar figure of the "Kiel week," christener of ships and maker of speeches.

He seemed to be flinging out words and phrases with his right hand over the wide dockyard, away across the coal- and rubbish-dumps. It was an emotional speech, with short, clipped sentences. But he was too far away for most of them to hear what he said. They only saw the short figure in the long cloak, and his vehement movements.

And they understood his concluding words:

"Three cheers for the German people!"

Evening in the casino: they were celebrating the Emperor's visit.

There were naval officers from the rank of captain down to sub-lieutenants. But no engineers' uniforms were to be seen. Because of their education and their great importance on board modern men-of-war it had been impossible any longer to refuse the title of officer to the engineers and technicians, but the privileged caste of naval officers still regarded them as inferiors, and they were not admitted to the casinos.

Dinner was over.

The stewards were clearing the tables. Dishes, cutlery, and plate, silver knife-rests, Rosenthal porcelain as light as paper. The guests no longer sat at table in order of rank and seniority, but had gathered in informal groups.

"His Majesty today . . ."—"Yes, brilliant again." "Did you hear, on the *Seydlitz* when he was distributing iron crosses, he said to a sub-lieutenant: 'Well, I expect it was pretty hot in that turret?' "—"Yes, you know the fellow, Lieutenant Walter. 'Yes, Your Majesty, several thousand degrees,' he replied."— "Several thousand degrees! Here, steward, wine; a large glass full."

"You were there, at the Commander-in-Chief's, sir?"— "Gad, but he banged his fist on the table. The direction and tactics were all wrong, and the *Blücher* a wretched old tub. He'd always known it."—"The cashiering of Ingenohl was really a bit surprising."—"Well, what can you say—"—"What can you say? I shouldn't like to be in Ingenohl's shoes. That Cabinet decree signed by the Supreme War-Lord with his own hand! 'His Majesty orders that the fleet be held in reserve and kept out of any action that might lead to excessive losses.' And then: '. . . inflict damage on the enemy, but always bear in mind that excessive losses are to be avoided.' Beat the enemy and inflict damage on him, but don't risk your own ships in the process. A damned difficult problem."

"His Majesty's health! The Navy is his own creation and has always enjoyed his special favour."

"His health, gentlemen!"

"To His Excellency!"

"To Admiral von Pohl!"

"To our new Commander-in-Chief!"

It was strictly forbidden to take shorthand notes of so much as a single sentence from the Emperor's speeches, and it was a silently accepted custom among naval officers to forget immediately the chance utterances of their imperial master. But after so unusual an event—the first naval battle of the youthful fleet! The loss of the battle-cruiser *Blücher*!

Rumour had it that the British battle-cruiser *Tiger* was also sunk. But that was only a rumour; it might suffice for the press and the general public. Here, in this initiated company, there was nothing to confirm it, no eyewitnesses. Here the rumour offered no consolation for the loss of the *Blücher* with all her officers and crew. But there was the wine-list—whisky, sherry, brandy, Danzig *Goldwasser*, and a plentiful variety of spirits.

"Your health!"

"Here's to the late—"

"A pause in the music!"

"Lieutenant—old fellow!"

"Evenin', Baron. Glad to see you."

"Still in the first squadron?"

"Yes. I'm fed up with this everlasting sitting tight and doing nothing. Still, we've got a new Commander-in-Chief now."

"A new Commander-in-Chief won't make any difference. The fleet's got political value, even if it stays in port. A fleet that's sunk has lost all value!"

"All the same, the whole thing's incomprehensible."

"What d'you mean? What's incomprehensible?"

"Now there's the *Blücher* again. I don't understand any longer what we learned at the Naval Academy. The most fundamental principles are turned topsyturvy. Why, we've known ever since the days of Nelson and de Ruyters that you mustn't send out cruiser effectives without supporting cover, except under special circumstances. And those special circumstances weren't present."

Suddenly the baron's expression became distant and cold.

"Excuse me—my attention wandered." At the same time he raised his glass and turned to another group, to a post captain: "May I drink to your very particular health, Captain?"

"Don't hash up your career," a friend whispered to the lieutenant. "Drink, and don't worry about naval tactics. Plenty of better men have given up being surprised."

The lieutenant hastily swallowed a glass of brandy.

"For instance, there's the commander of the first squadron. In the summer, when our light cruisers had got themselves into a tight corner, he put out to their support with all his ships, without orders, as a matter of course. When he received orders by wireless from the Commander-in-Chief and had to come back into port, he stormed to and fro on the quarter-deck, raging and swearing like a taxi-driver. And now—now he sits in his cabin and draws up memoranda and thinks the authorities right in all their strategy and policy."

The post captain at the next table was discussing the same subject. His voice rose. "For the second time we are confronted with the fact that German ships have been overwhelmed by superior force while the main body of our fleet never stirred!"

The captains sitting near him assumed the same blank expression as the youthful baron's before. One of them ventured on a remark.

"In our position it is hard to understand these things. What from our point of view may easily appear an oversight may be due to far-reaching political considerations."

"That is so. Far-reaching political considerations had a bearing here," snarled the baron.

At the lower end of the table a different problem was generating heat and causing excitement. The guests were arguing all the more vehemently because no danger to their military careers was involved. Is it correct and permissible for naval officers to take off the coats of their uniforms when they play skittles?

Strategy!

Politics!

The new Commander-in-Chief!

"Hi, steward!"

"Come here, too!"

The corks of champagne-bottles popped. The guests stood up and stared wide-eyed at the life-sized oil-painting of the Supreme War-Lord hanging above the table.

"Three cheers for His Majesty the Emperor!"

The lieutenant of the first squadron had swallowed immense quantities of brandy: "To hell with it all! I won't go on like this. I shall report for service on a submarine."

Germany was engaged in a vast struggle. The last reserves of the people's energies were mobilized; luxuries, food, and clothing were rationed. Here superabundance and ostentation prevailed, whilst prejudice and class arrogance paraded themselves. And the majority of middle-class officers vied with one another to imitate the feudal gentry in their own circle. Thus every gathering and every banquet was unutterably stupid.

The senior naval officers had withdrawn.

The atmosphere in the dining-room grew thicker and thicker.

The evening's festivity had reached its height.

A hoarse voice: "Five bottles of champagne—my skull's the hardest."

"Five bottles it isn't!"

"Eight—ten it isn't!"

"You're a wonder, Baron."

"A first-rate notion!"

They all wanted to have the thickest skull. They had to test it. A grand joke! The first couple stepped forward and butted against one another with lowered heads.

No one carried off the victory in the tournament. But the champagne was brought, a whole army of bottles, a French vintage from the occupied territory behind the western front.

"We've got to keep ourselves going. That's how we can be most use to the country."—"The fleet in being! The enemy's forces are held in check by our mere existence."—"But they'll come."—"Then we'll be ready for them. The whole fleet!"

The gentlemen stood round the table covered with bottles; each clutching his neighbour, they formed a solid block with hands and glasses upraised:

"To our meeting with the Grand Fleet!"

"To the Day of the High Sea Fleet!"

"To the Day!"

6. Spring Tides

THE month of March!

Stormy days—one cyclone after another swept across the Atlantic or broke from the polar regions of the North Sea. The unchained forces raced landwards. The German Bight was one foaming cauldron, the sky was blotted out, and the sea, a turmoil of gigantic, wild grey talons, scourged the dykes and the sand-dunes. The low-lying Frisian towns groaned beneath the raging winds, and their defiant square towers rang like steel.

The High Sea Fleet seemed immured in the estuaries. The burden of war service rested upon the submarines and the fishing-vessels. The submarines—metal tubs of anywhere from a hundred to six hundred tons displacement—put out into the roaring waters with crews of one and a half or two dozen men and a few torpedoes: against merchant ships. Fifty per cent never returned. The fishing-vessels were on patrol duty or accompanied the submarines a little way out into the North Sea.

These fishing-vessels passed through the locks in flotillas of eight, steamed in line ahead to their station, and then proceeded in fan formation on into the grey, troubled waters and were lost to sight beneath the wide sky.

Four days at sea.

Four days in port.

When they entered the lock, there were often only seven boats, or six, and sometimes fewer still. The rest never returned. But they were only fishing-vessels—worth thirty thousand dollars, with a crew of twenty-seven men.

And sometimes the bottle-cruisers got up steam and made raids into empty space. Risky manœuvres, useless from a military point of view and achieving nothing tangible.

But the Army! The glorious Army marching from victory to victory! The fleet had to accomplish something too.

The street boys in Wilhelmshaven sang:

> *"Dear Fatherland, mayst tranquil be,*
> *Asleep in port the fleet we see."*

The newly appointed C.-in-C. was seated in the admiral's cabin of the fleet flagship, writing a letter to his wife.

> *8.3.15. Wilhelmshaven*
> *On board S.M.S.* FRIEDRICH DER GROSSE

> *A thousand thanks for your words of com-*
> *fort. Nevertheless I am proud to have been*
> *given this command; but I feel as if I were*
> *confronted by a stone wall. I must wait for an*
> *opportunity; but when and where will it pre-*
> *sent itself? Even when I was Chief of Staff at*
> *the Admiralty I was oppressed by the conscious-*
> *ness that I was working with inadequate tools.*
> *But here the flaw confronts me at close quar-*
> *ters.*

It was long since this Admiral had had a command afloat. He had been Chief of Staff at the Admiralty in Berlin. It was only as a special favourite of the Emperor's that Admiral von Pohl could be promoted to such a responsible position in the High Sea Fleet.

On board S.M.S. FRIEDRICH DER GROSSE

*I do so want a stroke of success; I think and
plan for nothing else. Today I was off Heligoland with the first and second squadrons for
practice. The first squadron is still in the Baltic
for torpedo-practice. It was simply magnificent
standing on deck in the fresh air on a fine winter's day.*

It was simply magnificent standing on deck, Admiral! But
gun-drill in the casemates and armoured turrets of your ships
was not simply magnificent: it had been going on too long.

Yet the weapon must be kept sharp!

We know that: in order that it may rust at anchor!

For fifteen years, twelve years, and for many even of the
non-professional soldiers five years: "Hand on breech-handle,
right hand raised, left hand lowered! Open breech! Close
breech! Salvo—fire!" With blank shells—and that in the middle
of a war! And always the same. Every man could make the mo-
tions drilled into him in his sleep.

But the new C.-in-C. had to get accustomed to playing on his
new instrument, the new squadron-commander to handling his
ships, the new captain his crew. The commander, the gunnery-
officer, the division officer, the turret-commander, and the sub-
lieutenant who had just joined his ship, all had to grow accustomed to playing their instruments. They were perpetually
struggling for promotion in their careers, were promoted, and
joined some other ship appropriate to their new rank. Only the
coolies remained in the same place, grasping the breech-handle,
the spokes of the steering-wheel, or the coal-shovel.

Always the same.

Gun-drill under the gunnery-officer.

Cleaning the ship under the commander.

Drill with music under the division officer.

And in addition evolutions in squadrons, coaling ship, bag-inspection, and landing parties. Even landing parties, church, and time off duty were duties of sorts. Nothing was private.

"I do so want a stroke of success." "I am itching with impatience, but I must wait, and wait, and wait." "I could envy Hindenburg because of the great successes that have fallen to his lot," wrote His Excellency Admiral von Pohl.

And the lower decks of his ships lying in the Jade, in the estuaries of the Elbe, Weser, and Ems, and round Heligoland, were crowded with huddled humanity—a hundred thousand men! Inactive as regards the purpose for which they were crowded together, yet always busy scrubbing decks, or with gun-drill, rifle-drill, physical training. Packed into the narrow confines of the lower decks, they lived like the slaves of antiquity.

"The worst is my own burning eagerness. I am filled with a terrible longing for successes. We must not make peace too soon, much as I long for it. I must take the fleet into action first. I cannot say good-bye to the war till I have made my mark," wrote the Admiral.

"Whenever will this damned war come to an end?" growled the lower deck.

And the grey waves beat ceaselessly against the concrete sea-walls of Heligoland, against the heads of the moles and locks of Wilhelmshaven and Geestemünde, and against the planks of *"Alte Liebe,"* the pier at Cuxhaven.

Spring tides.

The plank flooring of *"Alte Liebe"* was like a sieve through which the water surged from below and foamed up as high as a man's head. Volumes of steel-blue air drove across the sea at the pace of sixty yards a second and swept the shore.

The elements were in the mood for battle.

Battle, too, was the cry of the men huddled together in the mess-decks. But the front had shifted. It was not England. That was far away, with four hundred miles of grey water between.

Here, however, were gold stripes on sleeves, and officers' caps embroidered with oak-leaves. A generation of admirals and officers of high rank had sprung up like mushrooms after warm rain. A spirit of miserable intrigue and of the pettiest egotism—often combined with inefficiency—was asserting itself. The labours of the Commander-in-Chief were confined to writing letters, making entries in the log-book, and drawing up memoranda for the Emperor.

On the other hand, the men were coaling, feeding the fires, and on duty for action. They had to perform the heaviest labour and at the same time drill and observe military form.

They were expected to combine hard physical labour with military parade.

Even in the big ships it gave rise to perpetual friction. On the fishing-vessels and patrol boats it degenerated into a bloodthirsty farce.

The North Sea patrol flotilla "E," consisting of seven fishing-vessels with their flagship, the *Blaue Balje*, lay alongside the coaling-wharf at Cuxhaven taking in coal. The sailors with their shovels and barrows ate into the mountains of coal and took their loads on board over the narrow gangways.

But they worked slowly and wearily.

There was no competitive spirit, no effort to beat the record, such as used to be customary when ships were coaling. Only occasionally, when an officer was at their heels, urging them on, one party would seize the barrows and defiantly run across the pier with the heavy load as if to show that they could if only they chose. But like the squalls that swept in from the sea and suddenly burst over their heads and were gone, they stopped again.

"What the devil's the matter?"

"Turn to, boys, jump to it!"

And the answer burst forth from the ranks of the crew, exclamations and half-spoken words. There was no saying from whom they came. But they reached the ears of authority. And that was what mattered.

"Fool's labours!" "Rifle-drill!" "Sunday duty!" "We want more time off duty!" "We want shore leave!"

The talk at coaling ship had changed. They had begun by saying: "We've nothing inside us!" "We want sausage, cocoa, beer!" "A fellow must have his fag now and then."

Now extra rations were issued when they went on duty. They had gained that point by *ca' canny*. The captain of each vessel made it a point of honour to be the first done at coaling, and they all had to agree to issue these extra rations. Later on, at sea, they had the chance to reduce rations and save what had been given out earlier. But this latest chit-chat was a protest, an assault upon the authority of the officers.

A gang of men stood against the *Blaue Balje* beside their empty barrows, and their hands rested idly on the handles of their shovels.

"And what was it that happened on the *Prinzregent* a fortnight ago?" asked Geulen, and gave the answer himself straightway. "She was lying here in the Roads and was shipping coal from the lighters. You couldn't work fast enough to satisfy them. You know, same as they always talk: 'Shift it, you lazy brutes! Damned loafers! Shovel up! Get on with it! Hurry up, men, hurry up!' They went on at the poor damned coolies all the time like that. The winches were working at full steam. The wire cables and the hooks carrying the sacks of coal just spun through the air. Suddenly one man got his foot stuck in the sling. The hook swung away and carried him up into the air.

"You ought to have seen that coolie! His head—it was smashed first against the lighter and then against the armour-plated side!"

"They can cart their own coal!"

"Anyway, what's the war to us? Fifty pfennig a day and broken bones!"

"So the higher-ups can get quick promotion and pocket big pay!"

The ship's band of the *Blaue Balje*, of which Geulen had prophesied months ago—it consisted of two trumpets and a drum —struck up a popular tune:

> *The sol-di-er, the sol-di-er*
> *He's the finest lad in all the State . . .*

And the matelots sang:

> *"Canned preserves are, canned preserves are*
> *What our State is built upon . . ."*

The commander of the *Blaue Balje*, who was the flotilla-commander's flag-lieutenant, approached the loitering groups: "You there, Seaman Gog, where are the men? Why the devil haven't they been reported?"

Able Seaman Gog, the acting P.O., spoke:

"Come on, now, get on with the job. It's no good."

"Shore leave, shore leave!" The cry rose from among the groups. Two cruises ago the captain had stopped all leave for the flotilla by way of punishment.

Wherever the commander appeared, the sailors bent over their work. They lifted their shovels, but dropped most of the coal noisily on the ground. When a few of them had, nevertheless, filled their barrows and had at last set them in motion, they stopped after a few steps.

The commander tried fair words:

"Come, Bülow, a smart fellow like you!"

"Yes, but—there's nothing but jam in my belly, sir."

"Look here, I'll show you how to get it across the gangway," boasted Geulen. He seized his barrow with an expression of the utmost zeal. What had Köbis said? "Show them your teeth, the damned skinflints!" And what had Kleesattel added? "But be wary!"

With cheeks puffed out Geulen had reached the middle of the gangway leading to the ship. Then his effort collapsed. He stumbled over a piece of coal, and the barrow skidded and fell right into the water.

"You clumsy lout! You'll be reported for that. Master-at-arms!"

Geulen assumed his most idiotic expression.

And from the background rang out the shrill demand:

"Shore leave! Shore leave!"

Captain Kessel was seated in his cabin turning over the routine orders for the past two months. He asked to see the extra rations for coal-heaving. "Sausages! Cocoa! Beer! And even cigars! And now they want shore leave!"

The commander and the sub-lieutenant of S.S. *Spiekeroog* were standing before him.

"How many tons?"

"Forty, sir."

"And how many in the *Spiekeroog*?"

"Twenty-five, sir."

The flotilla-commander sprang to his feet. He wore the Iron

Cross, first class, although all he had done was to send the other ships of his flotilla past Heligoland out into the deadly North Sea, sown thick with mines and alive with submarines.

"It's deliberate! Passive resistance! We must discover who's at the bottom of it. But let it pass for today. They shall get their leave today. I'm not going to bring discredit on myself over this everlasting coal. But we'll settle accounts with the crews at sea. We'll have no more of this!"

And with these words he dismissed his two subordinates.

The commander climbed on to a heap of coal. "All hands, 'shun! We have got in forty tons so far. If the rest is on board within two hours, the flotilla-commander has decided to remit the stopping of leave for today and to give shore leave to both watches, except the sentries. Carry on!"

The sailors began to dig furiously.

No more pressure was required. No more coal dropped from shovels, and nobody felt obliged to stop with loaded barrow and take a rest.

Two hours later the coal required for the flotilla had been shipped.

Now for a wash and shore uniform.

They did not even stop for a meal.

"Men granted leave, fall in for inspection!"

Captain Kessel himself inspected the men. The deck on which they stood was already shrouded in darkness as he walked along the line: "That neckerchief isn't properly tied!" "Those boots are not polished!" "That cap is battered." "That fellow has dirty finger-nails."

He picked out some twenty men with untidy uniforms and dirty finger-nails, and they, instead of going ashore, had to submit to bag-inspection.

"Who is on duty?"

"Seaman Gog."

"He is to oversee the repacking of the bag and to report to the master-at-arms each time."

"Ay, ay, sir!"

Leading Seaman Gog, the master-at-arms, and the twenty men were thus provided with occupation for the evening. The rest went ashore.

There was nothing much going on in Cuxhaven.

In the street you had to step down into the road every few paces in order to salute passing superior officers. If it were only the young officers of the mine-sweepers and submarines, it wouldn't have been so bad. They had other things to think of. It was no joke in the deadly mine-sown waters of the North Sea and the courses round the British Isles and far out into the Atlantic. These officers did not trouble about such petty details as salutes and a military appearance.

But the gentlemen of the city commandant's office and the officers of the fleet who lived a comfortable life at the base in their safely immured big ships—they had nothing else to do and they had established special street patrols with the sole object of seeing that the men saluted smartly during their short sojourn on land.

They came in companies from the harbour, the men of the *Spiekeroog* and *Langeoog*, of the *Blaue Balje* and the other fishing-vessels in the flotilla.

"Jan, I'm coming with you. I want to see somep'n like that," said the Square.—"We'll take Kuddl too," said Geulen.

"All right," replied Kuddl Bülow.

The three took leave of the rest.

"So long."—"Till this evening."—"Where are you going?"

"We're going to the Sun at the corner."

"We're going to the theatre with Jan."

"Well, good luck to you."

One group went to the corner public house, the Sun. Jan,

Kuddl, and the Square tramped up to the town. They had to hurry in order to reach the theatre before the play began.

Ibsen's *Hedda Gabler* was being performed.

The Square asked if it was something comic.

There were uniforms in the theatre lobby: officers, warrant-officers, petty officers, and sailors. Only the officers had women with them, and very few civilians were present.

"A standing-place," Jan requested. And Kuddl and the Square: "A standing-place."

They went in search of their places, holding the tickets in their big red hands.

"Across to the left and upstairs," the usher told them.

The three went upstairs. But before they had reached the curtained door, a petty officer appeared followed by three sailors carrying side-arms. It was a patrol policing the theatre.

"Your name?" asked the P.O.

"Seaman Geulen."

"And yours?"

"Seaman Bülow."

"Off caps!"

The three took off their caps, in which, according to the regulations, their names and serial numbers were sewn.

The P.O. took his note-book and entered the names and ship of the three sailors under the rubric: "The following men were seen in overcoats at the theatre."

Several men from submarine crews and from the mine-sweeper and patrol flotillas were already entered under the same heading.

"Now, look sharp and get rid of your tickets and then clear out as fast as you can. This will be reported to your captain tomorrow for disciplinary action."

"Do you understand?" asked the Square.

"Not me," replied Bülow.

"What's all this about?" asked Geulen of the naval police as they clattered off in their officer's wake.

"It's because of the order issued from the commandant's office. You're only allowed to go to the theatre in dress uniform."

The three stood open-mouthed, rooted to the spot, and stared at their overcoats, grimy with smoke and fog.

"Dress uniform—but we ain't got none! We've never had any."—"I've none either. And I don't go to the theatre," said the naval policeman.

At the box-office the three patrol coolies got their money back. And whilst *Hedda Gabler* proceeded on the stage in their absence, they sat in a public house a few streets off and ordered beer all round again and again.

In the Sun the men were celebrating the coal victory and the shore leave they had won. Thin war-time drink was served. You had to drink an immense quantity and then it had the same effect as peace-time beer and you forgot Captain Kessel and the commander and the whole damned service. The desolate grey tavern grew warmer, whilst the landlord and his fat wife stood behind the bar.

"And that Salvation Army lass!"

"What's that rot you're talking, Teddy?"

"The Salvation Army lass that came in and sold the *War Cry*!"—"Sold the *War Cry*? Well, what else? They all do that. It's just a kind of begging; no one's any the better for it. I wanted to sleep at a Salvation Army shelter once, in Rotterdam, when I was broke. I had to pay a lot."—"I don't mean that. But just look at her; and her hair—hasn't she extra special hair?"

"Just listen to him, he's plenty tight!"

A voice with a delicate, metallic ring:

"Twenty pfennig, the *War Cry*!"

"Give me one!"

"And me, too!"

"And me!"

The Salvationist sold her papers at every table. The patrol coolies paid their twenty pfennig, and yet none of them would read the paper. Confined as they were to ships and to the dock-yards in port, they were hungry for the merest chance contact with women. It was worth twenty pfennig to feel the eyes of this young woman resting upon them for a moment.

The seller of the *War Cry* had gone again.

"Bring some beer!"

"No, you leave it. I'll set 'em up all round this time."

Alrich Buskohl threw a solid five-mark piece on the table. "I've got another of those. You're surprised, ain't you? I've just sold my sea-boots and a pair of blue trousers."

"I've still got two blue serge uniforms."

"Get rid of 'em. What's the good of two pair of trousers? Only more to do at those cursed bag-inspections."

Turuslavsky of the *Spiekeroog* was there too. He sat at a table together with the two firemen of his watch, Klaus Möller and the coal-trimmer.

"That was a rare coaling. Every five minutes a barrowful was pitched over. I sneaked off and slept in the bunker."

The fireman Klaus Möller broke in:

"They dug like mad when the commander was after them. But none of it reached the bunkers. You can bet they made our flotilla-commander understand what they thought.

"You should have seen Jan Geulen of the *Blaue Balje*, Stan, how he sent his barrow toppling into the water."

Turuslavsky became uncommunicative:

"Do you know Geulen, too?"

"We've been ashore together once or twice; he's a smart chap."—"I don't know about that. Damn him!" replied Turu-slavsky.

Again the door swung open.

Some more men from the flotilla came in. Several of those who had been kept on board for dirty finger-nails were among them, as well as Able Seaman Gog, who had had to supervise the unpacking and repacking of the bags.

"Here we are. The skipper had visitors, two women. He went ashore with them."—"The commander sloped off, too."—"And the master-at-arms rolled himself up in a hammock."

A little later Bülow, the Square, and Geulen joined them. "Hullo, is the theatre over?"—"Theatre? There ain't none—not for us."

They recounted the affair of the overcoats.

"They're going to report us to our ship."

"That's pretty thick," said Gregory Gog.

Alrich Buskohl, Klaus Möller, and the rest crowded round the three. They made Jan Geulen tell the story over again. ". . . That's how it is; the theatre is only for officers," he concluded.

"And in the street the pavement is only for officers."—"And homes on shore and women are only for officers, too. My wife wanted to visit me a little time ago. They wouldn't let her leave the station. 'Because of the risk of espionage,' they said. Cuxhaven's a fortified town. I was allowed to spend four hours with my wife in the waiting-room, and then she went back again."

"But the officers' whores get passes."

"And even apartments!"—"And grub!"

"Yesterday our skipper's servant went ashore with two heavy trunks."—"It said 'dirty linen' on the pass. Dirty linen from the provisions-room!"

"Only you can't say anything now."—"But when the war's over!" "Then we'll let 'em have it!"

Not everyone could find an outlet for his anger in words. For instance, there was Alrich Buskohl, the East Frisian. He sat in his chair like a dumb log. He thought of the *Blaue Balje*, of the stupid service, and how he was shoved to and fro at drill. He listened to the turmoil of words and the accusations made, and his limbs grew heavy and his blood thickened.

"Well, Ali, you don't say a word."

Alrich Buskohl laid his second five-mark piece on the table and ordered drinks.

"How many? Two glasses?" asked the landlord.

"No, for everybody." That was his answer, his protest, and the expression of his sense of solidarity with all the seamen and firemen sitting in the bar and giving vent to their feelings.

"And Kuddl Bülow, he's another of that sort. You have to drag every word out of him."—"There he is at the back with the dockyard fellow."

Bülow took off his overcoat.

"Who wants this?"

"How much?"

"Three marks."

"Done!"

Bülow pocketed the three marks and the dock-labourer appropriated the coat.

Three marks—thirty glasses of beer! That would be enough to drown his annoyance.

"Landlord, a glass all round."

"Here, one for us too."

They sat about at the tables or stood at the bar. A few went and tried one or two other public houses, but they soon came back. "There's most doing here."

In fact, nothing was doing. Four bare walls, a picture of the old *Moltke* in the Kaiser Wilhelm Canal, a framed photograph of a fishing-cutter with spread balloon-jib, and a blackboard bearing the inscription: "Savings Association, The Full Money-Box." No comfort, no partitions, not even a pianola.

And yet it was here that most was doing.

This public house was favourably situated, and it was here that you saw the greatest variety of faces coming and going—men with a couple of hours free, quit of the constraint of military service.

One man sat apart: Turuslavsky.

"That's all rot what the fellow's saying," he suddenly bellowed across the bar.

Jan Geulen had been telling a story about whales. "And there they beat all our seafaring skill hollow—they cross the Atlantic in a dead straight line—round the Cape and up again, on the other side—and make a perfect landfall. There they meet . . ."

How that Geulen chap was showing off!

"That's all rot, I tell you."

But nobody answered Turuslavsky.

Nobody cared to have anything to do with him.

"You must ask Alrich; he's been to sea in a whaler."

But Alrich Buskohl had had enough for that day. He lay with his head on the table and snored and had no ears for anything further, whether whales or captains.

Besides, it was a holiday evening.

"Time, gentlemen, time!" cried the landlord.

Turuslavsky had already gone. The others moved off in groups, some walking abreast with linked arms. Geulen, Bülow, the Square, and Möller, the *Spiekeroog* fireman, were the last.

"We must take Alrich along too."

"Ali, come along! Get a move on! Up with you!"

But Ali didn't stir. And when they dragged him to his feet, he collapsed in a heap like dumped rubbish. "He's pretty far gone!" "I'd like to be as tight as that myself, once in a way."

In the end they took hold of him and dragged him out into the street. And they weren't so very steady on their legs themselves, either. Their knees were shaky and the pavement seemed like a ship's deck in a rough sea.

At last they got down to the harbour.

The sky was overcast and gigantic masses of cloud sailed above the sheds and coal-heaps, with the moonlight edging their arched tops, their peaks and towering summits.

"Good thing it's not much farther."—"God, but Alrich's a weight. Let's put him down for a bit."—"No, we needn't. Here's a barrow. We'll put him in that."

They laid Alrich Buskohl in a coal-barrow, and the four of them pushed him through the fishing-quarter, along the pier, and right to the gangway of their own ship.

Next morning at 4.30 the flotilla was to put to sea. At four o'clock the flotilla-commander was still in his bed ashore. "Wake me at 3.30. Set the alarm for 3.30," he said at night to his mistress, Helma. But when the alarm went off he blustered: "Stow it, damn it all. Confound the service—the fleet's to put to sea. Why, I should like to know!"

And then, after a time, when he had disengaged himself from his Helma, he gave an explanation of the need for early rising— an explanation that he had kept to himself the previous evening, for after all it did involve a movement of the whole naval force. The order given on such occasions is "strictly secret"!

"We shall be cruising farther than usual this time—through the mine-fields—the fleet sails through sixty miles west-south-west of Hornsriff—we shall stop there."

The blonde Helma had already slipped on her pyjamas, and now she lighted the spirit lamp. "You won't stay away longer than usual, surely! When you come back next time—there's no more of the sausages. And the cheese was good. And send some coffee too."

Helma was like a cow: grass, cheese, and coffee.

She took no interest in mine-fields and the fact that there was a passage through them sixty miles west-south-west of Tornsriff. It hadn't occurred to her hitherto that such knowledge could be turned into money.

But:

There were five thousand naval officers in the fleet.

And they occupied five thousand homes ashore.

As many women had found their way to the ports. And not all of those women were cow-like, not all were petty traders, content with a bit of sausage and a warm nest in return for their services.

The enemy espionage service worked admirably. Every movement of the fleet was betrayed, besides the whereabouts of mine-fields and the codes of the Secret Service.

And Admiral von Pohl issued orders:

"All the men's letters are to be subjected to strict censorship. The position of the ships must not be indicated in the address. The wives of the crews will not be admitted to the naval ports, which are to be regarded as fortified areas. . . ."

He never gave a thought to his officers, with their wives and mistresses. That was superfluous. Under the Navy orders the men and petty officers were subjected to punishment, arrest, and imprisonment in a fortress if they had mentioned in some tavern where their ship lay, or that she could not put to sea for the next fortnight because of boiler repairs.

"Send your letters direct to Cuxhaven," a fireman first-class wrote to his fiancée from the fishing-vessel *Langeoog*. Consequence: three days' double duty. It was forbidden to indicate the position of the ships.

About the same time His Excellency Admiral von Pohl was writing daily to his wife. He did not only write that he had slept well, that he was proud to be in command of so many ships, that he loved the fresh seabreezes and found them exceedingly beneficial; nor only that he breakfasted with His Imperial Majesty in the special train, he on His Majesty's left and Tirpitz on his right, that His Majesty conversed with him a great deal and Tirpitz turned quite pale, so that he was really sorry for him. Oh, no, the Admiral did not write merely about the state of his health, and how he had never before been so confined on board, and how life on his ship was odious—an uncomfortable berth, no hangings, no pictures, and all inflammable material removed.

His Excellency wrote more besides:

"Today my airships are flying across to England." "In the Baltic our ships have raided the Russian coast. I hope they will penetrate into the Gulf of Riga and destroy a few ships." "I can tell you in answer to your question about the fifty English ships that it was again a misleading report." "Tonight I am going to sea again with the fleet."

And that surprises you, country bumpkin! You don't understand. There's a difference between His Excellency Admiral von Pohl and Alrich Buskohl of the *Blaue Balje*.

And a lieutenant commander isn't a mere cipher.

When, in addition, he is flotilla-commander, the whole flotilla must wait for him. Captain Kessel had swallowed a cup of coffee and put on his sword and cape. Then he set out.

At 4.30 the flotilla was to set sail. The eight fishing-vessels lay with all their boilers under pressure and blew off steam.

"There he comes!"

"The skipper's coming."

"Tuit, tuit, tui, twit!" the boatswain's whistle shrilled. The petty officer of the watch in the *Blaue Balje* stood erect, thumbs in line with the seams of his trousers, and so did the men round the gangway.

The captain came on board.

The gangway was hoisted on board after him.

On the bridge a flag-signal was hoisted. Slack off on the lines!

Ahead slow! A touch ahead, a touch astern: ahead again!"

The ship was clear. The other vessels, too, were free of the pier.

Full steam ahead! The eight vessels steamed down the Elbe in line ahead, led by the *Blaue Balje*. To port on the flat shore the last sign of land, the tower of Neuwerk, rose to view and then sank again. The sea was choppy, with white-caps that leapt up sharp and jerky. The eight fishing-vessels ploughed through the wide, grey-green sea—heavy, sombre beasts of burden. They steamed north-west, altering course at accurately defined points as they made their way through the mine-fields. A broad belt of mine-fields shut off the interior of the German Bight.

By afternoon the fishing-fleet had reached its appointed position. It stopped outside the defences. The crew of the *Blaue Balje* were scrubbing decks; before that, gun-drill. In the morning, before they passed Neuwerk, they practised "Close watertight doors!" and "Fire-drill!" The crew were on their feet from four o'clock in the morning onwards.

The Square held a mop in his hand.

Geulen held a mop in his hand.

Buskohl held a mop in his hand.

Half the crew were distributed on the fo'c'sle and half on the after deck. They mopped up the water on the deck boards with their thick tow swabs. These small fishing-vessels were good sea-going ships. They lay easily on the rolling waters and rode easily over the waves. But every now and again the crest of a wave surged as high as the ship's side and swept across the deck. The seamen with their mops were kept busy. They had to dry the boards again and again.

Captain Kessel was settling accounts.

"The skipper's clean off his head."—"I suppose he thinks his old fish-tub is a first-class saloon."—"Always mopping. At this

rate we shall mop up the whole North Sea." Able Seaman Gog
was charged with the supervision. He would much have pre-
ferred to take a swab himself and slither about on his belly like
the rest, rather than be perpetually after them, urging them on.

As often as they could, a couple sneaked off to the mess-deck or
sought cover from the eyes on the bridge and watched the for-
gathering of the fleet.

The light cruisers of the scouting squadron, with a few half
flotillas of destroyers, had already passed beyond the mine-
fields and the fishing-vessels. They now deployed in steaming
formation and made a semicircle twenty miles in diameter. In
fan formation they pushed on ahead of the squadron of cruisers:
the *Seydlitz*, *Moltke*, *Derfflinger*, and *Von der Tann*, the reconnoitring units of the High Sea Fleet. The commander of the
reconnoitring units, Admiral von Hipper, flew his flag on the
Seydlitz.

Since the loss of the slow-moving *Blücher* the squadron could
steam at its full speed of twenty-eight knots.

The crew of the *Blaue Balje* was still cleaning. Everybody
on board was cursing. Buskohl stood at attention at the door
of the captain's cabin. The master-at-arms stood beside him,
and confronting him Captain Kessel with his conduct-book.

"You were brought on board in a wheelbarrow? Is that fit
behaviour for a seaman of the Imperial Navy?"

Alrich Buskohl stared helplessly into his captain's face.

"Is that fit behaviour? I ask you again."

Buskohl struggled to answer. He brought out the words with
an effort. "No, sir. It's like this, you see—I ought always to
stand by the bar. It doesn't do to sit down, else I just drop off
in a minute."

"That will do. Hold your tongue. Eight days' confinement
to ship for brutish drunkenness. Dismiss!"

Buskohl picked up his swab again and worked with clenched teeth. An hour passed, and nothing but smoke was now visible of the scouting squadron and the cruiser squadron, a broad smudge on the horizon. And now the "iron hounds" followed, ship after ship, squadron after squadron—the High Sea Fleet. In the centre came the flagship, *Friedrich der Grosse*, with the Commander-in-Chief.

At last His Excellency Admiral von Pohl had assembled the "crazy family, of which first one and then another member is absent," and with his whole force he was making a push out into the North Sea. These broad, flat monsters steaming across the water had been built for battle. The weight of their turrets, with guns, casemates, and armour-plating, made them rigid and clumsy in their movements. Their gigantic engines and the unceasing labour of the thousands who manned them endowed them with high speed and a sinister life of their own.

On the bridge of the fleet flagship balls were hoisted: signals handed on from ship to ship along the line. The grey giants increased their speed. Thick volumes of smoke were emitted from the funnels, sparks flew—red cinders that turned black in the air. The balls descended and the ships moved more slowly. Flag-signals were hoisted and passed on. Each ship in the long line, with its end still below the horizon, turned to starboard and changed from line ahead to line abreast. A fresh signal and they steamed obliquely. The great thirty-thousand-ton monsters moved about like obedient chargers and the Commander-in-Chief was linked with the line of reconnoitring units ahead of him through the wireless on his own ship, as also with the flank cover of light cruisers, which were so far away as to be out of sight.

Flag signals, Morse, wireless messages.

The Commander-in-Chief was growing accustomed to playing on his instrument. The fleet performed evolutions. The quadrants round Heligoland had been transformed into a barrack-square.

That continued all night and the following day.

On board S.M.S. Friedrich der Grosse

Tonight I am putting to sea with the fleet to see if I can discover any trace of the enemy. I shall be back tomorrow night. It is not a very promising beginning, for we have just received a wireless message that the Hamburg *has collided with destroyer No. 21 and has cut it in two. It really is too stupid that ships should ram one another; it is so unnecessary. But there it is—I have my anxieties.*

We are safe back again and are now steaming up the last section of the Jade, and this letter shall go ashore directly. I was with the main body of the fleet 120 miles north-west of Heligoland, but we never sighted the enemy. Unfortunately. They're hiding in their Scotch harbours. I should so have enjoyed ramming several of their ships and sending them to the bottom.

The *Blaue Balje* was on patrol duty.

She lay at anchor in fifteen fathoms. The moon had not yet risen and only a few scattered stars shone forth amidst the driving masses of cloud. The sentries tramped to and fro, behind the guns trained on the beam, one behind each gun. Four steps forward and four steps back, gazing continually over the water, penetrating the liquid darkness.

The fishing-vessel *Spiekeroog* lay anchored in the same line as the *Blaue Balje*, though her proper position was on the other wing of the flotilla. But the captain of the *Spiekeroog* had been promoted to the rank of lieutenant commander and the occasion had to be celebrated. For that purpose he had come across on to the *Blaue Balje*.

The eyes of the sentries ceaselessly swept the dark sea. Beneath the deck, in the flotilla-commander's cabin, sat the three captains in the flotilla. Bottles and glasses stood on the table, and there was a pack of cards.

"Clubs are trumps."—"How many will you go, sir?"— "Double."—"Diamonds!"—"Spades!"—"You've lost, sir." The two lieutenants divided the stake. Captain Kessel laid a five-mark piece on the table.

He yawned and stared at the ceiling.

"That blasted fan!" They could hear the hum of the motor that pumped the stale air from the lower decks, and at times the creaking and grinding of the chain cable.

Forward, in what had formerly been the fish-hold, the seamen, firemen, and petty officers were quartered. They were all asleep after their exhausting duties, except the sentries posted on deck. They lay fully dressed in their hammocks, ready to leap up at the slightest alarm. The permission to sling their hammocks whilst on guard on active service was a favour that they owed to the confined space. Side by side there would only have been room for a third of them. The hammocks hung one above the other in several tiers. The confused mass of hammocks and outstretched ropes swung in the dim, red light.

"That's my trick."—"Spades!"—"The destroyers were in a fine state of confusion coming back."—"Your deal, please."

"That damned fan!"

"Hi! Boy! Fill my glass."—"Here's to our new lieutenant commander!"—"We can't do it properly in brandy."—"That's

what I say, too."—"I've got a case of champagne in my cabin."
—"Yes, yes, sir, I'll trump that."—"Boy, bring the champagne."
—"Now, then, that buzzing must stop. Just go up and tell them
to stop the fan."

The noise of the fan ceased.

The iron ventilating shafts on the lower deck stopped work.
The air grew more stifling and oppressive to the sleeping men.
They responded by stirring slightly, undoing their buttons, and
baring breast and trunk. The perspiration settled in their pores
and they lay with open mouths.

In the centre of the deck there was just one passage through
which a man could make his way by bending down. At the end
of that passage was the petty officers' mess, only separated by a
wooden partition. Able Seaman Gog, as the acting P.O., slung
his hammock just by the door of this partitioned space. It was
an honour which had its drawbacks. For the higher a man's
rank, the more rigid was his backbone! And when the petty
officers had to bend in order to creep under Gog's hammock, he
often received a knock in the back. Gregory Gog didn't always
wake—you get used to that kind of thing. He only started from
his sleep at an especially hard jolt.

A change of the watch.

Two men made their way through the jungle of ropes and
swinging bodies bathed in red light, in order to wake the relief.
"Come on, Ali, out with you!" they shouted. "Jan, can't you
hear? Up with you!" "Now, then, shake a leg."

The sleeping men did not stir. One had his leg hanging over
the edge of his hammock, as heavy as a log, and another his
arm. Mouths and tongues were swollen. If one of the men
opened his eyes, he stared stupidly before him. "But there's a
stink like a monkey-house!"—"They're doped like."—"Those
brutes have stopped the fan again."

The gunner's mate entered the mess-deck.

"What's up? Where are the sentries? Have you called my relief?"—"Yes, sir. But we can't rouse him." The gunner elbowed his way through to the petty officers' mess and set the hammocks swinging in his wake. He had been in the service fifteen years and would soon be promoted to the rank of warrant-officer. He jolted against P.O. Gog so that his hammock started swaying violently.

"You clumsy lout!" roared Gog mechanically.

Clumsy lout—that from a seaman to a gunner's mate who would shortly be a warrant-officer! The gunner just saw red: "What are you thinking of? Are you mad? Stand at attention! Stand at attention, I say!"

Gregory Gog's mind was still befogged. He was stupefied by the exhausted air that he had breathed and he felt as if he had a heavy iron band round his head. With a convulsive effort he opened his eyes and realized: so he was to spring to attention when he was sound asleep in his hammock! And mechanically, as before, he reached behind his head, seized a sea-boot, and hurled it right in the gunner's face. This time he had really done what formerly he had only dreamed.

A dust-up in the lower deck!

The sentries had already gone up on deck. Gregory Gog was now sitting upright in his hammock, and others, too, started up out of their sleep. "The gunner made off with the sea-boot in his hand."—"But he's always knocking against the hammocks. Him in particular—he's swallowed a ruler."—"Bang on his nose! Pity it wasn't the skipper's."—"And he's stopped the ventilation again."

"What's it all about?" asked Gregory Gog.

"My stars! Him asking what it's all about!"

The sentries by the guns had been relieved. Buskohl, Geulen, and the Square stood behind the port guns. There were three men on the other side, too. No sentry was permitted to turn round; each one had to keep his eye on a particular section of the ocean surface. The moon was breaking through the banks of cloud on the horizon. The beating waves looked black, with bright white crests.

The three officers in the cabin had sent for a sailor with a harmonica. Drawing out his instrument full stretch, he played them the tune of a chorale, to which the three sang their own words:

> *"Furry, furry,*
> *Furry is the cat.*
> *And if the cat should lose her fur,*
> *She'd catch no mice, it's certain, sir!*
> *Furry, furry . . ."*

The captain clutched the table as he sang. The lieutenant commander from the *Spiekeroog* was pale, but he sat erect and bawled as loud as he could, together with the others. "Here's to the *Spiekeroog's* captain's prospect of joining the High Sea Fleet!"

The cabin-boy entered:

"The gunner's mate asks to speak to the captain."

"Let him in."

> *". . . Furry, furry is the cat."*

The gunner entered with blood-stained face, carrying a sea-boot: "I have to report to the captain: when the men were being called, P.O. Gog threw a sea-boot at me."

"A sea-boot?"

"Yes, this one here."

Captain Kessel's expression seemed to suggest that the laws of nature had suddenly been thrown into confusion and that he was confronted with a phenomenon of the first importance. "A seaman threw a sea-boot? Are you drunk, sir?" "Sir . . ." the gunner repeated.—"Gentlemen, the fellow must have—gone mad!"—"Yes, sir, mad."—"That is the only possible explanation. Arrest the man. Put him ashore tomorrow to have his mental condition examined.

"Let's go on singing, gentlemen," he bawled hysterically.

"Here's to—"

"The promotion!"

"To the High Sea Fleet!"

"To 'the Day'!" Kessel's voice was thick.

"To 'the Day'!" The captains repeated the fashionable toast among naval officers: to the day when the German High Sea Fleet would measure its strength against the English.

On deck the sentries marched to and fro. It was so dark that you could not see from one gun to the next. Geulen had left his post and groped his way to the next gun.

"Hullo, Ali!"—"Jan?"—"My head's buzzing."—"I'm better now. That was because of the ventilation."—"Did you hear the row? Gog with his sea-boot? And the catawauling aft?" Buskohl merely answered yes and gazed fixedly into the night. "We ought to tear out the firing-pins and chuck them into the water. Then we could all knock off and the skipper could sail home with his tub."

Geulen had returned to his place.

Buskohl stared at the shining blue steel of the gun-breech. Just one little turn with his two fingers and the firing-pin would be loose. If it dropped into the water, nobody would notice. But it must be done to all the guns, or else it would be pointless.

The moon rode through clouds half-way up the sky. Sometimes there was a break in the grey blanket of fog, and then for a time it was spectrally light on the ship. The stem of the *Spiekeroog* stood out, black and sharply outlined. She was still moored behind the *Blaue Balje*, and her position on the other wing of the flotilla was still vacant.

"Hi, sentry! Just come down here."—"I'm not allowed to leave my post," replied Buskohl.—"Yes, you are, it's the captain's orders. You are to come down," answered the captain's cabin-boy. Buskohl descended the steps to the cabin with heavy tread. The captain was seated at the table, holding his sides with laughing. Opposite him sat the two other captains, who had vomited all over one another.

"Seaman, fetch a bucket of water. And then wash down the two officers." Buskohl went and brought the water. Then he washed down the filthy sleeves of his superior officers. When he was back on deck, standing behind the gun, he gazed more and more fixedly at the shimmering blue parts of the gun-breech.

On the bridge an electric torch flashed. The signalman sent a Morse message to the *Spiekeroog* that a boat was to be sent to fetch the captain. All the sentries were called from the guns in order to get the boat away. The captain of the *Spiekeroog* stumbled and fell down, and lay beside the rope that moored his boat. But the captain wasn't drunk, nobody must suppose that. He knew quite well what was going on and was perfectly on the spot. He stroked the hempen rope, reiterating thickly: "My line, a fine line, a pretty line . . ."

"Come, my lad, up you get."

Buskohl gazed fixedly at a rising bank of cloud. Now it had reached the moon. A veil of darkness was drawn over the ship. The gun-sentries were amidships; two held the boat and the rest dragged the lieutenant commander across the deck.

Buskohl stood by the breech of No. 1 gun.

A little turn. Spring and pin slid into his hand. Silently they both dropped into the water. The same happened with No. 2

gun, and No. 3. When he stole across to the other side, he knocked up against Geulen: "All right! I've polished off this side. Now hurry up and get amidships."

They came just in time to lift the captain into the boat.

The patrol boats *Spiekeroog* and *Langeoog* were pitching through a choppy sea. Course: north-north-west, Orders: to await submarines a hundred and eighty miles north-north-west of Heligoland and convoy them into port. Each ship had a crew of twenty-seven.

If you looked across from the *Spiekeroog* to the *Langeoog*, there was sometimes nothing but the funnel to be seen, just showing behind a wave. The smoke moved level across the water and rapidly dispersed. When the ship climbed a mountainous wave, her hull rose up and the water gushed in broad, foaming torrents from her deck. Whilst she rode on the crest of the wave, her deck remained dry for a few moments and you could hurry to the centre of the deck. But then the *Langeoog* slid down into a valley and hid her nose once more. And if you looked from the *Langeoog* to the *Spiekeroog*, you saw the same.

In the fo'c'sle of the *Spiekeroog* sat the watch, just about to relieve. On one side were the seamen, on the other, at the table, the firemen. There were three of them—a grimy fellow from the engine-room and the two stokers Turuslavsky and Möller. The coal-trimmer had gone midships with the key to fetch their dinner.

There were rissoles, three apiece, and potatoes. The seamen had divided up their rations and were already busy chewing. They sat with their feet firmly planted on the deck and held their bowls of food in their hands; they kept their balance, swaying the upper part of their bodies with every movement of the ship. When she rose, it seemed as if they were suspended almost horizontally in the air.

The firemen were still waiting for their dinner.

The coal-trimmer stood with the dish on the upper deck amidships and waited for an opportunity to go forward. His cap was jammed on to his forehead down to his ears. The ship was riding over the crest of a wave. The coal-trimmer felt his way down the couple of steps, but already the *Spiekeroog* was plunging downwards. The man lost footing on the planks, sat down with a bump, and slid forwards down the steep incline as if it were a toboggan-slide. He held the dish firmly in his hands, pressed against his body. He tore open the door and arrived at the bottom together with a torrent of water.

"You clumsy brute!" snarled the seamen.

"At last!" grumbled Turuslavsky. He was partly satisfied, for at least the dinner was still in the dish. And when the coal-trimmer offered him his own share, because he couldn't eat in such foul weather, Turuslavsky was altogether mollified. Klaus Möller, too, gave up two rissoles to him. "I can't get it down right, neither," he said.

For a moment none of their spoons were raised. They lifted their heads and listened to what was going on above. It sounded as if someone were cracking long whips in the damp air: rifle-shots.

"Mines," said one man.

The sentries on the bridge fired at mines with captured Russian infantry rifles to explode them. In bad weather a great many mines got loose and floated uncontrolled in the North Sea.

The water that had got into the lower deck with the trimmer swished to and fro, washing about an overturned jam-pot, a paint-pot, some wooden clogs, and other rubbish.

"Submarines somewhere about! He won't get out of this, our flotilla-commander."—"He's not such a dud as that. There's no booze here—unless it's salt water if we run up against a mine."

—"But those fellows on the *Blaue Balje* pulled off something. I'd 'a liked to see his face when the gunner's mate came on to the bridge and reported: 'Ship unfit for action.' "—"And they stick together. Nothing's been found out."—"Quite right. I wouldn't say nothing, either."

"That's a dirty trick," said Turuslavsky. "In war time, and on patrol duty! I'd report the fellow if it were my own brother."

Eight bells. The watch changed.

They heard the eight strokes of the ship's bell fade away. The men pushed open the door of the fo'c'sle and hurried across the deck. The seamen relieved the sentries on the bridge and at the look-out. The firemen clambered down the ladder behind the funnel into the stoke-hold.

Half-way down, on the grating, they stopped to let the offgoing watch pass. Three grimy and weary men met them. When the ship lurched to one side, the three hung beneath the ladder like sacks:

"That affair with the breeches was a dirty trick, I tell you. And it's that Geulen that's at the back of it, and no one else," said Turuslavsky, as they climbed down, to Möller, his mate in the watch.

Two boilers, and three furnaces under each.

Today they could breathe in the stoke-hold. The wind driving across the sea penetrated into the innermost parts of the ship and drew off the fumes and gases speedily. But the tossing sea, and the efforts of standing and working in front of the furnaces with that tossing sea! The ship was six yards in breadth, and the space in front of the boilers the same, and barely six feet in height. It was a platform which tipped forty degrees downwards when the steamer pitched into a trough, and back again the same angle when she climbed up again; and there was the rolling in addition. It was a slab resting as it were on a needle's point at its unknown centre of gravity, rising and falling in all directions, yet always obeying a hidden but operative law by which it returned again to equilibrium at the centre of gravity on which it rested.

You have to have that hidden law in your bones.

Klaus Möller, the fireman, hadn't got it in his bones. Nor had the trimmer who had recently slithered down the deck carrying the rissoles and was now trying to push a full coal-barrow uphill. It was with a great effort that he pushed it up to the furnace. A supply deposited by the previous watch was still there.

Klaus Möller flung open the furnace door, gripping his shovel, throwing twenty pounds of coal each time—you have to scatter the shovelful widely and throw it right to the back. The incalculable slab lurched, the shovel was left suspended in the air, and the coal shot all over Möller's arms and body.

He was still dealing with No. 1 furnace.

Turuslavsky opened No. 3 furnace door.

He dug into the coal and lifted his shovel—three, four, five, The next. The stoke-hold lurched and seemed to plunge sideways into some abyss. Turuslavsky stood on one leg and turned a complete circle. Then he scattered the coal in the maw of the furnace with the whole weight of the lurching ship behind his shovel. Klaus Möller cursed; he was faint with pain. He had staggered against the furnace door.

"To hell with the damned . . ."

"Keep your balance, mate. Always keep your balance," bawled Turuslavsky. That was the whole secret, it was true everywhere. That fellow Geulen, and along with him that blockhead Butendrift, had given him a thrashing once. He hadn't forgotten. He'd be even with them and restore the balance there.

Turuslavsky shut his last furnace door with a bang. The

finger of the steam-gauge which indicated the pressure in his boiler was only just below the red line. He gulped down a bowl of cold coffee and lit a cigarette.

At last Klaus Möller had finished, too.

He had no time, and it was better not to begin standing still at all. Turuslavsky had already started stoking up. He thrust his long poker into the glowing coals, hoisted them up and broke the crust of cinders, drew it out, and then thrust it in afresh.

Möller didn't find it so easy.

"The clinkers! The cinder ash!"

They stuck in the fire-bars as if they were glued. The rags with which he gripped his poker began to smoke. The rod was getting red-hot and beginning to bend. Möller snatched it out with a furious oath and flung it away. The trimmer threw water on the cinders that were dragged out with it. Steam rose, hissing and filling the whole stoke-hold with foul, hot fumes.

"Come on, now, clear away those cinders."

The ship rolled from side to side. Pieces of coal clattered round their feet. In the bunker everything fell down from above. Uproar on all sides. The trimmer was at the end of his strength, and Klaus Möller was stiff in the small of his back. He had no longer sufficient elasticity to adapt himself to the ship's motion. In opening a door he lost one of his clogs and stumbled into a heap of hot ashes. He barely avoided the tongue of flame that leapt out of the furnace.

"Let it be, you're dead beat. Take a rest." Turuslavsky took the poker from his hand. As a matter of fact it was all the same to him. These firemen, these land-lubber firemen! The fellow might drop asleep and be buried in the ashes shot from the furnace for all he cared; or spew the lungs out of his body. Turuslavsky didn't care a damn. But he realized that now was the time when he might hear something about the *Blaue Balje* and

Geulen; now or never. Both Möller and the trimmer were friends of Geulen.

"I'll break up your furnaces a bit. Get along over there where the trimmer's sitting."

So now they were both lying with their backs against a heap of coal, and they both gave in finally. But in such weather activity is the only medicine.

Turuslavsky broke up furnaces, shoved barrows of coal, and fed the hungry mouths of the furnaces. White pillars of steam curled upwards. Tongues of flame leapt out and vanished in the air, leaving black smoke behind them. Not a shred on Turuslavsky's legs was dry. His tongue hung out of his mouth like a piece of wood.

"Sit down awhile; I'll manage that load."

"There are my cigarettes; you take them, Turu."

"Keep your cigarettes; I've some of my own."

Möller was glad to be able to sit a little longer. When the *Spiekeroog* plunged downwards, he always felt as if his stomach had been left behind under the deck above. The trimmer had relieved nature and vomited. You can't get into such a state on deck in the open air.

Turuslavsky worked with shovel and fire-poker. A red glow flickered on his face, on his long arms and his naked chest, which looked as if it were covered with wool. Sparks coruscated over his hair. He was attending to all six fires.

"Stan . . ."—"Eh, what's that?" "Next time we go ashore we'll have a drink." "Sure we will, Klaus. And we'll take that limb of Satan Geulen of the *Blaue Balje* with us."

Turuslavsky threw away the poker.

"You still go about with him?"—"Yes, often."—"He's not such a bad fellow. And, now I come to think of it, that affair on the *Blaue Balje* was mighty smart; they pulled it off neatly."

A furnace door came unfastened and flew back. The glowing

coals from the opening slid out with a rush, down on to the deck
—not the whole lot, only a couple of barrowfuls. The ship
trembled and lurched as if she were caught in the fiercely snap-
ping jaws of a monster.

Turuslavsky put matters right and came back again. "These
damned doors! The flotilla-commander ought to be stationed
here—here, in front of the furnaces, with a coal-shovel."—
"That's just what Geulen says."—"Does he—and what else?
What does he say besides?"—"That we oughtn't to put up with
such a lot of duties. We ought to stand up against it. There are
ways and means."—"Oh! there are ways and means? What are
they?"—"Well, for instance, when you're shipping coal—but
everyone must know that for himself."—"To pitch your barrow into the water, and suchlike?" "Yes, and besides—we've
no chow. And the captain takes sausages from the crew's rations, and flour, and sends them ashore."

An hour later the three firemen were relieved. They washed
off the dirt with a bucket of hot water and a cloth and lay in
their hammocks in the fo'c'sle.

Turuslavsky sat up again.

"Klaus, Klaus Möller!"—"Yes, Stan."—"Just to remind
you—you told me one or two things during the watch about
that cursed swine Geulen, and about the Square. When we get
into port, I shall report them to the flotilla-commander!"

7. Sky-Trippers

CAGE beside cage, twenty-four cells on each floor, and that three times over, one above the other, in three storeys. In the prison corridors it was like the passages of a stable: scraping, stamping, snorting. The men under arrest tramped to and fro ceaselessly in their cells. A cell is three paces long and two wide. Sometimes a man will stop and fix his eyes on one spot. Another will suddenly begin to rave, hammering with his fists and bellowing: "Warder, I must get out! Quick, else I'll foul the whole cell."

The warder does not come. He knows that trick. Twenty-eight days' brig on bread and water, without bed or light, is no trifle.

Jan Geulen had got twenty-eight days' brig.

The Commander-in-Chief had foretold that he would get several years in a fortress. But no proof could be adduced before the court martial that he had thrown the firing-pins overboard, and all that remained was a few phrases that he had once burst out with. The Square came off much worse. He got two years in a fortress because he had said the men "ought to do the same everywhere."

At first Jan lay quiet on his plank bed for several days. Whenever he opened his eyes, the walls of the cell closed round him like a thick black curtain. Only at one point a fine thread hung suspended. It was like a glowing electric wire. That was the light of day, for the window, fastened with iron bolts and locks, did not fit tight. He lay quite still. As long as you can bear it, that is the best thing to do. There are limits anyway to the program for subsequent days.

Every time the crack of light began to shine, Jan Geulen, lacking a calendar, made a knot in his shoe-lace. On the fourth day the window was opened for twenty-four hours. And so it continued: three days darkness, one day light. For two whole days he occupied himself establishing communication with Alrich Buskohl, who was serving his week of confinement for drunkenness in the same corridor. But when at last he reached him across four or five intervening cells, it was no use. Buskohl did not understand tapping signals and the Morse code. Then gradually Jan grew restless like the others and devised all manner of crazy occupations. For days he cleaned his shoes. Or he made speeches. He saw a gathering of thousands of p'or damned coolies rising out of the darkness. Until the warder flung open the door and threatened to report him. The petty officer in the next cell washed his handkerchief again and again and walked to and fro with it till it was dry. On the next light day Jan conducted a gunnery duel for hours. His ditty-box represented the enemy ship. He had rolled bread into balls for shells beforehand and left them to get hard. The little bread ball fell behind the box: "Overshot the mark!" The next fell in front of it: "Short of the mark!" Then the fun began: "Take aim! At the *Blaue Balje*! Eighteen hundred!" Geulen commanded. "Salvo —fire! Good, quick!" He bellowed like a madman, till the warder flung open the door again.

At last the twenty-eight days were past.

Geulen walked like a convalescent through the daylight streets of Wilhelmshaven at midday. They had ejected him from the *Blaue Balje* and transferred him to the sixth company of the Second Naval Brigade:

"Sixth company fall in for roll-call!"

The company-commander saluted:

"Thank you! Petty officer! Read the order of the day."

The petty officer opened the order-book and read in a monotonous voice:

". . . 2 p. m., march to mount guard at Mariensiel. Twenty

men to the kitchen of the men's mess in the first division to peel potatoes. The rest to scrub and mend clothes. Tomorrow, 7.30 a. m., clean ship. Eight a. m., working parties fall in in front of the barracks. Fifty to the docks, one hundred to coal S.M.S. *Pommern*. The rest to gather nettles. Those with anything to report or petition, fall out! Dismiss to mess."

The company turned about. The men went into the barracks and got their plates. Those with reports and petitions stood side by side. The company-commander strode along the line, behind him the petty officer with a note-book. First the petitions: home leave for betrothal, christening, or family business, or because of a mother's illness, and so on. All the petitioners met with refusals. In accordance with divisional orders, home leave was granted only in return for the delivery of gold coin. For one gold coin, one day; for five hundred marks in gold, three days; for one thousand marks, five days.

Then came the reports: "Seaman — reports his return from hospital." "Seaman — of S.M.S. *Nassau* returned from arrest." "Seaman — of S.M.S. *Ostfriesland* returned from arrest." "Seaman Mathiesen of S.M.S. *Strassburg* returned from arrest." "Seaman Geulen of the patrol boat *Blaue Balje* returned from arrest."

The company-commander's legs grew more and more rigid: "Petty officer!"

"Yes, sir."

The same thing happens every day after roll-call.

"At ease! Show identification tags."

A few produced their "death disks"—small metal disks stamped with their numbers, which should, according to the regulations, be hung round the neck by a cord. But the majority had not got theirs with them. And now the commander came out with his speech, a mechanical formula: "Your identification tags! I require you to wear your identification tags. Loyal service and precision in every detail—well?"

The petty officer whispered:

"They've had previous convictions, sir."

"Yes, previous convictions. Pull yourselves together. Loyal service in every detail. Once you are caught in the machinery of the law, it is too late. You won't escape then. The next step leads to fortress arrest.

"Petty officer, dismiss the men."

Those who had been newly transferred to the company turned about and got their plates. Commander "Death Disk" stalked across the barrack-square.

A very different spirit prevailed in the Naval Brigade from that of former days. Geulen noticed that at once. There was something queer about all the company-commanders. And there were many shirkers amongst the petty officers and men. For instance, there was a petty officer in his room, a tall, slender pseudo-lieutenant with a pale face. When Geulen entered with his sea-bag, a sailor was just engaged in polishing the buttons on his dress uniform. He even had a dog, a little beast with a coat like silk.

"Whose is the tike?"—"Our petty officer's."—"But what will he do with the beast when he's ordered to his ship?"—"Him ordered to his ship? You're an innocent! He'll stay here. He'll stick it out."

Some ten men were seated round the table mending clothes. The others from that room were out, sitting in the canteen or gone ashore without leave, with forged passes.

"How many days did you get?" asked the boiler-scaler Harry Mathiesen, who had himself come from arrest that day. "Twenty-eight days' brig."—"I got off with a week this time. But now we're well out of it. Nothing can happen to us here in the company. We can stick it out here till the war's over. But then we'll make straight for Hamburg."

After a time another sailor came in, Gregory Gog:

"Hullo, Jan. You here? Ali told me all about it. He's here, too, in the company."—"And what about you?"—"They kept me three days at the V.D. clinic and then sent me away. I've got to wait my turn here. They had me up once for questioning: violent attack on a superior officer."—"You're sure to get fortress arrest."

Gregory Gog gazed vacantly into space.

"I've got it coming too, six weeks," said another man, whom they called Jimmy. "I slipped off to Hamburg once without leave. But they won't take you, the prisons are all overcrowded."

"I'm off now, Jan. Tomorrow before working parties I'll come for you. Then we'll sneak off to the staff canteen and stay there till roll-call."

The first evening Jan did not go out.

He hadn't a penny in his pocket, and it was no fun just to saunter about the streets. He went to bed at nine o'clock. That night he lay like a log. Only once he started up when someone shouted: "Torpedo track to port!"

"What's wrong with him?" Jan asked the man in the next bunk.

"He's come from hospital. He was on the *Undine* when she was torpedoed."

Life in the barracks had undergone a change. The companies were only at half strength. Down below lay the recruits, pale, half-grown lads from inland. In the old sailors' rooms lay men broken by the war, whilst more and more men assembled there whom no captain would have on his ship after they had served their sentences.

Next morning in the staff canteen. All the tables were

occupied. Gog, Mathiesen, and Geulen were seated together. "We don't give a damn! We're well out of range."—"And what do we gain if we let them pound our bones to jelly? An iron cross? I'd rather have my bones whole."

The canteen had really been established for the servants and orderlies of the Second Naval Brigade staff. But as it was open from early morning and was situated within the barrack walls, it had developed into a favourite resort for those evading duty. The petty officer in charge of the canteen, who made a profit on the drinks he served, didn't mind whether it was visited by none but orderlies or also by skulkers evading duty. Some played *"Schafskopp"* and sixty-six, whilst others argued or read books. Every now and then a raid was organized and the men who were caught were brought to their company-commander for punishment.

"What's a week's arrest? You get through that lying on your behind."—"Besides, everything's chock-full. In the second company our petty officer penned the whole lot into one room and wrote 'Arrest' outside the door with chalk."—"They say there's a petty officer Weiss in your company?" Mathiesen inquired.— "Yes, Paul Weiss, a mighty fine fellow."—"I was with him on the *Ariadne*." Meanwhile Gog had concluded a deal on Geulen's behalf with a staff orderly. "Twenty cigarettes."— "Right; tomorrow morning, here in the canteen."

The next morning Geulen received a forged pass in exchange for the twenty cigarettes. A few more days and he had found his feet. He went into the town whenever he chose, lounged about the streets, or lay in the sun on the dike outside and gazed at the glittering surface of the Jade. At low tide the bay was transformed into a broad stretch of mud reaching farther than the eye could see. Only in the middle a narrow channel remained. Out in the Roads lay the fleet, always in the same place.

Once or twice Geulen was ordered to gather nettles. In parties of fifty they scoured the fields and the overflowing ditches where the nettles grew thickest. They did not gather many. It was no good to exert oneself. For the textile-manufacturers? They made a mint of money out of the cloth made from the raw material so cheaply obtained.

The nettles stung and the men's hands were blistered. There were no longer enough gloves for whole companies. Such times were past and gone. Germany was despoiled. You just had to catch hold firmly. And spittle is useful; it cools the stings.

The nettle party spread in skirmish line over the cultivated fields. Every man had a bundle stuffed under his left arm. Nobody bent down now to pick nettles, but only kohlrabi, carrots, and peas, which were just beginning to form in the pods. They swallowed everything, both the roots, still smeared with earth, and the green leaves.

Nobody's hunger was satisfied now by the rations in barracks.

And so the summer passed:

There was sentry duty beside the lock, or by powder-magazines, canals, and railway underpasses. Or they formed working parties for coaling and carrying loads. Midday dinner grew more and more liquid, and the bread ration smaller and smaller.

Once more the trees stretched long, lean arms up to the grey sky. Wilhelmshaven was immersed in wintry fog.

One evening in the Fleet Tavern: Jan Geulen, Butendrift, and the "Admiral." The war was their everlasting theme: "There's no end to the damned thing."—"Remember our good old *Lesbos*? That was something like a life."—"That Samos wine in No. 2 hatch! If we had a bucketful of that . . ."

A sailor from S.M.S. *Pommern:*

"You still ashore, Jan? How do you do it, honest, now?"—

"Honest now, I've done nothing at all. I've had one or two rows. After that they wouldn't have me on board. And now nobody'll have me."

"Did you see, Admiral? The *Möwe* has sunk three more ships. That makes twelve."—"She's the only German ship in the Atlantic."—"I saw the *Möwe* when she left the docks. She hadn't a name then. A.S. she was called, she was just an ordinary merchantman."

Kleesattel knew the captain.

"He's a type, I tell you, a real aristocrat. If his ship gets shot to pieces, he won't swim a stroke. He'll go down with folded arms like a stone."

The sailor from the *Pommern* sat down at the table: "You'll drink another glass with me?" Kleesattel wanted to pay for the second round. "No, no, I won't have that. It's my turn to-day. It's my birthday."

After the fifth round the landlord approached.

"God! I've only twenty pfennig left!" The "Admiral" wanted to come to the rescue; so did Jan and Dierck. "No, no, I ordered it. It's no damned business of yours." The sailor from the *Pommern* was literally mad with rage.

"What's that? You've got no money?"

"Don't you kick up a row, else I'll polish your mug for you. You can fetch the patrol, and that's all about it."

The patrol entered the tavern. Before he was led away, the man from the *Pommern* pressed the hands of the others round the table: "Boys, I mean to keep my bones whole, so when peace comes." And to Jan:

"So long, till we meet in barracks."

"That fellow's first class!"—"And he's right, too."—"I'm sick of lying for ever in the Roads. And look at all the lumber: benches, tables, trunks, sea-bags, all protected by armour-plate. Clear decks for action! Full speed ahead—to Heligoland and

back."—"The officers' mess have plenty of chow, and they get
extra war rations."—"The commander of the *Helgoland* is
right. 'Every seaman wants twenty stripes on the behind,' he
said."—"If only we could go into action for once. I don't mind
being smashed myself, if only that damned lot get knocked to
bits at the same time."—"I'd rather see if I can't get away from
my old tub."

"Landlord, more drinks! You needn't be anxious, we'll pay
on the nail." " 'I've only got twenty pfennig left,' he said! He's
no fool. You just wait and see, I'll be the next. I'll get a trans-
fer."

Jan Geulen went with Butendrift to the dockyard gates.

He told him the story of the *Blaue Balje* and the scouting
flotilla, and how the fireman Turuslavsky turned traitor. "And
there's no bearing it any longer in the company. We're fair
starved."—"Even so, it's still better than on board. We don't
get much more. And we see all the time how the officers live."

And when they shook hands at the dockyard gate:

"Jan, I'm through with it. I shall make some sort of a row.
If I don't come ashore for a while, you'll know why."

And Butendrift wasn't the only one.

The sailor from the *Pommern* wasn't the only one.

The prisons had long been too small, and now the buildings
newly taken over no longer sufficed. Breaches of discipline, arrest, and transference to the seamen's and firemen's divisions.

Hundreds came to the barracks.

Seamen ashore crowded the streets and taverns of Wilhelmshaven. A few variety theatres began their cabaret performances
during the day, whilst the men were still on duty. The company-
commanders' disciplinary powers were insufficient to punish the
countless acts of insubordination.

The problem of men ashore was growing more and more
urgent. And the admirals found a solution. Companies were

assembled and the white ducks were dyed field-grey. A few days' home leave, and then they were packed off to Flanders.

The solution of the problem was Flanders.

"Pack bags! March off to A.S. II!"

Such was the command which swept three hundred and fifty men out of the seamen's and firemen's barracks of Wilhelmshaven and welded them into a ship's crew. Officially "A.S." meant "Auxiliary Steamship." But in the canteens and taverns these ships had a different name, which cast a lightning-flash of illumination on their peculiar character: "Sky-tripper."

A skyward trip: that was another solution to the problem of the crews!

"Form fours! Squads right, march!"

Loaded with sea-bags, the party marched along the streets. Petty Officer Weiss of the second company was in command.

"I couldn't have stuck it any longer anyhow," said one man, consoling himself. "Cabbage or turnips every day and dried grass. There'll be no more of that now."—"If we only knew what there really is behind that 'A.S.'!"—"Just you wait, we'll soon know."—"It won't be worse than Flanders, anyway."

They marched into the dockyard through No. 4 gate, past barracks, workshops, and coal-dumps, till they came to a big freighter.

"Division, halt! Sea-bags down!"

Two lines of seamen and two of firemen. The petty officers in command of the seamen and firemen went up the gangway and reported to the officer of the watch:

"Deck crew ready."

"Engine-room crew ready."

The officer of the watch saluted and reported to the commander: "Crew await orders beside the ship."

The men standing on the quay stared at the ship, towering tall and black out of the water: four masts, two funnels. Many of them knew that ship's silhouette. They were standing at attention and might not move their heads, and yet word passed down the line like the wind. Everybody noticed something, and those who neither noticed nor knew passed on what their neighbours told them. "Do you see, my boy? The second funnel is just bluff, made of cardboard. You just keep a look-out, it'll all be as flabby as cardboard."—"Masts, funnels, upper works —the *Belgravia*!"—"Her name's scratched out at the bows, but she's the *Belgravia* all right."

And it really was the *Belgravia*, known to every sailor between Hamburg and New York as scrap-iron, sure to go down with man and mouse. More than one of them had refused at the Mercantile Marine Office to sign on for that ship. Jimmy had taken one trip in her. "With a shipment of horses! The poor beasts' legs were broken, the old tub pitches so."

And now the commander came down the gangway. He had grey hair, clear grey eyes, and an austere yet pleasant face. "A fine fellow!" said one man who had sailed under him previously. "The other chap with him is an ass."

"At ease!" ordered the commander.

The other, who was both gunnery-officer and personnel officer, began to call the roll: "Hans Peterson!"—"Here."— "Alrich Buskohl! Jan Geulen!" To each man his instructions were given and his station on sentry duty, when decks were cleared for action, at the guns, and when lights were screened, his place at mess, and his bunk.

Kuddl Bülow was there, too. He had joined the company only four days ago and was straightway enrolled. Dierck Butendrift hadn't been ashore much longer, a fortnight in all. When his name was called, Bülow did not step forward quickly enough for the gunnery-officer: "Back again! You've got to be a bit

smarter on our ship. I may as well tell you all that at once!"
The gunnery-officer had a gentle, melodious voice: "Stanislaus
Turuslavsky." Geulen pricked up his ears: Turuslavsky! He
nudged Butendrift. "That red-haired Turuslavsky, he's here!
Here on board with the rest!"

After the firemen also had been enrolled in divisions, they
all went on board. The men's quarters had been established forward in the between-deck which had formerly served as a
hold and, when a cattle-transport, as stabling.

Each man was allotted a locker, a place for his hammock,
and a place at mess. After half an hour to settle in, the bos'n's
whistle sounded.

"Working parties fall in in divisions!"

They stood on deck in grey dungarees, the first division on
the starboard side, the second on the port side. Paul Weiss was
petty officer of the port watch. His orders were brief and precise: "Two, four, six . . . ten, left face! Go ashore to carry
cases!" "The next ten bring on board the pile of planks beside
the ship!" "The next: carry ammunition! Sweep fo'c'sle! Clean
heads!"

He stood in front of Seaman Geulen:

"Can you write?"

"Yes, sir," replied Geulen, gulping down the "sir" so that
it was barely indicated. That was what Paul Weiss liked. To be
brief, decided, soldierly, that was enough. He didn't care a damn
for his position as petty officer or for any distinctions of rank
except in so far as they meant higher pay. "Very well, you're
my divisional clerk. Go down and prepare the lists for leave."

The ship was like an ant-heap.

Seamen, firemen, and an army of dockyard labourers. More
than a thousand men were swarming in confusion, carrying
iron, planks, ammunition, cases, and sacks. They hammered and

riveted and sawed. They shouted from on board down to the quay and from the quay up to the ship.

They took it in turn to retreat to the mess-deck, where they sat round the tables, drank cold tea, and exchanged discoveries. "They're fixing up eight six-inch guns and four torpedo-tubes." —"And it's all concealed, nothing visible from outboard."— "The old tramp'll never stand that."—"I wonder wherever they mean to take us." "That's as plain as day. There's to be another *Möwe*. The *Möwe* was fitted out here. She was just called 'A.S. I.' "—"We've stowed provisions on board, provisions for the tropics."—"And Jimmy bashed in one case." —Jimmy was there himself. "Just at one corner," he said. "It gave way right off. What was inside? Sun-helmets!"

Sun-helmets. Rifles. And mine-rails were being fitted up. "Not me, my dad's son ain't having any!" said Harry Mathiesen. "The steamship *Marie* put to sea from here in the summer with ammunition and guns for East Africa," one man declared, knowing the whole story. "No one ever heard of her again."— "And the *Libau* with Lieutenant Spindler on board, loaded full of rifles and ammunition for the Irish rebellion. Caught when she was unloading on the Irish coast!"

There was no end to the elaboration of their guesses concerning the purpose and destination of the ship. Groups of men who knew one another well sat together and considered possible means of escaping from the ship. They had to shout in order to make themselves heard. There were about a dozen heavy hydraulic riveting-hammers at work. And besides that the hiss of the oxy-acetylene blowpipes. Round holes were being melted in the steel-plated decks, and showers of red and green sparks descended on the mess-deck.

"Get along to work!" A petty officer drove the men from the tables; he was a sturdy fellow with short legs, a red face, and an unkempt moustache streaked with grey. He belonged to an older class, one of the naval reserve. The men rose unwillingly. It was already dark and the rows of electric lights had been turned on. "Just a few puffs more, sir."—"A minute for a smoke. We've only just come down below."—"That don't matter. Jump to it! Up on deck! Service is service, and drinks is drinks."

The ship's lights were screened above as a protection against an attack. The men went on working. The winches clattered and an endless train of coolies carrying loads moved along the raised gangway.

"That's that!" shouted the Hamburg boiler-scaler Mathiesen, and dropped a load of planks from his shoulder almost on a young lieutenant's feet. The long-legged Lieutenant von Birkhoff, wearing a uniform with an elegant waist, exclaimed: "Clumsy fellow!" He said no more and withdrew in silence. The captain had said that he valued good work and good seamanship in the men more highly than correct military form.

At last work was over, but only for the crew. The docklabourers worked in day and night shifts.

The riveting-hammers roared and scattered sparks of glowing metal beside the outstretched hammocks. The sailors drew their caps over their eyes. It was not till morning that sleep came. The exhalation from their bodies rose like a gentle flood to the deck-beams and enveloped everything. You could see the sky through the open hatch, overcast, damp, and smoky. But gradually dawn broke and it was time to wake the men. "Shake a leg! Jump to it, out you get! Lash up hammocks!"

Half an hour later was breakfast. There was coffee and plenty of bread. Each man even received a piece of sausage for his breakfast. "The commander saw to the relish." That commander, now, every way! "Yesterday evening I went ashore without leave. At No. 1 gate I met the commander. Now for the dust, I thought. Not a bit of it! He looked away, just as if he hadn't seen me."—"From today there's to be leave. Jan is making the lists."

"Working parties fall in!"

So they slaved away. By day they slunk off as often as they could to the mess-deck or the dockyard privies. The commander shut both eyes. Without these occasional opportunities for a smoke he couldn't expect his men to get through the extra work. In the evening they went ashore, often without washing, just wearing their short overcoats over their dungarees.

The work of fitting out the ship went on without a pause. It seemed like unregulated confusion, a fever that filled the days with noise and plunged the nights in fire. But in this chaos of planks, cases, and iron parts, something was coming into being. When the seamen and firemen had slaved for a fortnight filling the belly of this black, ten-thousand-ton monster with coal by day and celebrating noisy farewells by night or had listened in their sleep to the roar of the unresting riveting-hammers, the ship was ready for sea.

Nobody talked any longer of getting transferred.

The better food was one argument against it, and then there was P.O. Weiss. He could drink like a fish, but what a decent chap! In the other watch was P.O. "Alcohol," the moustached naval reservist, another definite type. No nonsense about being a petty officer in dress uniform, with shining buttons and gloves to go ashore. True, there were others, men with ox-like faces and wide, glassy eyes—"Yes, sir!" Heels together! Soft manners for those above, arrogant bullying for inferiors! Nevertheless, Paul Weiss set the tone, and he was supported by P.O. "Alcohol" and others.

And then the commander! Some of his men had followed him of their own free will from his former ship. "There's no one like him in the whole Imperial Navy," they said. "They've just

ordered him to our ship because they want to get rid of him."
The others on the bridge, with the long-legged torpedo lieutenant, the adjutant, and the gunnery-officer, were just felt to
be superfluous and to serve only decorative purposes.

The dockyard urinals opposite the ship were in use all day
long. With the adjacent privies there was room for fifty men.
But the days when you could sit in comfort were past. They had
reconstructed the seats and mounted them at an angle of forty-
five degrees. Nobody remained seated longer than necessary.
Your legs hurt, and with the slightest movement the hard edge
hit your back.

"These tilted seats, now, that's an invention! Who ever had
the luck to light on that?" "Some land-lubber admiral gone
mad. We've got a heap of them running round loose."—"They
design privy seats, but as for mounting guns! After the Dogger
Bank engagement they fooled about with it. They only increased their range by one kilometre. I heard that myself from
our gun-pointer."

The "Admiral" was there, too. The battle-cruiser on which
he was at present was likewise lying in dock for boiler repairs.

"Did your gunnery-officer bring his dachshund with him?"

"Yes, he takes it for walks on the quarter-deck."—"That fellow's got a voice like the tall girl that sings comic songs in the
Crown." The day before, Hans Grimm had had messenger
duty outside the officers' mess. "The gunnery-officer poked his
head round the door yesterday: 'Hi, you fellow,' he said to me,
'tell my dog Hans to come to the mess to me. Say I've got something for him.'" The whole privy reverberated with roars of
laughter: ". . . his dog Hans! Hansi!"—"If we go into action, the captain'll remove him from his command anyway."

The captain had previously been a gunnery-officer in the
Navy. They had hardly seen him yet—he was a post captain
with a goatee and dark, melancholy eyes. "The Lord alone

knows why they've put him in this old tub."—"I'd rather be
on one of the big ships, in spite of everything. We'll never put to
sea. Schillig Roads—no farther! And even if we do, there's
armour-plate nearly a foot thick, and us safe and dry behind
it."—"That tike Hansi! I'll chuck a plank at him before
I've done with the old tub," said Harry Mathiesen. He was
firmly resolved to be transferred. He had failed to salute and had
gone ashore without leave, but it was no good. "You can't do
anything worse: fortress."—"My dear chap, you're a duffer,"
said a sailor from a battle-ship. "It's perfectly simple, a touch
of the clap is enough."—"Yes, but if you want it, you don't
get it."

The pair withdrew into a corner. "But don't let on!"—"On
my honour, I won't," answered Harry, and made a note of the
address where a woman lived known by the name of "Gonococcus." "The destroyer flotilla have got one too," said the sailor,
and pocketed the proffered cigarettes. "But this one's enough.
Dead sure."

That evening the port watch had leave.

"Are you coming with us to the Crown?"

"No," said Harry Mathiesen; "I've got something else to
see to." He took leave of Jan and Dierck and went on his way
alone in the direction of Mariensiel. The lights were screened
above and all round. They cast but a faint light on the streets.
The pale yellow rays shone almost perpendicularly on the
pavement.

Outside the town the fields lay wrapped in darkness. Nor was
anything visible of the houses along the road, where lived dock-
labourers, small peasants, and the families of soldiers at the
front. All the windows within the military area of Wilhelmshaven were screened. The sentries had orders to throw stones
at insufficiently curtained windows. Mathiesen did not see the
block of houses till he was standing close in front of it.

He felt his way along the wall to the corner. It must be here.
He knocked. Something moved inside.

"Open!" called Harry Mathiesen.

An empty plate stood on the table behind a half-drawn curtain beside the iron stove, and there were quite a week's unwashed crockery and saucepans. That was the first thing that
Mathiesen noticed. He got no impression of the woman's face.
A colourless, shiny, grey rat's tail of a plait hung down her back.
Harry laid his parcel on the table and did not know what to
say after: "Good evening."

"That stove smokes," he began at last.

"Yes, it's not so bad today. Sometimes it's unbearable. The
landlord won't do a thing."—"The flues are clogged with
soot, they want sweeping out." He delivered an elaborate lecture
upon draughts and the proper treatment of iron stoves. "Oh
yes, and a good friend sent me here. And I haven't much time,
either. I've come ashore without leave," he lied. "I've brought a
parcel; there it is on the table."

She sat down beside him on the bed.

She couldn't manage without turning up her skirts, and as
sure as sure, she wore 8.8 sea-boots and flannel drawers belonging to the Imperial Navy. He had already observed that she
wore a sailor's shirt with the regulation blue stripe as far as
the collar-bone. "Gonococcus's" chief occupation was that of
potato-peeler in the cellar of a canteen. You could tell that
from the skin of her hands, and from the smell.

". . . I've been in Hamburg, too. I lived in Eimsbüttel."
Above the bed hung a photograph, a young girl in a white sailor
blouse with long plaits. Beside the photograph was an oleograph:
The last man on the keel of S.M.S. *Leipzig*. And there were
pictures from illustrated magazines: Admiral Tirpitz with a
long, flowing beard, and the Emperor in field uniform with
his wife on the way to Berlin Cathedral.

"That's no good. Can't we turn the lamp down?" He stood up and busied himself about the lamp, then returned to the bedstead. "Gonococcus" looked unreal now, like the picture of the girl with plaits up on the wall.

She wasn't paid much for her services. As it was, the coolies had to share one loaf among six. But sometimes one of them would add something to the bread ration. She always did her best.

Her aged body shook convulsively.

"That's all right, that'll do," gasped Harry Mathiesen.

He did not turn up the lamp again. He had brought half a loaf and a piece of sausage. "There, I'll leave the parcel on the table. Now I must hurry back to my ship. So long!"

Outside he nearly ran into a tree. He could see nothing except the distant, pale, luminous mist over the houses of Wilhelmshaven.

After he had been to a number of public houses in succession —brandy was to hurry things up. If only that damned *Belgravia* didn't sail too soon!—he landed at the Crown cabaret. It was a great barn with several hundred chairs, and yellow, stained tables. There were no women to be seen. There were no women in Wilhelmshaven, except those attached to the officers. Only seamen and firemen sat round the tables. They had weak, watery beer before them and weak, watery, wartime jests were declaimed from the platform. But after a certain amount of alcohol the tritest words assumed a deep significance.

It was rubbish that the two-hundred-pound Germania was singing on the platform. But the refrain that they all sang together—that was the thing. That expressed an irrefutable truth which Harry now grasped fully for the first time.

There were Jan and Dierck still, and P.O. Weiss beside them. All three were singing open-mouthed. All three were bawling the refrain of Germania's song so that the clouds of tobacco-smoke which filled the air of the shed began to vibrate. Harry Mathiesen joined in too:

> *"For this campaign*
> *Ain't no express train!*
> *Rub your eyes—*
> *With sand-paper."*

"Evenin', sir." "Why 'sir'?" Paul Weiss drew himself up up with a jerk and sat erect. "Oh, it's you. You just swill and shut your unruly mug." He pushed his half-filled glass towards him and ordered beer all round. "This Turuslavsky, now, the stoker crew will soon be even with him; it's a pity—a chap like that." With these words he ended the interrupted conversation. The waitress suddenly appeared at the table, bringing beer. The fumes of alcohol and clouds of tobacco-smoke made walls round them so that each separate table was like a room to itself.

"Your health, boys! Don't run away, little girl." And he touched her lasciviously behind.

The girl submitted willingly to familiarities from a petty officer. Humanity begins in the eyes of the Wilhelmshaven girls at the anchor and crown, with a petty officer's pay and prospects in the government service. Everyone below that mark is a coolie. She waited till the four had emptied their glasses. Paul Weiss ordered a bottle of wine; he had received his pay the day before. The wine was poor stuff, but the price was high enough. Li Arndt, the tall singer with whom Jan had been keeping company since he was in barracks, came back from her round selling postcards and sat down beside him.

"We may put to sea tomorrow," said Jan. "Betrayal of military secrets!" interrupted P.O. Weiss. "I've just sent

Blondy away," answered Li, and gazed in Jan's face. Paul
Weiss raised his glass and clinked it with his men.

"Old fellow!" he said, instead of "Your health!" He used
the familiar *"Du"* with emphasis and significance to each one
separately. In addressing Li Arndt, who had a thin face and
wise eyes and looked more aristocratic than any princess that
he had ever seen on Imperial ships in peace time, he used the
more formal *"Sie."* He actually made excuses to her: "Conduct
that can't be suitably characterized and that undermines discipline! That's what our gunnery-officer would say. . . ."
—"The gunnery-officer—Hansi!" bawled Harry.—"But what
am I to do? This lad here is my divisional clerk and my right
hand. Yesterday evening when the officer of the watch was
making his rounds, I couldn't say 'a' clearly. I just lay stretched
out on my back, dead drunk. Jan covered me with a whole
shopful of overcoats. Not a sign of Paul Weiss to be seen. Judge
for yourself, ma'am—my right hand! I can't say: 'You owl!'
to him. And here's Harry. It wasn't a mere pond we were on
together, but the North Sea. Harry, old boy, do you remember?
Our old *Ariadne*, how she suddenly turned turtle and her keel
and red-painted hull came up?"—"I should think I did, sir! I
had on a pneumatic life-jacket, and it burst."—"You see, miss.
Besides, Harry belongs to the honourable profession of boiler-
scalers. What would become of navigation without boiler-
scalers? And Dierck Butendrift: his fists and arms and shoulders! Just feel, miss. Judge for yourself."

They opened the second bottle.

On the platform a musical clown was tinkling out tunes on
beer-bottles: "Firm and faithful stands the Watch on the
Rhine. . . ." The Austrian and German flags which hung
crosswise on every pillar in the room were blurred by the thick
clouds of smoke.

"I've not got leave, but it doesn't matter," said Jan. And

Li answered: "Good, you come along with me. I can fix things up. Tomorrow may be too late."

Dierck sat heavily in his chair. He was thinking about the *Belgravia*. Suddenly he said, apropos of nothing: "Come what come may! It'll be good to get away from this dog's life. Maybe we'll have to get ourselves interned."

"We: that's it." P.O. Weiss had discovered the formula.

"We" is forbidden and entails punishment. Every jot of evidence gains double and treble importance if it presupposes community of intention. And Paul Weiss loved forbidden things. He had made his way to sea at the age of fifteen and signed on for twelve years. That damned naval propaganda! What he wanted was the sea and the comradeship of bold, seafaring lads. He had found barrack rules and drill.

"They've made me their tool, a head cleaner of guns, a head boot-black! A head sewage-pipe! Here, lass, another bottle!"

There was nothing else for it. What a true instinct these lads possessed! Merchant seamen get paid off if they don't like a ship, and stay ashore, wherever they choose. A.G.'s: irregularly and compulsorily enrolled in the Navy! "Your health, Dierck! Your health, Jan! Old fellow, we . . . and there it is. On board, of course you know. . . ."

P.O. Weiss assumed a military air. He leapt to his feet.

"Seaman Butendrift, Seaman Geulen! What are you thinking of? Keep your distance! Hands at your sides!" He bawled so that those at neighbouring tables looked up. The manager, an indispensable warrior behind the front, came running up: should he call the street patrol?

"That's all right. That's only manners on board ship." Paul Weiss motioned him away. "But, boys, you understand, just a sideways glance. We'll lull the baby!"

"That's agreed, Jan. I must go up once more. Then we'll be

off. I'll just leave the postcards." Li Arndt took leave of the others. A few more *Belgravia* men had joined them and sat down round the table.

"Tomorrow we put to sea," said the fireman Balten.

"*Maskie!*" shouted P.O. Weiss.

It was a word that the "Christian Voyage" had borrowed from some Malay archipelago, and its meaning amounted to: "There's an end of seamanship. Now we'll let the devil take the wheel." *Maskie!* And he emptied his purse on to the table. The seamen and firemen did likewise. "Landlord! Bring us drinks for all that, it doesn't matter what."

Jan and Li had gone. The table was covered with empty and half-empty bottles. The girls on the platform seemed to be dancing in another world. Everyone was drunk; only Butendrift, the fireman Balten, and P.O. Weiss kept up some sort of appearances. Paul Weiss stood up. The more he had emptied down his throat and the more the world seemed to sway insecurely, the straighter he stood and the more precise were his movements. It had nothing to do with discipline; it was the law of his being. There was no half-way house between standing erect and falling prone. He stood by the table as straight as a die.

"Paul Weiss, P.O. in the Imperial Navy, in the second division in S.M.S. *Belgravia* . . ."—"That's scraped off, '*Belgravia's*' scraped off," the fireman Balten cut in with a grin. —"In the name of three devils, then: Paul Weiss of S.M. Sky-tripper So-and-so is going to see the daughters of the land. Squads right! Course: Port Arthur!"

The other two watched him take the shortest way between the tables to the door. "He's thrown all his money on the table." —"So he has, but it doesn't matter. He'll pull through without money. Last week he sold his trousers. Came back on board in his drawers."—"Our chief engineer's a swine," said the fireman. They emptied the bottles into their glasses, drank them dry, and then roused their mates.

"That's the end. Come on, back on board."

The *Belgravia* stayed in dock four days longer. They were constructing a system of pipes and metal tanks, an apparatus to produce artificial fog and render the ship invisible on occasion. On the third day Seaman Mathiesen reported sick. On the fourth morning before it was light he left the ship.

An hour later the ship was ready for sea.

On the bridge were the navigating officer, the adjutant, and Hansi, the gunnery-officer. Forward on the port side were the commander, Paul Weiss, and the starboard watch; aft Lieutenant von Birkhoff and the starboard division with their petty officer.

Slack off on the lines! First the forward hawsers splashed into the water, then those aft. They were drawn in, hand over hand. The screw began to turn and the ship to move. Slowly the Imperial dockyard of Wilhelmshaven glided past. The morning sun flamed above that Babel of frenzied labour, all smoke and iron, and seemed to splash it with red ink. A half-finished cruiser lying on the stocks looked like a flattened ship's bottom lying at the bottom of the sea, and the red lights in her were like pools of blood.

The coolies and the stokers' watch below, standing on deck, did not know their destination. They only knew that they had provisions, tropical provisions for many months, and seven thousand tons of coal on board, that they were in a ship with two camouflage funnels and removable masts, and that guns and torpedo-tubes were screened from view. They didn't even know the ship's name, which still lay concealed in secret archives. One thing alone was certain, the ship's motto: Skywards!

The curtain of steam, oil fumes, and fog over Wilhelmshaven

was growing flatter. On the outer Jade the ship began to pitch. Her sides creaked. Some of the waves rose high and flung icy spray in the sailors' faces.

They had been steaming three hours.

"Clear the anchor—let it drop." The anchor struck into the sea's bed, the ship dragged round on the chain; she was anchored fast.

"All hands fall in on the forecastle!"

The first, second, and third divisions had fallen in, with the the stokers' watches and the officers.

"Gather round!"

The men gathered informally round the bridge.

"The work of equipping our ship has proceeded very rapidly. This is my first opportunity to greet the whole crew, and I now thank you for the labour achieved. We have cast anchor here in order to make a few more alterations in the ship. I cannot tell you anything about our appointed task, except that it is a particularly glorious one and that we have the good wishes of our Supreme War-Lord. Three cheers for His Majesty the Emperor!"

Three hundred and fifty gaping mouths down below on the deck:

"Hurra-rra-ra!"

It didn't sound very vigorous, but perhaps the wind, which just then broke through the snowy air, cut off the shout.

"I have one more thing to say—in general I am in favour of a military bearing and especially of military uniform. But in view of our peculiar task it is my desire that no uniforms should appear on deck. The master-at-arms has a store-room with jackets and civilian suits and caps brought from ashore, enough for the whole crew. Pick out clothes to fit you. Dismiss!"

The crew surged backwards.

"Our skipper's all right."—"He might 'a been speaking at

a funeral like."—"And he just gave the cheers because he'd
got to."—"He don't know neither where we're bound for."—
"No, he's got sealed orders from Berlin and can't open 'em till
we're out at sea." This information came from one of the officers' cabin-boys.

The barber had noticed how melancholy his eyes were.
"Well, what d'you expect, my boy? His wife died four weeks
ago, and to be captain of a sky-tripper on top of that!" The
barber was haunted by gloomy forebodings. He hadn't laid in
enough eau-de-Cologne, nor enough soap. If everything went
well, that meant a serious loss in his legitimate profits. But the
commissary chief wouldn't give him credit. "Oh, yes, but you
used to be on a battle-ship," they said.

The deck watch was busy making the final alterations in
the ship. Jimmy wielded an ax and felled the second funnel.
"The wind would have blown that down, anyway. It was only
put there for spies." Jimmy was already wearing his new civilian clothes. "Look at him—like an English lord."—"When she
settles by the stern, we must change our clothes quick, or else
the English'll string us up to the yard-arm as pirates."

A long metal strip along the ship's side, with scuttles made to
look like passenger cabins, was also removed, and the upper
works, which had been painted white with brown stripes in
port, were now recoloured black. They were as prodigal with
paint as if it were water. It ran down the sides in streams and
streaks.

In the midst of their labours a siren screached.

The men of the watch below came on deck. A ship's hull
advanced through the fog, black, with two masts and one funnel, whilst a second funnel was just being pitched overboard.
The ship cast anchor and turned round. Part of her crew stood
on the forecastle in woollen jerseys and caps.

"Them's civilians!"

"Rats! Coolies in civilian clothes."

The ship was rather too far away to be within shouting distance. But you could manage it if a number shouted in chorus. Some twenty men made trumpets of their hands and bellowed:

"Ship ahoy!"

The reply came re-echoing back:

"A.S. III!"

"Such presumption!" cried the gunnery-officer on the bridge indignantly. "Master-at-arms, find out the names of those men. They shall be reported. The fellows can shout all of a sudden; and just now when there were three hundred and fifty of them to give three cheers, there wasn't a sound."

The signalman, whose duty it was to signal to the ship, reported: "A.S. III, put out from Kiel."

Auxiliary Steamship No. III did not stay long. Before nightfall she weighed anchor and vanished in a northerly direction. A.S. II also weighed anchor, but she took a southerly course and turned landwards again.

The gunnery-officer had been relieved.

The navigating officer stood beside the lieutenant on duty; he was a grey-haired captain in the merchant service. He had known well enough that the *Belgravia* was an old tub. The short circle across the "Wet Triangle" had showed him that she was not seaworthy.

She was top-heavy. The guns and the torpedo equipment played the part of a deck-cargo badly stowed. The punt was carrying too heavy a load anyway. The navigating officer did not know whither they were bound, but seven thousand tons of coal meant a radius of action round the whole world. Some change might, perhaps, be effected by restowing the ammunition. He called the bridge messenger: "Ask the gunnery-officer to come up on the bridge for a minute or two."

But the gunnery-officer was in the bath-tub.

"The lieutenant can't come just now."

It was pitch-dark. The water was calmer. Noiselessly the *Belgravia* made her way through the fog. The second and third stokers' watch were at supper. A rumour passed round the table. Balten, who had been ashore with one or two of the sailors, had set it going. "The stoker that split about that affair in scouting flotilla E is here on board."—"In flotilla E! You know, off Heligoland, unfit for action."—"Their captain must have jumped out of his skin! They transferred him afterwards."—"He got another ship. He'll never bullyrag his men again."—"That stoker's here on board. In the third watch. You just ask the seamen. There's one of them, Geulen's his name, who was in the flotilla, and Butendrift knows about the affair, too."

A vacuum formed around Stanislaus Turuslavsky. No conversation flourished round his place at mess. He took up almost half the side of a table with his widespread elbows. The four who sat on his side were huddled together. "The food's better than when we were in the company."—"And there's relishes, too." But nobody was thinking of food and relishes. They talked to break the silence at that table.

Clear for general exercise! The sailors were at their action stations. Wisps of fog brushed across their faces. It was cold.—"We're on the Elbe, I can smell it."—"And the time's right, too." Paul Weiss's face moved dimly in the darkness. "Man the ropes! Kuddl, you'll pay out. Jan, you stay here by the cleat. Afterwards Jimmy'll work at the winch." Everything proceeded as on a merchantman, and it all went off first-rate. A long pier rose from the water, faint and shadowy. A few minutes later the great steamship was firmly moored.

The "*Alte Liebe*" at Cuxhaven.

"Look at those railway trucks."

The loading gear was ready. The cargo was taken on board from the trucks. Submarine mines! Great, egg-shaped things painted black. They were fastened to hooks and swung across to the ship. On deck the seamen received them. Each one consisted of a quarter of a ton of iron and explosives.

There were six hundred of them, another hundred and fifty tons of deck-cargo, the navigating officer calculated. Long live Imperial navigation!

Ease off on the lines! Ahead slow!

The iron hull began to vibrate. Engines and screws were at work. The *"Alte Liebe"* glided slowly past: at the far end were two dim lights and beside them the men who had unmoored the ship.

"So long!" they shouted out into the foggy air. Then they were gone. And the lamps, too, had vanished.

North-west course! Full speed!

"Watch below stand by hammocks!"

They stayed on deck a little longer, drawing in the air and looking at the foaming side-wash. "We shall have snow for sure."—"If only the fog lasts till we're through!"—"The old tub hasn't much speed. Twelve knots!"

The watch cleared the guns for action. One man from each gun was sent to the galley to make good, strong coffee.

The watch below had retired to rest.

Dirt glued their eyes and clogged the pores of their skin. They had kept on their clothes and boots. The ship rolled. Port—starboard! Port—starboard! The hammocks swung from side to side. Somewhere something that had not been fastened was clattering. Behind the thin iron sides the sea soughed and gurgled.

The hull was still passing over flat sand-banks. But her course was north-west, full speed ahead. Every half-hour the ship's bell sounded. Fainter and fainter it sounded, till at last it was no more than the falling of silvery drops.

Suddenly the boatswain's whistle pierced the air.

A signal was hoisted and a voice cried:

"Clear for general exercise! All hands!"

They turned over on the other side. They knew that game—the petty officer wanted to have an easy job rousing them. All hands! That way they'd be up quicker. A few exclamations came from the hammocks, short and sleepy. "Rot!—That's like you— You just . . . !"

How quickly the watch below had passed!

There was no evading getting up. They snuggled down into the darkness, just a few minutes more. The knowledge that no one was stirring was like a warm, protecting cover.

No one moved.

Yes, one man alone.

The ship's barber, Willi Rösler, was wide awake. He was like a taut spring that would inevitably snap and let fly. What did it all mean? Why had the petty officer gone away after blowing the whistle? The ship's position was different from what it had been when they came below. She lay broadside on in the sea. They had altered course. There was no sound up above. But why didn't the P.O. stay? Willi Rösler stared at the swinging hammocks. The hammocks vanished. Impenetrable darkness!

The dim red lamps that burned at night had gone out.

There was the boatswain's whistle again. A clatter of descending feet. P.O. "Alcohol."

He bawled:

"Will you come up? The ship's sinking!"

The barber was on the ladder, boots in hand. The whole watch below, firemen and seamen, were on the ladder. They surged up the ladder and through the hatch.

Kuddl Bülow managed to speak:

"Keep cool, boys! Keep cool! We'll all get up on deck."

Butendrift wasn't exerting his strength; he kept his place in the line. It wasn't till he got to the top that he remembered his fists and burst through the rusty trap-door.

The exit was thus enlarged.

A pale light fell on the men's faces.

Driving snow on deck. One or two of the watch ran past wearing cork jackets. On the bridge they were working a Morse lamp. Actually, an oil-lamp! The beam of light was intercepted by the thick snow. The ship was listing to port. Amidships steam rose in coils.

"Make way!" A lifeless form was carried past, wrapped in blankets, and then another. The engineer and a fireman, scalded.

A cloak and officer's cap—it was Hansi.

He wasn't giving orders, but explanations:

"The main steam-pipe has burst. The boilers may explode. The mines—"

The mines! Six hundred mines! Above the engines with burst steam-pipes! Above the boilers that might blow up at any moment!

Figures moved on the upper deck.

Boats were swung out. "Only eight men in my boat," bawled the officer in charge of the mines. "Eight! And professional seamen who can row." He had his packed trunks with him. But not a boat could be lowered. The short waves of the North Sea leapt up like wild beasts out of the driving snow. The ship listed more and more to port.

The position was reported to the captain:

"The ship is fast aground.

"But:

"Soundings show two fathoms of water amidships.

"Soundings show deep water fore and aft.

"Therefore:

"She is only fast aground amidships. Fore and aft she is hanging suspended. Her whole structure is bent and strained. Breakage at certain points. Broken rivets all over, details not yet ascertained."

So much for the navigating officer's report.
The engineer added:

"Danger of boiler explosion averted. The firemen have drawn the fires under the boilers. But there is water in the hull, observed in all compartments, water everywhere. One bulkhead is smashed. The ship is breaking up."

The captain—with the portrait of his newly lost wife on the wall, surrounded on all sides by symbols of misfortune—shook his fist at the unseen powers, at the dockyard, the Admiralty staff. "They've landed us in a nice mess!"

"Built in 1895 in an English dockyard," was the navigating officer's confirmatory report. "Germany wasn't equipped in those days to build such large ships."

You could hear the tearing of rivets. A clatter as of machine-gun fire.

"One bottle of beer, two cigars."—"One beer, two cigars." So it went on and on. The men crowded to the canteen. They were allowed credit. The canteen yeoman chalked up: beer, cigars, cigarettes, chewing-tobacco. . . .

An endless procession of faces at the window. The P.O. wrote patiently names and rank and the goods bought on credit. At last the ship listed so far to port that the bottles fell from the shelves and crashed down on the deck. The P.O. spat on his book, flung it down on the broken glass, and shouted as he walked off: "That's the end. Take what you like yourselves."

From the hand-pump in the prow issued a stream of water as thick as a man's arm. The level of water in the ship rose irresistibly. The men dropped the pump-handle. "It's no good. We won't go on."

Strokes of an ax in the canteen and a collapsing bulkhead. The way lay open to the officers' commissary: beer, champagne, saveloys, ham! Cases full were dragged to the mess-deck.

The engine was flooded. No heating, no light, and the wireless apparatus not working. They were sending up rocket signals from the bridge.

Aft the men were still pushing mines overboard.

They slipped on the snowy, slanting deck. The steel shells of the mines were icy cold. The men's hands were frozen stiff. As they shoved, the melted snow and the fresh paint that it washed off trickled down their arms and into their shirts.

Fewer and fewer kept on at the task.

"It's so quiet now," said Willi Rösler, exhausted by the unwonted labour. His gang of three left the mine and listened across the dark after deck. "There's nobody left here."—"We must look for the others." They clambered up the ladder and ran across the quarter-deck. The sentry still stood outside the officers' mess. "They've all swilled a rare lot," he said. "There's only the captain still on the bridge and the navigating officer and the officer of the watch."—"Where are the rest of our fellows?" "All fore in the mess-deck."

The hatch to the mess-deck was wide open.

From below, a dim light flickered of candles and ship's lanterns. Not enough to illuminate the large chamber. The three felt their way down the ladder, hungry and half frozen. Cases of beer-bottles broken open, champagne-bottles, sea-boots. The coolies lay on the floor wearing their pneumatic life-jackets and holding bottles and bits of sausage in their hands.

"Hullo, Soapsuds, there you are!" Something hit his belly, a great lump of smoked bacon. "Guzzle, boys, swill!"—"You've come too late. Those two have had a bout. You'd ought to 'a seen! But just wait and see, wait and see . . ."

Lockers crashed in. Bits of wood flew through the air. It was all whirling, confusion, a heap of wreckage. Two figures emerged: Turuslavsky and Butendrift.

There stood Turuslavsky, his shirt hanging in shreds, and Butendrift's lungs were working like a pair of bellows. You couldn't see their faces, only two great ragged silhouettes. Behind the pair hung a lantern.

They rushed at one another. "Don't get so near, Soapsuds." —"Once I saw two big birds in the air—claws and beaks!"— "God! That's first-class."—"And he's up again."

Turuslavsky had been forced down on his knees by a blow that grazed his skull and struck him in the neck. It was only for a moment; then he was up again. Blood flowed from his forehead. But he got a grip of his adversary.

Turuslavsky and Butendrift, three hundred pounds of bone and muscle in furious motion. Fragments flew in all directions. It was like a ball flung across the room against the wall, bouncing back and springing up again. More lockers crashed. And neither of the pair swore.

Not a word.

The sailors standing round had dropped into silence too. They had let go of the bottles and were holding the ends of sausage in their hands without taking a bite. They had forgotten the *Belgravia*, with her hull sinking deeper and deeper.

Smash! A blow across both eyes.

Butendrift's teeth parted: "That's for flotilla E!" And already he staggered. His hand gripped his adversary's throat; he would not loose his hold: "For flotilla E! For the *Blaue Balje* and your treachery!"

The ship lay across a sand-bank like the plank of a seesaw, vibrating very slightly. Rivets burst and their iron heads shot across the room like dumdum bullets.

Turuslavsky's face turned blue.

But at last he managed to seize his adversary's scrotum and crushed it in his fist. Butendrift reared like a bull and the sudden pain caused him to slacken his grip.

Turuslavsky was free once more.

Again the pair faced one another.

"Dierck—Stanislaus! You're a couple of fools. Both of you!"

Paul Weiss elbowed his way to the combatants.

"Who knows how long the old tub'll hold together? Half an hour—and it may be all over, and we shall go down to the fishes. Better swill."

Neither of the two would let his adversary be. Turuslavsky wiped the blood from his eyes and charged again.

"Bring along the champagne."

The corks popped.

Turuslavsky received a blow that laid him low. He collapsed gasping on to the iron deck and lay still.

Bottles clinked. Fists! Heads! Exclamations!

"Maskie!"

Turuslavsky!"

"Butendrift!"

"Champagne!"

"Ham!"

"Guzzle!"

"Swill!"

"Long live shipwreck!"

But the toughness of these old structures! It's the same as with old buildings—pillars and beams that seem to have been made for eternity. Just as if iron cost nothing in those days. The *Belgravia* held together after rows of rivets had burst and a number of stays had sprung from their joints. Her ancient structure bore the temporary transformation from a floating hull to a seesaw with a weight of five thousand tons on each end.

The lights on the mess-deck had gone out. Beneath the ladder hung a wretched, open oil-lamp and swung towards light. Day was dawning. All was confusion on the between-deck—scattered hammocks and banging locker doors.

All the men had gone.

The lockers were empty.

One man lay forgotten amidst the mops. He picked himself up slowly. His head was like a stone, simply like a stone, devoid of nerves or brain. What a drinking-bout, and plenty of grub too! How his head throbbed! Oh, yes—the *Belgravia*. Pack bags! All hands on the upper deck! Someone had shouted that over and over again.

But afterwards? What happened afterwards?

Seaman Hans Grimm raised himself up.

The empty lockers gaped at him. On the dark bulkhead somebody had chalked: "Moved away on account of dampness in the house."

Was that meant for a joke?

And now Hans Grimm was on his feet. He felt as if he were deprived of air. He had forgotten his head and his heavy, leaden limbs.

"My God! My God! . . ."

Thus he staggered up the ladder and came out under the grey sky. He knocked up against a row of men carrying a thick hempen hawser, and stared as if at a miracle.

"Well, Hans, you're staring like a stuck calf!"—"Don't stand about doing nothing! Lend a hand too!" snapped a petty officer. Hans Grimm was still dazed. He took his place in the line and helped to man the hawser. "What's up? You've packed your bag?" "Where were you, then?"

The hawser was dragged forward on the port side.

Five, six, eight—eight hawsers stretched so taut that they sang. At the end of each a destroyer.

The *Belgravia* was being towed.

There were boats on either side of her, too. They had passed chains beneath her hull, which lay tipped sideways on the water, emitting no smoke. Amidships were fire-boats, the *Retter* and *Goliath* from Bremen.

The aged Madam *Belgravia* returned from her last trip with water in her belly, listing heavily, and surrounded by a fleet of boats. She wasn't a pretty sight. Nor were the coolies on board a pretty sight.

The dropsical lady lay deep in the waters of the North Sea —too deep for.her structure. Something had to be done. They had thrown open her hatches and begun to unload her. Everything was transferred to the lighters lying alongside, mines and ammunition, and then the coal.

There was no end to the job.

And now everything had to be done without the aid of steam, by hand-labour alone. Spades and baskets and twenty-five men at every hawser. A derelict with four masts and a throng of grey labouring coolies on deck was towed up the Elbe. There were people standing on the banks: a girl with long plaits, children, and women. They waved.

More and more people gathered on the banks. You could hear cheering right down on the between-deck, even down in the hold where the crew were busy coaling.

"Whatever is up with them folks ashore?"—"We've just done our old tub in. That's no reason for cheering."—"That's the womenfolk. Got your prophylactic packet ready, Jimmy?" Jimmy grinned and his teeth gleamed white in his coal-begrimed face. "All in apple-pie order."

"We're passed Finkenwärder."

"There's the fish-market. Altona! Hamburg!"

A buzzing up in the air.

"Come up on deck; quick, though."

The sailors surged up on deck from every hatch and opening and stared up in the sky. A Zeppelin skimmed across the Elbe. The car passed the *Belgravia* at the same height as the navigator's bridge. The officers in the car behaved just as crazily as the people ashore. They snatched off their caps and waved. One of them raised a megaphone and shouted: "Three cheers for the *Möwe*, returning victorious!"

The captain stood rigid on the bridge of his derelict ship.

"Oho, so it's for the *Möwe*."—"That's what they've got in their heads."—"So that's the time of day! They think we're the *Möwe*." "Yes, the official news-bulletin said: 'The auxiliary cruiser *Möwe* returned safe and sound today to a German port after sinking fifteen enemy ships.' "—"The *Möwe*, Sky-tripper No. I! We're only Sky-tripper No. II."

The *Belgravia* lay in the Reiherstieg floating dock.

The captain made a speech, standing up above on the quarter-deck. The beams of the electric lights fell on the upturned faces of the crew.

". . . The ship will be unrigged. The crew will remain united and be transferred to another ship. I am resigning my command and handing it over to a man who may, perhaps, have been born under a luckier star than I. This evening there will be shore leave for all hands except the sentries. Dismiss!"

The men on leave crossed the river by the ferry.

On the far bank, on the pontoons, a crowd of people thronged up the bridge and out as far as the streets: men and women! Women!

"Hello! Welcome! Magnificent, magnificent! . . . One ship against the whole world! Hurrah!" Each separate coolie was lost in a confused mass of faces. Women clung to every arm —whole bunches of women: "Come along! Come along! Magnificent! Fifteen ships! . . ."

"Well, don't break a fellow's bones!" Jimmy resisted vigorously. He really wanted to go across to St. Pauli to see his little girl. "Let go! I'm not one of the *Möwe* crew," gasped another man.—"But you're from that ship over there in the dock?"— "From that old tub, yes, that's right."—"Well, then. Oh, we know, it's a military secret. You mustn't tell. . . . Come along!"

And then in the tavern and afterwards in the beer-palace:

"What will you have to eat? Waiter, bring drinks. Whatever these gentlemen order. I'll pay." The gentleman belonging to the firm known as "Jellied Eels" paid. People came from other tables and gave orders and paid. "Fifteen ships—congratulations! Your health! Our boys in blue! Here's to them! Come across to our table."

Our boys in blue looked so unwashed, with their ears and noses clogged with soot and coal-dust. They had merely given themselves a lick and a promise before coming ashore. They wore sea-boots and dungarees. Dress and undress blues had been sold long ago. Wihhelmshaven was a very different place. There, if you wanted drinks, you had to pay for them.

"I can't gulp the stuff down quick enough. It's crazier than on our old *Belgravia*. I shall stay here now. I shan't get the stuff so cheap again," thought Jimmy.—"What, this neckerchief as a souvenir? There you are, miss." Miss wore a ring on her right hand. Hans Grimm took off the neckerchief.

The band played:

"Proudly waves the black-white-red. . . ."

The coolies knew only the first stanza. The women and civilians sang all three. Balten was a swine. He had come ashore in dungarees. Just as he had clambered out of the flooded stokehold. "Know what she says?" he bawled across the table. "Mud from the Atlantic! We'll let that stick."

Mud from the Atlantic! But the sailor gents told no tales of their bold cruise, of gunnery duels and burning ships, and how their English cousins sank in shoals beneath the blue waves. The "Jellied" gentleman did not get his money's worth. "Hold yer jaw! I told you first thing I haven't sunk no ships. We've only run our old punt aground. That's all."

"He's a surly chap, that mate of yours," and the manufacturer turned with an air of gentle reproach to Jimmy. And he found what he wanted in Jimmy, who thumped him genially on the nape of his fat neck. "Bacon, prime peace-time quality! Always had plenty of bread-cards, ain't yer, and a bit over?" Beside Jan Geulen sat a pale woman with a delicate skin, wearing her red hair rolled up in a large knot. Jan saw the blood surge to her face. There was another woman beside Alrich Buskohl. Skirt and stockings of a silk mixture, and illness stamped on her face. She worked in a powder-mill and her name was Anna. Alrich played with her yellow hands and timidly called her Annie.

"You damned pot-belly, your carcass 'ud just do to feed the fishes!"—"Or for the trenches! What's he doing, still fooling round here, stuffed with grub!"

No, these sailors really weren't the *Möwe* heroes. And how dirty they looked! What indiscipline!

"Waiter, the bill!"

The manufacturer of canned foods took his departure. His friends and womenfolk left too. The pale woman stayed. So did Annie and the dark girl beside the fireman Balten, and the one beside Hans Grimm—all of them. Others joined them.

The sailors scraped together a few coppers from their trouser pockets. When that wasn't enough, one of the others opened her bag and added her contribution. *Möwe* or *Belgravia*—it didn't matter which. And better an unwashed coolie in your bed than a husband in the trenches.

When Jan Geulen roused the next morning, a hand passed across his face, his arm, his body—very gently. She had clear, calm eyes, this woman. A network of blue veins showed beneath her skin.

"I don't even know your name."

She bound up the red waves of her hair in a knot. Then she went out and came back with a little girl: "Lottie. She's fourteen months old. She spent the night with a neighbour."

Above the writing-table, beside the window, hung a portrait. a man in a helmet carrying a rifle.

"It was 1914. On the Marne—"

Jan buttoned up his overcoat. The little girl was playing with his cap-ribbon. "Daddy! Bye-bye!"

"It's getting late. I can't wait for coffee."—"But you'll come again, won't you?"—"I'll come—this evening. And I'll bring some paraffin. Tomorrow I'm off on leave."

"Hans Olrich. Lithographer," was the plate on the door.

At a corner Jan saw the large head-lines of a newspaper displayed:

GERMAN AUXILIARY CRUISER
IN ACTION AGAINST THREE BRITISH CRUISERS.

On February 29 an engagement took place in the northern part of the North Sea between the German auxiliary cruiser Greif *and three*

British cruisers, as well as a destroyer. S.M.S.
Greif torpedoed and sank a large British cruiser
of 15,000 tons and finally blew herself up.
CHIEF OF THE ADMIRALTY STAFF

Beneath these lines was an outline sketch of S.M.S. *Greif*.
"So A.S. III from Kiel has got a name now."

In Osnabrück Jan changed to the express. In Münster they
turned him out again: his ticket was only valid for slow trains.
On the second day he reached Mülheim in the Ruhr.

His mother lived in Styrum. The street ran right through
Thyssen's Rolling and Steel Mills. Workshops and blast-
furnaces, railway tracks, and clouds of steam, and beside it all a
dusty row of houses.

Jan had forgotten it all—the air, the blackened houses, the
balconies crowded with household goods. "Odol, best for the
teeth!" still shouted from the blank end of the row. And in the
front that crack in the wall still reached to the first floor, just as
it had done formerly.

Jan climbed the steps, very slowly. On the door was the porcelain plate with its brass rim. Nobody opened the door, and
the passage was dark.

Mrs. Höckens next door:

"You, Jan! Well, I never! And you grown so big! I'll have
to speak respectful to you. Yes, yer ma's on her shift till this evening. Come in, won't you? . . .

"Katie? She's gone after 'taters. . . . No, she may be a long
time. She went this morning. But sometimes you've got to stand
there till evenin'. She such a nice, nippy little girl."

"I'll just leave my bag here, Mrs. Höckens. Perhaps I can
find Katie."—"Men on leave get served first. There, where the

road goes under the railway. You see, where them women's standing."

When he was down one flight of stairs, she called after him: "Rudi and Johnny are playing down below." Rudi and Johnny had been crawling on the floor when he left home. Katie was just starting school; and now she must be thirteen!

Women! They stood in fours, a long queue, nearly a hundred. Children, one or two men, and here and there a few dirty field uniforms. Two policemen stood at the warehouse door. The door was shut.

Jan sauntered along past the queue. Those women—their skirts hung in stiff folds, and they wore heavy boots or wooden clogs. No figures, no faces—not feminine faces. They looked at Jan and remained quite hard.

"Another of them chaps——" said one woman behind his back, with something approaching hostility. Jan turned round. "Yes, I mean you. Brutes from the front! And then the sailors as well —get served first. And we've got to stand and wait." The woman's lean cheeks and the faces behind her, with their shawls and ragged hair, were blue with cold.

The queue began to move.

The warehouse door was opened.

Shoulders! Knots of hair! In the drab crowd, reaching to the women's waists, little girls with meagre plaits. They all pushed and shoved. They were afraid that the supply would be exhausted before their turn came.

Each one received twenty-five pounds of potatoes.

Jan walked round the crowd, searching.

Scraps of talk:

". . . shot through the lung. His mother had a stroke."— "Mrs. Schulze, that little, dark woman. Her husband had leave not long since. That was seven months ago. She's nearing her time, getting quite a size. And now the husband's killed."—

"What stuff he does smoke! It makes me retch."—"These 'yer men on leave! She left her husband at home with the wash. And he put in the paper shirts along with the rest. All gone to jelly when she came home."—"If I'd got the money, I could go to the hospital."

Jan saw a girl with smooth, brown hair, a girl of about twelve. The sailor and the child gazed fixedly at one another.

"Katie!"

"Jan—"

"It's you, Katie!"

She flushed red up to the temples and forehead, right to the roots of her hair. She couldn't say a word. But you could see her stature increase. "No, I've no basket. They always press on you so right here. I'd rather take a sack."

Jan had taken the sack from her. He was served directly. He carried the twenty-five pounds of potatoes in one hand. Katie held the other. She trotted lightly beside him. She was thin, with long legs and lean arms—she was such a nice, nippy little girl and could elbow her way forward so cleverly in the potato- and margarine-queues.

A woman was walking in front of the pair; she was pregnant and was carrying a basket of potatoes. "I know her, she's another of that sort, she's only shamming."—"What sort? What's she shamming?"—"She's only stuffed in a cushion. Then she gets served first. Last time they nabbed one.—And I can cook, too. Rudi and Johnny? They're mostly down below, always playing— That there on my neck? That's from the operation. Rudi's got one too. And they operated on Martha Höckens last week. . . .

"That's where Mam works, in number 7. I always take her dinner." Jan's eyes followed her glance. Long sheds with darkened glass roofs: turning-shops, open-hearth furnaces, rolling-mills.

They passed a blast-furnace.

The charge of ore and coke had just been brought up and tipped into the cone which closes the upper end of the furnace-shaft. The bell, moved by an unseen force, descended and the charge sank into the interior of the furnace. A pillar of flame leapt up. Smoke and fumes enveloped the men who were up above on the platform manipulating heavy tip-barrows.

There were eight or ten men with tip-barrows. Jan could see them clearly silhouetted against the sky. They were dressed in sackcloth and had no shoes; their legs and feet were wrapped in rags. A sentry with a rifle stood beside them.

"Russians," Katie explained.

The gangs who brought the ore and coke to the hoist, and those in the pig-beds into which the liquid metal flowed from the blast-furnace, were also Russian prisoners.

Katie knew everything.

Women stuffed cushions under their skirts! Those were Russians! In the barracks there the "yellow girls" lived, the "canary-birds." "What, don't you know that? The women from the powder-mill. They live there because nobody'll have 'em. They cough and spit so. But they earn a mint o' money. They always wear gloves and put on veils when they go marketing."

A week's home leave.

Jan asked no more questions.

When his mother came home from work in the evening, she tidied the room and cut the bread for the children. She always kept the smallest ration for herself. There wasn't much cooking to do.

Jan was wretched in this suffocating, sombre den, wretched with his mother and sister. At night when they undressed and went to bed—Katie and the two little boys—what skinny arms and big, protruding stomachs! Jan had seen children with stomachs like that in the famine quarters of Chinese seaports.

A week is a long time.

Jan fetched food-supplies, took his mother her dinner, and wandered round the sheds and over the open spaces in the works. There was a wagon of scrap-iron—wheels, buffers, steel rails —waiting to be melted down with the raw ore in the open-hearth furnaces; the men who were handling the wagons wore old infantry uniforms: German soldiers from the front undergoing fortress arrest.

Once Jan came upon a gang of Russians: bent backs showing the large prison numbers sewn on their coats, and hungry, sunken eyes. They were cooking a stolen cabbage on a heap of hot slag.

An army-boot pushed in between the bearded faces bent to the ground and trampled on the cabbage: "You damned dogs! Get on with your work!" With blows from the butt of his rifle the Landsturm reservist drove the startled Russians before him.

The furnaces vomited fire. The chimneys smoked. In the midst of the works was a concrete soaking-pit as long as a bowling-alley in which the new gun-barrels were reheated.

Prisoners of war! Men undergoing fortress arrest! Forced labourers from Belgium! Women!

The last evening at home:

The children were already asleep. Jan sat beside the bed in which his mother and Katie lay. "I shall get her exempted from school. The principal told me so. But they won't have Katie in the turning-shop. And I've been to the boss at the filling-station. She's too little still."

Jan glanced at Katie—her breasts showing beneath her night-gown like half lemons, on her neck the scar left by the surgeon's knife, and her childish eyes already old. He saw brown spots on his mother's head, made by the oil that dripped from the shafting and clogged her hair.

"We could try the switch-yard. She'd only have to stick labels on the cars there. That's easier than in the turning-shop. And that slave-driver, the boss, isn't there—"

The slave-driver! The boss!

Those bosses, foremen, reservists, standing behind the workers in the works, by the blast-furnaces, and in the mines, and driving pitilessly in their anxiety lest they should be sent to the front! Jan stroked his mother's hand helplessly—her fingers with the hard, gnarled joints.

She was dropping asleep, but suddenly she started up and gazed at him wide-eyed: "Jan, d'you think there's a God?"

Jan stroked her hair; it was as hard as glass.

It was his last day on leave. She struggled against sleep, but her eyes closed in spite of herself. She still spoke, in a low voice.

"There ain't no God. I mustn't go to sleep; there's the planer, I must stop the planer."

Jan turned out the gas.

From time to time, when a blast-furnace outside swallowed its charge, the walls and beds and objects in the room glowed red. White wisps of steam floated past the windows.

Here was a centre of production: armour-plate! Guns! Shells!

8. Jutland

RAISE steam for full speed!

It was two o'clock in the morning: Weigh anchor!

Over the masts the great mountains of cloud, characteristic of the north, passed slowly. The twenty-two battle-ships of the High Sea Fleet, and the five battle-cruisers, were making their way out to sea from the bays and estuaries.

They were steaming north at eighteen knots.

The wind was in the west, blowing with moderate force. On land it stirred the smaller branches of the trees; here it blew the the smoke rising from twenty-seven pairs of funnels to starboard away over the sea. A great bank of smoke was left in the ships' wake, blotting out part of the sky. Sometimes tongues of flame leapt up from the dark, stumpy funnels.

The forty-five thousand men of the crews lay in the casemates on armoured decks covered with linoleum; they were shut in a steel prison, like the shells and the charges. Now and then a sentry who had been relieved looked out through a sighting-slit, or a wave washed the deck, or a star appeared. Otherwise the night was uneventful.

The northern night was brief.

Day broke soon after three o'clock.

The ships stood out clearly against the water—a troop of grey monsters with rigid, protruding tusks. They swept through the surf, irresistible in their advance.

The battle-cruisers had detached themselves from the main fleet and were now leading. The five units—forming, so to speak, the head—sailed far in advance of the main body, surrounded by a cover of destroyers and, like outstretched antennæ, a scouting force of light cruisers in a semicircle whose radius reached far beyond the horizon.

It was a demonstration by the whole fleet; a naval advance—one of many. The British fleet made countless similar advances.

It was May 31 in the third year of the war.

Light clouds sailed across the sky. The horizon seemed far away and very clear. There was a gentle swell and the sea was like green, transparent glass, a gigantic, glittering disk with the five armour-plated monsters in the centre.

The North Sea consists of many thousand similar disks shining in the flaming rays of the sun, and the mightiest fleets can pass one another unobserved.

Not a wisp of smoke on the horizon, not the tip of a mast, not a trace!

In Admiral von Hipper's battle-cruisers the men were cleaning the guns, then going through gun-drill, with blank charges, as usual. The High Sea Fleet, under Admiral Scheer, a hundred kilometres distant, was performing evolutions and battle manœuvres. The officers off duty stood on the bridges, fanned by the gentle north-westerly breeze, whilst the rest, and the main bodies of the crews, were in the armoured turrets and casemates.

Three o'clock in the afternoon.

The light cruiser *Elbing*, on the extreme left of the scouting force, sighted a trail of smoke, then a funnel and two masts as fine as needles; it was a Danish merchantman. The *Elbing* sent out two destroyers to hold up the steamer and search her. The Danish vessel stopped her engines and blew off steam.

The ascending steam was sighted by a scouting ship on the extreme left of another advance squadron, by the British cruiser *Galatea;* astern of her, two squadrons of battle-cruisers and the British Grand Fleet were advancing.

That steam blown off became the pivot of the whole action.

The *Galatea* fired the first shot that day. Wireless messages were sent back to both enemy lines, to Hipper and to Admiral Beatty, in command of the English battle-cruisers, to Scheer and to Jellicoe, who were still nearly a hundred and fifty miles apart.

Orders were given:

Flag-signals! Dot and dash! Wireless messages.

The light cruisers kept in touch, and behind them the fleets advanced. The race began for the best place in the sun and wind.

The German iron-clads formed in echelon, steaming westwards at full speed. The destroyers now steamed behind the echelon. They were almost lost to sight in the heavy swell. The light cruisers steaming in advance left a heavy curtain of smoke behind them, shrouding the horizon.

Then the hostile squadrons of battle-cruisers hove in sight of one another, and the light forces quitted the field.

The smoke sank and dispersed.

The air grew clearer.

The battle-cruisers confronted one another. Admiral Hipper had the *Lützow, Derfflinger, Seydlitz, Moltke,* and *Von der Tann;* Admiral Beatty, the *Lion, Princess Royal, Queen Mary, Tiger, New Zealand,* and *Indefatigable.* Five against six. A broadside of sixteen thousand kilograms against twenty-four thousand.

The hostile squadrons altered course for action, sailing along convergent lines, but still nearly twelve miles apart—gigantic grey brutes appearing above the horizon, rendered small by force of perspective, yet mighty even at that distance. In the belly of the smallest beast in these two herds, forty-eight thousand horse-power was potent. Each one carried anything up to four thousand tons of coal, and an equal weight of steel and dynamite.

The range of the German guns was eighteen kilometres, of the English twenty-one.

Admiral Beatty had not yet opened fire. The German ships lay shrouded in the light mist. Hipper cast off from the enemy

line at a sharp angle in order to pass rapidly through the zone of
unilateral danger. The coal was conveyed to the stoke-holds on
rails, as is done in the galleries of mines. The funnels were transformed into volcanoes spitting fire and flame.

Not a face to be seen on deck. All the armour-plated doors
were closed and the sighting-slits wedged tight. Electric light
burned in the transmitting stations, turrets, and casemates. With
lowered visors, the adversaries boomed in close proximity. The
gun-pointers stood with their hands on the triggers, and their
eyes glued to the telescopic sights. The captains and gunnery-
officers stood beside the telescope sights, in which they could see
the image of the enemy magnified fifteen times.

Still Admiral Beatty did not open fire.

Twenty-four tons of iron against sixteen! And behind him
lay the fifth battle-squadron, which had misread a flag-signal
and had not yet taken up its position. Admiral Evan-Thomas
with the four *Queen Elizabeths*, the most modern ships in the
British fleet—a further addition of thirty tons for each broadside.

Hipper hoisted a signal. The blood-red battle-flag.

"Open fire!"

"Fifteen thousand!"

Fifteen kilometres!

The gunnery duel began, ship matched against ship.

The sixth cruiser of the British line had no adversary. Smoke
poured forth, curled and swelled to the magnitude of cumuli,
hung about the ships' sides and in front of the telescope sights
for a time, and was then blown past the ships and away. The
British squadron lay in the wind. The brown ochre smoke from
their guns hung motionless and obscured their view.

The impacts approached nearer. The jets of water they threw
up were of a poisonous green and yellow at the base, gleaming

white at the summit. The volumes of water hurled aloft covered and concealed the hulls. When they received a direct hit, the steel bodies vibrated and reverberated like strange, gigantic musical instruments.

And it was this that was so profoundly impressive.

Suddenly the wind played on the steel shrouds as on a harp. A tall wave dashed over the bows. It was a summer afternoon, and the sea was like transparent green glass.

Once again the guns were raised—maws breathing flame and rending the air. In the foretop, a hundred feet above sea level, the gunnery-officer was perched, and reported by telephone to the fire-control where the impacts fell.

The *Lion* was ablaze. Thick smoke was emitted from the *Tiger*. One turret was put out of action on the *Seydlitz*—eighty men died a bloodless death, leaving no mortal remains. When the jet of flame subsided, soft black flakes floated down.

The look-out in the crow's-nest, the gunnery-officer, and the captain—they alone knew. The rest knew nothing, saw nothing, but merely felt the rocking of their ship seeking to escape her adversary by desperate turns.

There were living souls in the turret, in the hatchways, in the passage-ways, the vital marrow of these monsters raging across the sea; rising or subsiding within the long tunnels of the ships!

At each volley, when the blaze at the muzzle cast its reflection and the interior of the armour-plated sides glowed dark red, the guns' crew formed a single, solid mass. When the air began to vibrate in the compartments, and the hulls to reverberate under the impacts like the hollow belly of a musical instrument, the whole crew became one vibrating mass.

The fire-control registered:

"One salvo every twenty seconds."

They had ceased to be humans beings. Numbers one, two, three, up to sixteen, at the guns, twenty-four at the conveyors, forty in the magazines—all formed a single interlocking machine. Load—fire! Load—fire! That was the heart-beat of the ship.

So long as the guns fired, she still lived.

A pause. She altered course.

The barrels were hot. The grey paint on them had partly blistered and turned brown. Lamps like glow-worms hung in the compartments. Dry, hot air rose from the magazines.

They were all thirsty, but the tea-pots were empty and the water in the fire-buckets was warm and foul. Nevertheless, the buckets were drunk dry in an instant.

The battle proceeded.

Slower.

The fire-control had to adapt itself to the new course, to wait and check the fall of shells and correct the distances accordingly.

Machine-like movements precise and rapid.

When the fever abated, nature reasserted its claims.

Eighty men cooped up in the turret suffering pressure on the bladder. They sought relief till the fire-buckets were full to overflowing. The battle continued for an hour. The men's physical organs and functions—blood, nerves, intestines—worked at the furious pace of the engines. The stokers relieved nature upon their shovels and hurled it into the fires.

The stokers:

The *Seydlitz* had twenty-seven boilers, eighty-one furnace-mouths, and two hundred and sixty square yards of grate-surface. The bunkers held three thousand six hundred tons of coal—that is, a train-load of three hundred and sixty cars. The proportions of the *Derfflinger* and *Lützow*, the *Lion, Princess Royal, Queen Mary,* and *Tiger,* were even more gigantic.

A running fight.

At thirteen kilometres.

The eastern horizon was even more thickly shrouded than before.

The German ships lay in a thin mist so that their outlines were blurred. The British battle-cruisers stood out in sharp outline against the western sky.

Hipper led his ships, southwards, towards the main body of the German fleet. Beatty stuck close to the German squadron, taking a parallel course.

S.M.S. *Lützow*, Hipper's flagship, was hard hit. Flames broke from the *Seydlitz*. The next straddle of the British buried her armour-plated hull beneath foaming waves—the column of water leapt three times the height of her masts—and extinguished the fire again.

One of the *Lion's* turret coverings was swept away. The thick plate described a great curve as it was hurled into the sea. The same projectile put a second turret out of action and the turrret crew were all burned to death except two men. The *Lion* steered out of the line, trailing a thick curtain of smoke behind her that glowed a rusty brown underneath.

Admiral Beatty transferred to another ship.[1]

A searchlight signal, flashes of white light:

"Destroyers to the attack!"

They issued forth in front of the British line, the light cruiser *Champion* and three groups of dark-grey boats moving at frantic speed, and were intercepted by the light cruiser *Regensburg* and the black host of German boats. They approached within a thousand yards of one another. Light guns, point-blank range! The projectiles flew over the shimmering water like flints ground flat. The stumpy funnels gasped. The water's surface was black with smoke. Damaged ships lay motionless and whirled in eddies like wounded ducks with wings outstretched. Even whilst they sank they discharged their torpedoes.

[1] *This is an error.*—TRANSLATOR.

It was a battle within a battle, for the curved path of the battle-cruisers' heavy projectiles arched above the frantic whirlpools and the greasy, gleaming smoke of the destroyer engagement.

Columns of water! Direct hits! Gas and fire!

The *Moltke* and *Von der Tann* concentrated their fire upon the *Indefatigable*, the last ship in the British line. Armour-piercing projectiles burst through her armour-plate and exploded in her interior. Her grey steel sides trembled like the flanks of a hunted animal. The *Indefatigable* settled by the stern and ceased to follow the movements of her squadron. There was no sign of fire or smoke. A dark, turbulent mass! It was a full half-minute later that flames burst from her hull. Wreckage was hurled aloft. The dark fragments of armour-plate described ponderous, unwieldy curves, and yet they flew mast-high. The *Indefatigable* heeled over and capsized. One thousand and seventeen men went down with her.

"Adversary blown up. Shift target left, on the ship with three funnels and two masts!" ordered the gunnery-officer through the voice-tube. ". . . blown up." Bent backs were straightened and men pushed aside the protective bandages from their noses. A hoarse roar issued from their dry throats, inflamed with powder-smoke. The voice-tubes reverberated with: "Hurrah! We're still going strong!"

But their exultant shouts were quickly stifled.

Twelve hundred ears listened as one.

A clear, sustained note rang through the *Von der Tann*. The ship began to vibrate like a gigantic tuning-fork, as if the air were her support. For a moment the light went out. She had received a direct hit in her stern-post from a projectile weighing eighteen hundredweight, fired by the oncoming *Queen Elizabeths;* this time it ricocheted like a ball. The four *Queen Elizabeths* advanced and opened fire from an immense distance, sweeping the light cruisers before them and concentrating their fire, two and two, on the two ships at the extremities of the German line.

". . . blown up!"

Charges, projectiles, hoisting-derrick, shell-grabs! The gaping muzzles of guns! Seventy seconds later the ship reared under the first salvo fired at her new opponent. Beneath the smoking barrels the men breathed in the rhythm of the sharp reports of the metal parts. The drums of their ears ceased to perform their function. Internal membranes and intestines vibrated under the shattering explosions. Each time they heard the crash of a salvo, they felt a sense of deliverance.

Salvo—fire! Salvo—fire!

And when that ceased, it left nothing but a mocking void.

The *Queen Mary* had a crew of 1,256 men.

"God save the King" sung by a doomed crew, or the thousand voices shrieking "Mother!" in a demoralized trench—it is all one and the same. And when a thousand tons of ammuntion explode, even such things cease—no patriotic song, no cry to God. There is no place left for rebellious flesh. The black specks flung up from the gaping hull are past all sensation. And yet there were three clearly distinguishable phases in the catastrophe:

Coal-dust!

Fire!

Smoke!

The ship bent like molten iron. The funnels and masts crashed inwards. Greasy shining coal-dust issued in puffs from a rent hull. Then a flame burst through the covering of dust and shot up like a dark-red scar. Lastly, heavy, curling smoke circled round the flame that rose sky-high. From each ball of smoke another ascended, till everything was smothered beneath a pyramid of black, monstrously inflated bladders.

Shift target! Bellowing voices down the voice-tubes!

Beatty signalled to Jellicoe's flagship:

"Submit: *Queen Mary* blown up."

The *Tiger* almost ran into the sinking stern with still whirling propellers. Masses of wreckage crashed down on her deck. The ventilators sucked in the poisonous fumes and pumped them out into the lower compartments. The smoke eddied in raging whirls and shrouded the *Tiger*, and then the *New Zealand*, in thick clouds. They were moving at full speed, and yet they continued for a time invisible.

In the German line the *Derfflinger* and *Seydlitz* had observed the explosion. The other ships kept their attention fixed on their own targets. Interlocked in blind fury, they swept across the field. The column of smoke rising from the *Queen Mary* was still over two thousand feet high, like the crooked trunk of a mighty tree, after the battling giants had vanished beyond the horizon.

The four *Queen Elizabeths* had found surer range. The last of Hipper's ships plunged into cone-shaped gulfs or lay motionless, confronted by barricades of water hurled aloft. Racing turbines of one hundred and ten thousand, of ninety thousand, horse-power—birds' hearts must beat like that when they are checked in their flight—till at last the propellers beat again in smooth water.

And now the van of the German High Sea Fleet had reached the scene of battle and joined in the engagement: the *König* class, the newest and strongest ships of the whole fleet.

Beatty turned round to north.

Hipper followed close in his wake.

The Englishman moved faster. The distance between them increased. The salvoes fell more slowly. The clouds sailed low in a sky that seemed near to earth. The air grew milder and more oppressive and the green sea assumed a dark, metallic appearance.

When the retreating squadron fired, the mist upon the sea glowed like blood-stained foam. Then the gun-flashes sank lower on the horizon. At last there was nothing to be seen but red flashing specks.

Beatty steamed out of the field of fire.

Hipper placed himself ahead of the High Sea Fleet. The squadron was closed up once more. Scheer's twenty-two battle-ships and Hipper's five battle-cruisers, with their flank guards and the screen of light cruisers and destroyers ahead, advanced northwards in a long battle-line.

Hipper's ships had been damaged in the battle-cruiser engagement. Torn wireless aerials and voice-tubes swung over the decks. A number of turrets were gutted by fire, charred and blackened like burned saucepans and marked with brown, greasy streaks by the bodies of the slain. There were gaping holes in the ship's hulls, and fire blazed in the casemates and compartments.

They managed to localize the source of the fire. The leaks were stopped with hammocks and with blocks of wood and fragments of wreckage. The decks were cleared and the wounded carried to the dressing-stations. The five ships had seen two battle-cruisers sink, and their own vital parts were undamaged. The engines were still running. The pumps kept the flooding in check. They led the main body of the High Sea Fleet at undiminished speed.

They steamed northwards, in the direction of Skagerrak.

Great banks of luminous mist still rested upon the sea's surface. The swell increased. The north-west wind beat upon the watery gulfs and hurled foaming mountains against the advancing mass. The red flashes continued ahead. Guns roared, light and medium guns, by which the enemy forces maintained contact. The fleets kept close together. The flashes increased in number, soon stretching in a gigantic sweeping curve from the northern sky to the east.

And they grew larger and more menacing.

Heavy guns, finding the range.

"Remember the glorious tradition of the first of June and avenge Belgium!" was the message transmitted by the commander of a British battle-squadron to the ships in his division.

The light cruisers of the German advance-guard were obliged to envelop themselves in smoke and turn away without having detected the enemy's formation and strength in the fog. Again the battle-cruisers were under fire. And one by one the battle-squadrons steamed into the zone of fire.

The tables were turned. Admiral Beatty had successfully performed a magnificent encircling manœuvre. The British lay behind screens of smoke and fog to the north and east. The German ships stood out distinct against the evening sky.

Course northward, no change. '

The line of battle twisted into a fresh curve. The former red flashes, like eyes watching from an ambush, now gave place to streaks of blazing red. The firing squadrons lay shrouded in mist. The German guns could only aim at the gun flashes, and every salvo raised a new curtain of smoke in their field of vision. And only the foremost ships could get within range.

The guns were wrongly mounted.

The angle of elevation was not enough.

It was the same earlier against the *Queen Elizabeths*, the same in the battle of the Dogger Bank, the same off the Falkland Islands: ships were under fire and could not defend themselves. Individual captains adopted any and every expedient. They "flooded" on one side, letting anything up to a thousand tons of water into their ships. The heeling, listing hulls presented a somewhat larger target, but they gave the guns a somewhat greater angle of elevation.

Admiral Scheer still pursued a northerly course. He steamed in the middle of his long line of battle-cruisers and battle-ships, till the horizon was aglow and the sky became one vast curve of flame. He was surrounded—only in the south-west was the encirclement not complete.

And now Scheer realized: this was not Beatty.

This was Jellicoe and the Grand Fleet!

This was "the Day"!

The Day of the High Sea Fleet!

Scheer—and Jellicoe:

Six hundred thousand tons against a million! A broadside of 2,000 hundredweight against 4,500 hundredweight. And that without taking into account a twofold superiority in light cruisers and destroyers; and the manœuvring speed of the English forces was greater by several knots.

Scheer was a pastor's son, ambitious and hard-working— home-baked qualities. He had outstripped his superiors, was a man who calculated with tangible quantities, but he lacked the fire of daring inspiration, could not recognize a bird by its flight. Fate denied him the genius to strike into the fog around Skagerrak, where the enemy squadrons were even now forming a line which, just because of its immense length, was still inflexible and slow of movement.

There was nothing in him of the boy David with his sling.

Nor was Jellicoe a Nelson. He had none of the reckless, pirate spirit of Old England, but was rather the Admiral of Scapa Flow, burdened and trammelled by the weighty responsibility of maintaining the greatest fleet in the world. He had been appointed Commander-in-Chief of the Grand Fleet because his predecessor, Admiral Callaghan, had given cause for uneasiness to the British Lords of the Admiralty: he was too incalculable.

A cool, calculating spirit was Jellicoe.

Scheer—and Jellicoe.

Mathematics!

Armour-plate!

Dynamite!

Naval coolies—one hundred and five thousand head.

The last glowing spark had become extinct over Skagerrak. Thirty thousand tons of hulls, sent into action in columns and pushed about like the quantities in an arithmetical problem. Armour-piercing shells—and when they crashed through the sides and exploded inside the ship, they shattered her vital organs. When they burst as they struck, the place of the impact turned white-hot. Fragments of armour-plate! Flowing lava! The bodies of men were turned into grey, boiling filth.

Whales have a coating of fat nearly sixteen inches thick, whilst the ribs of battle-ships are covered with nickeliferous steel twelve and a half inches thick. And the transverse bulkheads, iron diaphragms which divide the bodies into compartments, give the vessels a measure of security.

The German advance-guard was under heavy fire. Flames burst forth once more from the battle-cruisers. Hipper's flagship was struck by a torpedo which brought her down by the bow.

The Grand Fleet was still invisible. The horizon was streaked blood-red. Only isolated ships, worried out by the German guns, appeared in the field of vision:

Destroyers, light cruisers, and one armoured cruiser of an antiquated type crossed the stage in battling clusters.

A cleft appeared in a banked mass of rust-brown smoke. The battle-cruiser *Invincible*, the victor of the Falkland Islands, stood clearly outlined against the sky, over five miles distant from the *Lützow* and *Derfflinger*. Three minutes' concentrated fire! An explosion! Crashing masts! Flames! The leaping wreckage of the ship was darker and more cumbersome than the rising smoke and gases. Heads and hands were seen amongst the fragments of the shattered ship. Six men clung to a raft. Later they were picked up by a destroyer.

An immense grey monster broke through the cordite smoke of

the British line, circled madly round its own axis, and, helpless to control its own movements, advanced towards the German ships. It was the *Warspite*, hit in her rudder and with her steering-gear jammed. The blazing wreck was shrouded in its own trail of smoke, like a torch brandished in the air, and was thus saved from immediate destruction.

A shell struck the funnel of the light cruiser *Pillau*, putting four boilers out of action and half the firemen. The steam thus liberated rose in wreaths, and green, burning oil rained down in torrents. The chart-house and bridge were in ruins. But those compartments separated by bulkheads from the scene of the disaster still kept her afloat, and the *Pillau* continued her course at twenty-four knots. The little *Wiesbaden*, also, was still afloat. She lay between the fighting lines, her engines wrecked, a flaming signal visible far and wide.

One figure in Jellicoe's arithmetical problem was incorrect—an error in Beatty's reckoning. He struck the main German fleet twenty-five minutes too soon. The main body of his ships was still steaming in cruising order and only just beginning to deploy into battle formation. It took time to deploy this gigantic machine, and the Grand Fleet, irresistible when once its far-flung battle-line was deployed, was still inflexible and cumbrous at this phase of the engagement.

Admiral Scheer and his staff:

A plotting-table—dots marked in India ink: ships. Patches: squadrons. Blue and red shading: areas swept by gun-fire. Arrows and flags: courses, winds, direction in which smoke moves.

But here mathematics failed.

Here was an unknown quantity.

And who was the Lieutenant Bonaparte of the day? He went down in a destroyer or was roasted in an armoured turrret. Or he wore a coolie's uniform; half dazed, perhaps, with hands and feet planted wide apart, he kept his place on the steel deck of a conning-tower and wiped the telescope glasses which the powder-smoke was perpetually blurring.

Admiral Scheer saw nothing but the gigantic curve of flame. He saw it blaze with increasing brilliance and gave the signal to retreat.

And lost his one and only chance.

The apex of the fiery curve moved south with the retreating fleet. The Grand Fleet gained time, and now it had space to expand. Rust-brown mountains of smoke rose like an encircling wall on the horizon. The appearance of the sea changed; it was now dotted with dark mirrors. Balls of vapour and cloud islands arose out of nothing. Unaccustomed laws ruled the atmosphere.

What now followed was beyond human calculation. It was as if the hand of a God drew rainbows—God's stolen hand! The circle of flames which leapt up as the salvoes followed in swift succession cut a gigantic disk out of the surface of the North Sea.

Upon this God-forsaken surface the twenty-seven fugitive ships sailed. Iron hounds—they gasped and growled. Hulls, frames, and ribs trembled under the weighty impact of the salvoes. The boilers, turbines, and pistons pounded at a furious pace. Fires were fed with oil. Old and worn-out engines attained for one last time the speed of their trial runs, or even exceeded it.

Matter in delirious fever! Nerves chained to wheels, and levers strained to the uttermost pitch!

A sailing-vessel came across the disk from the south. She was a Norwegian boat with three masts and light, swelling sails. She passed the German ships and sailed across the disk, her timber and canvas a picture of a long-forgotten age.

The fleet did not reach the edge of the disk.

The encircling fire was moving no less swiftly. The forty-five thousand men of the High Sea Fleet were one vast cargo bound for the port of death.

And now Scheer aimed the blow that he had failed to strike

against Jellicoe's fleet before it had deployed. He turned his ships sharply in an easterly course and flung them against the centre of the enemy's line.

They were hounds no longer, but only rats, trapped, desperate brutes with bared teeth. Heavy guns, medium guns—a salvo every seven seconds. And the men! There were human souls in the casemates and magazines and on the burning platforms of the turrets. The tumult designed to shout down the fear of death had ceased. There is a limit, moreover, to horror. Only a cold fever remained.

Circling walls of armour!

Barking gun throats!

Armour-piercing shells!

Preparatory charges!

Main charges!

Twenty-seven thousand rounds! Fifteen thousand tons of ammunition! Out with it!

The *Lützow* dropped out of the line and listed on her side. Light cruisers and destroyers circled round the dying giant and shrouded it in a vast mass of black smoke. Once more the burning *Wiesbaden* lay between the High Sea Fleet and the Grand Fleet, her side torn open and her funnels collapsed. The wreck seemed to be floating upon gigantic, invisible bladders. A direct hit would finish her. But they let her drift—a sheep bound for slaughter.

A signal was hoisted on board the fleet flagship:

"Battle-cruisers charge the enemy, full speed!"

"Ram the enemy!" was the antiquated form in which the signal code paraphrased the order. If you translate that into terms of modern applied science, it means: Death. The destroyers are to be brought up against the enemy line and, in sinking, to cover the retreat.

With their superior speed the battle-cruisers and destroyers detached themselves from the main body of the fleet and made straight for the head of the Grand Fleet.

It seemed that the end of the world had come. Turrets gutted by fire smelled differently from casemates saturated with gas. Faces glued to drifting wreckage were like an idyll. The moaning of a lieutenant commander riddled with shot is nowise different from a coolie's. Distinctions were wiped out. Gold-striped sleeves or cap-ribbons, turnips or five courses, it was all the same now.

The *Lützow* lay astern in the wilderness of smoke.

The *Derfflinger* led, without wireless, without signals. All the flags were burned. The ship steamed towards the wedge of flame, and the other three followed. The Admiral, without a ship, raced along beside the squadron. He reached the *Seydlitz* and wanted to board her.

The boat with the admiral's flag and the battle-cruiser *Seydlitz*: twenty-eight knots. On the bridge of the battle-cruiser, illuminated by the glare of exploding shells, was a signalman, arms extended like a man crucified, signal-flags in his hands.

His message:

> TWENTY DIRECT HITS BY HEAVY GUNS, COMPARTMENTS AND DECKS WRECKED. COAL-BUNKERS FLOODED. AERIALS AND WIRELESS SWEPT AWAY. THREE GUNS STILL IN ACTION.

The Admiral raced on, but did not find a ship. The *Derfflinger* had still one turret, the *Von der Tann* one; the *Moltke* was flooded with a thousand tons of water.

Turrets of the dead! Casemates smoked out! Torn sides,

flooded hulls, monsters with teeth drawn and broken—thus they hurled themselves against the enemy line.

"Destroyers attack!"

It was not yet quite dark, but already the sea was like a black cloth. The boats showed pale in the glare of blazing searchlights—mere tin buckets with sides less than half an inch thick. A direct hit, and not much was left. The crews—a hundred, two hundred faces pressed close together—were trapped in wrecks so battered that they could only drift. Some officers struck up the song: "Proudly waves the black-white-red." They all joined in, roaring: ". . . on our ship's mast." They would have prayed or shrieked if anyone had started praying or shrieking. The oil bubbling up from the bunkers evaporated in fumes, a green, glowing gas. The tarred, living torches of ancient Rome, the deaths at the stake in the Middle Ages, proclaimed a religious faith. This was the shriek of burned flesh.

A British wireless message:

> HAVE LOST TOUCH WITH HIGH SEA FLEET. AM ENGAGED WITH BATTLE-CRUISERS— ENEMY BATTLE-CRUISERS BEARING S.E.— URGENT! AM STRUCK BY TORPEDO—ENEMY DESTROYERS TO S.W.—ALTERATIONS OF COURSE—BY DIVISIONS ALTER COURSE TWO POINTS AWAY FROM ENEMY—ALTER COURSE THREE POINTS TO PORT—ALTER COURSE FOUR POINTS TO PORT—ADMIRAL INTENDS TO STEAM TWENTY-TWO KNOTS—ADMIRAL INTENDS TO STEAM TWENTY-FOUR KNOTS.

The Grand Fleet turned away in echelon before the destroyer attack. The line was weakened. The circle of flame melted away.

That had nothing to do with equipment. That was Jellicoe's method, formal, tactical considerations. Day is for the strong! Night with its hazards gives opportunities even to the weak. The Grand Fleet possessed the world. It could win nothing new, but only lose.

The aged lion was too ponderous to spring.

Once more the Grand Fleet put out its claws.

Scheer's manœuvre had been successful. The High Sea Fleet had turned about. And now the battle-cruisers also altered course —only three of them. The *Seydlitz*, too, was a wreck. Under cover of the clouds of smoke and vapour of the destroyer attack, they successfully shook off the last British vessels keeping touch. The High Sea Fleet vanished into the far spaces of the starless night.

The Grand Fleet proceeded southwards, making for the German mine-fields, for it was beside them that Jellicoe proposed to await the German ships at daybreak. The High Sea Fleet proceeded south-west; then it turned aside and made a wide circuit in a south-easterly direction. The British ships sailed in parallel columns, the German ships one behind the other in line ahead.

Making south-west, the High Sea Fleet broke through between the columns of the British main body and its rear-guard. After midnight the attendant destroyer flotilla struck upon the German ships proceeding in line ahead. They were unaware who it was and made the recognition signals.

Searchlights cut cones of glaring brilliance out of the dark immensity of the sea and remained mercilessly fixed to the grey boats which dashed into the light like moths. Secondary armament! At that short distance every shot meant a hit. The cruiser *Black Prince*, straying behind the British line, likewise came upon the German ships and made the recognition signal.

The salvoes crashed out a dull roar. The whine of the shells was clearer and higher pitched. In the brightness of the searchlights the cordite smoke looked like blood turned to steam.

The *Black Prince* was ablaze.

So, too, were the destroyers.

An echelon of gigantic, crazy torches flared up into the night. And there were men in these blazing pyres of oil, cordite, and steel—two hundred, three hundred, seven hundred men.

Twenty miles ahead steamed the main body of the British fleet.

No signal reached the Commander-in-Chief.

On the German side the *Frauenlob* and the battle-ship *Pommern* were torpedoed during this nocturnal march. The *Frauenlob* sank, the *Pommern* blew up in fragments.

Eight hundred men in the *Pommern*.

The last victims.

Wounded: 1,181; dead: 9,526.

Many of the dead still lived.

Sixteen in the *Wiesbaden*. They stared at the fire as it slowly subsided. Only the wood and the papers in the ship's office still flickered. When that had died down, they felt their wet clothes, and the cold, and the sea, black like asphalt.

Forty in the *Lützow* were trapped in the forward turret, cut off from the rest of the crew. The armoured door was jammed. They had air to breathe. The electric light was burning. The forty clung to the voice-tube, their last connecting link with the outer world: "Two thousand tons of water. The pumps are still working. We are making slow headway."

Sixteen in the *Wiesbaden*, forty in the *Lützow*, hundreds scattered over the desolate wastes of the waters of Skagerrak.

Eighty or twelve hundred men in a column of flame: it is one flash, ablaze and extinguished simultaneously. Three or four hundred doomed faces in a sinking ship: the strange spectacle of decks rearing to the clouds, the fiery heat of the catastrophe, the common frenzy.

The air of a slaughter-house is oppressive with the ponderous warmth of blood and the hot vapours of stuffed intestines. It only takes a few minutes to drain the blood of a stunned ox. But to die as an atom drifting in the vast ocean!

The harsh roar of iron rent asunder—a fiery blaze. Not the highest that day, but a torrential rain of dark fragments of armour-plate. Splinters of wood and human limbs fly farther than iron.

A last blow from the brute's claws.

The ship maintains her course.

Air bubbles gurgle astern. A head rises, a green face with a blood-red gash across the forehead and through the left eye.

The ship proceeds on her course.

The face with the gash—two waving arms—clutching hands —wood, a piece of wood! His nostrils are distended: "I'm not made of stone! I'm no aristocrat! No, captain! I'm not! Wood floats!"

The waves are dull troughs of slaty blue.

Karl Kleesattel caught sight of the ship riding over the crest of a wave, her funnels vomiting dark smoke. Twice again he saw her. On the next wave-crest she was so far away that nothing was visible but the red flash of the salvoes.

"There they go, steaming on and firing, steaming on and under fire themselves—poor devils! An armour-piercing shell— did you see? Like at the photographer's. A flash-light snap. Only that it's all red, and suddenly your mouth's dry. Marvellous— you hear nothing and know nothing. The sides are thick. But you find yourself wallowing in water. And it's not so bad. You can breathe here. And the stink's gone.

"S.M.S. Kleesattel! Hurrah! Now we get along by our own power. Displacement o.o. Full speed: sixty revolutions a minute. But then I should have to let go the plank. No, that's no good."

The blood rose to the "Admiral's" head and flushed his skin. He did not feel the low temperature of the water. But the silence, and the great soft curve of the wave that raised him and plunged him down again! Suddenly he started.

"Good God, they're out of sight! How can they go on and leave me here alone? What a damned feeble shell that was. Perhaps only one casemate and one gun? 'Fifth port casemate no longer answers.' And then? Who cared about the first and second, about Anna and Bertha turrets? No longer answers. That's all about it. But there were twelve men to that gun. Where are the other eleven?"

The ship had disappeared. Firing had ceased. Not even a distant salvo roar—only the shapeless night and the dumb monotony of the sea. And now Kleesattel bawled—louder and louder:

"Fifth port exploded! Simply exploded!"

Those eleven! One at least must have survived and be somewhere near. The loader had just been relieved; he pulled down his trousers and was squatting over the fire-bucket. Kleesattel laughed, a deep laugh. Perhaps laughing was some good. Jolly company is always pleasanter.

His laughter remained suspended in the air.

He lay deep within the trough of a wave. Round about him the water rose like a wall, gleaming like the black enamel of a bucket in which a tiny mouse is drowned.

And the battle of Jutland counted 9,526 dead.

In innumerable troughs of waves, in countless watery gulfs, solitary, deserted souls spun in their last, despairing gyrations.

The doom of the *Wiesbaden*, too, was fulfilled.

Nobody could discover by what power the ship was enabled to survive so long. Holes as large as barn-doors gaped in her sides, and now the water had reached her upper deck. The *Wiesbaden* heeled over and went down like a full bucket, quite gently and without leaving an eddy. Three rafts remained. Heads and clutching hands.

And the forty men in the torpedo-room of the *Lützow*! They still clung to the voice-tube. There was only room for one ear at the receiver, only one tongue could call: ". . . Otto, lad! Otto! Boys! Boys! Can't you hear?" It wasn't the words, but the tone.

". . . is no one there? Does no one hear us?"

Silence in the adjoining compartment.

Silence throughout the ship.

Far away the engines vibrated. The light in the lamps burned more slowly by a few revolutions. The armoured bulkhead caved in slightly under pressure. The door looked just as usual, but it remained unyielding. Not a fraction of an inch would it move.

"Don't bawl like that. The captain has just been here himself. It'll be all right, and we shall reach port, he said." The ship conducted sound as clearly as the double bottom of a gigantic violin: wasn't that the clatter of feet, many feet, up the ladders? Why was everybody hurrying to the upper deck—and where, where was the sentry at the voice-tube?

"Hold yer mug; all of yer, hold yer mugs a bit—"

One man bawled for forty: "What's up? Captain! Sir! Dear sir!"

The tube was unresponsive. The distant vibration of the engines had ceased. There was no more clattering of feet.

The captain was the last to leave the ship. Down the gangway into the destroyer. The boat was black with thronging humanity, the whole crew of the *Lützow*, and not one of them spoke a word. As they pushed off, hands were stretched out, furtively caressing the armoured hull. A little way off, the boat stopped.

"How many torpedoes, sir?"

"All four."

A voice like a blow in the face:

". . . cheers for the S.M.S. *Lützow!*"

The thousand voices were dumb.

Four torpedoes discharged—an explosion—an immense cone-shaped gulf in the sea. The ship's wreckage was whirled down in circling, narrowing eddies.

Destroyer *G. 38* to the Admiral cruisers: "2.45 a. m. *Lützow* blown up and abandoned."

When the water rises to your neck, the sea looks different. The waves are bigger and man is smaller. In fact, there is only the bit of a head—nose, ears, hair.

If you take an albatross on deck, it sickens and throws up all its food. A human creature amongst the tossing waves vomits till there is nothing left, neither stomach nor gall. Luckily the intestines retain something, or he would lose his sense of up and down.

A few more men joined the sixteen from the *Wiesbaden*. During the minutes while the ship sank, they awoke from their stupor and escaped from that charnel-house. Twenty-two leapt overboard.

Twenty-two clung to the three rafts.

You can't hold out long in sea-water with a loosely bandaged stump for a limb. Even with sound arms and legs your time is limited. By morning only half of them were still clinging to the rafts. The others had wearied and let go.

How rapidly faces lose shape and form! Lips thicken, mouths and cheeks swell. The eyes become lustreless spots of jelly, reflecting external lights. In the morning they had been milky, now they were green.

The sea was a transparent green once more.

Those who had let go of the raft remained in sight for a time. Then they sank with arms, legs, and body all rolled to a ball. The

sky swung in perpetual motion like a gigantic pump. When the
men's heads were plunged deep down in a trough, it was like a
flat lid; when they swam over a ridge, it was a wide vault.

And the green, surging wilderness was in motion, too.

The three rafts were drifting apart. Two turned eastwards
with the current, the third remained behind. Heavy arms were
raised to wave a last greeting, hands and fingers swollen with
water.

There were three channels through the mine-fields into the
interior of the German Bight. Jellicoe had received no word
from the destroyer flotilla that had run into the German fleet on
their nocturnal course, nor was he aware that the German fleet
had broken through his own forces. He waited for Scheer by the
middle channel. But the High Sea Fleet lay on the other side,
by the eastern entry.

And the Grand Fleet was satisfied with the gesture.

When he failed to strike the High Sea Fleet by the middle
channel, Jellicoe turned back. In three separate columns the fleet
proceeded across the North Sea, back to its bases. Only the
cruisers, Admiral Beatty's light cruisers and destroyers, combed
the waters of Skagerrak once more so as to give the *coup de
grâce* to any derelict ships.

But the waters of Skagerrak are wide.

Beatty's ships had suffered damage in the battle.

They did not stay long, did not even sight the battle-cruiser
Seydlitz, smashed in her bow and lying under water up to the
foot of her bridge. The *Seydlitz* was still making slow headway,
dragging herself southwards stern first.

Rafts and wreckage are hardly objects of interest, and from a
man drifting in a pneumatic life-jacket it is no far call to a floating corpse.

The sea clears things up.

Of 115,025 British tons and 61,180 German nothing was left but shattered fragments. Human blood is a peculiar fluid. Even in distended bodies it pulses and labours and clings obstinately to wreckage. But when fingers are so thick that they stick together and hands become like fins, they are forced to let go.

The "Admiral" still struggled.

He clung to a block of wood.

He had seized a drifting cap, an English sailor's cap: "Hurrah! Them that fishes out corpses has won the battle!

"A hit: good! quick!

"Salvo—fire! Salvo—"

Press the trigger: you've got one arm and one hand! The lumps fly a distance of over nine miles. The world market's at stake—and my ditty-bag! And a place in the sun!

The British fired, too.

"For democracy! The freedom of small nations! Avenge Belgium! Famine in Ceylon! Baton charges for Dublin and Manchester! Damn it all, the breech is jammed! Number one, the breech is jammed! A splinter!

"Right, the gun's all right again. Load! Fire!—

"Loader knocked out! Number one, loader knocked out!"

Made of porcelain—the head's still there.

A thirty-eight.

"For freedom! For the peoples!

"The loader—why can't the fellow stop shouting? He hasn't violated Belgian neutrality. Nor was he a tax-collector in Ceylon. He didn't even know any geography.

"Fire: that's right, quick! Then the shouting will stop. No more party divisions! Queen soup with liver rissoles, poached eggs, spinach, roast meat, fruit, coffee—and turnips for the men's mess."

Kleesattel was exhausted with staring up at the far-away sky,

and hoarse with wet and cold. But he shouted. The air whistled
in his throat: whatever happened, he mustn't keep quiet. If a man
caved in, he was lost.

And all the time he lay heavily on his chest. His head swayed
to and fro, his eyes fell to in spite of himself. A wave reared and
buffeted him and he started up again.

"S.M.S. Kleesattel! Half speed—otherwise all well. A little
water in the hull. But that's because of the mounting of the guns.
The angle of fire. Those latrine seats in Wilhelmshaven—that
bold angle, extraordinary how they were mounted! Look at our
technical achievements: nobody would remain seated longer than
necessary.

"Shift target left!"

Not far from him a mine was drifting that had broken loose.
He had kept it in sight since early morning. It was drifting ahead
of him, in the same direction—only a little more slowly. He and
his log approached nearer and nearer to it.

I'd like to know if it's an English or a German mine: "Hullo!
You English?"

The mine nodded its broad head: "Yes, sir."

"Or German—perhaps from Cuxhaven?"

The mine swayed to and fro, to and fro: "*Ja, Herr!* Yes, sir!
Ja, Herr! Yes, sir!"—"We two understand one another. No
more differences of opinion.

"Only I'd like to know—"

When German mines detonated, a jet of water ascended like
a fountain, whereas an English mine shot up like a tree and then
branched out like a big umbrella.

"Are the women just the same in the English munition works
where they make mines—the same lemon-yellow faces and
hands as in Cuxhaven?"—"Yes, sir."—"And they don't have
children any more?"—"No, sir."—"And queen soup with liver
rissoles?"—"No, sir."—"But there's free trade, and cargoes of

merchandise, Japanese kimonos, shifts and stockings from Kobe, silk from Shanghai—black-eyed Milly in Newcastle didn't wear a shift. She was too cheap! Sixpence. That was my wages, fifty pfennig for a naval engagement, half a mark. I'll give it as a subscription to the Life-boat Institution."

Heavy puffs of wind across the water. The sun had disappeared, its rays veiled by the clouds.

A wave lapped softly over his shoulders.

"Asleep, my man! Cowardice in the presence of the enemy! That means the cells."—"Yes, sir—but Freddy gave me a souvenir of Malta, Café Tripoli. A cap-ribbon: H.M.S. *Indefatigable*. He meant to open a sweet-shop when he'd served his time—ices, bonbons, cigarettes.

"Freddy's all right; he knows what he wants.

"He may be somewhere about. Hullo, Freddy! Ship ahoy!

"Maybe you've seen Freddy?"—"Yes, sir."

The mine had approached nearer. Its four horns, the little glass tubes on the top, rocked to and fro.

"A little black submarine mine. A little black—you've just got to—just got to catch hold of one of the tubes. A little spitfire! It's just her way: yes—yes! No—no! I'm not going to put up with that any longer.

"Milly's different. Sixpence: up and at it!

"Shake a leg, the Emperor needs soldiers!"

The sun broke through a rift in the clouds. The world's boundaries were enlarged. The sea was an immense bed of soft silk.

Karl Kleesattel: hands green, face green, the gash across his forehead chalky white.

"Observation: S.M.S. Kleesattel unfit for manœuvres!

"Otherwise all well. Sun shining.

"I shall lead you on to a glorious era! His Majesty the Emperor, hurrah! Did he not tell you truly—the place in the sun?"

The mine approached nearer and nearer. It swung like a church-bell.

"Pardon, madam. A slight indisposition—I am already better again. A green silken bed, madam, what say you?—for us alone, just for us two.

"Yes, that's right, we've won the war. Shifts, stockings—poor Milly! And the Chinese women. They've no stockings either. Too cheap—they lay their babies to sleep under the looms.

"To sleep—and the sun's shining! Only I must know—an English lady or a German?"

The mine rocked close to his head.

"What, I can't pay? Sixpence apiece! And my kit-bag! Hamburg, 3 Hopfenstrasse. Those grand boots! I've only worn them one trip."

Karl Kleesattel snatched at the little glass tube.

"Keep quiet, ma'am. It doesn't hurt a bit—"

The mine detonated and shot up like a tree. Then it branched out like a big umbrella. Standing out against the sky, it resembled a gigantic mushroom.

9. The End

THERE were 9,526 dead at Jutland and 5,475 at the Dogger Bank, the Falkland Islands, Coronel, and Heligoland. They lay side by side in the mass graves of Wilhelmshaven and Rosyth or were shovelled underground without ceremony in the Patagonian deserts. The fishes ate the rest.

This is not a novel. It is a documented statement.

Besides—I was there myself.

Enrolled as an A.G. in 1914. Second Naval Brigade, Wilhelmshaven, fifth company, raider No. 143. On board S.M. Sky-tripper No. VIII.

Yes, yes, sir!

I didn't come as a volunteer. But I shall never forget the muster-roll. It is stamped on my memory in letters of fire, like the branded mark of a bagnio captive or the number of a gelding passed as fit for service.

But our case was different. We weren't castrated, our organs were whole. And that was the downfall of the Empire. Just a little operation on enrolment, and much would have happened otherwise.

You ask if I had had previous convictions?

Do you think I carried wine-buckets, ironed officers' trousers, washed sleeves foul with vomit, and grinned when gracious smiles appeared beneath caps worked with oak-leaves? No, no, don't suppose that. Very well: reprimand, double duty, confinement to quarters, the whole gamut till you get to twenty-eight days in the brig.

I can't make pictures of that for exhibition.

Two, five—fifteen years in a fortress! Men were packed off in truck-loads, or locked up in madhouses. Or the modern method was adopted of putting them behind barbed wire in the labour battalions of Schleswig-Holstein. As for me, I was given to wool-gathering.

But:

Those twenty-eight days were scarlet.

Even the twenty-one days were also.

Password, skywards: sent in companies to Flanders or in ship-loads to run the British blockade. And if you're in luck, away from dry land and harbour, over the five seas to a hero's death.

Sky-tripper No. VIII.

No. I was the *Möwe*, No. II the *Belgravia*, No. III the *Greif*. Of Nos. IV, V, and VI we have no record. No. VII was the sailing-ship *Seeadler*, fitted out in Kiel; No. VIII was the Bremen steamer *Wachtfels*, rechristened S.M.S. *Wolf*.

S.M.S. *Wolf*: seven thousand tons, one funnel, two masts, made twelve knots; there are hundreds of such steamers on the seas. The guns and torpedo-tubes were concealed behind the hand-rail, and when the British merchant-flag flew from our stern, no ship would guess that we were a German man-of-war.

I stood at the helm.

The ship sailed smoothly, a couple of spokes even in heavy weather. She rose evenly over the dark, mountainous waves and slid gently down into the troughs. We were in luck: heavy weather and fog in the North Sea. We passed the line of the blockade beneath a cloudy sky. Only once we saw smoke, a ragged, curling blot on the fog, and that was gone again in a moment.

I had only occasional need to look at the compass.

The officer of the watch and the gunnery-officer stood on the starboard bridge—the same man we'd had in the *Belgravia*, Lieutenant Hansi of the dachshunds! And on the other side stood our skipper.

We had weighed anchor nine days before.

And for as many nights the skipper hadn't undressed. He slept

behind the wheel-house in the chart-house. The least movement
on the bridge, and he was out, requiring a report of the officer
of the watch, and then stood in the lee shelter and gazed out to
sea.

An hour earlier:

"Ice right ahead!" shouted the man from the top. It drifted
towards the stem, vast and grey. Already the skipper was at the
engine-room telegraph. One stroke: "Stop!" A second stroke:
"Full speed astern!"

The violence of the collision was averted—it was as if the
ship had run against a cork-like substance. The ice-block scraped
against our starboard side and sheered off, as tall as a village
church. It shimmered blue as we left it behind us, and disappeared into the night.

That was a timely order to the engine-room.

And altogether: the skipper was top-hole. He had been in
command of a man-of-war previously. The admirals sent him to
the sky-tripper, just as they did us. The devil alone knows why.

But he put up a fight:

In Wilhelmshaven he fought the dockyard bureaucrats for
every bit of equipment, and didn't give in till he'd fitted out the
ship, for all their chicanery, with 5.9-inch guns, torpedoes,
smoke-screen apparatus. We stowed an aeroplane into our hold,
and he even secured a submarine to help us run the blockade. He
extended his measures to prevent espionage even to the ranks of
his own colleagues. He deceived the officers regarding the time
of his departure, arranging a farewell banquet and issuing in-
vitations for a certain evening whilst we, meantime, had weighed
anchor and run the British blockade.

Eight bells! Eight strokes of the ship's bell. The man of the
other watch climbed the ladder.

"West-north-west," I reported.

"West-north-west," replied my relief.

The watch stood on deck, nine men behind each gun, muffled in thick woollen jerseys and blankets.

"How's her head?" asked the look-outs.

"West-north-west. We are at the entrance to Denmark Strait."

In nine days and nights we had steamed through the North Sea and now we were at the entrance to Denmark Strait, between Greenland and Iceland in the Atlantic.

Only a few lamps were alight in the fo'c'sle. It was thick with tobacco-smoke and the smell of oil and paint, whilst the stench of bilge-water rose from the ship's bottom. We lay in our hammocks. For a while we listened to the beating of the waves and the frozen snow scraping against the port side.

Somewhere or other heavy boots were tramping ponderously. Someone shouted in his sleep.

When we went on deck again, the snow was on the shrouds, delineating a network of heavy lines against the night sky. Flakes were still falling, filtering the air and impeding the driving blast. The waves were still high, but they beat less fiercely against the ship's side.

We had lost the submarine. Little tin cockle-shell that it was, it had climbed the mountainous waves and plunged head-first down into the valleys. So it followed in our wake nine days and nights. And now it had disappeared.

We stopped and hove to for two hours. But we never sighted the submarine. So we proceeded on our voyage across the Arctic Ocean. Alone!

Twenty hours of night.

And four of sunless day. Evening and morning showed simultaneously in the heavens. Fragments of drift-ice passed in long trains. The look-outs beside the guns might quit their posts, for both guns and torpedo-tubes were frozen hard. Nobody gave a thought to the English; we were wholly engrossed by the ice.

It covered the sea with myriads of slender needles; then it thickened and closed in nearer and nearer. It was immediately before our bows and on our beams, heavy and leaden grey. There was still movement beneath the covering of ice, a buoyant rise and fall. Then suddenly all became rigid, a grey prairie as far as the eye could see. No one inquired the course of the relieved helmsmen; everybody inquired our speed.

"We're still making seven."

"Still making five."

The ice-blocks which the ship's bows broke in its advance crashed with a metallic ring. The snow-drifts to the right and left of our course were like milestones frozen blue. We could have disembarked and gone on foot beside the ship.

Still we lost speed.

The air sucked in by the ventilators was icy cold. The fires howled and cracked in the stoke-hold. Rivets burst off and the cylindrical flame-tubes were crushed in like opera-hats. The firemen set to work with a will, their backs bent, gripping pokers and shovels: a race against the ice.

After a battle you may be picked up out of the water. But supposing the pressure of the ice increased? Supposing boilers and screw were powerless against it? What had become of sky-trippers Nos. IV, V, and VI? And the submarine? There were forty men on board.

"There's not a man will volunteer now for them submarines."

"No, they all go under orders."

"I was in luck, I got away again," the fireman Stüven told us, who had made two trips in a submarine. "When I went on board, they asked me at once: 'What have you been up to? You murdered your father and mother too, eh?' Lord! what a trip —sixty or seventy days without light, and air supplied from bottles. And then the oil and acid, they eat things away. I had

brand-new boots, Hessians, up above the knee. They were soon
hanging in rags about my legs. And by the end of the trip there
was nothing left but the soles. Two trips—the oil! The stink!
You'd oughter seen the privy—when we had to dive because
of them damned water-shells. You can pump the filth out down
to sixty feet deep, but deeper'n that it's shut. Forbidden—but if
you can't help yerself! The empty tins lying about. And no air
but what you got from the bottles.

"Our cook, now: when they discharged a torpedo, he just
counted. And if there was nothing more to be heard and it didn't
explode, he'd bawl right away: 'Hurrah, another thirty thousand
marks gone west!' "

The submarine warfare, the strongest argument for the sub-
jugation of England! Germany opened her unrestricted submarine campaign with an immense trumpeting of advertise-
ment. "We shall envelop England within an iron curtain,"
declared Admiral Tirpitz to an American interviewer. The Admiralty spoke of two hundred and thirty submarines for this
purpose to the Federal Council in Berlin. But that included
the boats only laid down and budgeted for. In actual fact only
fifty-four were available, and some of those were only used
for training.

Those that were ready for service took weeks for the outward
voyage and weeks for the voyage home. When they returned,
they had to be overhauled. There were, therefore, only two or
three submarines on patrol on the main sea-routes west of England over a stretch of six hundred miles. That was Tirpitz's
"iron curtain enveloping England."

Whilst the submarine crews had to endure inhuman hardships, whilst the people were bluffed through the press with
record figures of enemy tonnage sunk, the officers in the higher
ranks sneered at submarine warfare as "the war of sub-

lieutenants and lieutenant commanders." Obstacles were placed
in the way of further construction, orders sabotaged. Submarines
require more of the younger ratings and offer no positions to
the older officers. Secretary of State Admiral von Capelle said
in the General Purposes Committee of the Reichstag: "You
must yourselves reflect and consider what the organization
and prospects of promotion would be in a navy in which large
battle-ships were replaced by aircraft and submarines."

For the officers prospects of promotion. For the firemen and
seamen fifty pfennig as a day's wage. For the people, a press
that told them of sixty-three thousand tons sunk, eighty-four
thousand tons sunk, fifty-nine thousand tons sunk. Buy War
Loan!"

But the radius of action of a submarine is limited. It is obliged
to return frequently to the home port in order to replenish the
fuel required by its complex machinery. An auxiliary cruiser
can obtain its supplies of coal and food from captured ships and
thus carry its warfare to the most distant seas.

We had passed through the lines of the British blockade.
Only the ice lay between us and the Atlantic.

There were two hundred of us in the seamen's fo'c'sle and
a hundred in the firemen's, ten at a mess-table. It was the entire crew of the derelict *Belgravia*.

Bacon and bread and hot tea.

Warmth radiated from the heaters.

In fact we were glad to have escaped the senseless drill and
no longer have the sight of the flat coast around Wilhelmshaven
forced upon us. Our cruise through the ice was a gamble, and
we might win back the stake, which was our lives.

To what purpose? That was another question.

"It's all a swindle. If we sit down to skat, I stake a penny, but I may win yours as well, and then I've got two. But what about it when the war's over? If Germany wins? My sea-bag is no bigger for that. And I shan't get more pay. I shall look out for a ship and go to sea, and it's all just as it was before. It's a swindle, I tell you."

Jan was right. I had nothing to say in refutation.

"Leastways we shall get out of this and have water beneath our keel and wind about our ears," said Alrich Buskohl; and another man: "Maybe we shall capture one of them fine whisky ships."—"And one with cigars."

Chief P.O. Weiss poked his head down the hatch.

"Come on deck, boys."

"What's up?"

"Ice, a real big lump."

Only the firemen at the boilers stayed below. All the rest of us stood on deck. It was dark again and the temperature had fallen rapidly. When you breathed, it felt like splinters of ice in your nostrils.

The first thing we noticed was something peculiar in the air. It wasn't a roaring sound, nor whistling; it wasn't very loud even; but a clinking like broken potsherds shaken together; and the same high, uniform note, never ceasing.

"Land!" called the look-out.

By now it was very near.

It looked like an island with sombre cliffs along the shore. A floating glacier. A bold coast with gullies. And there were bridges, gigantic sweeping arches, plains, and slopes. And how it gleamed, with a cold, blue light! That iceberg was larger than the island of Heligoland. It followed its own course and passed us at a rate of three miles an hour.

Watch on deck!

Watch below deck!

We sought a way through the channel opened by the ice-berg and sailed through long stretches of lagoon. On the edge of the world yellow rays of the aurora borealis flickered.

The channel opened out.

Brash ice and drifting ice-fields.

Another one hundred and eighty miles and we had open water before our bows. The sun shone and ahead of us lay the Atlantic Ocean, boundless and pure.

The fire of one boiler was extinguished for repairs.

We steamed southwards with two boilers at seven knots.

A British wireless message:

> ENEMY RAIDER SIGHTED. SHIP WELL ARMED, HAS TORPEDO-TUBES AND ONE SHORT, THICK FUNNEL. SAILING AT HIGH SPEED. UTMOST CAUTION NECESSARY.

This did not apply to us and our seven knots, but to the *Möwe*, which had put to sea a second time a few days before us and was waging war as a privateer on the sea-routes of the northern Atlantic. We crossed the sea-routes without attacking any of the ships that passed us.

The captain offered an explanation:

"Our primary duty is to lay mines. We shall have fulfilled our task only if we avoid firing a single shot during the whole trip."

A trip without a single shot—a pleasant command!

I was number two at No. 3 port. What is a gun?—a barrel, the charge of black powder, and a piece of iron in front. You put your hand on the trigger-lanyard and pull: your hand is turned to a clenched fist and smashes the deck of a ship away on the horizon.

Yes indeed, that is your hand!

Only you mustn't think of what follows. I have seen drowned corpses swollen to the size of a cow's belly. And those Jutland corpses—blood oozed from the heaps of dead like brown slime.

When the fleet put into port and Admiral von Hipper inspected his squadron, they threw sail-cloth over the heaps.

The Admiral made them show him the shattered armour-plated sides, the turret-training racks, and the engines. But he did not look at the faces and the glassy eyes beneath the sail-cloth.

For battered ships material is needed, and labour and time. For dead coolies they chartered the Wilhelmshaven coal-carts. Fifty were taken in each cart, lying piled up one above another. For living coolies they needed one steam-kitchen per thousand, and one brothel per ten thousand, or the run of a city twice a year.

We had received our first pay.

Five marks in nickel money for running the blockade and crossing the frozen sea. There was bottled beer and cigarettes and tobacco on sale at the canteen. If we drank one bottle of beer a week and smoked sparingly, the money lasted till the next pay-day.

We scrubbed the decks, went through gun-practice, stood watch at the helm and the look-outs. It was long since we had worn shoes, and now we had given up shirts and just had something by way of trousers. When we were off duty, we lay up on the fo'c'sle and gazed across the water or up into the sky.

We had sailed beneath the shimmering cloud mountains of the north-east trade-winds and the steel-blue sky of the Sargasso Sea, which seemed dappled with black flakes if you stared at it for long. Under the hot torrential rains and cloud-bursts of a becalmed sea we had a tremendous washing-day and bathed to our hearts' content. Now we had to be economical with our water-supplies, and even the drinking-water was under lock and key. We had thrown some of our provisions overboard—a few hundredweight of flour. The commissary chiefs in Wilhelms-haven had speculated on our being caught in the meshes of the British blockade and going to the bottom. When we undid the sacks, the flour was mildewed. We passed a derelict, a gutted iron hull without masts, and a scrap of sail-cloth still hanging from the jib-boom. Otherwise we saw nothing, not a ship, not a wisp of smoke. It was always the same—water and clouds. Always the same faces, at the guns, at mess, off duty. We al-almost forgot the war. And the idea of land somewhere behind the eternal blue wall grew dim and misty.

And then we saw a rock towering out of the sea.

Wide and square: Table Mountain.

It was the distinguishing landmark for Cape Town. The south-easterly trade-wind had dropped. A solitary bird, a wide-winged outpost of the southern cape, circled wearily in the op-pressive glare of the sun.

"Smoke in sight ahead!"

A broad screen of ships putting out to sea. Six trails of smoke were rapidly approaching. Six funnels appeared above the horizon.

The ships came from Cape Town.

We were making for Cape Town.

Below deck it was as hot as an oven. Naked backs, greasy and shining with perspiration. The men's faces had not their usual appearance; lips and teeth were parted. They took hasty gulps of cold coffee. Some of them filled their pipes.

The alarm!

Clear decks for action!

It was a convoy of six big steamers led by an armoured cruiser, and they were making high speed. We could recognize the

British white ensign at the cruiser's stern with our naked eyes. The British merchant-flag flew from our own stern.

Outwardly we resembled a common tramp collier. Our guns were concealed. The gunners crouched behind the hand-rail. On the bridge only the captain and the helmsman were to be seen. The captain wore a civilian's cap. The helmsman and the eight men aft by the flag were all without uniform.

At No. 3 port.

The gun was loaded. The voice-tube man had put on his ear-phones. We might not stand up, but crouched close together by the hawse-pipe and peered through the hole.

The six steamers had thick, yellow funnels. The battle-cruiser belonged to the *Berwick* class: fourteen six-inch guns. She would make short work of us. A single hit in the midst of our cargo of mines—we had six hundred on board—would turn our ship into a blazing inferno.

The sea was made up of polished disks, of a deep blue near at hand, violet and flaming yellow farther off; we could see far beneath the surface. Table Mountain and the outline of the coast were like glass against the evening sky. As I looked out, I touched the naked arm and shoulder of Kuddl Bülow, our loader.

He turned to me:

"Teddy—you know it's all a dirty show."

"If that there fires the first shot, I shall jump overboard," declared Jan, who was likewise stationed at our gun.

"Stand by!" reported the voice-tube man.

We crouched behind the gun, still bending down and in-visible from without. The *Berwick* lay on the beam. A flag-signal was hoisted on her bridge. But that was not for us; it was for the steamers following her.

The man at our stern lowered the flag, hoisted it, and low-ered it again—the customary greeting of passing ships.

All eyes were glued to the armoured cruiser's flag.

Would she accept our greeting or ask us "Whence and whither?"

The British flag was lowered.

Then it was hoisted again, very slowly.

The new signal from her bridge was addressed once more to the convoy: instructions for the night.

After we had passed the convoy, we slowed down, till the sudden tropical nightfall swallowed us in darkness. Darken ship! Not a lamp, not the flicker of a match. If anybody wanted to light his pipe, he went below deck.

We approached the coast.

The sounding-lead tested depths.

"A hundred and sixty-four fathoms."

"A hundred and fifty-nine fathoms."

At ninety-eight fathoms our labours began. Above our heads arched the vault of the African sky. Stars! Shimmering lights on the water! Reflections, silvery white on the mines and bluish on the men's bent backs. They shoved the mines across the after deck, two or three to each. At the shoot-hole the sharp command: "Let go!"

The voice-tube man reported:

"Tenth mine overboard."

"Eleventh mine overboard."

Across the water, so near that you could almost touch them, lay a chain of white lights, like a pearl necklace: the long mole at Cape Town. Shadows: moored ships. Through field-glasses you could recognize the tall houses by the harbour and the bright clefts that were streets.

We by the guns had nothing to do; we had only to stand by, ready for action in case of need. Kuddl Bülow turned to Jan.

"What you said just now about jumping overboard—it's not

worth while."—"I know. But I'm not going to make it worth
their while; they shan't make a stunt of it. I don't care a damn
about a hero's death, I'd rather jump in and just go down to
the fishes." Bülow looked across to Cape Town and the ships
making a dark pattern against the sea of lights.

"What if them there put out to sea this way and knock
against a mine . . ."—"It's not their fault, neither."—"No,
it's not, they're just sea-going people."

Again and again the water splashed up beneath the mine-
chute, and the egg-shaped objects, standing as high as a man's
head and capable of shattering the largest ship with their explosive charge, sank and cast anchor in the sea bottom at a depth
precisely gauged.

The voice-tube man sang monotonously:

"Forty-second mine overboard."

"Forty-third mine overboard."

The crew of the No. 3 port were squatting round the coffee-
pot. They were talking about Cape Town. "If only we could
go ashore! That'd be top-hole."—"We've been sailing eight
weeks." Shortly before the war Jimmy had been to the African
coast: "Them was the times! The black mammies—not Cape
Town itself, a bit farther north at a small port. You could have
one of 'em for a piece of Sunlight soap."

Bülow was still meditating: whose fault was it?

"It's not the mammies' fault. Nor the johnnies over there in
the Delagoa Bar at Daddy Donald's who'll knock against one
of our mines tomorrow."

"Stand by! Stand by at all guns!"

"Three hundred and twenty degrees a steamer! Fifty-five
hundred!"

We leapt to our stations by the gun. Jan laid his hand on the
elevating-handle. Kuddl seized a shell. I set the range up to
fifty-five hundred. Each of the nine of us stood at his action

station. But it was a passenger ship putting out from Cape Town with her mast-head and side-lights, her cabins and saloons, brightly illuminated as if the profoundest peace reigned.

We laid one more mine-field.

Then we bore away from the coast.

In the succeeding nights we laid mines at other points along the coast, finally off Cape Agulhas, the southernmost point of the continent, for which passing ships stood in.

We proceeded on our way, steering northwards across the Indian Ocean.

Once more we were off the sea-routes. The velocity of the monsoon blowing from behind was the same as the speed of our ship, so that actually we lay captive beneath a burning sky without a breath of air. The smoke from the funnel ascended skywards as straight as a dart. We were enveloped in thick coal-dust.

The hatches were open. The winches clattered. We were shifting coal aft from the bows. It wasn't English or Australian anthracite, but dry lumps. The dust rose in thick clouds and descended on our bodies. Each man in the watch below moved nearly two tons one hundred and fifty yards across the deck beneath a blazing tropical sun.

A couple of us clung gasping to the hand-rail. The sky seemed infinitely far away and the sea a liquid, luminous blue. A lump of coal kicked overboard seemed to remain stationery in the unplumbed depths. It was several seconds before it shrank to a mere speck and disappeared.

We resumed our work. Our skin was clogged with sweat, our tongues hung out like pieces of dry bread. We had ceased to swear. Several were carried away with sunstroke.

"The finest material, sir," the doctor had said in 1914 when the recruits were enrolled. And our gunnery-officer wrote in his notes for a war book: "The men joked and sang as they worked;

you never saw an unwilling gesture. Some of them took pride in carrying two baskets at once."

Some of them carried two baskets at once because after their work they would then have only five or six others with whom to share the few cubic metres of salt-water in the canvas bath. The thirtieth or fortieth had only warm, coffee-coloured slime to bathe in.

We stood in file beside the galley-stove with tea-pots, one for each mess, waiting to receive supper rations—unsugared tea, margarine, and bread.

"Have you seen the gunnery-officer? He's sitting on the starboard quarter-deck with his paint-box."—"The sort of picture you can't tell what's what."—"Waste of good paint."—"They'd oughter make him carry coal. And give him dried vegetables at noon and margarine for supper."

The bread ration was issued. It was full of lumps because of the mildewed flour. The smell of roast meat was wafted to us from the officers' kitchen.

We strolled on to the quarter-deck with the tea-pots, past the gunnery-officer. He was seated at an easel, trying his hand at the sunset, which lay red over the sea and had piled up ponderous domes and cloud formations along the horizon. I had seen one of his pictures once, the iceberg in Denmark Strait. "I saw that, too. The cabin-boy showed me. The iceberg looks like a plum pudding in raspberry sauce."

A gentle breeze blew across the quarter-deck.

The crew's quarters were in the forward hold. There was not a single port-hole, and the artificial light was generally burning by day. The tables and drinking-bowls were thick with coal-dust. We ate our meals hastily and then lay down on the benches and tables or on deck till the whistle blew for "Stand by hammocks." Our limbs were as heavy as lead, but the heat was so great that sleep was long in coming.

And so it went on, day after day.

Always the same routine.

Our work was a wild orgy. And when, after lying a few hours, we were roused from our sleep, we were still weary and heavy-eyed.

A cyclone broke the monotony.

The sky seemed to shrink and turn to a great yellow sack which frayed and soon lost its colour. The bursts of wind whipped the waves blindly till they rose to mountainous heights.

The hatches were closed and life-lines stretched across the the decks. The ship ran into great volumes of cloud as she rose, and then plunged down into the deep troughs.

We were right at the centre of a tropical cyclone.

The only posts still manned were those at the helm and the look-out; the firemen stood by the boilers; otherwise all work had ceased. The fo'c'sle was shaken like a box in a giant's hand. Nothing stood perpendicular except an oilskin coat that had been hung out, some sea-boots swinging from the deck-beam, and the men clinging to the tables and benches. We played skat and cursed the chow and this cruise and the war.

"Where ever is the skipper taking us to?"

To India; we knew that by the course. But afterwards? "If only we could go ashore, to one of them fandango-houses."— "In bed with a gal, just for once."—"Or at least to go along a street at night with all the lamps lit." "Or a street-car ride in a full car with women on both sides and opposite and all round. Just to get a whiff."

The longest voyage in a sailing-ship is ninety days.

We had already exceeded that period.

Pipe down!

Stand by hammocks!

The ship's frame creaked and groaned. Her iron side was like an immense, taut cow-hide, trembling and vibrating and reverberating again. The hammocks lurched, tossing and plunging. The blankets were like fevered hands. Men kicked off their bed-clothes.

The hatch was closed because the sea was washing over the decks.

One man came down from above with something blood-stained in his hand; it was a bird with broken wings. The raging storms tearing across tropical islands devastate whole villages and plantations and sweep birds and butterflies for hundreds of miles over the sea.

"It was dashed against the funnel," said the man with the bird. One or two peered out of their hammocks and looked at the drenched, blood-stained creature.

"If only we were where it came from!"

"When ever shall we sight land?"

Carrying coal! Scaling rust! Painting! And besides that keeping watch, polishing guns, and gun-practice. It seemed that the cruise would never end.

A hundred days!

We had laid mines off Cape Town and Cape Agulhas, Colombo and Bombay, and in the Watchbank, a shallow in the Indian Ocean where ships take soundings for orientation in stormy or foggy weather.

Two hundred days!

We had captured and sunk merchant ships. It was always the same story: a steamer moving solitary across the bright, smooth water. We approach. At a distance of a thousand or five hundred yards we hoist the flag-signal: "Stop at once or I shall fire." Then the order to one of the guns to fire: "No. 2 starboard—one shot across the bows—fire!"

An explosion, and a column of water rises in front of the steamer's bows. She lies stopped, and rocks on the swell. From the firemen's and seamen's quarters men emerge, run across the

decks, up the ladders, to the boats. They carry clothing hastily
bundled together, and sometimes quite useless objects, such as
a bird in a cage or the model of a ship. They cannot launch the
boats fast enough. They bring out knives and cut the falls, but
never simultaneously on both sides. The boats are left hanging
on one side and plunge down on the other, dashing the occu-
pants into the water. The same thing recurs regularly, alike in
every detail, in the cutting of the falls and the broken legs when
the men are pitched out of the boats.

After that matters proceed more slowly.

Our motor-boat takes a prize crew across to the ship, and
the fugitive crew returns on board. Half a day later, off the
route, we moor alongside and rifle our prize.

We need coal, provisions, ropes, medicaments, and everything found in ships that have come from a port. Our consump-
tion of coal remains constant, but every captured ship adds to
our need of provisions, for the crews remain on board as prisoners.

We had captured ten ships.

We blew up the iron, and it sank in five or ten minutes. Wood
we set on fire, and sometimes it remained afloat for days.

Twice we lost men.

Once it was twenty-six men in S.S. *Turitella*, which we captured on the route from Aden to Colombo. The ships, moored
together, lurched and their sides dashed one against the other.
On the *Turitella's* deck the men were slaving as if we were
lying in some dockyard instead of out at sea. We cut chutes in
her sides with oxy-acetylene apparatus; then we mounted a
gun and took mines across. The English captain and the mates
and engineers came on board our ship as prisoners.

Our commander with twenty-five men clambered on board
the steamer with their sea-bags and settled down. The Chinese
crew was gathered round the main hatch. Speeches, gesticula-

tions, flushed faces, pigtails flapping excitedly! After a consulta-
tion the interpreter declared: "German or English, all the same
to us. We don't go to sea for the flag. We go to sea for five
pounds a month."

And our skipper conceded them eight.

The Chinese never received their wages. And we never saw
any of them again, neither Chinese nor Germans. The steamer
laid mines at the mouth of the Red Sea. Then she was blown
up and abandoned while in flight. After the crew had drifted
for twenty-four hours, they were picked up by a British cruiser.
The German and Chinese coolies were tried for piracy and
murder in Bombay and sentenced to long years of penal servitude.

On another occasion it was an accident that caused loss of
life. That was in capturing a rusty old tramp. By order of the
gunnery-officer the guns were loaded before they were swung
out, while their muzzles were still pointing inboard our own
ship, and a shell was accidentally discharged and exploded in
the midst of our own crew.

A pillar of fire, and then another!

We scattered and dashed over the hatch, up the ladder on to
the quarter-deck, only recovering our senses while we were running. It was a shot from our own gun!

We turned back. One man was coming towards us with a
blood-stained face; another pressed his sticky, reddened shirt to
his abdomen. Butendrift, of the fourth gun, held his lacerated
arm aloft like a torch. The rest lay motionless beneath the still
smoking muzzle.

The sick-bay attendants came with stretchers. We grasped
nothing and had no time to reflect upon what had happened.

"Away port cutter!"

We launched the boat and put across to the steamer.

She was S.S. *Jumna*, unarmed, on her way from Spain to

Calcutta with a cargo of salt and three hundred tons of bunker coal.

The steamer lay alongside. The derricks were topped, the winches clattered, and the *Wolf* took her coal and provisions on board.

We were all occupied.

Fore and aft a party to repair the ropes, which snapped in the heavy ocean swell like violin strings stretched too taut. Others brought out rope and wire fenders to prevent the two ships from knocking against each other. The rest were busy with the loading-gear or in the bunkers.

I was one of the bunker party in the *Jumna*.

She was an antiquated ship, with old, irregular-shaped bunkers, no lighting, no ventilation; the air in them was dry and dusty and burning hot. The coal gleamed in the stuffy hold and we groped for the baskets.

There were two dead and twenty-four wounded. Two or three more would die, the doctor had said.

"This damned steamer!"

"And the war!"

"And the gunnery-officer!"

Perhaps it wasn't the gunnery-officer's fault. But was it necessary to load the guns while they were still trained inboard our own ship? And against a poor, unarmed merchantman, moreover? Besides, we all knew him, absorbed in his dachshunds, with his paint-box and pencil, or playing at photography.

"I'd like to have that chap down in this yere dark bunker." The man who spoke picked up a great lump of coal and hurled it against the bulkhead so that it was smashed to atoms. "They're all alike. Our division officer is just the same—he knows how to part his hair straight and polish his nails."—"They've never had to work, that's what's wrong."

The fo'c'sle had been transformed into a hospital. The

twenty-four lay in their hammocks, stretched flat on the iron deck, waiting for the surgeon's knife. Some of them were given injections till their screams ceased and we heard only a faint, childish whimper. Some lay quite quiet, merely showing their bared teeth. So soon had their faces turned grey.

There was the engine-man, Beierl, with his head and the upper part of his body burned. His eyes were gone and he flung his scorched arms about: "Take off my gloves—my gloves; I don't need any."

There was Dierck Butendrift with his arm bandaged; he had seen the gun go off and the smoking muzzle afterwards and knew where the shell came from. He stared at the deck-beam— always at the same spot.

Alrich Buskohl lay apart from the rest.

"It's all up with Alrich," said the sick-bay attendant.

His abdomen was torn open, and he could neither eat nor drink. From time to time he took a mouthful of sugared water and spat it out again. He did it cautiously, almost without moving.

Two surgeons and an operating-table.

The doctors worked without pause.

When the sick-bay attendant tipped the bucket full of blood-stained gauze and fragments of flesh overboard, the sharks lying in wait around the ship flapped their tail-fins idly once or twice, came nearer, and snapped it all up.

The steam winches clattered.

Wire cables, hooks, baskets.

Four baskets at a time were swung across from the *Jumna* to the *Wolf*. Three hundred tons of coal is not much, but it would take us two thousand miles on our way.

The gunnery-officer had drawn up a protocol. A metal splinter stuck to the bottom of the charge had pressed the percussion cap in closing and had caused the charge to explode. Only now did the gunnery-officer discover that it was easy for something to stick to the charges, which were greased in pursuance of his orders, and that a field forge was located near the "ready use" ammunition.

That evening we committed the first casualties, a fireman and a seaman, to the deep. I had seen the fireman, Stüven, that morning. He sat leaning against the hatch and had a pipe in his mouth. He was holding the bowl of the pipe and a lighted match in the hollow of his hand. At that moment the shell exploded. Afterwards he had only a tiny hole in his forehead.

Next morning the engine-man Beierl lay on the bier. We had a ten-minute pause in our labours and stood in a half-circle on the fore-deck, the bunker and whip parties and the men at the winches and derricks. Backs and legs were bare, black, and sticky with sweat. Baskets and shovels lay scattered around.

In the middle lay the dead man sewn up in sail-cloth, with a piece of iron at his feet. The commander read a prayer. We stared at the yellow glare of the ship's lanterns set out in solemn array, and at the outspread ensign. Two men raised the bier and the dead man slipped overboard. We heard the splash in the water.

Next day we sank the *Jumna*. We put an explosive charge in the top of the engine-room, and ten minutes later the vessel plunged nose-first into the water and disappeared.

Alrich Buskohl was still taking sugared water and spitting it out again. It was now the third day, in the dust and heat of the between-deck. He did not want to die and fought for life. He would not let a drop of fluid get into his lacerated intestines, and he never stirred unnecessarily.

He summoned Bülow with a glance:

"Kuddl—the ship's moving again—it's better now. And when we're through with this trip—"

Bülow brought his face close to Alrich's so as to hear every word he gasped out. He knew that Ali was near his end, and understood that he was talking so as to cling to something.

"You're on the mend, Ali. And that's agreed, when we're through with this trip, we'll look out for a whaler—"

The sweat stood thick on Bülow's forehead. He had to force the words out: "A Norwegian, Ali. We'll choose a Norwegian. They pay best."

Alrich Buskohl's head, lying on the pillow, looked as if it were moulded in pale clay, with the broad East Frisian forehead and the heavy cheek-bones; and he was as still as a modelled figure. His eyes were wide open.

"A Norwegian—a trip—and when they pay us off—to Vier-landen, we'll go there to see the trees blossom again."

An hour later Alrich Buskohl was dead.

And the gunnery-officer in his *War Book for the Youth of Germany* wrote a hundred lines about death, which was a fa-miliar guest amongst German seamen; he wrote of the beautiful white cloth in which the bodies were sewn, of the green turf over the mass graves in Flanders, and the cool depths of the North Sea. He quoted the soldiers' song: "I had a com-rade . . ."; half an hour later, when the engine-man was committed to the deep: ". . . he marched at my side"; and when Alrich Buskohl was laid on the bier, the third verse of the song: ". . . my hand I cannot give thee . . ."!

Propaganda for the next war. Jan Geulen was right that time off Cape Town when he said: "I shall jump overboard, if there's nothing else for it. They shan't make a stunt of my death."

Southerly course.

No land in sight, only water. Day rested like white fire on the sea, and by night its dark surface glided past.

Somewhere the world must be.

And still the war dragged on.

Sometimes we picked up a wireless message from ships putting into port or out to sea, cipher telegrams from war-ships, or the S O S of some craft in distress at sea. Our mines off the African coast and the Indian ports did their work. Ships put out and sank, ships carrying rice, sugar, miscellaneous merchandise, war material, human souls, and horses.

We still had two hundred mines on board.

And we continued our cruise. There were three hundred men in the forward holds and as many prisoners in the aft holds. Between them the raised quarter-deck was situated, with the officers' quarters, and over them the bridge, with the control-station and the captain's quarters.

The captain read Kant and Schopenhauer, and was the loneliest man on board. He had no social intercourse with anybody, not even with the officers. Once when he came into the mess whilst they were drinking on some festive occasion, his entrance cast a gloom upon the whole company; silence fell suddenly and the gentlemen sat facing one another like snow figures. He was a dry mathematician who escaped the pursuit and pitfalls of the enemy, not by speed, but by the incredible slowness of our ship's movements. The war-ships that chased us always passed us by in the immeasurable expanses of the ocean and searched for us a few hundred miles ahead of our actual position. He fired no shot, he eschewed reckless feats of arms and heroism and only acted where all seemed perfectly safe.

Moreover, he exercised a bloodless justice which was directed impartially against crew and officers. When we had the *Turitella* moored alongside, he suddenly shouted to the commander down from the bridge: "What are those men carrying? I should like you to ascertain that." And when the commander had reported that the cases being taken to the sailors' quarters contained pineapples from the *Turitella's* cargo, he addressed us: ". . . whatever we capture is State property. Anyone who purloins it commits theft. In war that is called looting. And if any man is caught at it after this warning, I shall string him up to the yard-arm." And therewith he raised his lean hand and pointed at the mast, where he proposed to hang us because we had seized upon a few tins of pineapple to add to our starvation rations.

On another occasion he turned upon the officers. A cargo of several thousand eggs of a captured ship had found its way exclusively to the officers' store-room. For days, for a whole week, the cabin-boys scurried from the kitchen to the mess: A beaten-up egg! Scrambled eggs! Poached eggs! At last the captain observed what was going on and thundered at the commissary chief: "How many eggs did we get from that prize? How many have been allotted to the officers' mess, and how many to the crew's?" The fat commissary chief could only report that not one single egg had found its way to the crew's mess.

There was nothing remarkable in that; it is the generally accepted point of view: all "State property" goes to the officers, and the crew gets only bare necessities. But paragraph fifty-eight, subsection ten of the Military Criminal Code reads: "Any-one neglecting to exercise due care in providing for the feeding of the troops . . . is liable to the death-penalty as a traitor in time of war."

He addressed his officers in the spirit of that paragraph, and the poor remnant of the egg consignment found its way across to the crew's galley.

The captain's isolation increased.

The crew had no affection for him.

The officers mocked at him.

The prisoners aft were as ragged and grey as we in the bows. There were Englishmen, Portuguese, and Negroes, men of half a dozen nationalities. They received the same rations as we, but they were confined more closely. Moreover, they had no work, which acted as a perpetual narcotic upon the crew. And if the end should really come, if one day we were attacked by a cruiser, their fate would be that of rats drowned in a trap. Whenever ascending smoke was sighted, they were sent below deck and lay in the hold like so much merchandise. The hatches over their heads were closed, wedged, and secured.

A sailing-vessel lay ahead. The sea was almost becalmed and her sails flapped. Unchallenged, she hoisted the flag-signal: "English bark *Dee* in ballast on her way from Mauritius to Bamburi." She had had a long voyage and wanted us to tell her the time by chronometer.

Instead we hoisted the naval ensign.

We sent a prize crew over.

The *Dee* was sailing in ballast. She had only stones on board, and very little food. We fetched the cases and barrels across in boats. The last boats brought the British captain, two French mates, and the crew, consisting of a dozen Negroes. The Negroes were tipsy. We had to draw up one or two of them with ropes, just as we had the sacks of flour a little earlier. No sooner had we got them on deck than they dropped down and lay prone.

A boat with the demolition party pushed off from the *Dee*.

A dull roar, and the fragments flew.

The captain on our after deck, a white-haired man of sixty, snatched off his cap.

How many ships we had seen sink! And it was always the same. The water penetrated into the hull where the projectile had torn a hole. The ship dropped astern, grew heavy, and began to sway unnaturally. Some go down bows-first, others over the stern-post; one, the *Wordsworth* from Liverpool, keeled over on her side and capsized.

The captain of the *Dee* stood motionless. The fine spray beat in his face. The Negroes lay round him. The other prisoners stood at the hand-rail, as well as the German crew, all watching the old bark's fight with the water.

The ship went down square, quite steadily.

The English mates laid bets with tobacco or cigarettes or a pair of trousers. "She'll sink over her stern-post."—"No, over her bows. I bet my calabash," roared a bald-pated Irishman.

The old captain had brought the ship from Scotland, and ever since, for twenty years, he had sailed the seas of the southern hemisphere in her with coloured crews. His face was like old leather. Tears coursed down his cheeks, and he never noticed it.

The *Dee* vibrated through her whole length.

Her fore-topmast crashed, her stern rose, the air compressed in her after part burst the boards of the deck. A column of water shot up. The *Dee* went down with the thunderous roar of a harpooned whale.

The captain dropped his cap.

The Irishman had won his bet.

A hundred days!

Two hundred days!

Three hundred days!

Cut off from land, cut off from women, an endless voyage.

The officers sat in their mess and sang: "No more red wine. . . ." P.O. "Alcohol" awaited his opportunity and slipped into the sick-bay: "Give me another, lad, now!" and the sick-bay attendant poured out a glass of spirit for him, ninety-six per cent. The ship's doctor was seated behind a thin curtain and observed the phenomenon. After the draught the man, who had entered with a distracted, stupid expression, was transformed. He left the sick-bay with poise restored and returned to his duties. Some day he would collapse, but for the time being, he carried on.

And the whole crew was in a like case.

Their natural reserves were giving out. A certain nervousness

appeared on all sides, which was symptomatic. Things couldn't
go on like that much longer. If, indeed, it were possible to
dope the whole company with poison like the alcohol-soaked
P.O., the cruise might have gone on a bit longer with the help
of some such narcotic.

But then there was the food: dried vegetables, dried potatoes,
rice, corned beef, frozen meat, and canned things; no fresh vegetables and no fruit. It was a diet without vitamins, with inevitable
consequences. When the doctor crossed the deck, he was struck
by the peculiar whiteness of many faces; and when he examined
the men, he found enlarged pupils and shortness of breath; some
of them already complained of swellings at the knee.

If only he could talk to the captain. But it was the doctor's duty
simply to report to the navigating officer. And it was not time
for that yet. So far the symptoms only indicated general anæmia,
acidity of the blood, and increasing physical weakness. But beyond
stood the spectre: scurvy! Beriberi!

The captain was looking out for coal to continue the voyage.
He had the charts of the South Seas spread out before him. The
main routes for sailing-ships carrying coal from Australia to
western America lay through this region of everlasting tempest.

The days were a grey, steaming chaos. By night a few isolated
stars peeped through the piled-up clouds. The wind blew from
the west, always from the west. The ship, with her half-empty
hold, rolled and lurched heavily in the swell.

The relieved watch came below, the helmsman and the look-
outs and deck look-outs in dripping oilskins, the others in torn
black rags—shirt and trousers and sea-boots or wooden clogs;
that was the party from No. 1 compartment. In No. 1 compartment the coal had ignited by force of its own weight.

Fire aboard! Nobody took much notice of that now. It had
been going on for weeks, and each watch in turn descended into

the smoke-filled No. 1 compartment or into the bunkers, found the source of ignition, and removed it.

The watch below sat on deck and ate their chow. Afterwards they played cards and lit their pipes. There was no more tobacco, but we smoked dried tea-leaves and all sorts of dried stuff, if only we could get a spark out of it.

A phonograph played:

> "*I want to be,*
> *I want to be*
> *In my home in Dixie land.*"

Then the needle turned blunt and there was nothing but scratching and scraping to be heard. We had got the phonograph from a captured steamer. We knew all the records, and all their damaged places, by heart. And if one of us opened his mouth at table, the others knew what he was going to say.

There we sat, ten of us, round the table. Dirty, thumbed cards: "Eighteen—twenty-two—I pass."—"Twenty-four—twenty-seven—your trick." The two cooks were washing up the crocks. Kuddl Bülow was carving a model of a sailing-ship. The others just stared in front of them.

"You'll never finish that sailing-ship, Kuddl."—"Oh, yes, I will," replied Bülow. He was chipping away at a capstan the size of a pea. He had been working for months at the same model, with great patience and concentration.

Jimmy flung the cards away: "Pass—to hell with the whole lot. I'm fed up, even if I get a grand with fours."—"I'd like to know how long the old man's going to keep us in the old tub."—"No grub, no tobacco."—"Why can't he get himself taken prisoner?"

"Damned mess," growled a man who was pottering about with the things on the mess-room shelves and found his tea-bowl dirty. The cook merely looked at him; such a remark would certainly have meant fisticuffs some months earlier.

Fisticuffs were a thing of the past.

Faces had grown grey and dull.

"I'll tell you why we're cruising round here," said Geulen. "Here's a captured English newspaper: 'Bombay harbour block-aded.' 'Mines in the Indian Ocean.' 'Warning: enemy raider in the Pacific.' And here's the main point; insurance premiums and freight rates have been increased as much as fivefold. We're slav-ing for the insurance companies and the shipowners. It's them that profits; and the dockyards, that have to build more ships. In fact, everybody that trades in iron and steel and sells pro-jectiles and guns."

"Hullo, what's up? Why are they running like that?"

"The wireless operator—a wireless message from the fleet. He's posted it up on the ladder."

"A wireless message: mutiny in the German fleet!"

Kuddl Bülow left his model and his knife. Jan Geulen, Jimmy, and the whole watch below thronged round the ladder. The captain did not suppress the wireless message, but had it posted up as an example of English lying reports.

One of the men read it out:

> *In certain sections of the German High Sea Fleet lying at anchor at Kiel and Wilhelms-haven the crews have mutinied. The mutineers attacked the officers in the* Prinzregent Luit-pold, *the* Westfalen, *and the fleet flagship* Friedrich der Grosse. *The captain of the* König Albert *was thrown overboard and his body salved in the North Sea.*

"In the *Prinzregent*! The *Westfalen*! The *Friedrich der Grosse*!"—"Them mutiny and throw their officers overboard!"

"You believe that? That's lies I tell yer." There was a perpetual crowd round the bit of paper. They came down from the deck and out from the bunkers and stoke-hold.

Everyone was discussing the telegram.

"Of course it's just English lies, but there's probably something in it."—"The Russians have knocked off and chucked their officers into the Baltic."—"But Germany's quite different."

"And we go on and on."

"When ever will the end come?"

At four o'clock in the morning we were roused out of our hammocks. We slipped on our grimy dungarees, all stiff with dried sweat. The fo'c'sle smelled foul as we changed our clothes.

On deck it was still dark.

Foaming crests of waves leapt up, chalky white. The ship was an eternal seesaw, up and down in a long-drawn-out rhythm. And we were no longer conscious of it. Perhaps we should be sea-sick if we suddenly found ourselves on firm dry land.

We clambered down into the hold.

It was as high as a church vault and the coal a tunnelled wilderness, cut through by passages. The lights hung suspended in wreaths of white steam.

We filled the baskets and dragged them along, through the door into the next compartment. When we uncovered a source of ignition, a hose was brought to it. Steam! Smoke! Too thick for the light to penetrate, so that we could not see one another. We just caught glimpses of a speck, a leg, a face.

Carbonic oxide! Our heads buzzed and our bones were like lead. It was an effort to lift our shovels. And when we stood below the wind-sail and breathed in the air, not one of us spoke a word. We just stared stupidly at those who stood and vomited.

Four hours, and then we were relieved.

In the fo'c'sle we lay on benches and tables, but there wasn't room for everybody. And we hadn't long to rest.

Then we had to wash the decks and clean the guns.

And down again to the bunker.

And back to the fo'c'sle.

Then the trouble began with me, too. At first it was only little pockets round my teeth. Other men's teeth were falling out and their flesh was turning flabby. And a few Portuguese from the prisoners' deck lay in the sick-bay with swollen legs. When the doctor pressed his finger against their thighs, he poked holes.

"To hell with it all! We're rotting by inches."—"Better an iron-clad right away."—"But one thing I do say; if we kick the bucket, there'll be others go with us."—"We'll just see who'll swing from the yard-arm." Dierck Butendrift was standing on the deck in the midst of a group of men; he raised his scarred arm and pointed at the bridge.

Up above, the officer of the watch was tramping to and fro. The captain was standing in the lee shelter, smoking a cigar. Two look-out men were perched up in the crow's-nest, scanning the rolling waves right up to the grey sky.

But no ship hove in sight.

Besides, a ship in these latitudes would only provide coal, no vegetables, no potatoes, no fresh food.

A tackle had been placed over No. 1 compartment, a gin-block; up above, the sailors were pulling the rope very cautiously. Arms were stretched out over the parapet to catch hold. A head appeared, then shoulders, and they hauled a man up through the hatch and laid him on deck, another, and a third and fourth. Coal-gas poisoning! Beneath the covering of coal-dust their faces and skin were ashy grey. The four men were borne lifeless to the sick-bay.

During the following week quite a number of men from No.

compartment sneaked away to the mess-deck. Twenty or thirty of them were lounging there. The petty officer on duty came down: "Come on, boys, it's only another hour."

But the coolies did not stir.

"We're not going."—"We're going to stay down here."—"Let 'em do their own dirty work."—"The skipper oughter get himself taken prisoner."—"Yes, he ought to. I'm not going to do any more."

Up above, the sub-lieutenant called to the petty officer: "Where are the men?"

Then he came down himself, long-legged, his uniform cut to an elegant waist. He was obliged to be "smart" with the men.

"Get up on deck! Damnation! What's come over you? I'll make you run!" But the coolies remained seated on the benches and took no notice of him. What great brutes they were, with their chests and arms! Like a pack of orang-outangs! And the stench in the fo'c'sle was like a stable's.

The sub-lieutenant shouted at the top of his voice:

"Second division get to work!"

"Second division fall in!"

The division did not stir. There was silence on the deck. A wave beat against the side so that it reverberated. Up above, the wind whistled in the rigging.

The sub-lieutenant was scarlet with rage. He glanced uneasily from one to another. He couldn't report the whole division. He looked for some individual of whom he might make an example. His eyes rested on Seaman Bülow. Bülow was the one to pick, a heavy fellow, all muscle and bone, and as clumsy as a young ox.

"Seaman Bülow, get to work!"

Bülow remained seated at the table. He only raised his head. His lips formed a sound, but it was a little time before he brought it out. And it was a declaration of resistance to his superiors, to the authorities, to the war:

"Bülow refuses to go on."

The sub-lieutenant felt the fo'c'sle spin round.

"I give the direct order—second division—Bülow—fall in—master-at-arms!"

Already the sub-lieutenant was on the ladder. Sea-boots flew after him. The sailors remained seated side by side, an inert pack.

The sub-lieutenant reported to the commander, and he to the captain.

The master-at-arms came on deck with five men wearing side-arms. "Bülow, report to the captain—don't make any row —it's no use!"

Bülow stared at the master-at-arms, at the five men. He found himself isolated. The others did not tackle their job, but stood aside and awaited developments.

Isolated exclamations:

"We've had enough."—"We won't go any further."—"We shall all die like dogs here."—"Better behind barbed wire!"— "The skipper must get himself taken prisoner."

The master-at-arms gave a command:

"Seize that fellow! Up on to the bridge with him!"

The five hesitated. Only slowly did they advance, their eyes glued to the deck.

"Come on, now, Bülow."

Bülow's ponderous face assumed a rigid expression. You could hear his voice in the remotest corners of the deck:

"If Bülow won't, then he won't."

With these words he seized his seaman's knife and plunged the blade through his hand. With his left hand thus pinned to the table, he stood leaning over and glared at the master-at-arms.

In the German newspapers steel soles were advertised, and dried milk and unrationed meat substitutes. Professors and dietetic specialists had discovered that the turnip was an excellent and nourishing food for the populace.

Coffee made of turnips!

Turnip soup!

Boiled turnips!

Every naval officer was allowed twenty bottles of wine a month. Three times a week banquets were held. In the ships of the High Sea Fleet there was one steam kitchen for every thousand or fifteen hundred men, but three officers' galleys, with the attached store-room for provisions and wines.

Snapshots in the fleet:

S.M.S. *Nürnberg*: the celebration of the launching of the newly built cruiser. The stewards hurried to the mess with hot dishes. Five meat courses, pudding, dessert, coffee. The wine-list offered a choice of seven vintages of white wine and two of red, besides port and sherry and ten varieties of spirits. Speeches were made about the ship's glorious traditions, about His Majesty the Emperor and the resolve to hold out till a victorious peace was won.

"The German sword will establish peace."—"But we mustn't tolerate any slackness. Occurrences like the recent disturbances in Kiel—a pack of rowdies running through the streets and shouting for bread—that sort of thing must be eradicated from the German body politic."—"We mustn't accept an unsound peace. We need guarantees."—"Coal, iron, land for colonization. We must retain the Longwy and Briey basins with their ores. The east must be colonized by German peasants. And Belgium must remain a German protectorate, with Antwerp, which constitutes the bridge-head and the gate for an invasion of England."

The officers were seated according to their rank, the sub-lieutenants at the foot of the table. It was not till after dinner, when the first bottle had been upset and had spilt over the table-cloth, that their spirits rose.

The steward who had swept up the broken glass muttered to the dish-washer in the pantry:

"If on'y they'd go up on deck when they begin to spew, the deck-hands could clear up the mess. They've divided up the map, now they're on with the women, and there ain't nothin' else in their noddles. If the hands don't talk of nothin' else, you can understand it; they ain't got nothin' else, and there ain't much they can do with their pay. One of the stokers, Willy in the third watch, went ashore to one o' them women with a lump o' coal. But the officers now! They're after the women every day. Just listen, now, how they're bawling—one of 'em's brought out his joke again, how he got one of 'em."

The musicians at the mess-room door each received one glass of beer per hour. In the mess-room buttons were unfastened and collars and ties loosened. There was one sub-lieutenant with a fair, boyish head and a pale face. Drink didn't agree with him, but he played his part with spirit.

> *We are of Flemish race,*
> *The German sets the pace,*
> *For a loaf of army bread and a franc*
> *He can have his way for hours. . . .*

The seamen and firemen in the hammocks could not get any sleep. Some of them lit their pipes, but secretly. Smoking after the order "Pipe down!" was forbidden and involved a penalty.

". . . that gang there!"—"Let 'em face the music and go to the devil in action."—"We're hungry. We're hungry."—"To hell with that jam!"—"And you can't say nothing, else you're packed off on one of them sky-trippers like the rest."

A few days later Lieutenant Commander Lerche addressed the lined-up crew: ". . . Several men have asked for more bread today. It's impossible, you must just go hungry. If one of you dies of starvation, I will gladly accord him a funeral with all the honours of war. Back to work. Dismiss!"

S.M.S. *Helgoland*, coaling: as a result of the rush to break records there were the usual skin wounds, one man's face battered in, and one broken neck. The commander proposed to make a present of fifty marks to the dead man's sister. "Twenty-five would do, sir," the third in command counselled him. On another occasion a party was behind time with coaling, and the officer of the watch imposed punishment drill. Ashore, between the coal-dumps, he kept his men with bent knees for several minutes at a time and made them clump round in goose-step and lie down again and again in the mud.

"I'll teach you to shovel coal! Call that goose-step? Out with your feet! Detachment—halt! At ease! Just look at that foul puddle!"

Before them was a puddle of rain-water.

"Lie flat—'shun! Lie flat—'shun! Lie flat—"

They lay with their foreheads in the coal-begrimed mud.

The squadron chaplain stood on the bridge of the flagship looking through a pair of field-glasses and studying the physiognomy of the men undergoing punishment drill.

"Double time! March, march! Lie down—'shun!" And that for a whole hour.

Seaman Stumpf of the same ship wrote in his diary:

> . . . I have, in fact, already recorded a similar case; but I will do the same again because this time the affair is much more scandalous.
>
> As usual, several men employed in the dockyard had come alongside the ship to get the

scraps of food. One of them was a disabled soldier with a stiff leg. One of the sailors gave this man half his plate of turnips. No sooner had the officer of the watch seen this than he summoned the soldier: "How dare you come here to fetch food?" "I'm hungry, sir." "I don't care a damn for that. You know quite well that it is forbidden. Orderly! Take the food from this man and tip it into the watering-trough." I clenched my teeth as I walked down the gangway with the disabled man. Suddenly he gave vent to his anger, exclaiming: "It's a low-down trick, that is!" But the stern lieu-tenant heard and made the poor fellow come back again and gave him a real dressing-down, repeating the order to me to throw away the food. Luckily the pot had a lid, so that it wasn't difficult to prevent it's being spilt.

I can't understand such hard-hearted con-duct. I am inclined to blame his upbringing rather than himself. As the son of a deputy surgeon-general he is doubtless ignorant of what it is to be hungry, and perhaps he learned as a child that anything associated with the word "labour" is contemptible.

The *Friedrich der Grosse*: at mess. There were dried vege-tables, following turnips, soup made of potato peelings, and dried cod, all in the same week. The cooks came with the dishes and dealt out the rations—warm water and green stuff and that was all.

The officers' galley was situated in the same casemate amidships. The odour of roast meat was wafted through the deck, with the fragrance of the apple fritters and sauces served to the Admiral, the fleet staff, and the ship's officers.

The soup seemed to splash about in your stomach.

You can't go on like that.

One full-grown man collapsed. He was begrimed from his work at the boilers. He lay on the linoleum-covered deck as white as a sheet. One or two others were busied about him.

"No wonder!"—"You don't need no privy after a soup like that—it trickles and sweats out of itself."—"Water! Rot! What he wants is a bit o' roast."

A steward passed by with a dish of meat. The long arm of a stoker wound itself round his neck. The dish fell with a crash. Bent backs and eager, snatching hands crowded round it. One mess got something to eat, and they kept part for the man who had fainted.

On another occasion the men purloined the officers' roast from the pan, so that the latter had to wait two hours while the cook prepared another meal. Hundreds of loaves and bushels of potatoes disappeared in the process of delivery. There wasn't a ship in the fleet where the provision-room hadn't been rifled. Men refused their rations and nobody fetched them from the kitchens. The officers in command summoned the crews and read them the articles of war.

One of these gold-bespangled gentlemen was standing on the covering of a gun-turret, legs wide apart: ". . . I need hardly tell you that your families at home have much less in the larder than you. These are hard times."

Down below one or two men nudged one another; they belonged to the cutter's crew who had fetched the speaker from ashore in the boat a few evenings earlier and had brought him on board drunk.

"You fellows down there—"

He fixed his eyes on one who, unlike the others, was not looking up at him. "I'll spit on your heads in another minute; I'll keep you on the run. Swine!" Then, turning to the firemen: "You foul swine! You knock-kneed curs! I'll teach you! You've got too soft a berth. What you want is more drill."

"Division officers!"

The division officers stood at attention.

"Read the articles of war to each division and give them each separate instruction."

They read the articles of war:

". . . forbidden, under penalty, confinement to quarters, brig, cells, degradation, the firing squad!"

But the food didn't improve.

And threats don't still your hunger.

In the *Prinzregent Luitpold*, July 31, ten p. m.: The third stokers' watch was coming off duty. There were fifty of them and they had scrubbed themselves clean as best they could with sand and soap-substitute. They were naked except for their wooden clogs, and carried in one hand, rolled in a towel, their dirty stoke-hold dungarees and their toilet gear.

They came like that into the mess-deck.

The group gathered round the notice-board.

"It's enough to knock yer down!"—"Is the engineer office crazy?"—"We're off duty tomorrow. It was our turn for the pictures."

But there it was on the blackboard: "Third stokers' watch tomorrow morning at 8.30, drill."

Infantry drill in the great drill-ground in Wilhelmshaven after their work in the stoke-hold. "Instead of the movies, they're going to keep our noses to the big grindstone."—"They've got you this time!"—"They've done that because we asked for more soap."—"The greedy hogs! They've got good toilet-soap in their drawers."—"That's right, they have—boxes of it. I've seen 'em myself."—"Do you know what the crew of the *Pillau* did? They was cheated too and got no leave. So the whole lot cleared off and didn't come on board again till evening."

"Just let me get to the blackboard."

One of the firemen elbowed his way forward. He had a piece of chalk in his hand and wrote across the order: "If there are no movies tomorrow, then we beat it without leave."

Next morning after breakfast the petty officer on duty gave the order: "Third watch fall in outside the armoury."

But the watch didn't fall in outside the armoury. They slunk off one at a time down the gangway and assembled ashore under the Jachmann Bridge. Forty-nine of them passed out of the dock-yard gate and marched through the town to the dike.

They went back on board for midday dinner.

"The best thing to do would be to stand the whole lot against the gun-turret and shoot 'em," declared a Chief P.O. as they came up the gangway.

At two o'clock they were reported to the captain. All forty-nine stood in line on the upper deck. The captain, the commander, and the division officer strode along the line and scanned their faces.

"Fall out!"

"Fall out!"

They picked out eleven men: "Fourteen days' brig! Twenty-one days' extra duty! Degradation!"

Eleven were punished and the rest dismissed.

That evening after "pipe down" there was no peace on board. The men sat in the dark beneath their hammocks and discussed the affair. And in the dockyard a number of them squatted in a railway car—deck-hands and stokers from the *Prinzregent*, one or two from the *Friedrich der Grosse*, and several from the light cruiser *Pillau*.

"Eleven out of forty-nine! And look how the division officer picked them out—big Willem because he goes unshaved—all of 'em men whose faces he didn't like."—"We can't submit to it any longer. These high-handed ways have got to stop."—"And the everlasting drudgery."—"And the hunger rations."

"A week ago when they was guzzling at noon on the *Thüringen*, we turned the hose on 'em. And plenty of pressure. Dishes and plates, all flew across the deck. And when the officers tried to get to the door, they got a stream of water in their mugs and on their bellies. Soon laid 'em out flat on their behinds."

"And what happened afterwards?"

"Nothin'! Went to their cabins and changed. Never gave a sign, no inquiry, nothin'! If that 'ad come out, they'd 'a got the sack. They all go about now with their Brownings in their trouser pockets."

There were some fifty seamen and firemen in the car talking over occurrences on the various ships: on the *Helgoland* parts of the guns had been thrown overboard, and on the *Friedrich der Grosse* painters and boat-falls cut.

The car door was shut and it was quite dark. It was only when a pipe glowed that you could catch a glimpse of a face; or when someone struck a match, the whole packed assembly, head beside head, became visible for a moment.

"Mates! We've met here on account of the eleven firemen on the *Prinzregent.* . . ."

"Either we'll all be punished or none."

"Hold your mug. Let Alwin speak."

Alwin Köbis began again:

"Mates! The deck-hands and stokers in the *Prinzregent* want us to suggest something. We must agree on what we're to do. How are we going to protest?"

"We'd better all beat it tomorrow, the whole crew, and leave the old punt without anyone."

"I'm entirely opposed to that. We must put that off till we're ready to strike a serious blow."

"Yes, Alwin's right. We mustn't frighten the officers too soon," Fireman Beckers chimed in. "I suggest we get the eleven out of their cells and demand immunity for them from the captain."

"No, we've got to show our teeth for once."

"We'll march."

"We'll march."

"But we'll keep ready for action and come back in a body in three hours. There's a bigger issue at stake, and it's not worth while to be hauled up for mutiny over this affair."

"Right."

"We'll march."

"To the dike. We'll be back in three hours."

"And if the captain doesn't set them eleven free?"

"Then there's still us on the Big Fritz. Then the *Friedrich der Grosse* will quit."—"And there'll be more breakages than just an accumulator on the *Pillau*," declared one of her crew.

"We're all starved together."

"And we've all got the same pack of officers."

Slowly the dawn outlined the ships lying in harbour, with their upper works, their bridges and turrets. The smoke issuing from their broad funnels was quickly lost in the grey atmosphere. A strong west wind, sweeping the sky, rapidly piled up masses of grey-blue cloud. Heavy squalls beat upon the decks.

The crew of the *Prinzregent* swallowed their coffee of burnt turnips. The men's quarters were gradually emptying. A stream of firemen and seamen poured across the gangway down into the dockyard. Suddenly the officer on duty noticed what was happening and had the gangway blocked.

One or two men were hurrying through the casemates, among

them the fireman Beckers. A few were still seated at the tables there or busy with their clothes. "Come on! No one's got to stay on board."

When Beckers reached the upper deck with the last party, several men came up to him: "Here's a nice mess! The gangway blocked! Nobody may go ashore for the present."

"What are we to do now?"—"We're not going to stay on board alone."—"Sure not! Wait awhile, I know a plan."

With these words Beckers seized a bulwark-stanchion and jumped overboard, and the others followed. They made their way across a wooden raft lying between the ship and the land, reached the quay wall, and scrambled up it.

Meantime the telephone had been busy. The dockyard gate was shut, with police, the fire-brigade, and sentries standing before it. But the *Prinzregent* men, gathering from all sides, formed a swelling crowd: four hundred, five hundred, six hundred.

"You make yerselves scarce here."

"Clear out, else there'll be a smash."

"And a couple of fists in yer mug."

They hustled the policemen aside. The sentries retreated of themselves. The gate was a heavy iron one twelve feet high. They set their shoulders to it, those behind pushed and shoved, everybody wanted to do his bit. The gate gave way with a crash and the wings flew apart.

"We're not going to climb the wall this time."—"The skipper'll go cross-eyed!"—"They can have their damned infantry drill to themselves." Halloing and bawling, the *Prinzregent* men poured out into the street. Outside they formed fours and marched in close order through the town. They passed the barracks of the marines and on to the dike, then up on the dike along the coast of Jade Bay.

Alwin Köbis, the fireman, led the troop.

On the previous evening he had expressed his doubts, but once
the matter was decided, he took the place into which he had been
thrust. Showers swept across the bay one after another and beat
upon the dike, upon the solitary rows of poplars in the fields, and
upon the marchers' faces. Alwin Köbis grew more and more
silent amidst his comrades' excited chatter; for many regarded
the march as a successful stroke.

The troop reached the Strand Saloon, a restaurant standing
with its floor on concrete pillars thirty feet above the sea and a
little above the dike. In the afternoon and evening the restaurant was frequented by officers. At this time of day, and in such
bad weather, it was quite deserted. The six hundred men from
the *Prinzregent* took shelter from the rain underneath.

A confused mass of faces, an exclamation, and a hubbub of
talk. At last they had broken loose—even the common herd refused now to tread the path prescribed.

"We'll see now if the skipper won't let them eleven go free."
—"The *Friedrich der Grosse* and *Pillau* are joining us."—
"Boys, it isn't that, it isn't the eleven. We've got to show 'em at
last that we're human, and if they trample on us, we've got to
resist."—"You've got to put up with everything, and there's
nothing that ain't forbidden, except holding yer mug."—"The
war'd have been over long ago if we weren't such stupid
cowards."—"Do you think they'll stand six hundred of us up
against the gun-turret? They can't. They need us."

They stood in groups of fifty and a hundred.

A few made speeches.

"It's not only in our ship and the others that it's like this. It's
the same everywhere, they all think of nothing but their own
bellies, or of their pay and the orders they want to win. . . ."

"We grow three times as many potatoes as we need for food.
But where are they? We produce such quantities of sugar that we
used to supply half the world. But where's that? We won't know

if we shall even have turnips next year. But it's quite certain that
we shall have no coal. There's plenty of coal in Germany, but
look at the way the authorities distribute it! They arrange it so
cleverly that individuals get nothing. But I'm quite sure they'll
find a substitute in the end for the coal they haven't got. For in
those ways Germany leads the world. . . ."—"Things can't
go on like this. The sensible thing to do now is to stop the war."
"Lord, man, how d'you expect sense all of a sudden in these
crazy times when lunatics rule the roost?"—"We must get our
names on the register and vote for peace."

Alwin Köbis stood erect, as grey as the concrete pillar behind
him. He spoke of their object in marching out, and of the war
that would never end of itself.

"Hunger-strike on the *Prinzregent*, soap demonstration on
the *Friedrich der Grosse* and other ships! And we've all been on
leave and seen the women, the potato- and jam-queues. And
there's the workmen, disabled soldiers with their nerve broken
down; I talked with one yesterday in the dockyard. I had to
shout at him; he was partly deaf and he could hardly hold the
pneumatic hammer. His hands shook and jumped, and it's the
same at night when he's asleep, he told me. And the starvation—"

"And in the mess they shout about 'Siegfrieds.' They want
Belgium and half Russia and whole tracts of France. Stick it out,
give all you have, go on letting them shoot you down, the military situation is favourable. . . ."

The other speakers in the Strand Saloon gave way. More and
more crowded round Köbis and listened to him. Outside, the rain
poured down.

"When it began, they said we must defend ourselves. Now we
need annexations. They've always cheated us. They understand
how to drill us, stand us on the turrets with our hammocks, drive
us over the main-top, and make our lives a burden to us day and

night. But they don't understand their own job, or if they do, they make much too much of a song about it.

"They lied to us and pretended that Jutland was a victory, and all the time they were in a blue funk and as glad as us when they saw a clear horizon next morning and no British ships in sight. They only went out to provoke the battle to justify their own existence and their brilliant, idle future.

"But what's that to us?

"Those officers, who pocket their pay, have a home ashore, and never went without anything in their lives—when I see one of 'em with his blue-shaven mug and his smooth neck—"

Köbis shook his fist.

"My fingers itch to grip hold and throttle 'em. But that's no good, we mustn't do that. And it isn't only the officers. There's them that supply war materials, the industrialists: steel and iron and leather. It doesn't matter what it is, they all make profits, and they've all raised their dividends.

"And that's what we're slaving for!

"That's what we're starving for!

"That's what we're going to the dogs for!

"We don't need a victorious peace and territory and wealth. It's the desire to annex that's our destruction; if it wasn't for that, we'd have peace. We'd be able to work again, and there'd be grub for us. And the others are human too. The peoples have got to get together and come to an understanding. This slaughter is senseless.

"The workers ashore are beginning to understand. They can't carry on, either, with empty bellies. It's beginning everywhere. That's why they make us do so much infantry drill. If the workers strike, we're to fire on them. . . ."

For minutes on end Köbis could not make himself heard. The substructure of the feudal Strand Restaurant reverberated to a hundred voices:

"We won't do that!"

"Field-grey don't shoot on field-grey."

"Nor on hungry folk."

"We'll turn the guns' muzzles."

"A strike in the fleet!"

"A strike in the fleet!"

Köbis went on speaking of the State and of militarism and of the rational common sense that must prevail in the end. He had Max Stirner and Friedrich Nietzsche in his sea-bag in the *Prinz-regent*, and what he said was inspired by a weighty, passionate faith. He concluded:

"We've got eighty admirals fussing round, and they're nearly all ashore, occupying positions that draw princely pay. And then there's the generals and the governors of the conquered provinces, and not one of them will give up his post if he can help it. And the shareholders and dividend-eaters earning millions on guns and substitute materials.

"The war's one vast business deal.

"And there'll be an end of the swindle when we recognize it and refuse to go on. Comrades! It's each for all, and all for each! Better an end with horror than a horror without end! Down with the war!"

The six hundred went back on board in pouring rain. They clambered up the gangway drenched to the skin and retired to their messes.

Already the ship was getting up steam.

The commanding officers took no steps. But the ship's routine continued: clear for general exercise! The ropes were thrown clear and the *Prinzregent Luitpold* put to sea. Outside she anchored in isolation, separate from the other ships.

Events took their course:

The rest of the fleet put to sea. The passive resistance of the firemen and seamen on the *Friedrich der Grosse* and the other ships could do no more than cause delay. By evening all the ships lay in Schillig Roads. The crews looked for the *Prinzregent*, but she lay far out at sea, beyond their sight.

Wireless messages passed between the *Prinzregent* and the *Friedrich der Grosse*. The captain and the admiral came to an understanding and took measures accordingly.

Next day at three o'clock in the afternoon a little steamer came alongside the *Prinzregent*. The crew stood at attention. Certain names were called.

"Fall out left!"

"Board the steamer!"

The steamer put off. Caps and hands were waved: "So long, Harry."—"Keep my bit o' stew for me."—"We're going to be interrogated; then we shall come back till the trial."

The *Prinzregent* was lost in a sheet of rain.

The steamer tossed over the muddy, yellow waters of the Jade. The prisoners crowded on the lee side and talked over the events of the last few days once more. "Anyway, we've shown that we aren't going to stand anything and everything."—"But, boys, keep a stiff upper lip before the examining magistrate. We've got to show these chaps that we're not afraid of their sentences."—"And that the right's on our side, even if they lock us up."

Köbis noticed the perturbation concealed behind what many of them said. He thought of the wearisome interrogations: "Just listen to this. It's no good more of us getting cells than need be. So just blame it all on me."

"And on me," Beckers added to his proposal.

The vessel steamed into the lock and came alongside.

The men from the *Prinzregent* clambered ashore.

They were met by a company of marines. Each fireman and seaman was led away between two marines.

Solitary confinement! Interrogation! Protocols!

The accused Beckers deposed:

"I am greatly interested in philosophy. My studies have led me to the conviction that war in any form is irrational. Consequently, I hold peace without annexations to be the aim for which we ought to strive, and, moreover, the sooner the better."

And others:

"I was hungry. They lied to us, about the objects of the war, and about everything. They cheated us and gave us drill instead of leave, and punishment duty instead of time off. Every sub-lieutenant can send us over the main-top or make us stand for hours on the gun-turret with a hammock on our backs. They censor our letters, and sub-lieutenants who are barely twenty read what we write to our wives.

"We have been hungry, deceived, cheated, and humiliated again and again."

The Judge Advocate paid no attention to all that. "What is your attitude on the question of resorting to violence? Are you a member of the Soldiers' Union? Who are the leaders? Who carried on propaganda for a naval strike? What sort of man is this Köbis actually?"

While they were interrogated, the accused had to stand rigidly at attention. The Judge Advocate sat behind a table and dictated protocols in a tone of unconcern.

He was an official who had never set foot on a ship, had never crouched behind a smoking gun, either at Jutland or at the Dogger Bank. He had no knowledge of the soul-destroying service and the hunger of the war years; he only perceived that this was a great case by which he might make his career.

At his suggestion spies were sent to the various ships of the fleet, and further wholesale arrests were made. The seamen and firemen were mere ciphers, mere material in the hands of the Admiralty; why shouldn't they also pave the road to success for a poor Assistant Judge Advocate?

"Aha! here's one of the candidates for death," he exclaimed, by way of opening the interrogation of the fireman Beckers. "Will you be so good as to stand at attention?"—"All that's no good now, sir. You've just said so yourself."

And when he was confronted with Seaman Reichpietsch and Fireman Sachse of the *Friedrich der Grosse*, he laid his revolver on the table and sketched a gallows on a sheet of paper: "As you see, this is a revolver and that a gallows. You may, therefore, be shot or hanged. But as hanging is a more shameful death than shooting, it depends upon your deposition whether you are merely shot."

Alwin Köbis stood before the examining magistrate.

He was asked a number of questions, about the meeting in the railway car, his speeches underneath the Strand Saloon and in the White Swan, his membership in any organization, and his association with a political party—a pure fiction, non-existent except in the judge's imagination and the spies' reports.

Köbis made no answer.

The Judge Advocate tried a different method, that of kindly persuasion. When Köbis still maintained silence, he sprang to his feet in a rage and shouted at him: "I shall certainly recommend the death-sentence for you, and the court will have to accept my recommendation."

Köbis stood stock still, only his arms suddenly hung like lead. There was the table in front of him, the grain of the wood, the clerk of the court sitting with his back to the window, and the light shining red through his ears—Köbis had never observed so closely before.

The Judge Advocate was seated again.

He was fingering the documents nervously. Those fingers, that yellow hand, would write the death-sentence. And those piles of documents on the table: *Prinzregent Luitpold, Friedrich der Grosse, Westfalen!* Where could all those documents have come from? The sheet laid ready for Köbis was still a blank, white in the rays of sunlight that played upon it.

"Now then, speak, Fireman Köbis!"

But Fireman Köbis was silent.

Someone called the clerk of the court away.

Dobring and Köbis were left alone in the room.

The Judge Advocate, whose great opportunity had come, who could speak in person with admirals and was privileged to work under observation of the highest authorities in the Empire —this Assistant Judge Advocate, Dr. Dobring, and the locksmith and fireman Alwin Köbis, confronted one another without the presence of witnesses.

And the spectacled eyes began to vacillate. The Judge Advocate could not bring out the military formula with which he meant to protect himself against that face.

What a clumsy, ungainly fellow!

And what a time the clerk was away!

The ticking of the watch on the table filled the whole room. Judge Advocate Dobring couldn't stand the silence and the immovable face any longer. He drew out his pistol. With his finger on the trigger and his other hand on the button of the electric bell he sat and waited till there was a knock at the door and the clerk re-entered. Afterwards Köbis met his comrade Beckers in the passage: "Dobring seems afraid of me. I suppose he thinks I shall grip him by the throat. I shan't, though, the brute's too unclean."

The trial of the eleven men in the third stokers' watch was held. There was one death-sentence, whilst the rest got penal servitude varying from two to ten years. Hundreds more of the crews of other ships who had assembled in empty coal-bunkers or in restaurants ashore to discuss the penalties, or had organized coaling strikes or practised sabotage or passive resistance, had been arrested and were awaiting their sentences.

The piles of documents increased in volume.

Where there had been in reality spontaneous outbreaks provoked by hunger or the insolence of the officer caste, developing into a desperate, unorganized resistance, the examining magistrates constructed evidence of a widely organized conspiracy, which had been introduced into the fleet through the medium of a political party. And it was not a difficult task. Not all the accused were like the fireman Köbis, who confronted the incomprehensible language of lawyers with iron silence. They could get anything signed by means of endless interrogations, threats of death, and stupid appeals to the "honour and courage" of sailors. But they failed to complete their work. The statements made by spies were not enough alone. They could prove no link with members of the Reichstag and the political party. And, indeed, there was hardly any such external influence brought to bear in the Navy.

Three years of war, the turnip winter, the gulf between the men's and the officers' mess, the gradual realization of the egotistical motives of the war-mongers—these were the causes, against these the crews spontaneously rose in revolt.

In the prison yard: the fools' parade!

They marched one behind another, round and round in a circle. In the middle of this "circus" stood the warders and saw that the half-hour of recreation was conducted according to rule. The men were forbidden to speak, forbidden to stand still, forbidden to step out of the ranks. Round and round, marching in even step and at precisely the same distance one from the other.

But the warders had grown grey and dull in their monotonous duties. The prisoners kept a sharp look-out and helped the man whom the examining magistrate had designated as a candidate for death to the best of their ability. Hans Beckers worked his way forwards, passing one man after another, till he reached the place behind Köbis, so that wary scraps of conversation were possible.

On the previous day Köbis had been called as a witness in the trial of the third watch. "Is it really true, Alwin? It can't be!" —"Penal servitude up to ten years. Death-sentence for Span-deren. He said when they set out on the march: 'We must come forward tomorrow and ask for a different division officer,' and he was at two meetings; that's all."

Death for that!

Those high walls! The strip of blue sky! No door leading out to the street and back to the ships. Always round and round in a circle.

"Alwin, he was at me again yesterday, trying to worm it out of me—you know, about the idea of violence. I said nothing. Ten minutes later the warder came back. The door wasn't even shut when Dobring jumped up and bellowed: 'You liar! You shameless fellow! Now I have proof, although you denied it so impudently. Don't hope for mercy. I shall thoroughly enjoy be-ing present at your execution.' And all the time his smooth face was quite white and he grinned at me."

"And it's for them we starved. It's for them we stoked the fires."—"We never ought to have left the *Prinzregent*, not alive, we oughtn't. Pitch the officers overboard, get up steam in all boilers, and out into the North Sea. That would have given the signal."

Köbis turned round.

"It's too late for that now—now we've got to be the signal ourselves. You, Hans—and I—and the rest."—"Yes, if they'd execute us publicly. But they'll shoot us in secret. Alwin! Mate, just listen! You mustn't take it all on yourself. You must speak —disprove the accusations. You can."

"That gang's not worth deceiving."

"No, they're not worth being told the truth."

Köbis only gazed at him:

"Hans! We dare not wriggle out of it now, we've just got to

go on to the end. It's only that way that our death will have any purpose."

The trial was held on a Saturday.

An hour beforehand sentries stood in the corridors with side-arms and pistols. The accused were Köbis and Beckers from the *Prinzregent Luitpold*, Weber, Sachse, and Reichpietsch from the *Friedrich der Grosse*, two from the Helgoland, and one from the light cruiser *Pillau*. The sentries had brought cigarettes and were distributing them: "It won't be so bad. A year or so in a fortress. And the war's bound to end some day. Then they'll let you out again."

The young Judge Advocate Breil—his face freshly washed, a bundle of documents under his arm—approached Beckers, whose death-sentence he had drawn up, and spoke genially to him: "Come, now, Beckers, admit that you did favour the idea of violence. Don't make difficulties."

The doors of the great hall were opened.

There were two benches for the accused. A crucifix was placed on the judges' table. The room was full of naval officers, judge advocates, clerks, and invited guests from the Admiralty staff and General Headquarters. The atmosphere was fusty and oppressive. Outside, the August clouds sailed past the windows.

It was a monotonous trial.

One after another the accused were made to stand up and make their statements on the various charges. They denied what they could and tried to extenuate or explain the offences proved against them.

The hours dragged on endlessly.

The judges found it dull; they clattered with their penholders and one drew on a sheet of paper in front of him. The officers of high rank from General Headquarters, in their tight stays, polished their monocles again and again. One of the admirals from Berlin yawned surreptitiously. The trial produced nothing sensational. For reasons of State the sentence had already been passed.

Suddenly the officers grew animated.

The naval chaplains, present because of their "interest in the cause," lost their seraphic expression. The witnesses—*agents provocateurs* and detectives who had stood by the furnaces disguised as firemen—stopped peeling the hard skin from their fingers.

Alwin Köbis had leapt to his feet.

The fireman Köbis, who had maintained an obstinate silence during the interrogation and even before the court, was now speaking. He could not go on listening quietly to his fellow prisoner Weber giving himself and their common cause and common aims away before these officer judges and so manifestly appealing to the court for mercy.

"That's all no good," he growled.

And he stood and spoke about the war, about life in the ships and the pan-German propaganda carried on by the officers among the crews: "For a peace of conquest, for the seizure of territory, for the oppression of other nations! That's not what we fought for. It's that we resisted."

The judges drank in every word. Even the grey-bearded admiral's pen scratched diligently over the paper. Hans Beckers trembled for his friend's fate. He gripped his leg and tried to recall him to his senses. But Köbis took no notice of him and maintained his defiant attitude. His face was white to the roots of his hair and he looked away past the judges' table and over the officers' heads.

"We don't want annexations. We want a peace of understanding. And we'll get it. If need be, by any and every means." Turning to a spy, he said: "I won't have cowardly blackguards like you reporting on my actions and I admit openly that I did everything in my power to cripple the fleet by individual terrorism, so as to force a peace." He searched for the most forcible word in his vocabulary and concluded:

"We are social revolutionaries!"

With a deep sigh of relief he resumed his seat.

It was nearing midnight. The prisoners were stupefied after the excitement. The judges glanced at the clock. The guests from General Headquarters leaned on their swords; they all remained in their places merely for the sake of form.

"Gentlemen! Do you imagine you would still be seated here if these men had accomplished their nefarious purpose? . . ." The prosecuting counsel, Assistant Judge Advocate Dobring, asked for a verdict of flagrant treachery in time of war. At the conclusion of his argument he expressed regret that it was impossible to get hold of the members of the Reichstag on account of their immunity: "But, that being so, it is our duty to inflict just punishment upon their tools, the accused."

Dobring asked for the death-sentence in the case of Reichpietsch, Sachse, and Weber from S.M.S. *Friedrich der Grosse.* Dr. Breil supported his argument and likewise asked for the death-sentence for Köbis and Beckers. For the remaining ten, twelve and fifteen years' penal servitude.

The sentences confirmed the recommendations of the Judge Advocates as they stood: loss of citizen rights, expulsion from the Navy, and death.

And again the cell doors were slammed.

The condemned men were in adjoining cells; they tramped restlessly to and fro. If the fireman Sachse lay down on his bed for a few minutes, he heard Reichpietsch's restless steps in the cell exactly underneath his own, one tier lower.

Later Hans Becker wrote:

> *The little cell was too confined. But the*
> *thought that they were going to shoot us like*

*mangy dogs—we only wanted peace and free-
dom and bread—made me wild. Hadn't we
been in the right? I had often thought they only
meant to threaten and frighten us. But no, it
seemed that the military authorities were not
simply making a threatening gesture. And I did
not want to die—not so soon and in such circumstances. I resolved to leave no stone un-
turned.*

*I asked to see Breil. He was very genial. I
asked for information about the forms to be observed in making an appeal and withdrew with
a sheet of official paper. After that my cell
seemed much less forbidding.*

*I wanted to win over the Commander-in-
Chief, Admiral von Scheer, who would have to
confirm the sentence. But what was I to write
to him? There was nothing favourable to be
said about me of a military nature. I had made
no frank confession, and I had called attention to myself repeatedly before the court by
speaking on behalf of Köbis. But that fine
phrase about our slumbering desire to fight a
second Jutland must indubitably find a place
in the appeal. It would touch his pride, for he
regarded himself as the victor in that battle.
A drowning man clutches at every straw.
And this Jutland straw was most opportune
for me. I considered it necessary to tell the
Commander-in-Chief that my participation in
the infamous movement was not inspired by the
hope of material advantage—my thoughts had
not been so wickedly human. Besides, our small*

pay was ample; no, I had engaged in these nefarious activities blinded by the glittering, deceptive hope of peace (I got that expression from the Weser *Gazette). A few more phrases, and then I begged. that the death-sentence might be commuted to one of penal servitude for life. Oh, I was modest; I hardly knew myself. Deeply moved, I concluded my appeal and gave it to Breil to send in. I asked the warder about Köbis. "Oh, well, what can he do? He sits in his cell and broods." I was grieved, sorry for the poor fellow. I had only just handed in my appeal and was already thinking of myself as reprieved, whilst my faithful friend must die. All at once my cheerfulness deserted me, and I ceased to believe in the success of my appeal. I turned over fresh plans in my mind. Besides, I had written my appeal much too naïvely, with too little eye to effect. I thought of a variety of things that I ought to have said. What a pity it was already gone! Certainly I should have written with more spirit now. A proper appeal for mercy, I reflected, ought downright to ensnare and drug the recipient. The evil-doer's penitence ought to strike the reader at once. And I had said nothing whatever about penitence in the petition.*

On the next afternoon I met my friend, sitting on a bench outside the court-room. We exchanged a hearty greeting and sat together nearly a quarter of an hour. Köbis was calm. I told him about my appeal to the Commander-in-Chief. He listened in silence, but when I

*begged him to do likewise, he shrugged his
shoulders resignedly and said: "It would be no
good." I tried in vain to persuade him. It
seemed that he regarded the whole affair with
indifference.*

*I asked him suddenly how he pictured our
end. "Oh," he said, "I'm not in the least afraid
of death, but I don't want to think of the crack
of the rifles; I can't bear that." And he turned
away from me a little and looked down, brooding.*

*Then I gripped his arm and said: "Alwin,
we'll manage it quite differently." I told him
about the splinter of glass that I had on me.
Hastily we discussed a scheme. We would
spend the last night together. They wouldn't
refuse us that request. Lying on the bed and
smoking a cigarette, we would pass our whole
lives in review once more. A vigorous cut in the
artery at dawn, and then let the executioners
come for us. Köbis was amused and burst out
laughing. It was the last time I ever heard my
friend laugh. At that juncture we were interrupted. We exchanged a glance and then were
forced to part. I never saw him again.*

The condemned men were brought before the examining
magistrate once or twice more; otherwise they sat in their cells,
still kept strictly apart.

To and fro, to and fro!

The cells were four paces in length and two in breadth.
They would stop tramping to and fro, sit down at the table,

resting their heads in their hands, and brood till their heads ached.

A rattle of keys, and the door was flung open.

A young man of ascetic appearance entered, the chaplain of the fourth squadron. He hardly had courage to address Beckers, who was seated at the table, till the prisoner raised his head.

"Chaplain, I wonder if you can tell who's in the right, we soldiers who stood up against injustice, or the military machine which crushes everything that stands in the way of its schemes of violence?"

The chaplain was more than ever at a loss.

Rhetoric was useless here.

Beckers liked his face and thought it expressed delicacy and sympathy.

"And then the Church in war time—"

The young chaplain flushed; then he pulled himself together and stammered: "Yes, but—all that may be more or less true— but it doesn't do away with the fact that at the present moment you need help. Speak to me, open your heart."

"I have no need of consolation; I don't want it."

And Beckers was left alone once more. Somebody opened the door of the neighbouring cell. The chaplain was with Köbis. Beckers stood close to his cell door and listened.

Köbis was pacing to and fro and did not stop for a single moment. After a short interval his door was locked again. Then. something crashed to the ground—the table or some other heavy object.

Then the tramping began again, Alwin Köbis in the next cell, then Sachse, the youngest of the condemned men, and beneath him the seaman Max Reichpietsch.

Darkness fell.

The clock struck twelve.

One!

Two!

You could see the bars and knobs before the windows again. The clock in the prison courtyard struck four.

Beckers lay in a stupor on his bed and heard the tumult as if it were far away. Sachse sprang to his feet. He was wide awake in a moment. He stood in the middle of his cell, feeling as though he must collapse in a moment. The walls and roof of the cell shut him in like a big, firm hand.

The clatter of nailed boots—a confused sound of voices—a command given in the corridor downstairs. Max Reichpietsch was taken from his cell. The steps came up the stairs, along the passage—many and hurried steps.

Sachse felt the pulsing of his blood.

Two thoughts filled his mind. He hadn't fastened his shoes, and he had promised Köbis to stand erect and proud, and given his hand on it. The party stopped outside the cells. A bunch of keys rattled. But it was the adjoining door, Köbis's cell, that was opened.

Silence in the corridor.

An officer's voice.

"Stand at attention!"

Köbis answered:

"My name has been struck off the Navy roll and I no longer consider myself a soldier."

Behind his cell wall the fireman Sachse held his breath. He heard the rustle of papers being turned over. Then silence till Köbis spoke: "I am ready; you can do what you choose with my body."

Chains clanked, locks snapped to, boots clattered loud on the flag-stones. The party descended the stairs.

Three days later. Naval Judge Advocate Breil pushed a document across the table to his clerk: "Put that in with the file of the fourth squadron."

Wahn Rifle Range
5 September 1917
In the presence of Naval Judge Advocate Breil
as presiding Judge:

This morning the death-sentence passed on
the prisoners Reichpietsch of S.M.S. Fried-
rich der Grosse and Köbis of S.M.S. Prinz-
regent Luitpold on August 25, 1917 was
carried out. At six a.m. both prisoners were
brought to Wahn by motor-car from the mili-
tary prison at Cologne. Both during the jour-
ney and during the last night each prisoner was
attended by a chaplain of his own faith.

For the execution of the sentence a firing-
squad in the strength of a company was de-
tailed. The proceedings were conducted by
Major von Mohrs.

At the place of execution, while the firing-
squad presented arms, the sentence and its con-
firmation were read aloud by the undersigned.
After the chaplains had again been permitted
to address the condemned men, their eyes were
bandaged. Then, at the word of command,
the sentence was carried out, ten men for each
prisoner, in double file, at five paces; the time
was 7.03 a. m. At 7.04 a. m. Dr. Werner of
the Reserves, detailed to attend the execution,
reported the instantaneous death of both con-
demned men.

The ship's doctor of S.M. auxiliary cruiser *Wolf* had put on
his dress uniform and asked to see the captain.

The captain received him standing.

The after deck was crowded with prisoners. There were hundreds of them, in rags, a monotonous grey throng, a medley of all races. It was only at meal-times that the mass showed signs of life. For the rest they squatted side by side like a company of great brooding birds, gazing at the sky or across the everlasting blue sea.

The doctor reported:

"The state of health of the prisoners is the more serious, but I find the same typical symptoms among the crew: dilation of the heart, muscular atrophy, pains caused by pressure on the nerves. Many are losing their teeth. All the beds in the sick-bay are occupied and a further hundred men ought to be admitted. Thirty are unable to stand on their feet. Every day several collapse. All show symptoms of scurvy. Unless the voyage ends within a few weeks, the whole crew is faced with death."

That was in the Indian Ocean.

Since then we had sunk more ships, rounded the Cape of Good Hope, and crossed the Atlantic. For the second time we lay at the entrance to Denmark Strait, this time at the western entrance.

Behind us lay a route three times the length of the earth's circumference and three hundred thousand tons of shipping sent to the bottom. Our holds were packed right up to the hatches with valuable cargo. Our engines were worn out, and the hull dented and leaky as a result of the constant bringing alongside and unloading of captured ships. Every hour we shipped eight hundred and forty hundredweight of water. The bilge-pumps kept pace with the water as it leaked in.

The wind blew from the north, bringing masses of drift-ice to meet us. There was ice everywhere, ahead, on both sides, beneath the keel. Droves of great grey blocks stretching farther than the eye could see. The hull groaned and creaked as we crashed against them. Sometimes the waves, sweeping over the deck, left a block of ice behind, which then swayed like a railway truck on an unsteady rail, smashing the upper works and bulwarks. One torpedo-tube was knocked to smithereens. The second cargo-winch was a wreck.

We secured the ice blocks and took advantage of the rolling of the ship to pitch them overboard. Wire cables, crow-bars, handspikes, and one hundred and fifty pairs of arms and legs! And our bones were hollowed by scurvy; we had only to bend down to be bathed in a perspiration of weakness. One prisoner leapt overboard; it was Captain Tominaga of the sunken Japanese steamer *Hitachi Maru*.

Another, Captain Meadows of the *Turitella*, stood on the after deck. He had been taken prisoner thirteen months earlier and had been the organizing soul of the resistance ever since. He dissuaded his fellow prisoners from helping our progress by their work. He helped his mate and first engineer to jump overboard in order to swim to an island of the Kermadec group. He threw countless messages in bottles overboard. All to no purpose. What was a bottle in the great ocean? How many chances, what long years, before it came into anybody's hands! When Captain Meadows came on board, he reflected that the British fleet was mistress of the seas and said: "This damned nonsense won't last long."

Most of the prisoners crouched below in the hold and crowded round the heaters. Captain Meadows stood on the after deck, swathed in rags to keep out the cold, an emaciated wreck, with his gnawed pipe in his mouth. He stared at the ice hurling itself against our hull. "A lucky gang. But they won't get through the ice. And there's the British blockade in the North Sea—"

Meadows had observed correctly.

Denmark Strait—

Denmark Strait was blocked.

The ice drove us southwards. Finally we attempted to reach the North Sea by the route between Iceland and the Shetland Islands. But our luck continued and we reached the Norwegian coast without sighting a single British patrol boat.

We sailed inside the three-mile limit, and at night we passed the lights of fishermen lying beside their nets.

Skagerrak!

Jutland!

The Lesser Belt!

In the Gulf of Kiel we cast anchor. We had been voyaging four hundred and forty-four days.

They had sent us to go to the bottom. The notifications of death were already written and had been sent to our relatives by the Admiralty. But now we had returned and put in to Kiel. A hospital-ship took off the sick, and another boat the prisoners. Twenty-six of the crew were in a Bombay prison, convicted of murder and piracy. The four victims of our own guns lay at the bottom of the Indian Ocean.

The rest of us lined up in divisions.

The commander of the Baltic Station, a white-bearded admiral, paced along the line and asked kindly questions, always the same: "What is your name?" "How old are you?" "What is your occupation?"—"Geulen, sir." "Twenty-five, sir." "Sailor, sir."

A telegram of welcome from the German Emperor was read to us, and the captain received the *"Pour la mérite."* Then iron crosses were distributed.

Two days later:

Our iron crosses and the captain's *"Pour la mérite"* had been taken away again. The Admiral came on board, this time with a captain of the "Propaganda Department for encouraging the military spirit in the homeland." They had brought a cinometograph and made a magnificent film of the captain, the pack of dogs, and the crew.

The photographer turned his crank. The Admiral distributed the withdrawn iron crosses a second time, asked the same idiotic questions, read the same telegram from the Emperor, and conferred the *"Pour la mérite"* on the captain over again. A gigantic farce! The highest military order that the nation had to bestow had been turned into a theatrical property. The captain, who was refused a marriage licence with his wife because she was an actress, was himself forced to play the part of an actor with the rest of the officers, including the Admiral and commander of the Baltic Station, as supernumeraries. An extensive and economical background was provided by the crews of the war-ships lying in harbour and the landing-stages, which were thronged in accordance with instructions. We shouted "Hurrah!" fifty times over, till we were hoarse, and all the time we were grinning: Propaganda to encourage the military spirit in Germany!

It provided five hundred yards of film for the homeland and for the hospitals. Our prize cargo, worth forty million marks, consisting of raw rubber, copper, human hair, rice, coffee, tea, tinned meat, groceries, and spirits, was not intended for the homeland or for the hospitals. The officers' casino at Kiel was interested in that cargo and fell upon us with a number of lighters, intending to begin discharging it. But the captain, being in command of a ship that sailed alone, took orders from no command and had the sole right to dispose of the goods. By his injunction the prize was unloaded in the free harbour of Lübeck, outside the control of the naval authorities.

We were decorated with orders. The kings of Saxony and Bavaria and Württemberg, and the Free Hansa Cities sent decorations on board in chestloads. The captain received his fourth gold stripe, which meant an increase in pay of eight hundred marks a month. The gunnery-officer got his second stripe and four hundred marks a month.

We remained coolies, at fifty pfennig a day. The prize-money due to us got enmeshed in the tangle of bureaucratic procedure. The Lübeck soldiers' wives who took us to their beds wore chemises woven from nettles, and washed themselves with army soap made without any fat. Their money was no longer sufficient to buy the rationed substitute food-stuffs. We stole all we could of the cargo, shared it with the customs' authorities and the police, and sold the rest to profiteers and middlemen who had forgathered from other parts. A retired naval officer of high rank resident in the town wrote to the Admiralty: ". . . the much fêted crew of S.M.S. *Wolf*—not heroes, but brigands and thieves! They pilfer State property. Every one of them, down to the youngest seaman, ought to be court-martialled."

But we were packed into a train and taken to Berlin, where we marched through the Brandenburg Gate with a guard of honour on either side. The city commandant made a speech. The Empress waved her hand whilst we were permitted to defile past her in solemn march. Women belonging to "patriotic societies" distributed flowers. The city gave us a dinner and Kempinski a supper. In Busch Circus, in the theatre foyer, and in the Zoo, we were almost suffocated by vast crowds of patriotic ladies thronging round us. The stage-managers of the whole performance were in the War Office. The entry of the auxiliary cruiser's crew into Berlin was only one of many items in the varied program of the generals for combating the growing war weariness.

A conference in the Leipzigerstrasse: Prussian faces of mathematical precision, representatives of the Military Cabinet, the War Press Department, the Imperial Chancellery, and the Ministries:

"The situation is exceedingly serious—we must pursue a vigor-

ous home policy—a press campaign carried out on uniform lines
—detailed and forceful instructions must be given to the clergy
and the teachers—the women's co-operation must be enlisted—
orders must be more liberally conferred, a cross for auxiliary
service for members of the committees of societies—more frequent visits of His Majesty to Berlin. It would be desirable that
the Emperor should evince sympathy with the working classes,
visit large works, and establish, perhaps temporarily, homes of
rest for munition workers in royal castles—the press must explain the hard work performed by the sovereign and his family in
fulfilment of their arduous duties, the simplicity of their lives,
their feats of arms, losses, etc.—rumours about the Crown
Prince must be suppressed—government measures in the field of
social welfare must be traced in the press as far as possible to
the initiative of His Majesty the Emperor and King."

Barfussstrasse, Berlin, middle building, fourth floor: I was unpacking my sea-bag—canned milk, corned beef, Australian
tongue. Half a hundredweight of State property. My mother was
shrunken and her hair had grown thin: "If we'd had that a few
weeks earlier, Father would still have been here. It couldn't go
on, he ate us out of house and home. There was no satisfying his
hunger. . . ." I held his photograph in my hand. Swollen
finger-joints, his suit hanging loose on his emaciated body, his
collar much too large round the neck. His face was altered, and
he used not to be so puffy beneath the eyes. Only the beard I
recognized. "He was standing there by the stove. It was the day
when the letter came from the Admiralty—the second one,
about the *Wolf*, saying she was lost and the crew to be counted
as missing. That came on top of Paul being crippled by a gun-
shot wound in the backbone, and Fritz's nerves all to bits.

"He stood there with his back to the stove.

" 'I shall never see the boy again!'

"And after a bit he began to whimper about the briquettes being

all used up again: 'I wonder what's wrong with me. My feet
are so cold again—and it's working upwards.'

"Afterwards he went to the doctor. . . ."

A doctor's waiting-room: women, one or two children, few
men. There is a smell of unwashed underclothing. An old man
falls from his chair and is carried in lifeless to the doctor. The
patients move nearer together and quickly relapse into gloom as
they wait.

An ambulance—the infirmary—the place where bodies are
collected.

I went to see the grave. There were long rows arranged alpha-
betically. Each individual grave had a number, ranging from one
to a hundred. Germany was well organized: there were mass
graves for those who died of starvation and for new-born babies.

Buy War Loan! Give up your copper kettles and brass fit-
tings at the collecting depot. Section forty-three of your food-
card entitles you to one hundred and twenty-five grammes of
war-time jam.—We believe that God has ordained this war.—
Anyone who strikes is a scoundrel.—We must stick it out! Carry
on! Hold our tongues!

The last copper had been requisitioned and had yielded profits
to a series of middlemen, till it finished by exploding as the
driving-band of a projectile. The front was as rigid as iron; there
was no more field warfare. Staff officers in civilian quarters in
occupied territory no longer had the opportunity of using table-
napkins instead of chamber-pots. They made up by emptying
French cellars of wine and enriching themselves by the seizure
of furniture, carpets, and works of art.

The wheel flew round till it began to generate heat.

Shuffling was going on in the Centre party; cabinets were
overthrown. Parliament and the civil government had become
mere executive organs of the dictator generals. Everywhere
cracks began to appear at the circumference.

There were munition strikes in Munich, Kiel, Hamburg, Bremen, Brunswick, and, indeed, all over the Empire. A scene in Dresden outside the powder-mill: strike-breakers collapsing on the pavement under blows from the women munition workers' wooden clogs. Women and children smashed the windows and plundered the food stores. The Berlin metal-workers marched through the streets distributing leaflets: "What our brothers in the trenches require of us is revolutionary action, not munitions!" Slogans were passed round: Abolish the state of siege! Freedom to strike and freedom of assembly! Liberate the political prisoners! The movement was crushed by sentences of penal servitude and, for the general mass, the trenches.

Prisoners of war, Russian, Belgian, French, Roumanian. Their fate was a pre-ordained sequence: blast-furnace, barracks, fever hospital, mass grave. Incidents were handled with expert skill. If a man collapsed at work, he was carried aside and allowed to lie there for a time with cold compresses on his forehead. If anyone swallowed gas in filling the furnace, he was given an emetic, and if that was not enough, the stomach-pump was used. All other cases could be dealt with by prison regulations and blows with the butt-end of the rifles of reservists, as had happened at Thyssen's in Mülheim. Over a hundred Russians were herded into the rubbish-dump and lined up. "Hands up! Any man willing to continue work, fall out." They all stood still with raised arms. If one of them grew tired and let his arms fall, he received a blow in the back from the butt-end of a rifle and fell into the ashes. After three hours of such treatment the prisoners were willing to work again, even though their demands—more to eat and some tobacco—were not fulfilled.

A fever hospital in Cassel: newly admitted patients were carried on stretchers or walked to the barrack-like building outside the city. Patients discharged were driven away by night. Between admission and departure were days with an ascending life-curve.

Those who were not seriously ill strolled along beside the fence; after dark they climbed over it and held rendezvous with women from the powder-mill, who were also housed in barrack-like buildings outside the city. The hospital was surrounded by barbed wire. The women suffered from skin-diseases, and their lungs were eaten away as a result of handling the powder. They came close up to the fence, and the barbed wire stretched above the couples lying on the ground.

We were given eight weeks' leave to recover our strength. Twenty per cent remained in hospitals, V.D. clinics, or prisons. The remainder of the crew of S.M.S. *Wolf* returned to Wilhelmshaven.

At the commander's office: "Fall in with sea-bags! In file, right turn! March at ease!"

In patrol boats!

In mine-sweepers!

Count Dohna-Schlodien, captain of the *Möwe*, was made aide-de-camp to His Majesty the Emperor after his raiding cruise across the north Atlantic on which he sank eighteen merchant steamers. The middle-class captain of the auxiliary cruiser *Wolf*, after a cruise over the five seas which was without parallel, after sowing mines outside important harbours in four continents and sinking three hundred thousand tons of enemy shipping, was made chief of the mine-sweeping service in the North Sea.

C-boat *212*.

She was like a cardboard box, and just as flat. When we put to sea with the rest of the boats, the men in the big ships knew what it meant: "The louse-squadron is putting to sea."

Whenever the fleet was going to manœuvre, the louse-squadron cleared a path through the mine-infested waters of the North Sea. Each sweeping-gear was drawn by two boats and consisted of a steel wire with a pair of shears. The steel wire got entangled and loosed the mines from their anchorage. Those which floated upwards were then shot at and destroyed. The nasty part of it was that we trailed the wires behind us and had to push ahead in front of them into the mine-fields.

There were eighteen of us on board.

When the sweeping-gear was out in the water, we squatted at the stern—the stokers' watch below, the deck-hands, but also the captain, a quartermaster whom we called "Sea-boots." We sat on the hand-rail, prepared to jump overboard. That way we halved the risk, which the firemen on duty and the man at the helm ran to the full.

No. *110* had been blown up on her last cruise. We picked up eleven of her crew. In Cuxhaven they were given new sea-bags and afterwards another ship. The sea-bag stood ready packed in the barracks. The lost men were replaced by one or two from the fleet and one released from prison.

The summer was over.

We were arrested three times for every once on leave. We had been given a new ship. The *C 212* had been blown up with her firemen, helmsman, and cook. After that we were allowed to call our quartermaster "Sea-boots" even when he was present.

The system was breaking down.

The Emperor made a speech in Essen to fifteen hundred starved workers in the heavy industries: "My dear friends in the Krupp works . . ."

Troops sent to the front as reinforcements wrote on the railway cars: "Cattle for slaughter; Wilhelm and Sons."—S.M.S. *Nürnberg* on patrol duty in the North Sea: Everyone in the mess was tipsy. The commander made them smear his naked seat with mustard and hold it out of the window while the sub-lieutenants proclaimed: "That's our latest searchlight." Banquets were still held in the naval officers' casinos, and there was music every evening at dinner. Sentences had been passed on men in the Navy amounting to one hundred and eighty-one years' penal servitude and one hundred and eighty years' imprisonment, besides the death-sentences, and the court martials were still busy.

October 28, 1918!

Quartermaster General Ludendorff had resigned his commission. The newly established civilian Government had offered an armistice to the Entente. The entire German High Sea Fleet was concentrated at Wilhelmshaven and in the Roads.

The mine-sweeping flotillas were instructed to clear away mines, and the squadron commanders had received sealed orders as follows: "High Sea forces to engage in attack and action against the British fleet."

In the first, second, third, and fourth squadrons they were getting up steam for full speed. The ships steamed out and volumes of black smoke curled up to the starless sky.

At ten o'clock in the evening they were to weigh anchor.

S.M.S. *Thüringen* had her lights screened. Not a ray of light escaped. Nothing was visible of the ship anchored next to her in the line. Someone called through the foggy air: "*Thüringen* ahoy!" A boat emerged from the fog, a steam pinnace, then another, and a third and fourth. The first moored by the gangway. The rest proceeded to the other ships. The officers were returning from the casino ashore.

Up by the gangway of the *Thüringen* stood a group of seamen and the stokers' watch below with critical faces: "They're all boozed again."

The men sat in the casemates under the outstretched hammocks. Electric light, steel bulkheads, steel decks. Nobody lay down to sleep. Four and a half years of war! Military collapse had come. But what matter?—it meant peace!

Yet something was brewing in the depths of the hull, in bunkers and stoke-hold. Coal was being carried, fires stoked, and boilers, pipes, and turbines began to vibrate.

Why had the mine-sweepers been sent out?

Why was the fleet lying in Schillig Roads?

Why were they getting up steam?

Something was in the air.

The seamen and firemen wandered from one casemate to another, crossed the decks, watched the bridge, and made their way aft under cover of the darkness to the quarter-deck.

In the officers' mess the festivities were at their height. The gentlemen found it so warm below that they had had the skylight opened. A phonograph was playing and they were singing.

Champagne-bottles popping, glasses, a confused buzz of voices!

Suddenly the phonograph ceased playing. Somebody had kicked it over. Those of the officers who were still able to stand sprang to their feet. The stewards refilled the glasses.

The seamen by the skylight looked down into the mess. They forgot all caution, and their faces were rigid. They drank in every word spoken below.

Lieutenant Commander Rudloff stood up, glass in hand: "We shall fire our last two thousand rounds at the English and then go down gloriously! Better an honourable death than a life of shame!"

"Rather ten years of war than such a peace!"—"Lawyers and shopkeepers and newspaper scribblers want to rule us now!" —"We don't care a damn for the Government. The fleet and the Commander-in-Chief are absolutely free to act on their own initiative!"

Pale faces and voices hoarse with excitement.

"The *Thüringen* must go down! Comrades, gentlemen! Our honour is at stake, this glass—"

"To the death-ride of the German fleet!"

"To our last cruise!"

"The last two thousand rounds!"

The seamen withdrew from the skylight. They ran through the casemates, and the seamen's and firemen's quarters, shouting at the top of their voices what they had heard. Groups collected on all sides. If anyone was asleep, he was dragged out of his hammock.

The same thing was happening on the *Helgoland*, the *Ostfriesland*, and the *Oldenburg*.

On the other ships, too, the men had observed the signs—the putting out of the mine-sweepers, the getting up steam, and the uproar in the officers' mess. It was the bellicose slogan of victory or death. Crews of a thousand men were carried away by the same impulse to rise in revolt and make an end of it, or else they lay overwhelmed and stupefied in the dim casemates and waited.

The new fleet flagship was S.M.S. *Baden*, the largest and most modern of the battle-ships, with fifteen-inch guns and tripod masts. The *Baden* lay in the inner harbour beside the quay wall. Her crew were asleep. Suddenly somebody shouted: "Escape if you can! The officers are blowing up the shell-rooms!" The rumour flew through the casemates, a hysterical alarm: "Officers . . . shell-rooms . . . escape . . ." The fifteen hundred men surged up through the armoured hatches, rushed across the decks, and scrambled ashore.

The men's mood in all the ships was one of horror-stricken expectancy.

Ten o'clock at night in S.M.S. *Thüringen*:

Bos'n's whistles blew. Orders were shouted.

"Second cutter's crew weigh anchor!"

"General quarters!"

The second cutter's crew climbed on the forecastle and went to the windlass. Levers were turned. The windlass creaked as the steam was turned on. Link by link the heavy cable was shortened in through the hawse-pipe. In the darkness

there was nothing to be seen of the bridge, occupied by officers, but only the thick clouds of smoke issuing from the funnels.

A throng of seamen rushed up on to the forecastle. They had
stopped for nothing, were only half dressed, and some barefoot.
"Boys! Boys!"—"It's madness!"—"Hands off the windlass!"
—"We won't put to sea again!"—"Let 'em do it themselves!
Let 'em go down alone!"

A sub-lieutenant, a lieutenant, and officers hastened to the
spot, and pistols were pointed threateningly. The cutter's crew
yielded to superior force and the discipline inculcated through
long years. The cable groaned and creaked and grew shorter.
The anchor hung free and thumped heavily against the ship's
armoured side.

Sparks flew from the funnels.

They saw the outline of a ship float past.

Then another. The fleet was under way.

The night was rent by a shriek—the shriek of a single individual. The cry was echoed from hundreds of throats, a cry
of rage and despair. The upper deck of the *Thüringen* was
black with seamen. At that moment the other anchor fell; one
or two men had dropped it. The cable rattled through the hawse-
pipe, and the ship was anchored once more. And now the stokers appeared. They put out the fires. No more trails of smoke
were seen, but steam issued from the funnels.

The masses began to move.

They stormed through the casemates, into the forward battery, lashed the anchor-chain, closed the petty officers' compartment, which was below the crew's quarters, and wedged the
hatches firmly to. They cut the lines and cutter-falls so that
no boat could be got out. Officers who came down from the
bridge were pelted with all kinds of things—wash-basins, boots,
and boiler-scrapers. Arms and fists were raised. The portrait of

the "Victor of Jutland" was torn to shreds. Lights were smashed, rifles and cartridges distributed. Men called for ammunition for the secondary armament.

The casemates reverberated with shouts:

"We mean to have peace!"

"We mean to have freedom!"

"Down with the aristocrats! The cut-throats! Down with the Imperial Navy!"

A searchlight! Morse signals!

S.M.S. *Helgoland* answered:

"Stick it out, mates. We're doing the same."

The *Thüringen* remained in Schillig Roads.

The *Helgoland* remained in Schillig Roads.

The fleet, battle-cruisers and battle-squadrons, put to sea. The commanding officers succeeded, within the white beams of brightness emitted by the searchlights, in dispersing the crowds on the decks and ensuring that anchors were weighed. The naval officers made a last appeal to the men's sense of duty, speculating on their credulity: "No, we won't sail against England. We'll only go mine-sweeping. There are still ninety submarines out at sea. They don't know the channels. We must bring them home."

The fleet proceeded in line ahead, a long train of ships.

Slowly! The stokers kept steam low.

Twelve to fourteen knots is enough for mine-sweeping and bringing in the submarines. As they left the Jade estuary, a wind rose. There was a rift in the clouds, and watery stars appeared. The ships rolled in the ponderous rhythm of the sea. They altered course. The wind blew from the opposite side. You could feel it, even down in the casemates.

North-westerly course!

Against England!

Orders were given, but not from the bridge: "Out of your

hammocks! To the forward battery! All hands to the forward battery!"

There a man was standing on the chain-locker:

"North-westerly course! An attack! There are charts of the east coast of England on the navigating officer's table. On the shelter-deck there's paint ready to paint the funnels. They've swindled us, as usual. Four and a half years' war! Now it's at an end. Their careers gone to the devil, their brilliant, idle existence. They're afraid of the future and want to take their own lives.

"This attack is suicide. And they expect us to be in it. To give our lives for that!"

The ship rolled in the ocean swell.

Half a dozen men clung to the chain-locker in the forward battery. Mutiny meant death. A group was sitting round one of the six-inch guns, trying to calm themselves by singing: "I want to go home again. . . ."

One man made a speech, then a second and a third.

And now the commander appeared.

"Only one of you can talk with me, or two at most—I am a South German, I have been in the Navy eighteen years. I love life—somebody threw something at me. That's not decent—comrades! Comrades!"

"Swindler!"

"Suicide!"

"At him! At him!"

Electric bulbs were smashed.

The forward battery was plunged in darkness.

There was a stamping of feet, a hustling of many men.

"You damned cowards, stop that singsong!"—"Where are the stokers?"—"In the stoke-hold. To the fire-extinguishers! Open the fire-extinguishers!"—"Put out the searchlights!"

"Lights out!"

"Fires out!"

For a brief moment the searchlights lit up the figures of the men surging up from the armoured decks and the packed throng rushing across the decks. Then the beams of light swerved skywards and went out.

A wireless message from the Commander-in-Chief:

"Enterprise to be carried out at all costs."

The reply: "Enterprise not to be carried out."

A siren blew.

The between-decks and passages to the stoke-hold were thronged with seamen. The staff engineers beat a retreat, with lumps of coal flying after them. Petty officers were defending their stations.

Wheels! Handles! Weights!

The fire-extinguishers were opened.

Furnace doors flung open.

The alarm! Telephones!

A last effort on the part of the officers:

"Clear for action! All hands to battle-stations!"

The attempt to delude the men no longer succeeded. Immense volumes of steam ascended in the stoke-hold. The flicker of the dying fires illuminated confused masses of struggling men. Engineers and chief mates were crushed by the mass.

The last boiler was out of action.

The ship was stationary.

One ship after another sheered out of the steaming line and lay crosswise upon the waves. Drifting and rudderless, the vessels seemed like giant, distended animal corpses.

There was an end of the naval attack.

The fleet staff were transferred from the great battle-ship *Baden* to the inner harbour on to the office-ship *K.W. II*, which had neither masts nor engines.

Fog lay over the Jade, and in the Nordostsee Canal and the

Gulf of Kiel. The surface of the sea looked like flowing, watery milk. Gulls flew behind the slowly moving ships, shrieking and fighting for scraps of food thrown overboard, then quickly disappeared with the wind. The squadrons had separated, and each was steaming back to its base, to Wilhelmshaven, Cuxhaven, Brunsbüttel, and Kiel.

On the office-ship *K.W. II*:

The staff officers were glued to the telephone lines. Typewriters clattered. Orderlies ran to and fro. Telegrams and wireless messages were dispatched: "Clear plenty of room in the prisons at Fort Schaar, Gökerstrasse, and Heppens. The North German Lloyd steamer *Frankfurt* has been secured to accommodate a large number of men. There can be no question of solitary confinement.—To the Judge Advocates . . . the clerks of the court with typewriters on board the *Schwaben*. Embarkation by special instructions.—A company of marines at war strength to be embarked on two harbour steamers to arrest the mutineers.—Unless the men voluntarily obey the order to come up on the forecastle, a torpedo-boat is to fire a projectile into the forward battery. In case of need a submarine is to be placed near the *Thüringen*."

A lieutenant commander, Captain Spiess, in command of a submarine, managed at last to find the naval staff and reported for service with *U 135* to the Chief of Staff, Admiral von Trotha.

The Chief of Staff had already packed his trunks.

He was not deserting his post: four weeks earlier he had been detached to General Headquarters, and this juncture, when the fleet was in rapid dissolution, seemed to him a proper one to make a hasty departure. He never reached General Headquarters.

"Can you rely on your crew?"

"Yes, sir."

Admiral von Trotha explained to the submarine captain what was required of him: "Put out and ensure the arrest of the mutineers in the *Thüringen* and *Helgoland*." "Put out," "ensure"—such expressions did not satisfy the lieutenant commander. For it was a question of torpedoing and blowing up our own battle-ships. He asked for written instructions.

The Admiral answered:

"There are none."

The submarine captain understood: he was to act at his own risk, as he had so often had to do. The higher authorities refused to shoulder the responsibility. He could not get clear orders even from the Commander-in-Chief, only a brief salutation and a bow; then he found himself outside the door again. Half an hour later the *U 135* was steaming in line ahead behind the steamer carrying the marines, out into the fog.

Three hundred men in the *Thüringen* were arrested, and an equal number of the crew of the *Helgoland*.

The fleet returned: battle-cruisers, battle-ships, and destroyers, not in steaming formation, but just in herds like fugitive animals.

A great battle-ship with turrets and fighting-masts!

The naval ensign floated from the flagstaff.

The crew wore dungarees—shirts and trousers—and sea-boots; they were unwashed, unshaven, emaciated, and big-boned; four and a half years of war and blockade had left their stamp on the men's faces; they were like a grey stream sweeping over the decks.

A reservist officer was speaking, a man incapable of reading portents: "Must it come like this, boys?—I worked my own way in 1914—as a coal-trimmer, from New York. . . ."

Crow-bars, handspikes, side-arms!

The cells were smashed.

The prisoners surged forth into the daylight.

The reservist officer was trampled underfoot. The crew surged aft like an avalanche. There was no resistance; the officers had entrenched themselves under the armoured deck. There were fourteen hundred seamen and firemen; above their heads floated the ensign, black on a white field with the iron cross in the left-hand corner.

Nobody let go the ensign halliards. A mass of arms and outstretched hands!

The halliards parted. Down came the ensign.

Several arms raised a swab, used to mop dirt from the decks, old and frayed, thanks to the sweat of countless coolies condemned to punishment labour.

"The swab—fix it on!"

"Ready—all hands! Hoist away!"

The swab flew aloft and hung from the flagstaff: on the gaff where, for the four and a half war years, and ever since the establishment of the Navy, the symbol of the Empire had floated.

And in the other ships the flags were lowered. Swabs, coalsacks, and red flags were hoisted.

Five thousand naval officers had sworn loyalty to the flag. At uproarious banquets, raising glasses filled with champagne, they had repeated again and again that they would stake their lives for their flag and Emperor.

Five thousand admirals, captains, and officers!

Only three defended the flag.

It was on S.M.S. *König*, the captain, the commander, and the adjutant, a sub-lieutenant of twenty. The three stood on the quarter-deck, pistols in hand, abandoned by all the rest. They shot one seaman dead. Then a grey flood swept over them, striking and shooting, a confused medley of bodies, arms, and legs.

The captain and commander were wounded and collapsed.

The adjutant lay dead.

The Emperor's flag was lowered.

The red flag was hoisted.

All the ships yielded without a struggle.

The naval depots on land yielded without a struggle.

The Admiralty in Berlin, with the Secretary of State, the admirals, captains, commanders, and several hundred officers, armed with swords, pistols, hand-grenades, and machine-guns, and supported by a loyal company of rifles at war strength—capitulated to a petty officer and six men.

And the Supreme War-Lord, Wilhelm II, *Imperator Rex*?

After he had fled across the frontier in a motor-car, his aide-de-camp, Lieutenant Colonel Niemann, asked why he had not gone to meet his death at the head of his troops. He replied:

"The days of heroic gestures are past."